OUR *first* CHRISTMAS

DL GALLIE | D.M. DAVIS
HARLOW LAYNE | KATE RANDALL
KATIE RAE | K.B. BARRETT | LISAMARIE KADE
L.M. REID | MAY GORDON | VI SUMMERS

A Pucking Good Christmas

BY DL GALLIE

This is a work of fiction. Names, characters, organizations, places, events, and incidents are products of the author's imagination or are used fictitiously. Any resemblance to actual events, locales, or persons, living or dead, is entirely coincidental.

Copyright @2022 by DL Gallie

No part of this book may be reproduced, stored in a retrieval system, or transmitted in any form or by any means electronic, mechanical, photocopying, recording, or otherwise, without the express written permission of the publisher.

This book is licensed for your personal enjoyment only. This book may not be re-sold or given away to other people.

Cover Design: Ya'll That Graphic

'Tis the pucking season.

Kallen finally has the girl and they're about to celebrate their first Christmas as a married couple. And Chelsea has a present for Kallen he'll never forget.

However, when his rivalry with Stefan Däuchmen spills over from the ice into their personal lives, it threatens to not only melt their careers but Chelsea's surprise for her husband too.

CHAPTER 1
KALLEN

... EARLY OCTOBER

With my eyes still closed, a smile appears on my face as I register what's happening beneath the covers. My wife—fuck, Chelsea is now my wife—currently has her lips wrapped around my dick, sucking me to the back of her throat. This is the best way to wake up on the first day of our honeymoon.

Lifting the sheet, I glance down to see my wife's beautiful hazel eyes staring back at me. She throws me a wink and then focuses on the task at hand. Her head bobs up and down as she sucks on my shaft, the tip hitting the back of her throat, causing her to gag a little. Call me a dirty asshole, but that sound has my cock hardening further. She cups my balls and presses on THAT spot close to my no-go zone and from the evil glint in her eyes, she did that on purpose. "You'll pay for that," I hiss, which turns into a moan when she rakes her teeth gently along my length.

My cock slips from her mouth and she shakes her head. "No go for you. No go for me." Then she swallows my dick again and all thoughts about the no-go zone evaporate as I focus on the pleasure my wife is currently sucking from me. *How the puck did I get so lucky to score a wife like this woman?*

Gripping my cock at the base, she squeezes as she sucks the head. It doesn't take long before my balls begin to twitch. "Do it," she mumbles around my shaft and as if my body is in sync with her words, the first spurt shoots into her mouth. She sucks and swallows every last drop before my cock pops out of her mouth. She wipes at the corner and sucks her finger into her mouth. I know I just came but seeing her do that has my dick sparking back to life.

Beckoning to her with my index finger, Chels snakes her way up my body, dropping kisses along the way. She straddles my chest and stares down at me. "You beckoned, husband?"

"I did." I nod. "I want you to come up here and sit on my face. Once you've come on my tongue, I'm going to fuck you hard and fast from behind and then make sweet, sweet love to you for the rest of the day."

"As you wish." She lifts herself and hovers above my face, giving me an unobstructed view of her dripping pussy.

"Did that turn you on, baby? You're dripping."

"Maybe, but less talking, more licking."

"As you wish." I grip her hips and slide her to my mouth. Licking her from taint to clit, she moans when I circle my tongue over the sensitive bundle of nerves at the top. She lifts her hands and plays with her tits as I suckle on her clit.

"More," she demands, and I know exactly what she wants. Sliding my tongue down her slit, I thrust it inside her, flicking it around before sucking. She swivels her hips and rides my tongue and face. Gazing up at her, her eyes are closed and she's giving herself over to the pleasure building. Her arousal is dripping down my chin, she's never been this wet before. I could drown in her juices and I'd die a happy fucking man.

"Kal," she cries, "I'm … I'm coming." Just as she says this, a torrent of her arousal soaks my face. I lap at her pussy like a starved man as she rides out her orgasm.

She leans forward and rests her head on the headboard, panting and still sitting on my face. "That," she pants, "was amazing."

"Mmmhmpf," I reply against her pussy. She giggles at the vibrations and lifts herself off my face and collapses to the mattress beside me. Looking over to her, I find her staring back at me with a blissful grin on her face.

"Good morning."

"Good morning, indeed." Rolling to my side, I lean over and press my lips to hers. What starts out slow, quickly turns heated. "Pussy and penis breath kisses are the best."

"You're disgusting," she mumbles against my lips.

"You love me."

"I'm questioning my love right about now."

"Too late, we have a piece of paper that says, 'til death do us part and you, Mrs. Jones, are not dying until I've had my fill of you."

"And how long will that be?"

"For at least fifty years. Minimum. But in all honesty, no amount of time will ever be enough with you."

"Kal, that's beautiful."

"You know what else is beautiful?"

"What?"

"This." I roll on top of her and my cock easily slides inside her and we make sweet, sweet love together. I know I said I'd fuck her hard and fast from behind first, but we have our whole lives for that to happen AND it's only day one of our honeymoon. I still have four uninterrupted days with her before we have to get back to New York to continue preseason training.

I'm lucky my coach also happens to be my wife's dad and he gave me a few days off to get married and for us to have a quick honeymoon. We could have waited until the next off-season to get married, but I couldn't wait another minute to be married to this amazing woman. So, four months to the day I proposed, we became man and wife.

Marrying Chels was the best day of my life, even better than the day I was drafted to the Crushers. Hockey won't be forever but what Chelsea and I have, it will last till the end of time, and even then, it won't be enough.

CHAPTER 2
CHELSEA

... LATE OCTOBER

The new hockey season is underway and the Crushers are currently at the top of the leader board. I love watching hockey but I hate it when the Crushers play the LA Legends because my ex, Stefan Däuchmen—affectionately nicknamed Doucheman because well, he's a douche and lives up to the douche in his name —plays dirty, on and off the ice, especially when it comes to my husband.

You'd think he'd have given up on his grudge now that we're married, but nope, he's still a douche with a capital D. It's not as volatile but it's no picnic in Central Park either, and I think that's due to his handler, Wren Brooks. Yep, Stefan now has a babysitter. Wren was hired by the LA Legends management and board to keep him in line and work on his image. She seems like the nicest girl ever, and I feel sorry for her having to babysit him.

On the ice, Stefan is an amazing player but off the ice, well, he's not so amazing. For the most part, since she started working with him, he's kept himself in line on and off the ice, but once a douche always a douche. I really hope they're paying her big, super-huge bucks because I have no doubt she's working twenty-four seven, three hundred and sixty-five days of the year keeping his douchey ass in line. I bet she's thankful that leap years only happen once every four years, and we just had one. Hopefully, by the time the next one comes around, she will be free of the douche and his antics.

We are in the final period and there are two minutes left on the clock and these two minutes are turning into the longest two minutes of my life. My heart is racing. My palms are sweaty and I feel like I'm going to throw up, again. This game is intense.

There's only one minute remaining and the score is tied, three to three. Doucheman has the puck and he's headed straight for Kal in the net. The rest of the Crushers seem off in la-la land because Doucheman easily makes his way through them. Weaving in and out of them, the only one who's trying to stop him is JJ.

We're now down to twenty-six seconds left in the game and it's all going to come down to this shot. Everyone in the stadium is on the edge of their seat. The atmosphere is electric and my heart is beating so fast, I'm expecting it to beat through my rib cage and land at my feet. "Come on, baby, you've got this," I chant to myself over and over. I'm now rocking back and forth in my seat watching Doucheman skate closer and closer to the net, and Kal.

He raises his stick and swings, executing a perfect slap shot. I jump to my feet and watch the puck sail through the air. Kal reaches out just as the siren blares and there's a collective gasp from those around me.

"Where's the puck?" someone from next to me asks. Just as they finish their question, Kal opens his glove and the puck falls to the ice, he saved it. They will now go into overtime.

The Crushers fans go crazy, as does the rest of the team on the ice. They all skate up to Kal and slap him on the back and helmet, while Doucheman stands there in shock that the puck was stopped. From the look on his face, he's pissed. No doubt Wren will be scrambling to stop him from going into douche mode as soon as the game is over.

Five minutes later, they take the ice again and Doucheman is out for blood. He's returned to the ice like a raging bull with a red flag waving in his face. He's body checking left, right, and center, determined to not let the Crushers score. He's just Kronwalled JJ into the plexiglass and has the puck, he makes a breakaway and is headed for the goal and Kallen.

Once again it all comes down to Kallen against Stefan.

Like the last period, my eyes are locked on him as he makes his way down the ice. He really is a great athlete, it's just a shame about his personality and persona. Kal is watching him intently, much like I'm watching them.

Stefan is flying down the ice, he's got some speed behind him, rather than launching into another slap shot, he heads straight for Kal and the goal. He's going for a wrap-around this time and skates to the right, knowing that Kal's left isn't as good as his right. He circles the back of the net and with a flick of the wrist, hits the puck, and it sails past Kal into the net.

The Legends win.

"Puck," I mumble to myself as I jump up from my seat and quickly make my way into the belly of the stadium to wait for Kal. He's going to be devastated. Losses always suck but when he loses to Stefan, it's always harder to take.

It feels like it's taking him forever to come out. His teammate, JJ, and Lexi, the team's physical therapist and now JJ's girl, exit first. "How is he?" I ask, pushing off the wall to walk over to them.

"I think you know how he is," he replies. His face confirms what I thought, Kal is pissed at himself for the loss.

"Puck," I mumble, just as a wave of nausea rolls over me. Racing over to the nearest trash can, I empty the contents of my stomach. This bug is just lingering, every time I think I'm better, it strikes again.

"You okay, Chels?" Lexi asks me, running her hand over my back.

"Yeah, that bug I picked up in Cleveland last week is still hanging on. Add in the nerves of the game just now, and well, my nachos decided I needed to taste what they're like on the way up. FYI, not as good coming up as going down."

"Duly noted, let me get you some water to wash away that nacho-flavored vomit."

"Thanks," I mumble as I wipe my mouth with the back of my hand.

"I'll get it," JJ offers. I watch as he reenters the dressing room, leaving me to lean against the cinder block wall. Closing my eyes, I take a deep breath, willing myself not to barf again.

"Maybe you're pregnant," Lexi teases from beside me.

"Yeah, nah, it's just that bug. Dad was sick too if you remember."

"True," she agrees, "but you and your husband do bang a lot."

"I can't help it, have you seen my husband?"

"I have." She suggestively raises her eyebrows at me. "Your husband is H O double T, hot." And she's right, my husband is the hottest player in the NHL and he's all mine. There's no better feeling in the world than waking up beside him each and every morning. Actually, the best feeling is waking with his head between my legs and that magical tongue of his sliding through my folds before thrusting inside of me. Man, I wish I didn't feel like death warmed up, I could do with a tongue-induced orgasm right about now. I mean, it's been fourteen hours since his tongue was inside of me, that's forever in tongue time.

"Aww, thanks, babe," JJ coos, kissing Lex on the cheek as he hands me a bottle of water. "I think you're H O double T, sexy as fuck too."

"Thanks, but for the record, you're only H O T hot, no double T for you," she teases him. He fakes being hurt and then the two of them proceed to discuss JJ's hotness and the hotness ranking of each other.

Unscrewing the water bottle, I take a sip and watch the two of them bicker back and forth. I'm so glad the two of them pulled their fingers out and got over their issues. If two people are meant to be, it's those two.

Me throwing up again pulls them apart, and just like last time, Lexi rubs my back while my body expels the water I just drank.

"Chels, babe," Kallen voices, rushing over to me. "Are you okay?"

"I'm fine," I tell him. Wiping my mouth on the back of my hand, I turn to face him and smile. "That bug from Cleveland is still hanging on and kicking my ass, but YAY, I didn't vomit during the game."

"That's good, hope it's not anything more serious."

"Maybe she's—" JJ's sentence is cut off when Lexi covers his mouth with her hand.

"… going to be okay," Lexi says. "I was thinking I'd take her home and you two can meet us there after you wrap things up here." She pauses. "Maybe also go and have a few drinks with the boys, let Chels and I have some girl time."

"Thanks, Lex, I appreciate you looking after Chels like that, but as her husband, I should be looking after her."

"I'm not an invalid," I add, "I can get from the stadium to home by myself."

"I know, babe, but I just worry about you."

"And I'm fine," I sneer, hoping he can't tell I want to vomit again.

"Chels, throwing up in the trash can twice isn't fine," JJ states. "To appease us, please let Lex look after you and I'll look after your man."

"I'm—"

"Please, babe," Kal says, pulling me into his arms. He slides his around my waist and I drape mine over his shoulders. "For me?"

"Fine," I relent.

"Thank you." He places a kiss on the tip of my nose. "Now go home and warm the bed up for me. Then when I get home, we can—"

"LALALALALLALALALA," JJ singsongs, putting his fingers in his ears. "I don't need to hear about you two bumping uglies."

"Why?" Kal asks. "We all heard you and Lex in her treatment room yesterday before training."

Lexi's eyes widen and her cheeks darken in embarrassment, meanwhile, JJ grins like the guy who scored ... and technically he did. "What can I say? My lady is—" Once again, Lexi covers his mouth.

"Do not finish that sentence, James Jameson ..."

"Ohhhhhhh, you just got full named, you're in trouble now," Kallen teases and I smack him in the stomach. "What?"

"Be nice, otherwise, there will be no ..." But before I can finish that sentence, I throw up again.

"Doesn't look like you'll be getting any tonight, Jones," JJ teases him.

"And you won't be getting any either, Jameson," Lexi throws back at him. "Come on, Chels, let's get you home."

"Thanks, Lex." I turn to Kal. "Play nice in the press conference and then enjoy your night with the guys."

"You sure?"

Nodding, I smile and reach up to cup his cheek. "Very sure. Now go and get your drink on."

"Love you." He leans in for a kiss, but I cover his mouth with my hand and shake my head.

"I have nacho-flavored vomit breath and before you say anything, that's worse than morning or pussy breath, so don't even try to argue with me."

"Fine," he hisses against my palm. "But tomorrow, when you're feeling better, I'm going to kiss your pussy and then share a pussy breath morning kiss with you before we spend naked Sunday together. And FYI, I might kiss your pussy several more times with both my mouth and my dick."

"What is it with you and my hoo-ha?"

"I'm addicted. One taste and I was hooked."

"Lucky I love you, Jones."

"That I am. And for the record, I love that you love me, Mrs. Jones." It's still surreal to be called Mrs. Jones but I wouldn't have it any other way. We've only been married for a few weeks now, but it's perfect in every way.

"Let's go, Jones," JJ yells as he's joined by Jett and Cliff from the team.

Kal kisses me on the cheek and then walks off with the guys. Lexi links her arm with mine and we watch them head toward the press conference. When they're out of earshot, Lexi leans into me. "First things first, we need to get a pregnancy test."

"I'm not pregnant," I snap.

"For me, please pee on a stick?"

"Fine," I relent, "but I'm not pregnant."

FYI ... I'm not pregnant, the test was negative. It's just a bug, like I keep telling everyone.

CHAPTER 3
KALLEN

Leaving Chelsea with Lexi just now isn't sitting well with me, but I know my wife, when she's made up her mind, there's no changing it. Well, except for that one time I made her date me … and then marry me, but that's all moot now. I slapped a ring on that and she's mine forever now. And one day, she'll carry my babies and we will live happily ever after.

"Dude, you okay?" JJ asks, slapping me on the back. "You were off in your head just now."

"Just worried about Chels."

"Dude, it's just a bug. She'll be fine."

"Yeah, I know but …"

"But you love her and want to make sure she's okay, blah-blah-blah."

"You can't tell me if it was Lexi throwing up like that, that you'd be okay."

"Hell fucking no. I'd flip the team off and be there to hold her hair back while she vomits her guts up and then I'd feed her chicken soup and rub her feet."

"You're so whipped," I tease, bumping him in the shoulder.

"Like you're not?"

"Well, I'm here—"

"Only because she demanded you come here. See, whipped." He makes the sound of a whip cracking.

"Damn straight, I am. Have you seen my wife?"

"I'm not falling for that again, last time I agreed with you, you whacked me in the leg and I could hardly walk for a week."

"And I stand by that whack. No one ogles my wife except for me."

"And the millions of people who see the two of you on Page Six every time one of you sneezes. If it isn't baby watch, it's saying that her and Doucheman are sneaking around behind your back."

"Hell will freeze over before that ever happens." JJ laughs at me but it's true. Chelsea will never go back to him and it's not just because she's with me, but because he broke her trust and her heart.

"Speaking of hot, have you seen his babysitter? She's H O double T hot and what adds to her hotness? The way she stands up to and handles Doucheman."

"Yeah, seeing her all feisty and in his face does things to me that I shouldn't be feeling." Everyone nods their heads in agreement over Wren Brooks. "And if Chels ever asks, I will deny this conversation ever occurred."

"Dude, none of us will ever admit that to our ladies. I don't know about you, but I like my balls where they are," JJ states.

"What, in Lexi's handbag?" Jett teases, causing us all to laugh.

"Fuck off, assholes." JJ flips us off and then cups his balls to reiterate the fact they are between his legs. "As you can see, my balls are firmly attached to my body."

"Physically yes, metaphorically speaking, they're

currently at my place firmly in Lexi's grasp. Now that we know the location of your balls, can we stop talking about your balls?"

"I can't help it if you like my balls."

"I'd like to kick you in the balls right now."

"You wound me, Kal, you wound me."

"Fuck off, asshole."

We spend the next few hours at Squires drinking beer and ribbing each other at every turn.

When I finally make my way home, I find Chelsea sound asleep in our bed. Leaning against the doorframe, I stand here and watch her sleep. Her chest rises and falls with each breath she takes. I want nothing more than to crawl into bed and make sweet, sweet love to my wife, but I know she's not feeling well so I just stand here and watch over her.

She's so pucking beautiful, and I thank my lucky stars every day she gave me a chance. She swore never to fall for another player after Doucheman screwed her over but from the moment I laid my eyes on her, I was pucked. Unfortunately for her, I'm a persistent bastard and I wore her down. Now we're married and have the rest of our lives together.

"Are you watching me sleep again?" she mumbles.

"Yep," I reply.

"It's still creepy." She taps the mattress next to her.

Pushing off the doorframe, I walk over to her side of the bed and sit on the edge. "How you doing, baby?"

"Feeling a little better now. Lexi thought I might be pregnant ..." My eyes widen and I'm pretty sure my heart stops.

"And?"

"I'm not, it's just a bug ... like I keep telling everyone."

"Ohh," I dejectedly reply. "For a minute there, I was excited you might have been." Pulling back the blanket, I cover her stomach with my hand. "I can't wait for the day your stomach swells with the baby we created together growing inside of you."

"I am too, but for now, I want to be selfish and have you all to myself." She raises her eyebrows at me in that 'I want you to devour me' kind of way and it has me sitting here sporting a semi. One eyebrow movement and my cock's a goner for her.

"Are you sure you're up to it? A few hours ago you were vomiting in the trash cans at the stadium."

"That was a few hours ago. Right now, I feel fine and I really really want to practice making a baby with my sexy as puck husband." To reiterate she wants me to fuck her. She sits up and pulls her Crushers tee over her head, baring her gorgeous tits to me. Lifting her hands, she cups her boobs and with her middle fingers rubs her nipples. "But before we get to the baby-making, I want you to fuck my tits. I love feeling your dick slide between them."

"What my wife wants, my wife gets."

Quicker than *The Flash*, I strip out of my clothes and straddle my wife's chest. With my eyes locked on hers, I stroke my dick while she continues to play with her tits. "You ready, baby?"

"Always," she breathlessly pants.

Shuffling forward, I guide my cock to her tits and slide the head into the soft cushioning of her mounds. A moan slips free when her tongue glides over the tip of my shaft. Sliding it back, I push back through but this time, she lifts her head up and sucks on the head. "Fuck, babe. Your mouth and tits are phenomenal."

"Only for you, baby, now fuck my tits."

"As you wish." I throw her a wink and then I do as she requests. Undulating my hips back and forth, I fuck her tits.

My shaft slides in and out and sooner than I would have liked, my balls begin to tingle. "I'm close," I grunt.

"Do it," she hisses and as if her words are the detonator, I come. Milky white streams splash across her tits and chin.

Wiping her chin, she sucks her finger into her mouth, and seeing her do that has my cock once again coming to life. "Really, already?"

Shrugging at her, I grip my shaft and stroke him back to hard. "What can I say, I'm an addict when it comes to fucking you. Now, remove your panties, it's your turn to come."

"As much as I'd love to, I'm spent and need sleep. Can we settle for a shower and a snuggle?"

"A sexy shower? A naked snuggle? Both?"

"With us, anything is possible, but right now I need a shower to rinse off the mess you made all over me."

Chelsea naked and wet, yes fucking please. Climbing off my wife, I offer her my hand. Pulling her up, I cup her face and slam my lips to hers. Pushing my tongue into her mouth, she wraps her arms around my neck and pulls me into her. Her cum-covered breasts press against my bare chest. My cock hardens further and when Chels whimpers into my mouth in that 'I need you to fuck me' kind of way, I know I'm going to get a sexy shower.

Unfortunately for me, it wasn't a sexy shower but I did get naked cuddles, and a naked Chelsea is better than nothing.

Blissfully happy, I drift off to sleep with my naked wife's body wrapped around mine. The next morning though, I get a wake-up blow job, followed by a sexy shower and a full day in bed ... naked ... with my wife.

CHAPTER 4
CHELSEA

... MID DECEMBER

Lexi and I are sitting in Squires waiting for the guys to get here while Margot, my best friend and current drinks wench, heads to the bar to get a pitcher of beer. The guys played against LA earlier tonight and they kicked LA's ass. Like thrashed them, thirteen to zero. I think that's a history-making loss, better look that up because if so, that's a marketing dream come true. The promotion from that will be amazing. Doucheman was sent off in the last period for being, well, a douche. Poor Wren is going to have her hands full with him tonight. I remember what he was like when they'd lose when we were together. He's like a two-year-old throwing a tantrum after their balloon flies away.

Margot arrives with a pitcher of beer and I could kiss her, my throat is dry and I'm thirsty as hell. "I ordered wings too."

"Awesome, I'm famished," I tell them as I pick up the pitcher and begin to pour us each a glass.

"How are you famished?" Margot asks me as she takes

a seat across from me. "At the game you ate an order of nachos, half of Lexi's, three hotdogs, and two giant pretzels."

"What can I say, I'm a growing girl."

"Yeah, outward," she teases. I was about to hand her a beer so I stick my tongue out and hand it to Lexi instead.

"Maybe you're pregnant," Lexi adds from beside me and thanks me for her beer. A sense of déjà vu washes over me, of her and I having this same conversation a few weeks ago but this time, I think she might be right. My boobs have been really sore the last couple of days, the nausea first thing in the morning is horrendous, and I'm hungry all the time. Like ravenous, I'll stab a bitch, hungry. My eyes widen and I flick my gaze between her and Margot, covering my mouth in shock.

"Nooooo, I'm not ... am I?" They both stare blankly at me. "Surely, not?"

"I don't know, are you?" she questions.

"I ... I don't know. I'd know if I was, right?"

"Well, when was your last period?"

"I don't know, I don't get one. I'm on that birth control that stops them to help with my endo."

"Babe, no contraception is one-hundred-percent effective," Margot unhelpfully adds.

"Abstinence is," I throw back at her.

"Yes," Lexi deadpans, "you and that hunk of a husband of yours refrain from sex all the time. NOT. Did I not catch you two in the locker room a few days ago?"

"Well, yeah, but I hadn't seen him all day."

"Case in point, right there, as to why you might be preggers, you two hump like it's an Olympic sport."

"So do you and JJ," I throw back at Lexi.

"We are talking about you right now." She points her

finger at me. "You know, I'm surprised you don't already have a billion babies."

"Riiiight?" Margo unhelpfully agrees. "I've thought the same thing on many occasions."

"You two are crazy, let's reduce that number to three, three baby Kallens I can handle."

"Three billion," they both say at the same time, fist bumping before falling into a fit of giggles while I continue to freak out that I may in fact be pregnant.

Lexi looks at me and when she sees me in freak-out mode, she sits up straight. "Look, Chels, I seriously think you'd know if you were, so have a great night tonight and let future Chelsea worry about it."

Nodding my head, I smile. "Yeah, you're right. I'd definitely know if I was, it's just my mind running rampant 'cause the heroine in my current read is pregnant."

"Exactly, now drink up." Margo lifts her beer and proceeds to chug it back. Shaking my head, I sit back in my chair and lift my drink to my lips but for some reason, I don't take a sip. I stare into the bubbly amber liquid and internally freak-out. Lexi and Margo start discussing a girls' trip away but I can't focus, I just keep thinking about the fact I might be pregnant.

I'm not, am I? Sure, Kal and I hump like rabbits but we're newlyweds and he travels for work. Surely not.

Before I fall into full-blown panic mode, the guys arrive. My husband sweeps me off my chair and into his arms before he smashes his lips to mine. For a few brief seconds, I stop my internal panicking and focus on the man currently squeezing the life out of me. Then I quickly push away, what if I'm pregnant? He'll squish the baby if he squeezes me like that.

"You all right, babe?" he questions, worry etched on his beautiful face.

"Yeah, I'm fine, I just need the bathroom." Looking to the girls, I shout louder than necessary, "Bathroom. Now."

They both look at me with confusion but they sense the silent pleading/impending freak-out I'm spiraling into because they both jump up and drag me out of my chair. We loop arms and the three of us walk away from the guys toward the restrooms.

When the guys are out of earshot, 1 whisper-hiss, "I think we need to get me a pregnancy test."

CHAPTER 5
CHELSEA

"Come again?" Margot questions when I flip the lock on the main bathroom door. Sorry, ladies who need to pee, but I need one-on-one noninterrupted freak-out time with my girls.

"I ... I think I'm pregnant." They both stare at me wide-eyed and open-mouthed. I've left Margo speechless, something I've only managed to achieve a few times in our life.

"With a baby?" she finally asks.

"No with a pucking gorilla, of course a baby."

"We were only teasing you." She adds, "You don't have to get so momma-bear."

"I know but ..." I shrug and subconsciously cover my stomach with my hand and begin to gently rub circles.

"Holy puckballs, you really think you are, don't you?" she squeals when she realizes I really think I am.

Nodding, I stare at my two bestest friends and smile. "I ... I really think I am. My boobs are sore. I feel sick all the time—"

"And earlier today you ate as much as Kallen and JJ combined."

"I didn't eat that much." They both give me the 'really'

look. "Okay, fine, I did overeat a little but forget about that, what am I going to do?"

"I can duck out to a pharmacy and get you a test," Margot offers as she takes my hand in hers, squeezing in that reassuring best friend kind of way, letting me know it's all going to be okay.

I shake my head from side to side. "I'm not taking a pregnancy test in a bar's bathroom."

"Well, how about we head home early?" Lex suggests.

"No." I shake my head again, but this time the action causes a lump to form in the back of my throat, and I feel like I want to vomit. "I can't duck out, I need to be here to celebrate tonight's pucking amazing win."

"But what if you ARE pregnant?" Lexi asks me, she looks worried that I'm considering waiting to find out.

"I'll still be pregnant tomorrow, Lex. Tonight, I'll play wife and tomorrow Chelsea can play the 'what if I'm pregnant' card."

We all nod in agreement and when we open the door to the restroom, we come face to face with Wren. She looks on the verge of tears but before we can see if she's okay, she darts past us into the restroom. Then we hear a frustrated growl from a deep voice at the end of the corridor. Hearing that makes me really want to check on her and make sure she's okay but before I have to make a decision, the door opens behind us.

Spinning around, I come face-to-face with Wren. She smiles at us and mumbles, "Excuse me." Lowering her head, she shuffles past us only for an arm to reach out, grab her, spin her into the wall of the corridor, and their muscular body cocoons her in.

My eyes widen and then I take off toward them, just as I hear her sneer, "Back the fuck up, Stefan." She presses her hands into his chest but he doesn't move, even though the tone of her voice means business. Stopping mid-stride, I stare at them when I realize who she's fighting with. I really don't want to intrude so I stand here and watch them. I'm once again shocked when I hear Stefan utter two words that I never thought I would hear him utter, much less to a woman. The words "I'm sorry" just passed through his lips. What the actual fuck? Stefan Däuchmen just apologized.

From beside me, Margot grabs my upper arm and digs her fingers in and whisper-hisses, "Did ... did Doucheman just apologize?"

"Mmmhmpf," I reply, nodding.

"What the actual fuck?" she sneers in shock. Her words cause both of them to snap their gazes toward us.

Offering a shy smile, I remove Margot's hand from my arm and take her hand. Dragging her and Lexi past them, I offer a small, "Excuse us" as we exit the restroom corridor. When we step back into the main bar area, Margot once again hisses, "What the actual fuck?"

A laugh breaks free. "You literally just said that, Margot."

"I know but, fuuuuck. Wren is a fucking miracle worker if she's getting him to utter the 'S' word."

"She sure is." I nod in agreement as the three of us walk back to our table. All thoughts of me being pregnant vanish when I reach my husband, who is laughing with his friends and teammates.

CHAPTER 6
KALLEN

"What is it with chicks and going to the bathroom in groups?" I ask JJ as I take the seat Chelsea just vacated.

"Beats me, maybe it's a safety in numbers thing."

"Who knows, but whatever the case, it's fucking weird."

"What's weird?" Jett asks, placing the two pitchers of beer he's carrying down on the table, while Cliff places the glasses down and the two of them proceed to pour beers for everyone, handing them out like the good beer wenches they are.

"How girls all go to the pisser together," JJ says.

"You really are crass sometimes," I tell him, bumping his shoulder and causing him to spill his beer.

"Fucker, you made me spill my beer."

A commotion nearby snaps my attention and when I turn my head, I see Wren and Doucheman having a heated argument. "You really are a douche," Wren sneers at Stefan and from the look on his face, he's hurt by her words.

"And you're a stuck-up bitch who's riding my ass every five seconds."

"It's my job to ride your ass," she snaps at him. "Stefan, you're this close ..." She holds her fingers millimeters apart, "... to losing your career. To losing everything you've worked so hard for. I don't want to see everything go up in flames because you act like a Neanderthal, hot-headed dickwad."

"More like you don't want your reputation marred if I fail."

"Yes, I'm so shallow that I'm all about the 'look at me' crap. I'm not conceited like you. I actually fucking care." She turns and walks away from him. After a few steps, she spins back to him and gets up in his face. "You really are a self-centered, egotistical prick."

"And you're a sexy, uptight bitch."

They stand there, in the middle of the bar, staring at one another. Each of them breathing heavily but the air has changed from heated anger to simmering with desire. Chels was right, there IS something going on between them, she'll be pissed she's peeing right now and missing this.

"Huh, didn't see that coming," I mumble, but clearly it was loud enough for them to hear because they both turn their heads toward me. Both stare matching angry daggers in my direction.

"Fuck off, Jones," Stefan snarls, "she's my handler. That's it."

Wren's head snaps back to him and there's hurt etched all over her face. She shakes her head and as she turns to leave, I notice tears welling in her eyes. Stefan stands there and watches her leave.

"Go after her, you fool," I shout at him.

"What?" he questions, confused at my words.

"For puck's sake, you two clearly have the hots for each other. Go. After. Her," I enunciate the last three words, spelling it out for him.

"Do not," he refutes, but his words are high-pitched and the tone used tells a different story. I see the moment the light bulb goes off in his head. "I—"

"Go," I tell him again and it sparks him into action. He turns and heads in the direction Wren raced off. He looks over his shoulder, indecision on his face. I nod in Wren's direction and then I sit here and watch as he goes after his girl.

A few minutes later Chels returns. "What'd I miss?" she asks, stopping in front of me.

"Babe, you will never believe it." Pulling her between my legs, I rest my hands on her hips. Placing a kiss on her forehead, I then fill her in on what we just witnessed.

"No pucking way," she says when I finish telling her. "That explains him saying 'I'm sorry' to her just now."

"Didn't know he knew those two words."

"Maybe Wren is perfect for him, professionally and personally," I say and then we rejoin the team to celebrate our massive win tonight.

* * *

It's nearing on close so we decide to call it a night. All us guys are well past tipsy but we're not yet shitfaced. The girls keep whispering like schoolgirls and my Spidey Sense is telling me that Chelsea is hiding something from me.

"Let's go home, husband," she declares, sliding her arm around my waist.

"Only if I get to fuck you in the as—" She covers my mouth with her hand and shakes her head from side to side.

"You know the answer to that, not happening … ever … unless I can—" Now it's my turn to cover her mouth with my hand. The cheeky minx winks at me and proceeds to lick my palm, circling her tongue over my skin. "I can do that to your dick," she mumbles against my palm.

"Taxi," I shout from behind her hand. This causes her to giggle and, fuck, I love that sound. Gripping her wrist, I remove her hand from my mouth. "Chels, we need to get home now before I take you into the bathroom and fuck you here."

My hand is still covering her mouth and she mumbles, "Taxi" just like I did.

Laughing, I bend down and throw her over my shoulder. Slapping her on the ass, I turn around and start toward the exit but I bump into someone and in my slightly inebriated state, the three of us fall to the floor. Chelsea grunts while a deep voice sneers, "Whats tzhe fusch asschole."

My eyes widen when I register that the voice belongs to a very drunk Doucheman and I mumble, "Fuck," to myself as I offer my hand to Chels and pull her up.

"Wants a pieced of me, pricks?" he dribbles, clumsily pushing himself up into a standing position. Clearly he's had a few too many tonight. I look around for Wren but I can't see her anywhere. Looks like the two of them didn't kiss and make up after all. "You dids thatchs purpse."

"It was an accident," I snap back at the douche. "And you're drunk."

"Amsd snot," he throws back at me and then giggles. "Schnot," he repeats, chuckling to himself as if saying schnot is the funniest thing on earth.

"Where's Wren?" I ask. That was obviously the wrong thing to say because before I can process what's happening, his fist flies toward my face. I stumble backward from the hit and he comes at me again, causing the two of us to fall to the floor. He sucker punches me and my head bounces off the cement.

Someone pulls him off me and Chels drops down to see

if I'm okay, but Doucheman gets free and knocks Chels to the side, trying to get to me. He stares down at me and I growl, "The fuck, man?" Jumping to my feet, I get up into his personal space, pissed off that he just pushed my wife. He's angry and drunk, his face red with anger and inebriation. Spittle forms at the corner of his lips and before I can say anything, he swings at me again.

"Ohh, it's on now," I growl through clenched teeth.

Curling my hand into a fist, I rear it back and slam it into his face. This pisses him off even more and he launches himself at me. The two of us crash into a high-top table before we roll and grapple on the ground. We go hit for hit and it isn't until someone separates us and shouts, "Break it up!" that we both stop.

Falling to my back, I breathe heavily, trying to catch my breath as I stare up at the ceiling of Squires. Rubbing my chin, I groan. I'm going to be bruised and sore tomorrow. I can't believe I just got into a fight with him, but the view and my internal processing is interrupted when an officer comes into my line of sight and hovers over me. "You're under arrest ..." *Ahh fuck, my wife and Coach are going to have my balls.*

CHAPTER 7
CHELSEA

"Mom, this is all a mess," I cry as she slides a cup of coffee across the island counter to me. Dad is currently down at the police station, working on bailing Kallen out. Wrapping my hands around the mug, the warmth seeps into me but it does nothing to ease the anxiety coursing through me.

Bringing the mug to my lips, I take a sip and as soon as the liquid hits my tongue, I begin to gag. Placing the mug down, coffee sloshing everywhere, I race down the hallway to the guest bath and barely make it to the toilet before I throw up. Resting my arms on the seat, I continue to heave into the bowl.

A wet washcloth appears on my neck, followed by the rub only a mom can do on my back. "That's nice," I murmur just before I throw up again.

Mom continues to rub my back and finally I stop vomiting. Closing my eyes, I rest my head on my arms. Not quite game to move just yet, that is until Mom asks, "How far along are you, honey?"

My head snaps up and I turn to face my mom. My mouth opens and closes a few times before I finally mumble, "I ... I ... I'm not pregnant." Wiping at my mouth with the back of my hand, I stare at her and smile. She returns the sentiment and offers me the washcloth for my face. "Thanks."

Taking the cloth from her, I wipe my face and hide behind the cool, wet cotton in my hand, avoiding Mom's stare.

"I think you might be pregnant, Chels," she says, and I know I have no choice but to face this now. She drops to the floor next to me and takes my hand in hers.

Removing the cloth from my face, I lean over and rest my head on her shoulder. She squeezes my hand in that Mom way and it immediately comforts me.

"How did you know?" I whisper.

"That reaction just now to coffee was exactly how I was when I found out I was pregnant with you."

"I ... I haven't done a test yet."

"Why not?"

"Because my husband got arrested for brawling in a bar with my ex-boyfriend."

"That's a good excuse."

"Mom," I plead, "what if I'm pregnant?"

"What if you are?" I nod absentmindedly at her words. "Surely you and Kallen have discussed children?"

"We have. We want three, but not for a few years yet."

"Well, when you have sex, pregnancy tends to happen."

"I'm on birth control," I defend.

"And no birth control is one-hundred-percent effective."

"Why do people keep reminding me of that?" Mom looks quizzically at me. "Margot said the same thing earlier tonight."

"Why didn't you test then?"

"I wasn't doing a pregnancy test in a bar's restroom."

"Fair enough." We fall silent but Mom breaks that a few moments later. "Okay, I'm going to run down the block to CVS and get you a test, no time like the present to see if I'm going to become a nanny."

Nodding, I sit here while Mom runs off to grab me a pregnancy test.

Twenty minutes later, Mom gently shakes me awake. "Sorry to wake you, honey, but A. You're asleep on the floor in the bathroom, and B. My neck hurt looking at you just now, and C. You have a test to take."

"Is it wrong that right now I'd rather do an algebra test than a pregnancy test?"

Mom laughs. "Chelsea Jones, I never thought I'd see the day you shy away from something."

"I'm not, I'm just … scared."

"Welcome to motherhood. Not a day goes by that I don't worry about you."

"But—"

"Nope, no buts, you will understand when you become a mom. You worry constantly—"

"You make motherhood sound amazing," I deadpan.

"It's the most amazing job I have ever done. From the moment I saw that pink plus sign, I was in love. There hasn't been a moment since that day that I haven't thought about you. You are my greatest achievement, Chelsea, and I thank the puck gods every day for giving me you as a daughter. I love you baby girl."

"Mooom," I tearfully cry. "I love you too."

"I love you too, honey. Now that we know we love each other, it's time to pee on a stick."

CHAPTER 8
KALLEN

It's lunchtime the following day and I've just made bail thanks to my coach and father-in-law, David. We climb into his car and the atmosphere is awkward, I can tell he's pissed off at me because I'm pissed at myself too. Brawling in a bar is not anything I've ever done before, but when it comes to Stefan Däuchmen I lose clearheaded thinking and I become a Neanderthal … just like him.

Neither one of us utters a word as we pull out into traffic. The silence is deafening. I don't know what to say but what I do know is, right now, he's disappointed, frustrated, upset, and ashamed of me. I could go on with the descriptive words but of all the ones I've mentioned, it's the disappointing him part that is the worst thing about all of this. Actually, above all of that, not being there for my wife after she got shoved is the worst part, but disappointing Coach is a close second. I need to be a better husband and player, and right now, I don't know if he's angry at me in a son-in-law way or as my coach … it's probably both, truth be told, which means I'm doubly screwed.

Fifteen minutes after leaving the precinct, we silently

pull into the underground parking garage of my building, and I pull on my big boy panties and break the silence. "I know you're disappointed in me, you don't need to say it, Coach, I'm disappointed in me too."

"Wasn't going to say a thing," he nonchalantly replies from the driver's seat as he pulls into one of my guest parking spots, but his tone says it all. "But since you mentioned it, as your father-in-law, I'm pissed that you didn't look after my little girl. She's fine, by the way."

"I know she's fine, the arresting officer let me know."

"I expected this shit from *him,* not from you. You're better than that, Kallen."

"He started it," I snap like a petulant child. Like *him.*

"So mature of you, Kallen. Guess now's the time to let you know that you've both been scratched for three games. You will each also be fined ten grand and at the upcoming Christmas charity day for underprivileged kids, you and Däuchmen will be required to give a talk on team bonding and how to deal with big personalities. Hopefully, doing this will prevent WWF matches between the two of you. Wren has arranged for both teams to be there as a buffer, we can't trust the two of you alone together. Coach Barber from the LA Legends and I feel it's time you two learn to play nice together."

"But—"

"No buts, Jones, this rivalry between you two has gotten out of hand. It's either this or indefinite suspension, I will not have the Crushers' name marred by you or him."

"Fine," I relent, "but I guarantee you, he won't be happy about this."

"I don't give a puck about him. I want you to man up and be the player and man I know you can be. Don't let Däuchmen and his antics bring you down. Kallen, you've worked too damn hard to let this rivalry dash your dreams."

"Fine." I huff, hating that he's right. I could lose it all if shit like this happens again. "You coming up?"

"Yep, Ness is upstairs, she stayed the night with Chelsea. Wanted to make sure she was okay after being shoved, since you were otherwise indisposed."

"You just had to rub it in that I was a shit husband last night."

"No rubbing when it's the truth. Now get the fuck out of my car, you stink and you owe my daughter an apology. I hear she likes books with half-naked men on the cover."

Just like that, I know Coach and I will be fine. Now, I have to go upstairs and face my wife.

CHAPTER 9
CHELSEA

The front door opens and in walk Kal and Dad. Jumping up from the sofa, I race over and throw myself at him. Thankfully, he has quick reflexes and he catches me as I wrap my legs around his waist and hug him for dear life. "Are you okay?"

"I'm fine, baby, but the question is, are you okay?"

"I'm fine," I tell him, but then I push on his chest and he lowers me back to my feet. He hugs me again and I gag, pushing myself away from him I cover my mouth. "Ugh, Kal," I mutter through my hand, "you stink."

"Told ya," Dad chortles as he walks over to Mom and envelops her in a hug. "How you doin', sweetness?" The two of them whisper together and then they start kissing, my parents are still so in love with each other it's sickening at times.

"Are you sure you're okay, baby? You took a pretty hard knock when Doucheman and I got into it." He cups my face and I cover his hand and smile up at him.

"I'm fine, Kal. No scratches or boo boos. Did you get everything sorted?"

"Well, I'm out," he dejectedly replies. He pulls me in

for another hug and even though he smells like a dumpster, I hug him back. "I missed you last night," he whispers, kissing me on the head.

"I missed you too, please don't get arrested ever again. I was so worried."

"I'm sorry to have worried you, and I promise to never ever get arrested again."

"Good, so what happens now?" I ask him but before he can reply, Dad does on his behalf.

Turning to face him, I can tell from the stern look on his face, he's pissed off and I'm glad I'm not Kal right now. When Dad's pissed, it's not a pretty sight.

"Luckily for them both, no charges were pressed by Squires because Kallen and Stefan are going to head over there this afternoon and repair any damages themselves."

"That seems fair." I nod. "Anything else?"

"They both have been scratched for three games, each have been fined ten grand, and at the charity event next week, he and Däuchmen will be giving a talk on team bonding and how to deal with big personalities."

"Really, Dad? You couldn't go lenient on your son-in-law?"

Kal hugs me from behind. I snuggle back into him even if his stench right now is turning my stomach. I love being in his arms and I didn't realize how much I missed him until now.

"It's because he's my son-in-law that I imposed all that. I can't be seen as showing favoritism, besides this feud has been going on long enough. It's time to let bygones be bygones. What if you'd been seriously hurt, Pumpkin?"

"I'm fine, Dad," I argue with him, but when David Maxwell has made up his mind, there's no changing it.

"Your father's right, Chels, it could have been a lot worse for you," Mom interjects. I can see from the look on her face, she's referring to the fact that I'm pregnant and not that I'm a damsel in distress.

"I'm not made of glass," I snap, "and you both know that Kal would never let anything happen to me."

"I know, Pumpkin, but you're my baby girl. I will always worry about you." Dad pulls me from Kal's arms and wraps me in a hug. I stare over at Mom and I realize they're right, it could have ended badly for me … and the baby. "When you become a parent, you'll understand."

My eyes widen when he says that. Does he know? Did Mom tell him? Pulling away, I look over to Mom. "Umm, Mom, can I get your help with something?"

"Sure, honey." She follows me down the hallway and as soon as I close the door, I whisper hiss, "Did you tell Dad?"

"No." She shakes her head. "I would never spoil your news but, honey, you need to tell him."

"I know I do, but what if he doesn't want kids yet? We've only been married a few months, it's too soon."

"There's no perfect time to have children, sweetheart. It happens when it happens, but you need to tell him."

"I know … I think I want to wait. What if …"

"Nope, no what-ifs. This baby is a fighter, he, or she is a combination of Maxwell and Jones. Can't get any stronger than that. You need to share this with your husband. Your husband, who loves you to the moon and back, he'll be happy. Trust me."

Smiling, I nod and for the first time since I found out, I'm not freaking the puck out. "You're right, Mom, thank you." I pull her in for a hug. "I … I think I want to give him the news as his Christmas present. Can you keep a secret for a little longer?"

"As much as I want to sing it from the rooftops that my baby is having a baby, I can wait, BUT please let me buy one baby thing for Christmas?"

"That's fine and thank you, Mom, you're going to make a fabulous granny—"

"No, I'm not Granny, I want them to can call me Nanny, Nanny Ness."

"And Dad can be Grumpy."

"I like that, but I think he'll be Grandpa ... just like his dad is Grandpa to you." She takes my hand and squeezes. "I'm so excited, Chels, but how are you going to gift this surprise to Kallen?"

"I have the perfect plan," I tell her with a smile. I just hope I can keep this secret for a little longer because I'm not very good with secrets.

CHAPTER 10
KALLEN

"He's such a douchehole puckwit," I complain to JJ for the millionth time today.

"And you're acting like said douchehole puckwit." I eye him but he ignores me and tacks on, "Come on, man, you're better than this, and him. Three more hours and we're done."

"We still need to give our talk," I whine like a three-year-old who doesn't want to leave the park ... even though I'd be more than happy to leave right now. "How can I talk about being all buddy buddy with him when all I want to do is kick him in the nuts?"

"Fake it 'til you make it," JJ unhelpfully offers. "Look, you can either suck it up or face the wrath of Coach, your wife, and an indefinite suspension. I know what choice I'd make."

"When did you become the levelheaded one?"

"About the same time I pulled my head out of my ass, manned up, and faced my feelings for Lex."

"Pussy-whipped," I snigger.

"Too right I am. Have you seen my sexy as sin girlfriend?"

Ignoring that question because we all know it's an opening for a punch, I go with a much safer question. "When you going to put a ring on that?"

"I've been thinking about it, but when's the right time?"

"When you know, you know," I truthfully tell him. I don't remember the exact moment I decided I wanted to marry Chels but as soon as the feeling hit, I had to do it. Hence why we had a short engagement, I didn't want her coming to her senses and changing her mind.

"That's not very helpful."

"Well, Christmas is coming up, an engagement ring would be a pretty amazing Christmas gift."

"Yeah, but then I puck myself over for future Christmases."

"New Year's?"

"Too cliche."

"Fuck, you're picky ... how about January third?"

"Why that date?"

"I just picked a date, you can't pick one so I did it for you."

"I kinda want to do it this year."

"Then December twenty-eighth?"

"But that date has no meaning."

"Puck me, JJ, you're so annoying. Just pick a date and slap a ring on it."

"I need to ask her dad first, but he's a scary dude and I'm kinda scared that he'll say no."

"If I can ask Coach for Chelsea's hand, you can ask Mr. Knight for Lexi's hand in marriage."

"Dr. Knight."

"Whatever, just man up, ask him, and then ask her ... on December twenty-first."

"I thought you said December twenty-eighth?"

"Pucking hell, just do it."

"Fine, I'll call Dr. Knight now."

"Good luck, but I'm sure the good doctor will be happy to give his blessing to the man who broke his little girl's heart before he finally grew a pair and swept her off her feet."

"You're a real piece of work sometimes, Jones. Go back to pucking Canada."

"I will, next month when we play the Vancouver Vikings."

He rolls his eyes at me, turns, and walks away with his phone to his ear. Like a creeper, I stand here and watch him, gradually sliding closer so I can hear him ask. I've never seen him look so nervous but after the question passes his lips, he holds his breath. He looks like he's gonna upchuck, glad I'm not in hurling distance, but suddenly he's smiling. I'm telling you, Ronald-freakin'-McDonald McSmiling. Clearly, Dr. Knight has given him the okay to marry his daughter. JJ offers me a thumbs-up, and I find myself smiling back at him.

"What's got you smiling like Ronald McDonald?" Chels asks me, sliding her arm around my waist and resting her head on my chest.

I chuckle to myself at her Ronald reference since I just used it myself. "JJ just asked Dr. Knight permission to ask Lexi to marry him and he gave his blessing."

"No pucking way."

"Yes, pucking way, and now you need to keep it a secret until December twenty-ninth?"

"Why not Christmas?"

"'Cause he doesn't want to ruin all the Christmases thereafter, hard to top a diamond ring for a gift."

"This is true, but why that date?"

"It's random and one I totally made up. I actually have no clue when he's going to do it."

46

"He needs to do it now 'cause I can't keep this secret." Looking up at my husband, I eye him. "Babe, you know I can't keep secrets."

"Even though you're keeping one from me now?" Her eyes widen and then it hits me, she IS keeping a secret. Pulling her closer, I stare into her eyes. "What are you keeping from me, Chelsea Jones?"

"Nothing, I'm—" She doesn't get a chance to finish her lie because we're interrupted by Wren and Doucheman.

"Sorry to interrupt," Wren says with a smile, "but Kallen, it's time for you guys to give your speech."

"Sure," I reply with a nod. Looking back at my secret-hiding wife, I place a kiss on the tip of her nose. "We'll finish this later," I tell Chels before I follow Wren and Doucheman to the front of the room.

We stand to the side of the makeshift stage and Wren begins explaining what's about to happen but I don't pay attention, I keep staring over at my wife. Worry is etched on her face and that in turn makes me worry because she's hiding something. And as she said, she's the worst secret keeper in the history of secret keepers, so the fact that she IS hiding something means it's big.

"Focus, Jones," Doucheman growls at me. "I don't want you fucking this up for me, you've already nearly cost me everything, I won't have you do it again."

My face scrunches in confusion, what did I almost cost him? He's the one who got drunk and threw the first punch. He's the one who landed us in this predicament, not me. He's such a douche, but I don't have time to worry about that or my wife and her secret because, it's go time.

CHAPTER 11
CHELSEA

Shit! Shit! Shit! I internally repeat as I stand here and watch Kal and Stefan follow Wren. He knows I'm keeping a secret and the hurt I saw in his eyes was a kick to the va-jay-jay. I know this secret will be worth the surprise, but maybe I need to tell him now. Christmas is still a week away and I don't know if I can keep lying to him like this. "Puck me!" I mumble.

Someone walks past me and heads toward the kitchen, the scent of raw meat hits me like a freight train and my stomach begins to churn. That 'ohh shit, I'm gonna vomit' lump forms in the back of my throat. "Be right back," I whisper to Lex and before she can say anything, I turn and race away from her toward the restrooms.

Just as I enter the restroom corridor, I hear her whisper-shout, "It's starting soon."

I make it as far as the family restroom and I know I won't make it to the ladies, so I slip inside. *Technically, I'm a family,* I think as I race over to the toilet. Dropping to my knees, I empty my stomach into the bowl. Whoever called it morning sickness has a pucking sick sense of humor because I feel sick all the pucking time. How Kal hasn't clued in yet is beyond me but then again, he has been preoccupied with today.

Dropping forward, I rest my head on the edge of the toilet seat and take a few deep breaths; in through my nose and out through my mouth. It works for a few fleeting moments but then the last of lunch decides to make an appearance.

Finally the wave passes and I push myself up. Walking over to the sink, I wash my hands and rinse my mouth. Drying my hands under the hand dryer, I spin and lean against the wall. Dropping my head back, I wipe my hands down my face. Keeping my face covered, I take another deep breath. Feeling somewhat human again, I swing open the door and step out into the hallway only to come face-to-face with Stefan. "Shit, Stefan," I pant, "I'm sorry, I didn't see you there."

"Are you okay, Chels?" He reaches out and rests his hand on my arm. That caring gesture reminds me of the man he once was.

Shaking my head, I quickly refute his claim and offer a smile, which I know isn't coming across as sincere. "I'm fine, Stefan."

"You look a little green, Chels. You sure you're okay?" I nod my reassurance again and then he tacks on, "For a minute there, I thought you might have had a bun in the oven."

My eyes widen and when he sees my reaction, his open too, mimicking mine. "Fuck me, you're pregnant?"

"Yes," I hiss, "but Kallen doesn't know and you can't tell him. Don't be a douche and ruin my Christmas surprise."

"You are the worst secret keeper ever. How does he not know?"

"Please," I plead with him, ignoring his secret jab. "I ... I, please don't tell Kal."

"Don't tell Kal what?" the man in question asks, stalking toward us like a man on a mission.

"That she's still in love with me," Stefan cockily taunts my husband.

"Yeah, I call bullshit on that." He looks to me. "What are you not telling me, babe?"

"I ... I ... I was sick again, Kal."

"Again?" he repeats, concern laces his one-word reply. He steps in front of me and rests his palm over my forehead, checking my temperature and being all swoony. "I really think you need to go to the doctor, you've been sick lots lately, baby, and I hate seeing you like this. You don't have a temperature, so that's a good thing."

"I'm fine," I tell him, sliding my arms around his waist for a cuddle.

"Maybe she's pregnant," Stefan unhelpfully adds. Looking over my shoulder at him, I glare and give him the evil eye. *Pucking douche*, I think to myself.

Kal pushes on my shoulders and grips my upper arms. "Are you?" he asks, staring intently at me.

My mouth opens and closes. I'm at a loss for what to say. I want to give him this as a Christmas present but I also know I'm a shitty liar and I don't want Kal thinking the worst of me. I'm so pucking screwed, looks like I'm going to have to ruin my Christmas surprise. However, before I can confess, Stefan begins to gag from behind me and then he rushes into the bathroom I just exited. From where we are standing, we can hear him dry heaving through the door.

"Maybe you both have food poisoning?" Kal voices before stepping over and knocking on the door. "You okay, Däuchmen?"

"Fine," he yells out before heaving again. Hearing him heaving sets me off and I race into the ladies' restroom, but I don't make it to the toilet, I throw up in the sink. A hand begins rubbing my back and I know it's Kal. "Kal," I whisper, "this is the ladies' restroom."

"I know, but my wife needs me." *Swoon*, how can my va-jay-jay swoon to life when I have vomit mouth? "And I'm not going anywhere."

"But your wife needs water, can you go get me some? Please?"

"Anything for you, baby." He places a kiss on the back of my head and leaves me to dry-heave in peace. Looks like my stomach is finally empty.

Kal returns a few moments later with water and Lexi. "Babe, I need to leave you with Lex. Doucheman and I have to do our thing now." He pauses and scrunches up his face. "I really hope he doesn't vomit on me."

"I'm sure you'll both be fine. I'll be out in a moment to watch you shine."

"You just look after you." He leans in for a kiss but I turn my head and vomit again, clearly my stomach wasn't empty after all. He pats my head and leaves me with Lexi. "Ugh, this better pass," I tell her.

"It will and if it helps, strong morning sickness is a sign of a healthy pregnancy."

"Doesn't really help, but I guess this ongo—" I don't get to finish because I throw up the water I just drank.

"I really think you need to tell your husband, he's so worried about you."

"I know, but it was going to be his Christmas present. Lex," I whine, "I don't know if I can wait 'til next week."

"So give him his present early," she suggests like the pucking genius she is.

My head snaps up and that light bulb clicks in my mind. "That's perfect, why didn't I think of that?"

"Probably 'cause your head is always in the toilet or you're stuffing your face with food. How it hasn't clicked, I will never know."

"Stefan guessed right away," I tell her, "And … and I think he covered for me just now."

"Huh?" she questions as I stand up and lean against the sink.

"Just before, I ran into him after throwing up and he said, I was pregnant. Pretty sure it was a joke, but he knew from my facial expression that I am. I asked him not to tell Kal and then Kal arrived and he heard me say that. I was at a loss for what to say, but then Stefan started to fake vomit, well, I think it was fake."

Turning around, I wash my hands and think over what just happened. He was teasing me and then he was retching, did he just help me keep my secret? Or is he really sick? "Whatever the case, he just saved my ass."

"Let me get this straight, Stefan Däuchmen just helped you keep a secret?"

"Yep."

"Stefan Däuchmen didn't throw you under the bus?"

Slowly I nod. "Mmmhmpf."

"Are we in *The Twilight Zone*? 'Cause, what the puck?"

"I know, right? But whatever the case, I need to get out there so I can see my man shine, and then I'm going to give him his Christmas present early 'cause secrets and me aren't good." I nearly spilled the secret I know about her, but my brain kicked into gear and I kept my mouth shut. Look at me, I can keep a secret. We really must be in *The Twilight Zone* after all.

"Okay, let's do this." Lexi links arms with me and we head out of the bathroom.

CHAPTER 12
KALLEN

Being up here with Stefan, I find myself in awe of the guy as I listen intently to his speech and that's something I never thought I would do. He's a douche, plain and simple, but as I sit here and take in his words, I realize he really put thought into this presentation. Now I kinda feel bad for ignoring most of his texts and calls this past week.

"… and with that being said, I'll wrap things up but before I do, I need to offer an apology." This piques my interest and I sit up straighter in my chair. "I need to apologize to my former teammates and coach. I really was a douche when I was playing here in New York. I thought my shit didn't stink and that the world owed me. I hurt a lot of people along the way. Sorry for not being the teammate and man I should have been, but I guess it worked out well for you, Kal, because you married a pretty great chick." He turns to face me. "Kallen, you're pretty great too, but your wife's better. I know we've had our differences, on and off the ice, but that's all in the past and I hope that one day we can become friends." Then he turns to Wren. "I also need to thank this amazing woman here last. Wren, thank you for keeping my ass in line and putting up with me, but most of all, Kallen and I need to thank you guys, our fans. Without fans we wouldn't have the desire to win like we do. You guys cheering us on is always the push we need to play at our best. Sure, some of you root for the wrong team." My teammates and I boo him. "And yes, I know I used to be a Crusher, but I'm now with the far superior team." His teammates cheer. "But rivalry is good when it's handled professionally and left on the ice. I think Kallen will agree with me, life is much simpler when we don't have management, or Wren, riding our butts."

"I don't know about Wren riding my butt 'cause, well, I'm not a douche, but I do have a wife and father-in-law who keep me in line."

"Yeah, boys and girls," Stefan singsongs, "don't hook up with the coach's daughter because Coach will push you harder, on and off the ice."

"It's worth it if you ask me." Finding Chelsea at the back of the crowd, I blow her a kiss. She smiles and air kisses me back, but I notice an odd look on her face. She's here but she's not here, and that causes my worry for her to increase. Then I think about her throwing up all the time and her general offness lately, is she sick? Is she dying? What the puck is going on? What is she hiding from me?

JJ shouts, "You guys are whipped," from the back of the room, earning himself an elbow to the ribs from Lexi.

I realize I tuned out and missed the rest of Stefan's speech, but he's wrapping it up now, and I'm thankful for that because I need to be with my wife. "Life is hard," Stefan says, "we aren't always going to get along with everyone and that's okay, but we need to treat each other with respect. Life is difficult enough as it is, without making it harder for ourselves by focusing on the negatives." He pauses and looks to Wren, a look of contentment appears on his face. "A wise woman once told me to show respect to everyone, even those who don't deserve it because it reflects on you and your character in how you treat them." He then turns to me. "Jones, I'm sorry for being a jackass to you." He looks to the crowd and finds Chelsea. "And especially you, Chels. I let my insecurities fester and it wasn't until I was about to lose it all that I realized, I, and only I, can change what happens in my life."

"I ... ummm, wow, I don't know what to say."

"You don't have to say anything, just know, I'm sorry and I'm sure you'll make a great dad." My eyes widen at him mentioning kids and then he adds on, "One of these days."

"Thanks, man, and truth be told, I'm sorry too."

"What are you sorry for?"

"I'm not sure exactly but after your heartfelt speech, I felt like I needed to say it too. I'm sure I did just as many douchey things as you did."

"Let's leave the past in the past and focus on the future?" He offers me his hand and I take it, shaking it.

"I'd like that."

The crowd claps and when I look up, my eyes find my girl. I notice that she's wiping at her eyes as she starts to walk toward Stefan and me as we climb off the stage. "You guys, that was amazing," she says when we reach her.

"I meant it, Chels, I'm sorry. I was horrible to you when we dated and the things I did to you, I'm ashamed of myself."

"As you said, it's in the past. I've moved on ... and I think you might have too." I head nod toward Wren, who is talking with one of the organizers.

"I'm trying but she's stubborn."

"Is she worth the fight?" I ask him and before he even answers, I know what he's going to say.

He nods. "Yeah, she is."

"Then don't give up," Chels tells him. "Be the man I first fell in love with and she'll have no choice but to fall."

"How and why are you being so nice to me?"

"Because I'm happy and, Stefan, that's all I ever wanted for you. Sure, you and I didn't work out and you did the worst thing possible to a girl, but I never wanted you to be alone and unhappy. Everyone deserves happiness, Stefan, even douches who cheat."

"Thank you," he tells her. Chelsea then shocks him and wraps her arms around him, she whispers something to him and he nods, smiling at her when he pulls back. "And, Jones, thanks for today. It was eye-opening all around."

"It was. Thanks for making it fun because I was really dreading this."

"You and me both, but as it turns out, you're not so bad after all but just know, the next time we play you guys, I'm going to wipe the ice with your ass."

"And the douche is back," I tease him.

"Once a douche, always a douche," he replies nonchalantly. Waving us goodbye, he steps around us and walks over to Wren.

Turning to face Chelsea, I find her smiling, her eyes bright, something I haven't seen for a while now. "What are you smiling about, babe?"

"Nothing in particular but I have a surprise for you. Will … will you come with me?"

"I'll go anywhere with you, Chelsea Jones. Any-pucking-where."

CHAPTER 13
CHELSEA

Lacing my fingers through Kal's, we say our goodbyes to everyone and after pulling on our winter coats, we head out into the chilly December afternoon. We jump into a cab and leaning forward, I give the driver our home address. Kal looks at me inquisitively. "Just need to grab something from home quickly."

He nods and I can tell the suspense is killing him. It's not often I get to surprise him because, well, I suck with secrets and the fact I'm giving him this earlier than planned confirms I can't keep my mouth shut. The driver pulls up and I climb out, quickly racing upstairs to grab the present for Kal, ever so thankful I already wrapped it.

With the gift safely tucked into my bag, I race back downstairs and ask the driver to take us to Rockefeller Center. "What are you up to, Mrs. Jones?"

"You'll find out soon, Mr. Jones."

Leaning into his side, I snuggle in and breathe him in. Nerves are starting to build and I feel like I could throw up again, but I swallow the lump down and concentrate on the gift in my bag. We finally pull up and Kal climbs out first before turning back to offer me his hand. "Such a gentleman," I coo as I take his hand and walk toward the tree. My heart rate increases the closer we get and my stomach begins to flutter with nerves and not the feeling to vomit —go me!

Arriving at the base of the tree, I tilt my head back and Kal wraps his arms around me from behind. Together we gaze up at the tree, enjoying the intimate moment.

"Ever since I watched *Home Alone 2* when I was little with Kendall, I've loved this tree. I can't believe I've lived here for as long as I have and I've never been here before."

"Well, I'm glad to pop your tree viewing cherry." *And in a minute, I hope you love this spot for a whole new reason.* Taking a deep breath, I spin in his arms to face him. "Merry Christmas, husband," I whisper and hold out the narrow gift box.

"Christmas isn't 'til next week."

"I know, but I want you to have this now." He stares at the box, then at me and then back at the box again. "Open it," I encourage him. He tugs at the bow on the top and is struggling to get it undone. I shake my head and laugh, covering his hand, he looks at me. "It's a gift box, you just lift the lid."

"Ohh, oops." He shrugs and then proceeds to remove the lid. He stares down at the positive pregnancy test and then lifts his gaze to mine. "You gave me a pregnancy test." Nodding, I wait for him to register that it's positive, but his face remains neutral. He lifts it up and that's when I realize it's upside down, the pink positive sign is facing me, he's looking at the plain white plastic side. Reaching up, I spin it over so he can see the positive sign. He stares at it for a few beats and then his eyes widen. "Are we? Are you?"

Nodding, my grin widens. "Yep, we, well, I am."

"Are you pucking with me?"

Shaking my head from side to side, I reach up and cup his cheek. "I'm not pucking with you, Kal, I'm pregnant."

"With a baby?" I laugh, it's scary how much alike he and Margot are.

"Yes, with a baby. Your baby."

"Are you serious?"

"Mmmhmpf," I reply with a nod. He just stares at me, his expression neutral and I can't tell if he's excited, angry, or what, but then the biggest of big Kallen Jones smiles appears on his face and all my worries flutter away with the snowflakes that just started to fall. It snowing right now makes this moment perfect in every way.

"This is the best pucking present ever, Chels, and it explains why you've been so sick."

"Pretty much."

"Why didn't you tell me as soon as you found out?"

"'Cause you were in jail and I wanted to give you an amazing Christmas present to end the year on a high."

"Best present ever, and I'm definitely ending the year on a high."

"Merry Christmas, Kal."

"Merry Christmas, Chels." He scoops me into his arms and spins us around. "I'm gonna be a dad!" he shouts into the air. Placing me back on my feet, he stares into my eyes. "I pucking love you."

"I pucking love you too, now take me home and ravage me."

"With pucking pleasure." He dips me backward and presses his lips to mine for a kiss that leaves me breathless, before he whisks me home and we have a pucking good night, naked and sweaty between the sheets. Kal can play my body with precision. He knows exactly where to press, where to suck, and he pucks like there's no tomorrow.

I'm the luckiest gal in the world.

This is gearing up to be a pucking good Christmas.

CHAPTER 14
KALLEN

"So are we going to tell your mom and dad at brunch this morning?"

"Well, Mom already knows—"

"What? How?"

"Well, the night you and Stefan got arrested and Mom was here with me, I threw up when she made me a coffee. She did the same when she was pregnant with me. She ducked out, grabbed a test, and one lil' pee later, it was confirmed."

"Ohh, right," I reply with a nod, hating that while I was in jail for brawling, my wife was alone when she found out she was pregnant. "So, we'll tell your dad today?"

"Yep. Are you scared?"

"Well, I wasn't 'til you said that."

"Are you scared he's going to kick your ass for defiling his Pumpkin and knocking her up?"

"Puck yes, I am, he's scary when it comes to you."

"Who knew the big bad goalie for the New York Crushers is scared of his coach and father-in-law?"

"We can't all be perfect like you," I tell my amazing wife. "Now, if you don't go and put some clothes on we're going to be late. 'Cause, babe, you are sexy in lingerie at the best of times but when you're pregnant and glowing in lingerie, you're pucking phenomenal."

She stalks over to me and I'm rooted to the spot, trapped in her seductive web. She traces her finger down my chest and toys with the knot in my towel. "You like what you see, baby?" she breathlessly whispers before dropping to her knees and removing my towel. "'Cause I definitely like what I see and I think he's happy to see me too." She places a kiss on the tip of my dick before opening her mouth and sliding her lips down my shaft. Raking her teeth gently on the way back up.

"Puck me," I groan as her head bobs up and down. Sliding my fingers into her hair, I grip her head and guide her back and forth. The tip hitting the back of her throat causes her to make that gagging sound that turns me the puck on. She reaches up and cups my balls and it's game over for me. With a guttural grunt, I come down her throat. She sucks every last drop from me. My dick pops out of her mouth and she wipes at the corners of her lips before sucking on her finger. I may have just come, but the carnal look on her face has my dick springing back to life.

"Your turn," I inform her, but she shakes her head.

"Later, because we'll be late if that tongue of yours touches my body." She stands up and turns to get dressed.

Reaching out, I grab her wrist and pull her back to me. Hugging her from behind, I lean forward and whisper, "Then we're going to be late because I need to fuck you with my tongue now." Spinning her around, I drop to my knees, throw her leg over my shoulder, and I kiss her through her panties.

"Kal," she moans, rocking herself against my face.

"Yes, wife?"

"Hurry up, I need you now."

"As you wish." Moving her panties to the side, I spear my tongue deep inside her. She grips the sides of my head and shoves me into her, grinding herself on my tongue and chin. Sucking on her clit, she moans in a guttural way that has my cock coming back to life. I need to fuck her and I need to do it now.

Pulling away from her, she whines in protest as I drop to my ass. Gripping her hips, I tear her panties off her body and guide her down onto my cock. The head slides between her folds and the two of us groan in delight as she sinks down to the hilt. She grips my shoulders and begins to ride me like a bucking bronco. "Yes," she pants as I meet her thrust for thrust. "Harder," she demands as she slams herself down on me.

Chelsea has always been a sweet lover but seeing her lose control like this is out of this world amazing. She throws her head back and howls as she crashes over the edge. Seeing her lose control sets me off, and together we draw out our climax, milking every last drop from each other's body.

She collapses onto my chest and I wrap my arms around her. "We're definitely gonna be late now." She giggles into my chest. "We can blame morning sickness," I reply into her hair, causing her to lift up and slap my chest.

"We cannot blame our baby for what just happened."

"Milk it while you can," I say.

She slaps my chest again. "Kallen Jones, that's terrible … but depending on Daddy's anger, it can be our backup plan."

"Deal, now we better get moving, otherwise, we'll be really late … much like the first brunch with them."

Thirty minutes later and only ten minutes late, Chelsea and I walk hand in hand into the diner and over to Coach and Nessa. "Morning," I singsong as I slide into the booth.

Chels joins me after kissing her mom and dad hello. Slinging my arm over her shoulder, I pull her to my side and kiss her temple. It feels like since she told me she's pregnant, I've fallen in love with her all over again, but in a more intense way.

"You two ever going to get out of the honeymoon phase?" Coach asks, hailing the waitress and ordering four coffees.

"Just tea for me," Chels says, and then she looks to her dad. "And you are one to talk, you two are still all lovey-dovey and you've been married for eleventy billion years."

"Ease up there, Pumpkin, I'm not that old."

"Yeah, you are, Grandpa," I tease, earning myself a whack in the stomach from Chels and a glare from Coach.

"Speaking of Grandpa," Chels says, taking a deep breath, "you're going to be one."

All eyes are on Coach as we await his reaction. He doesn't utter a word. Just sits there rapidly blinking. No one breathes, we all wait for him to make the first move. "Did you just say I'm going to be a grandpa?"

"Yes, Daddy. You're going to be a grandpa and Mom's going to be Nanny Ness."

His gaze snaps to mine. "You knocked my daughter up?"

"Dad," Chels complains.

"David," Nessa berates him with a slap to the arm.

"Yep," I timidly reply with a head nod.

Again, silence falls over the table. The waitress appears. "What can I get ya?" She's oblivious to the silence right now.

"Can we have a few more moments?" Nessa politely says to the waitress.

"Sure, whatevs," she nonchalantly replies, moving on to the next booth.

"Say something, Daddy," Chelsea says after the waitress leaves.

"I'm gonna be a grandpa."

"Yep," I reply and just when I think he's going to yell at me, a smile graces his face.

"I'm gonna be a grandpa." He turns to Nessa. "We're gonna be grandparents." He excitedly voices, "Chelsea has a baby in her tummy. My baby's having a baby." He slaps the table, causing the cutlery to clatter around. "My baby's having a baby," he repeats as he slides out of the booth and pulls Chels up into his arms. "So pucking happy," he murmurs into her hair.

Nessa and I sit here grinning as we watch Chelsea and her dad embrace. He grips her head in his palms and places a kiss on her temple. Then he turns his attention to me. "You hurt either one of them, I hurt you."

"Understood, sir," I reply with a nod, slightly shitting myself at his warning. He didn't go this daddy bear when I asked him permission to marry Chels.

"Good." He nods and then looks to Chels, who is still standing, tears welling in her eyes. "You okay, Pumpkin?"

"Perfectly happy," she cries as a tear cascades down her cheek. "My hormones are hormoning and I'm starving."

"As luck would have it, babe, we are in a diner, so sit down and we can order."

Chelsea drops down beside me and when the waitress returns, she orders what feels like one of everything off the menu. When my baby momma is full, we exit the diner and begin walking down Broadway. "So, when's your first ultrasound?" Nessa asks, just as a deep voice shouts, "You're pregnant?"

We all turn toward the W Hotel and see Stefan and a sheepish-looking Wren staring at us. "I ... umm, yeah, I am," Chels replies, not sure if she should be confirming the news, especially to him. I know yesterday we kinda mended fences and all that, but it's not like we're buddy buddy and he'd be the first person I'd want to know.

He smiles. "Guessed it," Stefan cockily replies. "Seems you're not a very good goalie after all, you let one slip past the goal ... but then again, in this instance, I think you want to miss, right?"

"Stefan," Wren berates him. "Don't be so rude and crass over something so exciting. Congratulations to you both," she offers with a smile to Chels and me.

"Thanks, it was a shock but we're happy," I tell them.

A silence envelops us but the moment is interrupted when a kid comes up to us. "Mr. Jones, Mr. Däuchmen, can ... can I get your autographs?"

"Of course," I tell the kid and I drop down to a knee so we're the same height. Chels hands me a pen and I sign the card in the kid's hands. I notice it's a birthday card. "Is it your birthday today?"

He nods and grins. "Yep, I'm ten today."

"Well, happy birthday, lil' man." I ruffle his hair and then Stefan takes the pen and card from me and signs it.

"Can I get a pic too, please?"

"Sure," Stefan says.

Stefan and I pose with the boy while Chelsea chats to his parents. "She's pretty," he whispers to me.

"The prettiest," I agree.

"One day I want to play hockey like you and I'm going to have an even prettier girlfriend."

"You do that, and I'll be in the stands cheering you on." He races over to his mom and excitedly tells her what I just said. Chels looks over and I throw a wink at her. She blushes and it reminds me of her cheeks from earlier this morning when she was riding me. My cock begins to twitch and I have to think of a naked Doucheman to deflate him.

"You really are going to be a great dad," Stefan says, his words shocking me.

"Thanks, man ... you will too ... one day."

He laughs. "One day, but not anytime soon. I still need to work on me first."

"Well, you're doing a good job, keep at it."

"Thanks, Jones."

"You're welcome, Däuchmen." With that, we say our goodbyes and I whisk my wife home for an afternoon on the sofa, eating ice cream and binge-watching *Stranger Things*.

* * *

Chelsea is sound asleep in my arms when there's a knock at the door. Sliding out from under her, I answer to find Phil, the doorman, standing there with a gift box. "Delivery for you, sir."

"Thanks, Phil."

I take the gift and head back inside, placing it on the island counter. I lift the lid and inside is a mini hockey stick and a onesie. Lifting it up, I read the front and it says, 'Future LA Legends player.' "Get pucked," I mumble as I notice a card. Pulling it out, I read.

Congrats to you both!
Thought I'd get the lil' man a gift, hope he loves it as much as I do.
Let's go Legends.

"That pucking douche," I growl.

"Who's a pucking douche?"

"Who else, look what that puckhead got the baby." I hold the onesie up and show Chels, she begins to cackle.

"Ohh, I love it," she says. She picks up the hockey stick and turns it to face me, it has 'BABY JONES' etched into it.

"That's cute," I tell her, "but our baby is not wearing that shit." I toss the onesie to the side.

"Don't be a douche," she teases me. "We just got rid of one, we don't need another."

"Fine," I huff. "But how does he know it's a boy?"

"He's just guessing, time will tell. Now, come snooze with me, Momma is still tired."

Sweeping her up into my arms, I whisk her into our bedroom and we have a snooze … after we get our puck on.

CHAPTER 15
CHELSEA

... CHRISTMAS MORNING

Lying in bed, I keep my eyes closed, willing the sickness away. Cracking open my eyelid, I let out a breath and smile when I don't feel the need to vomit. Slowly, I sit up and from the corner of my eye, I see a packet of saltines on the side table and a glass of water. My husband is the best.

Grabbing a cracker, I nibble on it and then I hear the banging that woke me again. With cracker in hand, I slip my feet into my slippers and follow the noises down the hallway, but I notice the door to the spare room is slightly ajar. "Kal," I call out as I push on the door.

The door swings open and my eyes widen at what I see before me. Our spare room is no longer a spare room, it's the most amazing nursery I have ever seen. The walls have been painted light gray and along the center of the back wall is the most gorgeous glossy, white wooden crib, which is decked out in Crushers blankets, complete with hockey-themed mobile. On the wall next to the crib is a hockey stick art piece that I can see a rocker chair in front of. On the opposite wall is a Canadian, a US, and a Crushers flag and there are many more cardboard boxes.

This is not what I envisioned my child's nursery to look like but now that I've seen this, it's perfect. My eyes well with tears and when a set of muscular arms slide around me, I smile. Kal leans in and nuzzles into my neck. "You like?"

Spinning around to face him, I gaze up at my sexier-than-puck husband and nod. "It's perfect, Kal."

"I was hoping to have it finished before you woke up as a Christmas surprise, but that pucking stick thing took forever to make."

"You made that?" I ask him.

"Yep, with my bare hands." Those hands are currently squeezing the peachy globes of my ass. "Merry Christmas, babe." He drops to his knees and whispers to my belly, "Merry Christmas, Bug." Kal and I chose to call the baby Bug while we wait to find out if we're having a boy or girl. The thought of referring to him or her as 'It' just didn't sit right, and since we thought I had a bug, Bug seemed like the perfect name.

He stands back up and wraps his arms around me again. "Merry Christmas, Kal," I whisper, lifting to my toes to press my lips to his for a kiss. A bang on the front door pulls us apart. "Who would be here at eight on Christmas morning?"

He shrugs at me. "Guess we better answer it and find out." His response is cryptic and I wonder if he knows something I don't, but he looks just as clueless as me right now. Pulling out of his embrace, I pad down the hallway toward the front door when they impatiently bang on the door again. "Coming," I mumble. When I swing the door open, I come face-to-face with a huge pile of Christmas presents that has legs and two hands.

"Hello?" I question by way of greeting.

"Pumpkin," my dad says from behind the pile. "Grandpa needs you to let him in. Please?" Yes, in the few days since Dad found out, he's been referring to himself as Grandpa ... and in third person. It was funny to begin with but now, it's just annoying.

"Nah," I tease, "I'm just gonna stand here in the doorway all day and stare at this massive pile of presents with hands and legs that talks."

"Pumpkin," he warns, and as he growls, a present from the top topples to his feet. "Shit," he hisses, "I hope that wasn't one of the breakable ones."

"What the puck?" Kal says, joining us.

"Dad went overboard with presents."

"Grandpa did not."

"I see we're still on the third person thing," Kal states with an eye roll, all of us sick of the third personing.

"Mmmhmpf." I nod.

"Kallen Jones," Dad growls, "if you don't let me in, I'll bench you for the rest of the season."

"Like you'd let your star goalie warm the bench," I scoff, "but in the spirit of Christmas, come on in, Dad."

"Grandpa thanks you, Pumpkin," he says, somehow shuffling through the doorway and not dropping any more presents.

Bending down, I pick up the dropped one and look into the hallway for Mom. "Where's Mom?"

"At home sleeping, she looked so peaceful and I didn't want to wake her."

"You left Mom at home to wake alone on Christmas morning?"

"Well, yeah, I had to drop off the presents for Cletus the Fetus."

"You did not just refer to my baby as Cletus the Fetus, did you, Dad?"

"Grandpa did because saying It felt too impersonal."

"And Cletus the Fetus is personal?"

"Well, what should Grandpa call him then?"

"SHE," I emphasize that word, "is being referred to as Bug."

"Bug, Grandpa likes that," Dad says as my phone begins to ring. Walking over to the kitchen island, I smile when I see Mom's face. "Merry Christmas, Mom."

"Merry Christmas, honey, is that husband of mine there?"

"Yes, Grandpa is here and he has the whole of Toys R Us with him. Why did you let him go crazy?"

"Try stopping that man, ever since your ultrasound, he's been telling everyone." I had my first ultrasound two days ago, turns out, I'm twelve weeks along. Remember that mini freak-out back in October, yeah, well, I was pregnant then. The test I took after the Crushers lost to LA was a false negative because it was only early days. It seems that I conceived on our honeymoon. Since Kal is a celebrity, when we were seen coming out of the doctor's clinic, within minutes, the whole world knew too. That night we were all over the entertainment channels. The joys of being married to a pro player. "Give me ten minutes and I'll head over."

"Take your time, Mom, we'll be here when you get here."

"Love you, Chels."

"You too, Mom." Hanging up, I turn around and my eyes widen when I see all the presents laid out, when there's another knock at the door. "I'll get it." Shuffling over, I open it and once again, I come face-to-face with a pile of presents. "Dad, what the puck?"

"Phil, thanks for your help," Dad says to our present-laden doorman, ignoring me. He ushers Phil in and helps him unload the presents.

"Merry Christmas, Chelsea and Kallen," Phil says with a nod before exiting our apartment.

"Dad, this is too much."

"Never. Grandpa is going to spoil Bug and it all starts with her first Christmas."

"You do realize that right now, she's the size of a plum?" *Ohh plum, I could go for a plum right now* I think to myself as I stare at Dad, who is placing a hockey puck under the tree. "Daaaaaad, she won't need that 'til she's—"

"Born," Kallen interrupts. "Need to start on the next generation of Jones hockey players."

"Puck me." I rub my stomach. "Bug, I'm so sorry that your family is crazy."

"Grandpa heard that, Pumpkin," Dad says as he walks into the kitchen and over to the coffee maker. He sets about making coffee for everyone, and a tea for me, while Kal starts arranging a fruit platter. Walking over to him, I pinch a strawberry off the plate and take a bite. Closing my eyes, I moan as the sweet juices explode and dance on my tongue.

Opening my eyes, I see Kal staring at me, a heated look is reflecting back at me, and suddenly I'm no longer thinking about plums. I'm thinking about my husband and all the sexy things I want to do to him on the kitchen island. He and I screw on this counter more than we eat at it, which is probably a good thing for sanitary purposes.

Thankfully, there's a knock at the door and it bursts the connection because we cannot do that on the counter right now, not with Dad currently arguing with the coffee maker. "I'll get it," I say again.

This time, when I open the door, it's Mom, with no

presents. "What, no presents?" I tease. "The last two people to arrive were laden with presents."

"Sorry to disappoint, sweetheart, but I can offer you and Bug a hug?"

"Bug and I would love that." Mom envelops me in a hug and I embrace her back just as tightly. "Merry Christmas, Mom."

"Merry Christmas, baby girl." She pulls back and stares at me, she's smiling brightly and I find myself grinning back at her. Linking my arm with Mom's, we walk into the apartment and her eyes widen when she sees all the gifts. "I'd like to state, I had no part in this present explosion."

"No, but you did go crazy on Baby Barn ordering clothes," Dad informs us, trying to show that Mom is just as baby crazy as he is.

"I'm a nanny, it's my prerogative to spoil my grandbaby with clothes."

"And it's my prerogative to spoil my grandbaby with anything I want," Dad throws back at her.

"We've created grandmonsters," Kal whispers as he wraps his arms around me from behind, resting his hands on my tiny baby belly.

Our first Christmas as a married couple started off rocky, thanks to a rivalry on the ice that threatened to derail Christmas with an arrest. But now, the air is clear, paving the way for a bright future, on and off the ice. The rivalry between Kal and Stefan is finally over, something Bug and I are extremely happy for.

As I stand here in my husband's arms and watch my parents bicker about the arrival of their grandbaby, I realize that it's a pucking good Christmas and next year is going to be so pucking great.

The Pucking End!

Want to read the story of how Kallen and Chelsea fell in love? Grab I Pucking Hate That I Love You now.

FACEBOOK ~ INSTAGRAM ~ BOOKBUB
GOODREADS ~ WEBSITE

ALSO BY DL GALLIE

STAND ALONES

Antecedent

Doc Steel

Oops

Off the Books

Fractured: A driven world novel

Deck…the Balls

Secrets and Sunrises

Love Me Like You Do

Never Let Me Go

Seven Nights

Seven Kisses

* * *

PUCKING NOVELS

I Pucking Hate That I Love You

A Pucking Good Christmas

…and a few pucking more

* * *

FALLING NOVELS

These men make it hard not to fall for them

Falling for Dr. Kelly

Falling for Dr. Knight

Falling for Agent Cox

Falling for Agent Cruz

Falling: The Complete Collection

* * *

THE UNEXPECTED SERIES

When it comes to love, expect the unexpected

The Unexpected Gift

The Unexpected Letter

The Unexpected Package

The Unexpected Connection

The Unexpected series: The Complete Collection

* * *

THE CASTAWAY GROVE COLLECTION

Love has arrived in the Grove

Oasis

Unequivocal Love

Five Words

Broken Rules

…and a few more to come.

The Castaway Grove Collection, Vol 1

* * *

THE LIQUOR CABINET SERIES

Liquor has never been so disturbingly saucy

Malt Me (Book 1)

Tequila Healing (Book 2)

Wine Not (Book 3)

The Final Shot (Book 4)

The Liquor Cabinet: Series boxset

A BLACK OPS Christmas

by D.M. DAVIS

Part of the **OUR FIRST CHRISTMAS** Anthology

Copyright © 2022 D.M. Davis
A Black Ops Christmas by D.M. Davis
Published by D.M. Davis

All rights reserved. No part of this publication may be reproduced, scanned, distributed, or transmitted in any form or by any means, including photocopying, recording, or other electronic or mechanical methods, without the prior written permission of the author, except in the case of brief quotations embodied in critical reviews and certain other noncommercial uses permitted by copyright law.

www.dmckdavis.com

Editing by Tamara Mataya
Proofreading by Mountains Wanted Publishing & Indie Author Services

This book is a work of fiction. Names, characters, places, and incidents are either the product of the author's imagination or are used fictitiously.

This story contains mature themes, strong language, and sexual situations. It is intended for adult readers.

ABOUT THIS BOOK

Join the *Black Ops MMA* alphas and their women as they celebrate Christmas on the slopes, vying for alone time while juggling kids and holiday festivities.

For my Divas. 💋

CHAPTER 1

GABRIEL AND FRANKIE

Gabriel grips my hip, moving in to bracket my backside with his warmth. My hold on the railing tightens as I close my eyes, block out the extraordinary winter wonderland before us, and suck in air cold enough to burn my lungs. "Big Man," I sigh and sink into his chest, knowing he'll support my weight.

"Angel." He skims the space behind my ear, the place he loves—I love—with tender kisses. "I need inside you." His gravelly plea echoes in my chest and zings between my legs.

Yes, do that. Please. Now.

It feels like an eternity since I've felt his powerful thrusts—

"Really? Is this how it's gonna go?" Rowdy pulls us from our moment of coupledom.

How long has it been since it was just Gabriel and me? Nearly four years, I suppose, if I'm counting back to before Maddox was born.

"We're coming," my man grumbles, wrapping me in his arms. "Who agreed to no babysitter?"

"You." I turn and kiss him quickly before the moment is completely gone.

He teases and takes, then gives and softens. "I'm a fucking idiot."

I laugh, patting his chest. "You're the love of my life and the father of my children."

"And a fucking idiot for not realizing how much more we need than only a handful of moments to ourselves." He squeezes my hand as we head inside.

"We'll figure it out." We always do.

"You hungry?" He steals another kiss.

"Starving." Breakfast on the road didn't stick with me.

A wail from the end of the hall stills his departure and pulls me in the direction of our baby girl Maddyn. "She's hungry." I press my hand to my breasts, my nipples tingling as the milk lets down.

Gabriel's gaze flicks between my breasts and my face. "You feed Madd. I'll get lunch started and Ox fed before his nap."

Nap? Maddox, at nearly four, has decided naps are for babies, and *he's not a baby,* as he likes to point out to his larger-than-life father. "Good luck with that." I turn to leave but stop when his hand engulfs mine.

"We'll find time, Angel. I promise." His soulful blues tell the truth of his commitment even if I didn't believe his words—which I do.

"I know." I want to lean into him, steal another moment —but our girl's cry is tugging at my heart, keeping me from sharing that we girls have talked about trading babysitting duty. We all want some adulting time with our better halves.

I love our life. I love our kids.

But I do miss being able to indulge in my man at the drop of a hat. Now it takes planning, stealth, and sacrificing precious sleep. He has no problem with missing sleep. Me, not so much. I've been known to nod off during the day even with a full eight hours in the tank. Now, after two kids, it feels like I'll never catch up.

As I get Maddyn soothed enough to nurse and settle into the rocking chair in the nursery, screams of laughter stream up from the first floor. All our boys are close in age, ranging from almost two, Killian, Rowdy and Reese's oldest; to two-and-a-half, Cade and Wade, Cap and Cher's twin boys; to our Maddox, who'll be four in February. We only have two girls in the mix: our Maddyn is nine months, and Iris, Cap's youngest, is fourteen months. I hope Rowdy and Reese, and Landry and Taylor have a girl or two to round out the mix.

I run my hand over Madd's silken-haired head. Her blue eyes flutter closed as she fights sleep. The soothing touch is as calming to her as it is to me. I set a timer on my watch to switch sides in case I fall asleep and lay my head back. It won't hurt to rest my eyes for a few minutes.

* * *

When thirty minutes pass and my Angel hasn't come downstairs, I take them two at a time and stumble to a stop when I find her sleeping in the rocking chair with Madd still sucking away. I hope she switched boobs. Sometimes my wife drifts off and misses switching sides before Maddyn falls asleep again. She's on solid food, but our girl savors this time with her mom as if she knows it'll soon come to an end.

I gently graze Frankie's cheek. "Angel."

Her eyes pop open. "Dammit. I'm sorry. I didn't mean to fall asleep."

"It's okay. We're on vacation. There's no rush. Did you switch?"

"Yeah, I set a timer on my watch. Thanks to you."

Frankie kept falling asleep while nursing our first and wouldn't have any idea how long he'd fed, and he'd be knocked out and not nurse the other tit. I suggested her frustration could be eased by setting a timer, so she could relax and know to change when her watch vibrated. Simple. Effective.

I smile and kiss her cheek. "I'll change her diaper. Go grab some grub."

"Did you eat?" She unlatches my girl and hands her to me before hiding her succulent tits from view.

"Nah, I was waiting on you." I cuddle Madd to my chest, getting a loud burp before I even pat her back. "That's my girl." I kiss her head, breathing in her sweet baby scent.

"I'll see you downstairs."

"Right behind you." I lay Madd on the changing table and smile at my heart who yawns and chews her fist like she's still hungry. "Maybe some peaches and green beans will fill you up?"

Her smile and babble hit that place in my heart only for my kids. Never thought I'd have this. My Frankie Angel gave me life, hope, purpose, and then she gave me a family.

"You're gonna sleep good tonight, Maddyn. Daddy needs some Mommy time. Okay?"

Madd coos and reaches for me.

"I'll take that as a *yes*."

At the bottom of the stairs, Taylor stops me. "Can I hold her?"

"Did you eat?"

She pulls Madd from my arms. "I'll eat after you and Frankie."

I hesitate, not wanting to turn down the offer, but... "I was gonna give her some baby food."

"Can I do it?" Taylor lights up like a kid in a candy store, only this is a baby, and feeding my little angel can be both messy and fruitless, depending on Maddyn's mood.

As far as I know she and Cowboy aren't trying, but Taylor is always up for watching the kids, particularly the babies. They haven't even been married a year, yet she might have caught a little baby fever from the rest of us.

"You sure?"

"Yep. Set me up, and I'll feed her." She kisses Madd's cheek and nuzzles her neck, setting off Madd's giggle button.

I catch my Angel's approving gaze over Taylor's shoulder, making me forget what I'm supposed to be doing until my *little* angel grabs my attention with a gurgled, "Dadadada."

"You hungry, Lil Ang?" I ask, knowing she can't answer except with a squeal of excitement. I think Taylor's feeding experience will be a good one today. My little bundle is raring to go. "You want to put her in her highchair? I'll be right there with the food."

After getting Taylor and Maddyn situated, I feed Frankie and myself. Her eyes never leave Madd or Ox for long. Her motherly instinct is focused and trained on the most important people in our lives.

A glance out the window has me smiling. "It's snowing." My woman has only seen snow a handful of times. None of our kids have seen it except on TV.

"Snow!" Ox, Kill, Cade, Wade, and Iris nearly kill themselves and demolish anything in their path to get to the sliding glass doors, faces and hands pressed to the glass in awe, excitement buzzing all around them.

"Shoes!" Cap orders before anyone even thinks of racing outside.

"Coat and gloves too," Rowdy adds as he picks up the fallen chairs the kids knocked over in their haste.

The kids scramble to don their winter gear. A glance shared with Rowdy has him offering, "I've got Ox." He motions to Frankie. He knows how much she loves all things winter and Christmas.

Taylor cleans up Maddyn as I take my Angel's hand, urging her to the front door.

"Shoes." She frowns at her socked feet.

"I got you." I toss the blanket from the back of the couch around her shoulders and pick her up before she can step away.

"Gabriel," she whispers into my embrace, her breathiness has my cock stirring, wanting to hear my name in that same throaty way as when she comes.

Not yet.

We make it down the porch steps before anyone else comes outside, taking in the winter surrounding us. Stealing another moment—just for us.

"It's so beautiful." The catch in her voice has me pulling her tighter.

"It is." *She* is. My woman tips her head and closes her eyes as fluffy flakes fall around us, lightly dusting her hair and lashes.

"It'll be great skiing tomorrow." Rowdy stomps outside with Reese at his side, holding Killian and Ox's hands. "But it'll make a great snowman tonight." His eyes light up as he calls the older kids out to get started.

"You wanna help, don't you?" Frankie's nuzzles my neck, her cool nose reminding me I need my jacket and gloves.

My smile captures hers for a quick kiss. "I kinda do."

"Set me on the porch. I'll watch for a minute, and then make hot chocolate."

"You sure?" I'm reluctant to release our moment, to trade it in for one with our kids, nieces, and nephews.

Memories. We're making them every second of every day.

She kisses my cheek. "I love you holding me, Big Man, but I love you playing with our kids too. It's snowing." Her eyes shine with emotions and... happiness.

Damn, I'm gonna love on her good tonight. "Who's on kid duty tonight?"

Taylor's hand pops up. "Me! I want to be on kid duty."

"Really?" Cowboy frowns at her before deciding his grumpy ass would do anything for her. "We do." He smiles, shaking his head.

He has no idea what these rowdy kids can get up to. Honestly, they'll probably be worn out from the snow, so Tay and Lan might have it easy.

I set my girl down just inside the door, stealing one more kiss. "It's you and me tonight, Angel."

Her blush is perfect as she bites her bottom lip. "I can't wait."

Neither can I.

I grab my coat and gloves, catch the sight of the boys making snow angels as I slip back outside and close the door to the girls giggling in the kitchen.

I don't know who suggested a family vacation for Christmas, but I think it should become a tradition. I'm loving every second of it so far.

CHAPTER 2

ROWDY AND REESE

"You okay, Kitten?" His concern is unwarranted but welcome. He's attuned to my every mood and seems to know what I need almost before I do.

I sigh into his warm, wet embrace. A bath with my Shadow is exactly what I needed. "I'm perfect."

But he's not asking about my mood. I've been feeling yucky. It started on the drive up. I'm not prone to car sickness, but I guess there's always a first time. Plus, I've never been to this altitude before. Never even been out of Vegas until his mom's funeral and then our wedding and honeymoon. I love the snow, but give me a beach, and I'm one happy clam.

"Need to drink more water. It'll help with the altitude."

"Yes, Dr. Durant. As soon as we're out of the tub in, say, an hour or so."

He nuzzles my neck. "Maybe two."

Maybe. I'm in no rush.

I wrap my arms around his and close my eyes. He sinks lower and rests his head on the rise of the tub. His heart thrumming behind me eases me, centers me, comforts me.

The love of my life has been going through a bit of an identity crisis since he found out Cap was his biological dad. For the most part, he's made peace with his mom and Barrett. But the turning point—the last puzzle piece—was deciding to change his legal name to Durant, after Cap. It was a difficult discussion with his dad, Barrett, but one he had no intention of backing down from. He's still Jenkins—his adopted name from his best friend in high school who died—in his professional life, but with family—his everyday existence—he's a Durant.

In support, I changed my name too. I'm Mrs. Durant. An honor I share with Mom. Kinda weird. And kinda perfect... she and I still having the same last name—through marriages neither of us felt worthy of or even dared believe possible. But it is, because we found two amazing men who happen to be father and son... matching hearts, only a generation apart, our other halves.

Warm, knowledgeable hands stop me from drifting off as one slides lower and the other cups a breast. "Kitten." He presses his lips to my ear, warm and teasing as he lengthens between us.

On a groan that shivers through me, I open my legs to his talented fingers, needing him in ways that still surprise me—the depth, the yearning, the dirty, dirty thoughts. I push his hand lower, his fingers closer... "Need you."

He sinks two fingers inside, squeezing my breast. "You've got me."

Years of loving, of only knowing his touch, of training my body to respond to him take over. His words fill the air, echo in my ears, and land on my heart. His body, his hands, his mouth, his cock fill, knead, suck, twist, thrust, grip.

Deeper and deeper.

Harder and harder.

Smooth and loving, sexy and primal, he takes me, and takes me, and takes me.

Racing hearts and grunted passion, we're one entity, convulsing, cajoling, consuming, riding the wave, each other, so high.

Higher.

Higher.

"Oh… Shadow—"

"Fuck, yes, Lion. Squeeze me."

Christ on a cracker. He steals my breath in a searing kiss and fills me to eternity.

Forcing.

Forcing me.

Over the edge.

Willingly.

Willingly.

Plundered. I explode into a million pieces… and yet, I'm whole, complete as he shoots his release, filling me, filling me, filling me.

"Fuck, baby." He peppers my face with kisses. "Fuck. Fuck. Fuck." He lifts his hips, holding me tight, shallow thrusts sending goosebumps along my skin. "Not done, Kitten. Nowhere done loving you."

No. No. Never be done.

"Shadow."

"I know."

He always knows.

He's my ride or die, and I always ride.

* * *

Leaving her sated and barely able to keep her eyes open, I kiss her shoulder before slipping out of bed to check on the little cries coming from somewhere beyond our haven. I don't think it's Kill crying, sounds too young, but I had my time with my Kitten. If I can help Gabriel or Cap have a moment with their wives, then I'll do what I can to comfort whoever needs it.

A groggy Cap blinks up at me as he soothes my sister, Iris, gently patting her rump as she wriggles and burps on his shoulder.

I secure my hair in a bun and reach for her. "I got her. Go to bed."

"She's barely started her bottle," he protests.

"We're good. I need a little bonding time with my sister." I urge him to go as I settle Iris in my arms. She's already looking for the bottle and getting pissy that I'm not fast enough. "It's coming, Itty Bitty. Have patience."

Cap laughs. "Yeah. Patience is not her strong suit." He stifles a yawn, eyeing me for another second. "You sure you don't mind?"

"Nah, we're good." Having a baby is hard. Having three kids under two and a half is even harder. "Get some sleep or love on your woman." I'm sure he could use a little of both.

"What about you?" His concern is genuine and reminds me how lucky I am to be a part of his family by choice and blood.

"Already took care of one. I'll sleep as soon as Iris conks out." Which I'm predicting is in about fifteen minutes after she gulps her bottle and releases a giant belch. I've never had much trouble getting a baby to sleep. Gentle rocking and steady patting always gets them in the end.

He nods his silent thanks as he creeps to his room, whispering, "Goodnight," before his form is swallowed by the darkened hallway. Iris' room is right next to theirs, not that it matters. We have baby monitors set up in each of the kids' rooms.

Maddox, Killian, Cade, and Wade are in bunk beds in the loft. They're all close to the same age and threatened by Gabriel to sleep and not fuck around—not his exact words but definitely his meaning. Then Maddyn and Iris have separate rooms so one doesn't wake up the other. When they get older, they'll bunk together too. Though I imagine, like most younger siblings and cousins, they'll want to be with the boys. I just hope the older ones take their family bonds seriously and take care of their sisters, cousins, each other. We've got a brood going, and it's only going to grow. And I can't wait.

It takes a little longer than anticipated for Iris to settle down. A full tummy, a fresh diaper, and a good burp has her lolling to sleep on my shoulder in the end. After settling her in her crib, I watch her closely to be sure she'll stay asleep before I tiptoe to the kitchen for waters and then back to my Kitten.

Naked, I settle in behind her warm lusciousness and fill my nose with her scent with a little hint of me and sex, making me ache for her again. Pulling her close, she settles in, her leg over me, putting her pussy teasingly close to Cocky. A nuzzle of her mouth against my neck, a swivel of her hips, and a soft moan have me sinking into her welcoming heat.

Lazy thrusts and pleading hands, sounds of making love fill the room, making me harder and her wetter. A firm grip on her ass, grinding her against me has her coming in record time, soaking me, riling me.

I flip her over. Flat on her tummy, her hips undulating, pleading for more, I enter her from behind, sinking in slow, groaning through every delicious inch as she takes me, consumes me. "You need more, Kitten?"

She pushes back, twisting her neck to lock on me. "Yes, hard this time."

"Fuck." She had to go and unleash my beast. I sit back and pat her ass. Without verbally asking, she rises till her ass is in the air. "That's my girl. Cross your ankles."

What a beautiful sight: ass high, pussy glistening. I want to eat her out, but it's late, and she's not feeling all that well, though you'd never know it by the spectacular orgasms she's gifted me—I mean hers, not mine. Though mine rock, I count my success by her pleasure.

Gripping her ass cheeks, I enter her pussy slowly.

Tight. "So fucking tight," I groan, pushing through her tremors, echoes of her last orgasm.

"Oh, fuck…" she breathes into the pillow, her head buried, gripping the sheets.

Once I'm fully seated, I slip in and out slowly, painfully so. Her moans grow with each intake. I kiss up her back and whisper, "You sure you want hard, Kitten? You seem to be enjoying slow tonight."

She clenches and quakes, offering a breathy, "Cam."

Jesus. She's primed. I reach round, circling her clit. "I got you." I kiss her neck and bite her shoulder as I slowly pump in and out, rounding her clit.

In and out.

Round.

In and out.

Round.

In.

Round.

Out.

Round.

"Ohmygod!"

"Fuck." That's it. She steals my pleasure I'm trying to give her, taking it and turning it back on me.

My fucking *Wendy*. Taming me. Sating me.

I fuck her into two more orgasms before Cocky finally lets go and feeds his pretty kitty all of our cum.

"Oh my god, Cam," she pants. "When I… can breathe… Can you do that again? Just like that," she gulps. "Again."

Fuck. My Lion. My heart. My wife. "Yeah, baby. But I need a taste first."

"Oh my holy—" her words die as I lick her from seam to ass, flip her around and suck on her clit until she's begging me to come inside her.

She never needs to beg, but damn if I don't love it.

My girl is hungry.

And I'm always up to feeding her.

Filling her.

Loving her.

My Lion.

My Shadow Whisperer.

CHAPTER 3

CAP AND CHER

Watching my Plum with our littles is one of the greatest joys in life. I'm lucky to have found a family in the grown men and women who work for me, surround me. But I've been doubly blessed to find out Rowdy and Taylor are mine too, and then to be triply blessed with the three munchkins gifted to me by Cher and the powers that be.

I'm one lucky motherfu—but the only mother I'm fucking is the mother of my children. I kiss her shoulder, breathing her in. "You sure I can't talk you into going with me? I'd stick with you, keep you safe." I could probably prop her on my skis and ski downhill with her glued to my front if she'd let me.

"I'm sure." She pushes her ass into me, trying to get me to back up as she fixes breakfast.

I grip her hips, securing her to my hardening length. "Shoving me with this ass isn't going to convince me to back off."

She laughs over her shoulder, granting me her electric-blue eyes for a hot second before her attention returns to the stove. "Not trying to convince you." She nuzzles into me with her head as she cooks scrambled eggs. "I can't ski. You'll have more fun without me. *And* I can't leave Ree with all the kids. Six is too much for one person to handle."

Especially with our six ranging from nine months to nearly four years old.

"Boys," I command.

Four little heads pop up from the long table big enough to hold all of us. Their eyes zero in on me.

"What's your job today?"

"Obey Aunt Ree and Granplum," Maddox, the oldest, is quick to reply, encouraging nods from the other three.

"That's right. And when Maddyn or Iris cry?" I ask.

Wade raises his hand. My little lover, always kind and respectful. With a nod from me, he answers, "Asks how we can helwp."

"That's right." I sit at the head of the table, keeping their attention. "And when it's naptime?"

"We're quiet even if we can'ts sleep and are too olds for naps," Cade, my little fighter, chimes in.

I rumple his golden hair that grows darker with each birthday. "Even then." He's not too old for naps. He only *wants* to be. He'll sleep for two hours after lunch. He plays hard. He sleeps harder. "Naps are important for growing boys and girls."

"I naps." Iris plops a slobbery hand on my knee. "I eats now?" Her brow crinkles, concerned she might miss her next meal. Not a chance.

"Yep, Itty Bitty." I lift her as I stand, kissing her cheek. "Breakfast is almost ready. How about a grape?"

"Yes, pweez." She waits patiently after I get her in her highchair to pass out the fruit Cher prepared as part of their breakfast.

I divvy up a couple of bananas, grapes, cantaloupe, and apple slices between everyone, giving extra care to the size for Maddyn. At nine months, her enthusiasm for eating often has her swallowing bites before chewing—or gumming. Near mush is a must.

With Eggs, bacon, and biscuits plated up, they dig in and are half done before the rest of the adults join us, dressed for hitting the slopes—except Reese. Like Cher, she's never skied before. I thought she might try, but doesn't look like it.

"Reese, I'm happy to stay back if you want to go today." I pull Cher into the chair next to me, needing a minute before I leave her for the day—or at least until lunch. We're taking it easy today. None of us have skied in a few years. Gabriel is the furthest out, but he's also probably the most athletic of the bunch. Don't tell Rowdy I said that.

Of the kids, Maddox is the only one who nearly qualifies to take kiddie ski lessons, cutoff being four years old. The kids will stay back today while we check it out and see if we can get Maddox, Killian, Cade, and Wade into some sort of ski lessons since they're all bigger than most four-year-olds—and athletic, if I do say so myself.

"No, I'm good," she's quick to shut me down, her gaze following Rowdy as he fills his plate with more eggs.

"Maybe we can go snowmobiling or tubing," Cher suggests to the room.

"Or a spa day." Taylor sighs dreamily.

"Yes! I second a girls' spa day," Frankie is quick to respond.

I kiss Cher's cheek. "I'm sure we can make that happen."

The girls don't know we already bought them a spa package for the day after Christmas. The guys will relax with the kids as our wives indulge in a little me-time.

After breakfast, we linger at the door, reluctant to leave

our wives and kids. "When did we get pussy-whipped?" I grumble more in awe than a complaint.

Cowboy chuckles as he pulls Taylor out the door. "The day you met your other halves."

"What about you?" She hurries to keep up.

"Songbird, you pussy-whipped me when I was seventeen. The only difference is, I get to take you with me."

"Good answer." She jumps on his back for a ride to the truck.

"I'm taking mine with me too." Gabriel takes one last look at his kids, then wraps his arm around Frankie. "But damn, if it isn't hard leaving our kids."

"Come on, Big Man. I'll sit on your lap as you explain the fundamentals of skiing."

"You could just ride my back down the hill," he offers, not even joking a little.

I laugh because I had nearly the same thought about Cher.

"We could stay, you know." Rowdy waves at Reese cleaning up Killian's breakfast face.

"We could, but then what was the point of coming to a ski resort if we don't actually leave the cabin or do stuff we can't do at home?" I grip his shoulder. Together we make our way out the door.

"We're coming back for lunch, right?" he confirms.

"Yeah, I'll be due for a Plum fix by then."

"Hear that."

The sooner we get this show on the road, the faster we can get home to our other halves and our littles.

I catch Cher waving as we pull out. My heart pangs.

I've said it before.

I'll say it again.

I'm a lucky—blessed—SOB.

* * *

The kitchen clean, Reese and I settle on the couch, the kids playing on the floor around us. I sip my coffee, watching Reese as much as the kids.

"You feeling any better?"

"Mmm, not really. Food helped. I think." She yawns. "I don't know. Honestly, I think I could sleep for a week."

"Cameron made me promise I'd ensure you drink more water."

"He thinks I have altitude sickness."

"What do you think?"

She seems transfixed by the fire dancing in the fireplace. "I think I might be pregnant."

My heart skips. I was hoping but didn't want to say it—put the idea in her head if she's not. They've been trying for a while. Each month, when her period comes, she's disappointed, though she does a good job of hiding it.

"Do you have a test with you?" I could ask the guys to stop on their way back, but they'd have to go to town. I doubt the ski shop carries pregnancy tests. Though, you never know.

"I do."

My brows shoot up. "Why haven't you taken it?"

She rolls her head toward me, sinking farther into the couch. "I'm scared it will be negative. If I don't take it, I can live in the *land of possibility* for a little while longer."

I understand living in denial. "Give it a few more days—or wait until we get home."

"I was thinking of taking it on Christmas Eve. It would make for a great Christmas present for Cam."

It could be a huge disappointment for them too. I don't point that out. She knows. Probably why she's really waiting.

"Well, there's time. We have ginger. I could make you some tea." It helped her through the nausea with Killian. She even had ginger suckers she kept in her purse and pretty much within arm's reach all over their house.

"That'd be nice."

She must be out of sorts if she hadn't thought of it. As I get up to make her tea, Killian climbs in her lap. "I tired." He snuggles into her chest.

"You ready for your nap?"

"No. Can I lay wiff you?"

"Of course."

"I'm kinda tired too." Ox yawns, followed by Cade.

Wade eyes the two of them before walking to me. "Movie?" His shoulders rise with his expressive brows. My intuitive little man. So young, but already a caretaker of his brother, sister, and cousins.

"That's a great idea. Why don't y'all get comfortable on the couches while we put a movie on?" I touch Reese's shoulder. "I'll make the bottles too." The girls will be ready for their bottles before their morning naps. I doubt any of the kids will make it through the movie.

Maybe not even the adults will.

CHAPTER 4

LANDRY AND TAYLOR

She's limping. I don't even think she realizes it. The idea of taking a family ski trip sounded so fun months ago. I hadn't considered the state of Taylor's physical readiness to actually ski. I don't think she considered it either. It was an automatic *yes* when Cap brought it up, and when he started planning, our excitement only grew.

Now, watching my girl walk in ski boots and carry her skis and poles, her limp seems more pronounced and a lot more concerning.

I don't want to hold her back. I don't want to overreact, undermine her confidence she worked hard to repair right along with her body.

I also don't want to underreact, chance a setback by injuring herself skiing too soon.

The doctor said it was up to her.

Frankie said she's physically ready.

I say wait. We'll have a hundred other chances to ski. But how fair is it for me to say she can't ski and then go out and have a blast doing what I said she shouldn't?

Damn, I just don't know.

"Lan, are you coming?" Gabriel calls as he heads to the ski lift with Frankie.

"I'll meet you." I turn back to Taylor, finding her eyes already on me.

"I'm good, Dually. Go. Have fun. I'll find you." She looks so cute in her hat, all wrapped up in her ski pants and jacket, her cheeks already rosy.

"I don't like leaving you." We've gone round and round on this. I want to stick with her. She wants me to leave her to concentrate on skiing without being self-conscious under my ever-present watchful eye. I'd never judge her. And me not taking my eyes off her is not only about her safety. She's hot as fuck in and out of clothes, but especially now all bundled up and adorable, she's irresistible.

"I'm all grown up, *Daddy*. Go." She pushes me the other direction.

Daddy? I know she's teasing, but, damn, if I don't want her to make me a daddy. I give in. I can't be the reason she doesn't try. "I love you. Be careful."

"You too." She turns, taking her glorious face and stunning body the other direction to catch the easier slopes. "Love you!" she throws over her shoulder right before she slips but catches herself.

Reluctantly, I make my way toward the lift Gabriel and Frankie took, all while looking over my shoulder until Taylor disappears from view.

My gut turns.

Am I making a mistake?

* * *

As soon as I'm alone, no longer able to feel Landry's assessing gaze, I'm swarmed with uncertainty. Am I making a mistake? Am I confident or stubborn, unable to admit I'm not ready?

The doctor says I'm good to go. So does Frankie.

Then, why don't I *feel* ready?

Each step to the chairlift feels weighted. My leg aches, but no more than normal. I will say these darn ski boots are not comfortable. I have a custom pair at home, in Texas. I didn't anticipate needing ski boots and skis in Vegas. Silly me.

If I survive today, maybe Dad can ship them to me.

As the lift ascends the mountain, I catch sight of Cap and Cam racing down the slope like idiots. Cam barely takes the lead on his snowboard. He never cared for two skis. He was always a good at both. Took to it right away. Our oldest brother, Drake, too, for that matter. I was slower in taking to it. Not because I couldn't do it, more because I was good and I felt a sense of bravery that scared me.

I have no doubt if I were in the military or a police officer, I would get myself killed. I'd be overconfident in my abilities, make a stupid mistake, and get shot. Or worse, get the people around me killed. I was a reckless kid. So was Cam—that's why his nickname is Rowdy. But somehow, he always managed to come out on top.

I did too, until Landry. That spring break my recklessness caught up with me. Though, I didn't feel reckless. It felt perfect. He was perfect. He *is* perfect for me—then, now, forever.

I glide off the lift and stop at the second-to-easiest hill, moving aside to allow those more eager than me to pass.

This hesitation isn't me. And it's pissing me off.

I don't know if it's physical discomfort that's making me hesitate, or if my gauge of what's reckless or not is broken since Beau.

I *let* him in my car. I *welcomed* him.

It was stupid.

It was *reckless*.

What was I thinking?

It's hard to breathe. I can't…

What am I doing on this mountain?

I can't ski.

I'm not ready.

Oh, shit. What do I do now?

A gravely "Songbird" hits me a second before Landry's strong arms envelop me.

Ohmygod. "Dually." I crumble.

He catches me, gets me off my skis and sequestered in his arms away from the drop off. "I got you," he whispers as I fall apart in his arms.

"How?" I sniffle, swiping at my face while digging in my pocket for a tissue.

"I couldn't just walk away. It didn't feel right. You were—aren't okay." He cups my cheek. "You have nothing to prove to anyone—not even yourself."

"I want to ski," I pout.

"And you can. But let me be by your side to support you if you need it, lift you up if you fall, cheer you on when you don't."

I lay my head on his chest and close my eyes for a brief moment, reminding myself I have a life partner in Landry. I'm not alone. He's my rock, my steady, my reason.

"I'm scared." The admission doesn't hurt as much as I feared.

"I know." He tips my chin. "But why are you scared?"

"I have all these doubts in my head. I don't trust my judgment."

He frowns, considering. "Judgment about what?"

"Is it too soon?"

"To ski? Or to believe in yourself?"

My surprise has him cupping my face, keeping my focus on him. "You believe in yourself, always. What happened in your past is in your past. You trusted the wrong person *one* time. It doesn't mean you have bad judgment. It means you have a caring, open heart. You don't see strangers, Taylor. You see potential friends. Don't let Beau keep you from doing anything you want, not even skiing."

"You think I'm ready?"

With his eyes still locked on me, he smiles. "It doesn't matter what I think. It matters what *you* think."

"I want to be ready."

"Then *be* ready. Fear doesn't mean you're not ready. It means you're smart enough to know there are potential dangers."

I look out over the hill. It looks higher from up here than it did at the bottom. "You'll come with me?"

"Absolutely." He squeezes my hand. "We take it slow, snowplough down if that's what it takes to build your confidence. Then, the next time, you'll go side to side if you're ready."

"Okay."

"Yeah?"

"Yeah."

He helps me back into position, skis and poles in place before he gets himself situated. "Take it slow. If you get going too fast and can't stop, sit down." He chin-nods down the hill. "I'm right here, the whole way."

Slowly, and I mean sloth-slow, I start down the slope, snowploughing for the first minute or so. Then, gradually, I start to traverse from side to side. I don't take my eyes off my destination, but Landry is right beside me the whole way, talking to me, telling me, "You're doing great."

I am. I'm doing it. My leg doesn't hurt. My fear diminishes the closer we get to the bottom. What feels like hours is, in fact, only a handful of minutes till we reach the base. Not giving me time to second-guess myself, I head straight to the chairlift to do it again, Landry at my side.

On my second run, I relax and actually look around, taking in my surroundings. "What?!" I'm shocked to see Cap and Rowdy behind Landry, then Gabriel and Frankie behind them.

Landry laughs at my surprise.

"We wanted to be sure you were okay." Cap's smile is full of pride—for me.

"You can pass me. I don't mind." I don't want to hold them back.

"Nah, we're good." Cam turns backwards, making wider turns to slow his pace.

I blink away pending tears. I can't believe them.

At the bottom again, Landry kisses my cheek. "They love you, Songbird. They believe in you even when you doubt yourself."

"True, but we're also hungry." Cam nudges my shoulder. "One more run, then lunch?"

Already? I must have taken longer to build up my courage than I thought. "Yes, please."

This time we take the lift a little farther up the hill. Still not black diamond like Cap and Cam-worthy, but it's black diamond enough for me.

They all stick with me, all the way down.

I feel lighter, like a weight I didn't know I was carrying has been lifted.

This is my husband and my family.

They carry me when I am too heavy.

They glide with me when I fly.

My family by blood.

My family by choice.

CHAPTER 5
FRANKIE

It's been three days of trying to keep up with Gabriel on the slopes and falling asleep at night while nursing Maddyn. He's carried me to bed every night, me barely able to keep my eyes open, insisting we make love because I need it, and sleep—I'm just not sure which to prioritize. He simply chuckles indulgently, kisses my nose and tucks me in with a commanding, "Sleep, Angel," before leaving to hang out with the guys or getting the rest of the kids to bed.

Three. Days.

We came on this trip hoping to get alone time.

If you call skiing side by side, surrounded by hundreds of strangers, alone time, then, yes, we've hit the mark.

I, on the other hand, believe drastic measures are in order, which don't include weaning my little girl off the tit while on vacation. Or getting railed against a tree on a foray down the slopes as my sweet hubby tried yesterday. Thankfully, we were only kissing before the ski patrol stopped to be sure everything was okay. Then they strongly encouraged us to be on our way after determining we were short of breath from making out, not injury or illness.

It's starting to feel like a conspiracy.

I'm feeling a bit desperate for that sweet connection only found in my Gabriel's arms.

Yes, he touches me. *Yes*, he tells me he loves me. Every. Day.

Yet, it's not the same. I'm needing an intimate joining of the bodies only he can provide, and it's more than a quick encounter in the shower. We've been stealing moments for months. I need a good, long, sound fucking—like we *used* to have.

"Hey, you okay?" Reese slides in next to me on the second-floor balcony.

I just finished nursing Madd, then Gabriel took her downstairs to feed her solids along with Maddox. Tired and worn out, I stepped out here needing a minute for a pity party before putting on my adulting hat and making the best of my sexless existence. I nod and swipe under my eyes. "I'm good." I'm tired as fuck, but I'm good.

She nudges my shoulder. "Yeah, I can see that. How can I help?"

Help? She's the one not feeling all that great. She's only come out with us once when we went snowmobiling and threw up right after. "I feel like I should be asking you that." I take a sip of coffee and offer her my mug. "Feeling any better?"

"Nope. Not even a little." She smells the coffee, grimaces and hands it back.

That doesn't look like altitude sickness... "Are you...?" I leave the question hanging.

"Don't know." She quickly looks over her shoulder and over the railing to the lower-level balcony then shrugs. "I'm waiting till tomorrow to find out."

"Why? You can still wait to tell him." Or is there another reason?

Her smile is endearing. "I can't keep a secret from Cam to save my life."

"Hear that." Especially one as big as this. We're all in baby-making mode. I think Taylor even has the bug.

"I'm staying here today. I need to catch up on some sleep or at least not expend more energy than I have," I admit, having just come to that conclusion.

She laughs. "I imagine Gabriel is hard to keep up with."

"Not usually," I consider. "Though, I don't spend all day doing athletic things with him. So, in reality, I probably never could keep up. But I'm blaming it on Madd and lack of sleep."

"Sounds like a plan I can get behind. I'm staying in too. Maybe Cher would like to go today if you're okay watching the kids with me."

I turn to head downstairs. "Considering two of the little monsters are mine, seems only fair I should contribute."

Then tonight, Gabriel is all mine.

* * *

"Fuck, Plum, this mouth." I grip the shower wall instead of her hair, my body urging me to ram my cock down her throat, my heart telling me to let her do as she wishes.

It's a battle, but her touching me—in any way—is a win.

"Fuck." I reach for her but stop as she circles my head, licking the seam before sucking lightly then taking me deep. My abs and ass tighten, fighting the need to thrust, feed her my cock one deep rail at a time.

Head back, eyes closed, I groan when she tries to take all of me. Her choking has me pulling out. "Cher, baby." I cup her cheeks and swipe at her tears. "Did I do that?" Did I unconsciously do what my mind was playing over and over in my head?

"No," she gasps, wiping the saliva from her chin and mouth.

Whether I did or not, she's done. "C'mere." I lift her in my arms.

"James—"

I squelch her protest in a searing kiss, finally letting loose, feeding her my tongue like I wanted to do with my cock. Like I plan to do when I'm inside her sweet, sweet pussy. I love her mouth on me and the *idea* of her choking on my cock, but in reality, I feel like a tool when she does.

"No more, Plum. Need inside you."

"You were—"

Nope. "Not the way I need to be." Not the way that brings us both boundless pleasure. She may like sucking me, teasing me. But I prefer her pussy over her mouth any day of the week. My sweet Plum.

Her legs wrapped around me, I pin her to the shower

wall, slipping in, not gently in the least. Her head falls back, hitting the tiles as she gasps, "Cap."

Fuck. Love her calling me that—still.

Her head rolls to the side, focusing beyond the glassed-in shower, biting her lip. A small moan escapes.

I follow her gaze and grin when I catch our reflection in the bathroom mirror. "You love to watch, dontcha, baby?"

"Yes. So much."

I twist her nipples, watching the live version while she focuses on our duplicates. If we had more time, I'd fuck her over the sink so she could watch up close and personal. But as it is, Iris will be up soon. I'm sure someone else would grab her, but I love those morning cuddles. Now that she's not breastfeeding, I get the first love and cherish feeding her a bottle.

"Harder," my wife begs.

"Everything." I steal her mouth, sucking her tongue and nipping at her lips until she tightens around me. I back off enough for her to turn her head. "Watch, baby. Watch me make you come."

"Ohmygo—" she loses her voice as she comes undone, her eyes locked on the mirror, her hold tight on me as I pump and pump into her release, giving her my seed.

Maybe one more kid…

"Love you so hard, Plum," I breathe against the softness of her sensitive neck.

"So hard," she pants.

CHAPTER 6
REESE

"I'm staying here today." I fill my glass with orange juice. "Frankie is staying too. We were thinking you could go out with Cap today or go shopping if you'd like." I eye Mom and don't miss Cap's smile.

He's awful chipper this morning. As a matter of fact, so is Mom.

"Really?" She plops in Cap's lap. "Did you hear that?"

He doesn't miss a beat in wrapping an arm around her waist and feeding her a bite of bacon. "I did. Sounds like our girls are giving us a day together, Plum. You game?"

"Always." She giggles into his neck when he squeezes her backside.

"Um, Mom, Cap, little eyes," Gabriel growls.

Cap and Mom don't pay him any mind as their embrace turns into a heated kiss.

Gabriel's eyes flash to Frankie, the disappointment right there in his sparkling blue eyes. "You're staying home, Angel?"

"Mmm-hmm, need to rest." She keeps his gaze, not backing off, giving in to his desire to have her with him. If

I hadn't talked to her earlier, I wouldn't be able to read her silent plea. He's wearing her out and not in the good under-the-sheets kinda way.

I find my Shadow in the mix of the kids, wiping one's mouth, cutting up a fried egg for another. He's such a good daddy, brother, and uncle. His head pops up as if he feels my gaze. His worried brow deepens as we share our own silent embrace.

Love you, I mouth.

He kisses Killian's head and rises to his impressive height, eats up the distance between us, picks me up and carries me out of the kitchen and down the hall until we're alone. Pulling my legs around his waist, he leans in, stealing my breath as I hit the wall. Not hard, but the move is packed with heat and primal claiming.

"You're not coming with me?" He's so close I can barely focus on his eyes. His yummy bacon and maple syrup breath wafts over me.

I run my fingers through his long hair, holding him in place so I can lick and nip at his mouth till he grunts and gives me the kiss I need.

Tender and slow, he savors my mouth, pressing every inch of his body to mine. I'm overcome with emotions—his —mine.

My breath hitches on a sob. It hits out of nowhere, and unwelcome tears fall.

"Kitten." My big protective man holds me, cupping the back of my head as I hide in his neck.

What the hell is wrong with me? There's no reason to cry. We're on vacation, having a great time.

"I'm staying with you today. Frankie can rest, and you and me will take care of the kids. I need you close." He kisses my hair. "Not leaving," he whispers as if he needs to reassure me. He doesn't. He's never let me down. He's always what I need. Most of the time, he knows it before I do.

"I'd like that." I sniffle and hug his neck tighter in case he's thinking I'm ready to be set down. I'm not.

He doesn't ask me why I'm crying. He doesn't need to. I've been out of sorts. He probably suspects. I'm surprised he hasn't handed me a pregnancy test by now. Maybe, like me, he's waiting on me to find out. Or maybe he's not ready to be disappointed again.

Drying my tears with his shirt, he pats my butt. "Come eat. I'll make you some tea."

"Hold me a minute more."

"Yeah," he sighs into my neck. "As long as you need."

* * *

GABRIEL

Pressing my lips to my Angel's forehead, I linger, not wanting to leave without her. She's tired as fuck, and I need to expel some energy. We're not on the same page. If I stay, I'll rut on her like it's mating season. And that is likely what has her in this tired state.

"Go, Big Man. I'll be fine. Have fun with the guys." She presses my chest like she can move me, persuade me she's fine. She can't, 'cause I'm unsure, hesitant to leave her.

"You promise you're okay? It's nothing more?" She wasn't this tired after having Maddox.

Her silken hair tickles my hand on her lower back as she tips her chin, granting me her silvery gaze. "I'm sure. I'll rest today, eat healthy, and be a new person when you get back tonight."

"I don't need a new person. I just need you, Angel." I kiss her nose and step back. "Promise."

Her smile is indulgent. "I promise. Now go." She swishes me away with her hand. "Love you. Be careful."

I stop mid-step and turn. "Love you." I capture the back of her neck and pull her to me, kissing her soundly. "More than life." Landry honks behind me. I flip him off. He can fucking wait. "If you need me, I'm here."

"I know. Now go before I make you nap with me."

I groan at the thought. "If I *nap* with you, the last thing we'll be doing is sleeping." I hover and press my mouth to hers one more time. "Rest, Angel."

I hurry down the steps before I can change my mind and decide to stay. Fucking Rowdy. He gets to stay. Why can't I?

Because you're horny as fuck and need to exercise.

"Who's hitting black diamond with me today?" I slam the door and buckle up.

* * *

It takes five runs before I'm feeling more like my calm, in control self. Taylor stuck with me for the first run, then opted to hang back with Landry for the rest of the morning. Mom and Cap are off doing their own thing. They said we *might* see them for lunch. I'm not holding my breath. We're all cut from the same cloth. We don't mind socializing, but when it comes to spending time with our women, we prefer to keep it to a party of two, especially when alone time has been cut short with all the kids we've been having.

The ache in my chest is back. I've a niggling feeling there's more going on than Frankie being tired. Maybe she's anemic. I make a note to buy some steaks and a home iron deficiency test.

Or I could ditch afternoon skiing, get a ride to the closest market and get home earlier. I'm starving, though. Food first, then decide what to do the rest of the day.

CHAPTER 7

FRANKIE AND GABRIEL

It's like a dream—no, a nightmare—as we rush to the emergency room. In all the years I've known Gabriel, I've never once seen him in the hospital, or even really hurt, for that matter.

A car.

He was walking out of a store, arms full, snow falling all around him, when some idiot in the parking lot didn't see him until it was too late. Slamming on his brakes, sliding on the mix of snow and ice, he hit Gabriel.

With his car.

Knocked my larger-than-life man off his feet, slamming into the windshield and bouncing off the car to land hard on the curb.

Unconscious. That was all they said on the phone.

I pace the hall, shrugging off Rowdy and Cap's concern for me to take it easy and sit before I wear myself out. I'm already exhausted. But I can't stop moving, and I can't make eye contact with Reese and Cher. They're a mess, crying the tears I wish I could but refuse to.

Landry and Taylor stayed at the cabin with the kids.

Oh God, Maddox and Maddyn. What'll I do if he dies?

No. Don't think like that. This is Gabriel.

He saves people. He's a rock—a Stone. He doesn't let a thing like getting hit by a car keep him down.

"Mrs. Stone?" a man in scrubs calls as he looks around the waiting room.

"Yes." I rush over. "That's me. Is Gabriel okay?"

"Come with me." He eyes my family at my back. "Only you, for now."

Hours later, I send everyone home. He's still out. The doctor said he has a head injury, a broken hip, femur, and fractured ribs. They've put off surgery until he's more stable and the swelling diminishes.

More stable.

My man is the most stable man I know. He can't possibly be *more* stable.

It's well into Christmas Eve before he regains consciousness. His heavenly blue eyes find me instantly. "Angel."

I can't stop the tears. "Big man." I press a kiss to his hand I haven't stopped holding since I entered the room. I don't care if I'm in the nurses' way. They can work around me. I'm never, *never* letting this hand go. "You scared me."

"S-shteak. I was buying you shteak?" He frowns, struggling with his words.

Oh no. His speech is lazy like he had a stroke.

"Steak?" Why was he at the store buying steak when we had plenty of food?

"An-n-nemic," he stutters.

Oh, holy Jesus. Does he have brain damage, or is it the drugs?

"You were buying steak because you're anemic?" That can't be right.

"You."

I shake my head. "I'm not anemic. I'm pregnant."

God, I haven't admitted that to myself or dared to say it out loud. Maddyn is only nine months old. I shouldn't be pregnant again. Not so soon.

"Preg-a-nant?" He waves off his stutter, eyes shimmering, and kisses my hand before a tear slips free. "Angel."

Angel. He sounds like my Gabriel when he says it. What are we going to do? I need to call Cap and Cher. But it's too late—or too early. I shouldn't wake them up.

"I…" I step back, fighting back my tears. "I need to call your mom. Tell her you're awake—" my voice cracks. I turn away, my whole body shaking as silent sobs erupt.

He's broken. My Big Man is broken.

I'll love him anyway. Always. Even if he can never lift a finger again. I'll love every inch of him no matter the damage.

But he's—oh my god, how will he feel about—

"Angel," his bark has me pivoting, coming to his side. "You don't hide from me. My body may be broken…" He taps his head and his heart. "But I'm still the same man you love in here."

"Gabriel," I sob, breaking down, falling into his arms.

"I'm the same man, Angel. You need to br-reak down, y-you do it wiff me. I'm your avenging angel." His hold tightens.

"I'm sorr—"

"Frankie." A firm touch. "Frankie! Wake up."

"What?" I shoot straight up, blinking at Reese as the hospital disappears. *Reese?* "What… where—"

"You were crying in your sleep. I came in to check on you but thought I should wake you up. Your dream didn't seem all that pleasant."

"Gabriel!" I jump out of bed and scan the room for my phone. "I have to call Gabriel."

"Here." She dials on her phone and hands it to me.

Ringing.

I fall to the side of the bed and wipe my face with the sheet.

It was a dream.

It was *only* a dream.

* * *

GABRIEL

My arms full of grocery sacks, I fumble for my phone. "Ree?"

"Gabriel!"

"Angel?" I check my phone to be sure it's Reese's number calling me. It is. "What's wrong?"

"Where are you?"

"Shopping."

"Inside?"

"Why?"

"Stop!" she screams. "Oh my god, please stop. Are you inside the store still?"

"Yes. What's going on?"

"Don't move. Gabriel, don't move!"

Her panic has me stilling, placing my bags back in the cart. "I'm not moving, Frankie. Tell me what happened. Why are you crying and panicked?"

"You're still in the store? You didn't go outside?"

"No, baby. I'm here at the doors, but I'm still inside."

"Is it snowing?"

What is going on? I glance outside. "Yeah, Angel. It's snowing."

"There's a car—"

"What the—" I jump back as a car slips and slides, skidding sideways, barely missing a guy walking to his car, but his cart is not as lucky. The car slams into it, sending everything flying, stopping feet from where I would have been if I'd exited the store. "Shit!"

"What happened?! Are you okay?"

"Yeah. Yeah. I'm okay. A car nearly hit a guy in the parking lot."

"That was you."

"What?! No, it was some *other* guy. I'm fine."

"My dream. I had a dream you were shopping and came out of the store carrying bags and didn't see the car coming. He hit *you*," she sobs. "You... Gabriel... you were—"

"Hey. Hey. Angel. I'm okay. The car didn't hit me. It was a dream." It's not real, but damn if it doesn't feel a little too real. If I had stepped out—

"But if I hadn't called you?"

"Well..." It could've been me in the parking lot instead of some stranger. "I'm coming home. I'll be there in twenty."

"Wait."

"Yeah, Angel?"

"I think I'm pregnant."

Well, shit. I didn't see that coming. It's gonna take hours for my heart to stop racing. "I'll get a test. Go play with Maddox and Maddyn. They'll make you feel better until I get there."

"Okay."

"And, Angel?"

"Yeah?"

"No car could take me out. I'm a tough asshole. I'd come home to you no matter how broken my body may be. You feel me?"

"Yeah." I can hear her smile. "Yeah, Big Man. You're too tough and stubborn to let a car take you out."

"Damn straight. I'll see you in a few."

"Love you, Gabriel."

"Love you so fucking much, Angel."

CHAPTER 8

LANDRY AND TAYLOR

She skied a black diamond run today with Gabriel. She ate up that slope as I snowploughed my way down. She was confident and owning her shit.

At least that's what I'd thought until we got to the bottom. Gabriel went up for more. She and I headed inside. She was shaking. Scared.

Seated by the fire, sipping hot cocoa with a mountain of marshmallows, she lets out a deep sigh. "I'm not ready for double black. I may never be."

I cup the back of her neck, squeezing softly. "It's okay, loads of people, like me, don't feel comfortable skiing at that level. You can still enjoy skiing on easier slopes."

"Yeah." She lays her head on my shoulder. "I'm tired. I think I'm ready to leave."

"*Leave,* leave, or head back to the cabin?"

"The cabin." She smiles up at me. "I'm not cutting our trip short because I can't ski like I thought I could."

That's good to know. She's a fighter. She's shown me that every day. Today is no different.

"I'm way better than I was the first day. I'm okay with being a mediocre skier. It's not like I could ever keep up with Cam anyway. I'd rather ski easier and enjoy it than ski expert and be a nervous wreck."

"Me too." I kiss her nose. "How about we just relax here a bit before we head out? I'll text Cap and see if he can pick us up on his way home. He wasn't planning on staying out all day anyway. Or we can catch the shuttle."

"Sounds good."

As I wait for Cap to respond to my text, we sip our cocoa, watch the fire and the skiers coming down the hill to either catch the lift back up or come inside to warm up.

"There's Gabriel." My Songbird points out the black dot getting larger as he descends. "He looks lonely."

"He always scowls."

She laughs. "Not when Frankie is around."

"True." I grip her shoulder, pulling her closer. "We're better men when our women are around."

"I think that's a good thing." She leans forward, following Gabriel as he heads to the lift. "He still seems lonely. He didn't want to leave Frankie today." She eyes me over her shoulder. "Do you know why?"

"Songbird, I don't want to leave you either. That's not hard to understand. But Gabriel has energy to burn—if you catch my drift. If he'd stayed at the cabin, I don't think Frankie would have gotten much rest."

She plops back. "You mean sex?"

"Yeah, I don't think he's getting much of that with how tired Frankie has been. You've seen her. She can hardly make it through dinner. He's put her to bed almost every night after getting Maddyn down. Then he stays up shooting the shit and helping with the kids."

"I guess I didn't think about it. Didn't notice."

Guys have sex on the brain. We can tell who's getting it and who's not. And my man Gabriel is not getting it.

"We should help with their kids more. Give them time

to themselves. I know tomorrow is Christmas Eve, but maybe we can take their kids in the morning, so they can sleep in."

"I think that's a great idea." My phone buzzes. I check my text from Cap and shoot a text off to Gabriel to let him know he can have the car to leave whenever he's ready. We're catching a ride with Cap. "Cap said he'll be here in a few hours."

Her sultry green gaze locks on me. "What are we going to do to fill our time?"

I've got an idea or two. "Come on."

* * *

"Dually, ohmygod!" I can't stop shaking. He's filling me from behind, holding me against his chest as jets of water from the multiple shower heads pelt my nipples and clit. My skin not being touched or covered by Landry is inundated by water in all directions, but it's the ones hitting my most sensitive parts that keep me coming and coming.

Landry booked a couples massage. When they brought us to a cozy room with two massage tables and a shower for two, he kicked them out, promising them a large tip to leave us alone and keep quiet.

The male masseuse eyed us up and down. "There's bottled water in the mini fridge. I'll be back in an hour. Enjoy."

"Damn, do you think I can book *him*?" the female masseuse whispered—not too discreetly—as they walked off.

"Fuck, Songbird, you keep squeezing me like that, and we won't need this room for the whole hour."

"Or," I gasp, "you could eat me on the table until you're ready to go again." I'm generous like that.

"Baby, you have the best ideas." He slaps the side of my ass, squeezing and drilling home.

"I do—*oh my god*—don't I?" I grip his arm and brace a hand on the wall, curling forward, coming again, trembling and shaking in his hold.

"Fuck. Fuck. Fuck." He slips out, turns me around, lifting and slamming into me, holding and holding as I clench around him. "Never tire of feeling you come on my cock, baby."

"Never tire of coming on your cock, Dually." Truly. They should make this an Olympic sport. We'd win. I'm positive.

Still seated inside me, arms wrapped around me, he exits the shower and lays me on one of the massage tables sideways so my head is hanging off. He grips my hips and fucks me relentlessly. I search for something to hold on to, but when I find nothing substantial, I grip my knees, holding my legs open, sending him deeper.

"Fuuuuuck," he groans. "That... is spectacular."

Spectacular? I'd laugh if my upside-down view wasn't messing with my head, my equilibrium, sending pleasure to all my hot spots. "Lan."

"I got you." He grips one breast and beats a rhythm into me. "Gonna fuck your mouth just like that after you come again."

Oh fuck. Yes.

"You're clenching me. Does that mean you like that idea, baby? You want me fucking your mouth, tasting your juices all over me?"

"Dually!" My orgasm hits so hard, I lose sight, my ears ring, and the only sensation is the pleasure of his cock filling me as he rubs my clit, sending ripples of ecstasy along my nervous system.

"Open, baby." Something wet and warm nudges my lips.

I open my eyes to sight of Landry's cock and balls in my face. I grip his sides and pull him closer as I tilt farther back. "Don't kill me." Kinda teasing. Kinda not.

I'm incredibly vulnerable in this position. He could easily choke my airways as he fills my mouth with short thrusts. A lesser man would get off on that.

He massages my breasts and down my stomach. "I got you, Taylor. You tap me if I go too deep." He squeezes my hand on his waist. "Okay?"

I mumble my okay around his cock, making him groan, "Fuck. Hum a few lines while you suck, Songbird."

I'm so turned on by the idea of driving him crazy. I start humming the first song that comes to mind, "Always Been You."

His grip on my breasts is tight as he squeezes my nipples and twists, making me moan, messing up my song. He doesn't stop thrusting, and I don't stop moaning when one hand travels down my stomach to my slippery wet center, sliding along my slit, around my opening and back to my clit, over and over in time with his cock slipping in and out of my mouth.

"Fuck, baby, you feel so damn good." Nipple pinch. "So primed." Slip inside and out to my clit. "I want to fill all your holes at once."

Gah, yes. I want that too. His dirty talk has me ready to blow.

"Wrap your lips around your teeth when you come. Don't bite my cock off."

Never. I suck him harder, deeper, begging him to come down my throat as his fingers work me. My feet placed firmly on the table, I raise my hips, flexing them, forcing his fingers deeper, touching that spot only his cock can set off. He pumps faster—his fingers and his cock.

"Gonna come. Want you with me."

A strangled cry escapes when I feel the first stream of cum down my throat. It's my trigger. Convulsing, I explode around his fingers, gripping him tightly as he growls his release.

Spent, he slips from my mouth. Then he picks me up, lying on the table with me splayed out on top him. "Gonna fuck you one more time, Songbird, once I catch my breath."

I pant, trying to catch my own air and close my eyes. "I'll hop right on that dick as soon as I can move."

He chuckles and skates his fingers down my back, making me arch, pressing into him. "Love you, Songbird."

"Love you, Dually."

CHAPTER 9
GABRIEL AND FRANKIE

I sit as patiently as I can on the couch, watching the kids play, even though I want to pace the front porch and pounce when Gabriel drives up. Maddox seems to sense my unease. He keeps showing me toys and laying kisses on my cheek. I try to reassure him I'm just tired, but he still keeps glancing my way.

He'll make a wonderful husband someday. He's intuitive like his daddy and not hindered with a turned-off heart. I pray it stays that way. Though Gabriel's difficult upbringing made him the man he is today, I wouldn't wish that on Maddox or any kid. I have to believe our love and encouragement will still make Maddox a good man, full of loyalty and honor like his father. His character-building moments will come in other ways. I worry what they might be and pray we don't break him or Maddyn like our parents did us.

I'm so lost in thought, I miss Gabriel driving up, and it's not until the door opens that I spring into action, leaping over kids and toys to lunge into his arms before he gets the door closed.

"Angel." He breathes into my neck. "It's okay, baby. I'm here."

I sniffle and hide my face, feeling all kinds of silly. "I'm so relieved."

He sets me back. "I see that." He squeezes my hands before letting me go to remove his coat and shoes.

"Hey." Rowdy and Landry greet Gabriel then gather the grocery bags I didn't even notice on the floor. "We'll get these."

"Thanks, guys." Gabriel pins me with his worried gaze. "Let me say hi to the kids and family. Then it's you and me, Angel." He cups my face and plants a kiss on my forehead.

"Yeah, okay."

Guiding me through to the living room, he releases me to catch Maddox flinging himself at his daddy, much like I did a moment ago. "Hey, big guy. You doing okay?" Gabriel hugs him tight, kissing his head.

"Mommy was worried." Maddox locks on Gabriel's face, the concern in his eyes matching his daddy's.

"I'm all good. Where's your sister?"

He points to Cap, who has an enthralled Maddyn on his lap, reading her a book. Cap looks up, giving me a nod, before continuing to read to our little angel.

Maddox goes back to playing as Gabriel heads to the kitchen, asking me, "You need food?"

"Maybe later." I'm too emotional to eat, but I am hungry. I just need time with him to reassure me he's fine after my horrible nightmare.

He snags a small grocery sack and some waters. "Y'all okay to watch the kids for a bit?" he asks Rowdy and Landry.

"Yeah. We'll save some dinner for you," Landry advises, pulling Taylor into his side. "Oh, and we'd like to watch the kids in the morning so y'all can sleep in."

Gabriel's eyes bug out. "All of them?"

Taylor only smiles. "Yeah, it'll be fine."

"I'd like to nurse Maddyn before bed, so please knock if we haven't come out to get her."

"Sure thing." Taylor gives me a quick hug. "Everything's good. We've got Madd and Ox. Go. Have some hubby time."

Sequestered in our room on the second floor behind a locked door, the world slips away as he leads me to the bed.

"First things first." He kneels in front of me. "Tell me about your dream."

I run my fingers through his hair. I love playing with it, especially since he wears it longer now. "It was a nightmare. It felt so real." I fight my emotions, still a bit strung out. It *felt* real.

He undresses me and himself, guiding me to the shower as I share as many details as I can remember. Like most dreams, the more you think about them, they seem to evaporate, slip away, but the slur of his speech still rocks me.

"I'm fine, Angel." He presses my hands to his chest as the hot water sprays around us. "Feel, baby. I'm solid and all here. My speech is fine. Not an inch of me hurt." He encourages my hand lower, wrapping around his cock. "Except maybe here. I ache for you."

"Yeah?" I tighten my grip, loving the grunt that escapes his parted lips as I stroke up to the swollen head and spread the moisture around his slit and down.

He pushes me against the warming tile wall. "Not going anywhere." He teases my neck as my head falls back with tender kisses. "I'm here, baby." His hand slips lower, between my legs. "Let me love you, wash away your fears."

"Please." I sigh into his hold as his fingers separate my folds, finding my center.

"That's it," he coaxes. "Spread your legs. Let me in, Angel."

I moan when he slips his fingers inside, his thumb rubbing my clit. He kisses and licks up my neck to my jaw and finally latching on to my mouth.

This is it.

This is what I've missed.

Slow, languid kisses mixed with needy hands and ragged breaths.

"Fuck. You feel so good. So wet." He bites my shoulder, "So mine," then licks and sucks till I'm trembling, ready to explode—or quite possibly implode.

I grip his shoulder and the back of his head, holding him to me, lifting my leg to wrap around his hip. "Now, Gabriel."

He growls as he lifts me by my thighs, slamming into me as he presses me to the wall.

I moan my contentment. He gives a few quick thrusts before setting in deep and stilling. "Need your mouth." Not really a question but a statement of fact.

We lock lips, and he tandem fucks my mouth as he rocks inside me.

"So good. So full," I pant into our kiss. "I've missed you."

"Too long, Angel. I'm sorry." He picks up the pace, stealing my voice and taking me higher, making me forget I've missed him, making me forget my name.

Harder. Harder.

Frenzied and fast.

He fills me.

Obliterates me.

Completes me.

He swallows my moans as I consume his, gripping his

ass, thrusting into him, meeting him, joining with him. Over and over.

I come undone when his hands squeeze my ass, separating my cheeks, rubbing my back entrance. "I want in here," he growls, pressing, sliding lower to capture my arousal and pressing back to my rosebud.

"Gabriel. Oh, fuck, Gabriel."

"Yes, Angel. Take. It." He thrusts through my clenching orgasm, squeezing him till he groans, almost painfully. "So fucking tight." His plays with my ass through a few more thrusts before he explodes. "Fuck, Angel. Fuck. Fuck. Fuck." He pumps and swears till he's spent and I'm languid and content in his arms.

I've missed him so much.

"I've missed you too." He kisses my forehead then cleans us up and dries us off.

I'm of absolutely no help.

* * *

I set her on the bathroom counter. "Stay here." I kiss her bare shoulder and grab the bag I left on the bed. "Here." I hand her the box inside.

"You bought one."

I smile at her surprise. "You said you might be pregnant, so, yes, I bought you a test." I turn it over and point to the directions. "It says you can take it at any time of day. Do you think you can pee?" I brought water in case she needs help getting there.

She nods, her sexed-up gaze landing on the vicinity of my cock. She squeezes her legs together. "Do you think I'm pregnant?"

Loosening her towel to fall away, I press her back, slipping my hand between her legs. "It's possible." She's so wet. "Does the idea of me getting you pregnant again turn you on? Or is it only hormones hitting you already?" I slip two fingers inside her.

"Oh, god," she moans, widening her legs. "Don't know, but I am insatiable. I need you, Big Man."

Yes, my Angel needs me. "Hold on." I pick her up, dropping her on the bed. I need more room to devour my wife than the bathroom counter allows. Plus, my knees are sore from skiing. I might have overdone it today trying to expel my energy. So, kneeling on the hard bathroom floor isn't going to happen.

I drop my towel and prowl up her body till I reach her tits, her beasts full of milk for our daughter. I lick lightly but don't suck. I know every drop is liquid gold for our girl. I settle between her legs, pushing her open with my shoulders. The first lick is for me. Her taste, I can never get enough of. I swear she's sweeter when she's pregnant—just like she is now. Does that mean she is?

I harden at the thought. Not even trying, I could have knocked her up like when I did with Maddox. Maddyn was planned. But any and all babies with my Angel are wanted no matter how scheduled they are.

"Gabriel." She grips my hair, longer for this very reason: so my girl can guide me where she wants me, where she needs me.

She rubs her pussy along my tongue, begging me to make her come. When I fill her with my fingers, rubbing her G-spot, her hips bow off the bed. I have to pin her down with one hand on her mound, while I lick and suck her clit and come-hither her insides.

"Jussst—"

Just like that. I know, Angel.

I know my girl and what gets her off quick and what builds her up to an ear-rattling orgasm. Her G-spot is one, her taint and asshole are another. I talk a big game, but I've never fucked her ass, other than with a finger occasionally. It's hot as fuck to tease, but in reality, I'm not sure she's really into it. I've never pushed it since her ex abused her so badly in that way. I'm game. But nothing could be as good as her warm, wet pussy wrapped around my cock.

But if she wanted my cock in her ass, she'd get my cock in her ass.

Whatever floats her boat is my pleasure to deliver.

"Oh, oh, oh!" She writhes and floods my hand with her sweet juices before she twists under my hold and comes.

Sweet Mother Mary. I love my girl coming on my hand, my tongue, and my cock.

When she's settled, breathing coming back to normal, I start again. Working her up till she squirts, then I fill her with my needy cock. Hard, ready to burst.

I take her on my knees, her on her back, lifting her ass in the air, nearly in a back bend, hitting that spot deep above her cervix. It gives her a totally different kind of orgasm, or so she says. They're all impressive in my opinion. I crave them like my next breath.

When she comes again, I settle over her, seated deep, and swivel my hips in slow, languid strokes. "I'm gonna love you all night, Angel. Keep filling you up. If you're not pregnant, you soon will be."

"Gabriel," she moans.

Yeah, my girl loves my cock, but she loves getting pregnant with our kids. It settles something deep inside her. For a man who never wanted a wife or kids, me giving her both over and over again only affirms how much I'm hers. I'd still be hers even if we weren't married or were childless.

But thankfully, we're neither of those things anymore.

Fuck. She's so wet, each thrust sounds and feels like

suction around my cock, pulling me back in. "Gonna fill you up, Angel. Need you to come with me."

For me.

Need to feel her sweet walls squeezing the cum from my cock, begging me for it.

I slip my hand between us and rub her clit.

"Just like that," she pleads.

Yeah, baby, just like that. I thrust faster, working her up. Taking her mouth, I steal her moans, her tongue lashing more from me, her hands pulling and begging me to get her there.

I'm so close.

I slip my hand below her ass. She's so wet. I barely need to tease her asshole to slip the tip of my finger inside.

Fuck. So hot. So fucking hot.

"Tell me you want me to take this ass with my cock, Angel."

"Yes, stop teasing me and do it already."

Jesus Christ. "Coming," I groan as the zing slides up my ass to my balls.

"Yes, Gabriel," she breathlessly pants in my ear. "Fuck my ass."

I'm done.

I come so hard, ramming through her tight muscles as she clenches and falls apart, joining me, riding the wave of our pleasure—our dirty, dirty, amazing, remarkable pleasure.

"Fuck," she exclaims and falls limp on the bed. "I have to be pregnant after that."

Chuckling, I extract myself and fall to the bed beside her.

I give us a minute to recoup, then wash my hands and clean us up. I offer her my hand. "You ready?"

"To pee on a stick?" She arches a brow. She loves teasing me.

"Yeah, Angel, to pee on a stick."

"Well, you asked so nicely." She kisses my cheek and leads the way to the bathroom.

Watching my Angel walk naked before me is an otherworldly event. If my dick wasn't wornthefuckoutbymyoneandonly, it would salute her.

I wait patiently as she does her business then hands me the stick as she wipes. After two kids, there are no parts of her I haven't seen, nor bodily function I haven't experienced with her. And I love her all the more for each and every one of those trust-filled, comfortable moments.

She washes her hands and comes to lean on me as we watch one line fill the window.

I hold my breath as another pink line appears.

"Oh, my god. You got me pregnant."

"*We* got you pregnant."

She beams up at me. "I guess we did." Her head falls to my chest. She has to hear the racing of my heart.

I rub her arms and up her back. "You okay, Angel?"

"I'm relieved." She looks up, her chin resting on the center of my chest till she leans back so we can make eye contact. "I'm so tired. I was really starting to worry something was seriously wrong with me."

I cup her cheek, letting my forehead fall to hers. "I'll do more, take more of the parenting and household load off you. Hire a full-time nanny. Whatever we need to do to allow you to rest and feel better."

"I feel like you already do so much—"

"I can't grow babies." I splay my hand across her abdomen. "I can't breastfeed. I can't kiss booboos away like you can. But there's lots more that I can do to let you focus on the things *only* you can do, Angel." I kiss her forehead. "We got this. I got you."

Her relaxing into me steadies my heart. She hears me and trusts me. "Climb in bed. I'll bring you Madd to feed while I get us some dinner." Joggers on, I kiss her softly before heading out.

"Big Man." She stops me at the door.

"Yeah, Angel?"

"Can we not tell anyone tonight?"

"Yep. Wasn't planning on sharing. I'll be back. Try to stay awake."

She yawns and sinks into the bed. "I can't make any promises. Just stick Maddyn on my boob. She knows what to do."

"That she does." Chuckling, I head out to get my little angel fed so I can feed my big Angel.

She made me a daddy all over again. I'm not a bit sad about that. And I'm relieved as fuck to know why she's been so tired. Need to get her some prenatals. Stat.

Sweet Maddyn is gonna have to wean before our new one arrives. She's gonna be pissed about that. My little girl is fierce like her mommy, tough like her daddy.

She'll be okay.

We all will.

CHAPTER 10

ROWDY AND REESE

The second I open my eyes I'm filled with excitement at the idea, the possibility of being able to tell Rowdy I'm pregnant.

Or I have the stomach bug.

I've been pregnant before. You'd think I'd just know. Right?

Laying around isn't in the cards if I want to take the test before Cam wakes up. Plus, my bladder has demands of its own.

Quiet as a mouse, I slip on my robe and head to the bathroom. I open the cabinet and find the box I hid in here last night. There're three tests. I grab one and hide the box again.

I do my business and pee on the stick. Then wash my hands and face while I wait.

And wait.

And wait.

Three minutes seems like an eternity.

One line appears.

Tapping on the door has me scurrying to hide the test in

my robe pocket, along with the wrapper. I quickly scan the bathroom to be sure all evidence is hidden.

Unlocking it, I come face to face with Taylor.

"Hey, you're up early." I open the door wider.

She looks both ways down the hall and slips inside, closing the door behind her. "Uh, yeah, I was hoping you were up." She twists the end of her sleep shirt, her gaze flitting between me and the space behind me.

"What's wrong?"

"Um, do you by chance have a spare pregnancy test?"

Christ on a cracker. "Wow. I do." I pull the box out of the cabinet and hand it to her. "Use all you need."

She sees it's open. "You—"

"I don't know yet. I was just—"

"Oh, right." She goes for the door. "Sorry to interrupt. I… uh… see you later?"

She's gone before I can reply. What are the chances she's pregnant too?

Wait. Too?

I don't know if I'm pregnant *yet*. Reaching into my pocket, I lock onto the stick.

Knock. Knock.

Oh, for fuck's sake.

"Yeah?" I open the door rather unceremoniously to a prancing Frankie.

"Hey. Are you done?" She crosses her legs. "I really need to go, and I didn't want to wake up Gabriel. We're supposed to be sleeping in."

"It's all yours." I let her in and step out.

"Oh my god, thank you."

The door shuts, and I hear her sigh seconds later.

Her relief makes me giggle. Finding a free bathroom with this many people can be tricky. All of the adult rooms have an ensuite bathroom, but with two people in each room, morning bathroom habits usually have us needing the bathroom at the same time. Finding an open hall bathroom can be challenging, especially if the older kids are awake. All the boys are potty trained, but when they need to go, they *need* to go.

Warm arms wrap around me the second I enter our room. "Kitten. I'm glad you're back."

"I didn't want to use our bathroom and wake you." I grab his hands wrapped around me, ensuring they don't drop lower and graze my pocket.

He kisses my neck. "You don't have to sneak around. I like waking up together."

I know. And I love that about him. He's not grumpy when he's woken up—that's me.

"But now that we're up, I'm starving." He releases me to throw on a t-shirt and sweatpants.

"I was thinking I'd make German apple pancakes."

His eyes widen before a dimpled smile takes over. "Please."

"Would you help cut up the apples?"

"Done." He graces me with a quick peck to the lips. "I'll make coffee while you get dressed."

"Sounds good. I'll be right there."

* * *

Besides sex, there's not much I enjoy more than watching Reese in the kitchen. She's free in a way she's not anyplace else. Cher is the same. I've never thought that about Gabriel, though he's a great cook too.

The German apple pancakes look amazing when we pull them out of the ovens. She made four, each in sixteen-inch cast iron skillets the size of pizzas, with brown crusty edges and caramelized apples fanning out in circles from the center. She squeezes fresh lemon juice across the tops before following it with powdered sugar. They look and smell fantastic.

"Have you ever considered opening a restaurant?" I'm half joking but kinda serious. Cher has her bakery, but they could expand into the store next to it or find another location. All three of them are exceptional cooks. I've never had a bad meal from any Stone. I'm not a picky eater, but I know good food when I see and taste it. I've no doubt they'd be successful.

Reese's blues meet mine before skipping across the room to Cher—who just smiles—and then land on her brother, walking in the room. "I'd consider it if Gabriel and Mom would do it with me."

Cap and I lock gazes. He likes the idea. The restaurant business can be difficult, but there are a lot of mom-and-pop-type places that make a good living. We're in Vegas. I've no doubt they'd succeed with Cap's connections, Gabriel's fame and their kitchen skills.

"Consider what?" Gabriel heads to the coffee pot. "Morning, by the way." He hands the first cup to Frankie, who shuffles in behind him.

"I was suggesting Reese open up a restaurant with you and Cher." I hand Frankie the creamer from the fridge.

"Thanks." Her smile is slight but genuine. She looks happy and sleepy. For that matter, so does Gabriel.

"Food's ready if y'all want to help get everything to the table." Reese hands me the egg casserole—one of my all-time faves. I carry it and help corral the kids not already at the table waiting somewhat patiently for breakfast.

Once we're seated and the kids have food, eating contently but not too quietly, we dish up the food for the adults.

"You outdid yourself, Kitten. It all looks delicious."

"Thanks. I didn't do it alone. You helped, and Gabriel made the egg casserole last night."

"You did?" Frankie stops mid-bite. "When?"

"When you were feeding Maddyn. Taylor and Landry helped."

"Barely," Landry says around a bite of pancake. "Holy shi—" he catches himself. "…man, this is good. Yes, please open a restaurant."

I catch Gabriel eyeing Frankie as he chews. Slowly he reaches out and touches her. Her head pops up, and her megawatt smile is all the confirmation I need. Whatever's been going on with them is all good now. My best friends are fine.

I smile at my Kitten, hopeful that whatever's been making her sick this week has run its course. She's eating well. I think she may be enjoying the pancakes as much as me.

"Ree?" Gabriel has everyone's attention, waiting on his sister to look up from wiping Kill's sugar-coated face.

"Hmm?" she absentmindedly replies before she realizes all eyes are on the two of them. She reaches for my hand that I gladly offer. "What's going on?"

Gabriel pulls Frankie into his side. "I really am interested in pursuing this restaurant idea with you further—partnering with you and seeing how we can fit Mom's baked goods into the equation. But I think it will have a better chance of succeeding in a few years after I quit fighting and our kids are older—yours and mine."

"Agreed." My girl is happy and relieved he's interested but not wanting to pursue it right away.

"Count me in as a silent partner—or whatever you need," Cap offers, kisses Cher hand and continues to eat.

"I think it's a lovely idea." Cher looks on the verge of

tears. I don't think she ever imagined her life—the life of her kids—could have turned out so fruitful and loving.

Cap has amassed an amazing family. One we're all blessed to be a part of. "I'm in. Whatever you need."

My girl kisses my cheek and laughs as Kill adds, "I'll helwp too!" Which brings in rounding support from Maddox, Cade, and Wade, with a head nod from Iris. Only little Maddyn appears oblivious to the potential multi-family, generational business waiting to bloom.

"I'm in no rush. I love the idea of our kids having so many options to work, grow, and succeed in—if they choose." Reese beams.

Her happiness is all I need to feel complete, but our kids growing up in Black Ops MMA, Sugarplum's, or Stone Café—*or whatever they name it*—sounds like the perfect conglomerate of talent and success.

"Don't leave us out of the deal," Taylor chimes in.

"Never," Cher assures her. "We'll need a good lawyer too."

"We're gonna need a bit before we start planning. Angel and I are gonna be a little busy with a new baby on the way." Gabriel drops a bomb that has the room exploding with cheers and a meaningful look between Frankie and Reese.

"What's that look about?" I whisper in my Kitten's ear.

"Um, I'll tell you later."

I turn her to face me. "Tell me now," I grouse, then soften it with a kiss and a tamer, "Please."

"It appears you and I are also going to be busy with a new baby—"

"Holy, shit. You're pregnant?" I can't hide my excitement. We've been trying. But—

"Yeah, Shadow, you knocked me up." She nods to Frankie, whose elation only grows.

"Yeah?" Frankie asks.

"Yes," my girl confirms.

"You hear that?" I bellow to the room. "We're having a baby too!"

More cheers, hoots and hollers from everyone except Maddyn, who gets scared and starts crying.

My Kitten is pregnant. We're having a baby.

I bend down to Killian's level. "You're going to be a big brother, Kill."

He smiles and points at mommy's tummy. "I want a puppy."

I chuckle and pick him up. "Your mommy and me don't make puppies, but we'll see what we can do about filling that request when you're old enough to take care of one."

I hug my Kitten close as we congratulate Gabriel and Frankie and accept hugs and congratulations from Cap and Cher.

It takes a moment before I realize my sister and Landry are gone.

CHAPTER 11

TAYLOR

I had to leave, if only for a moment to compose myself. Both Frankie and Reese are pregnant. *Again.*
Just this morning I had hoped—

"Taylor, wait." Landry reaches for my hand, but I quicken my pace to our basement-level room. I want to step out back to get fresh air, but I can only hold off my tears for so long. There's no way I want to dampen their happiness with my petty, self-indulgent crying. Plus, a dark, pillowy bed seems to fit the bill for my mood.

He manages to reach me before I make it to our room. With graceful ease, he sweeps me off my feet, snuggling me close. "You thought you were pregnant." Not a question.

"How did you—"

"You snuck out of bed early, returned and slipped into the bathroom. I wasn't snooping. I saw the pregnancy test in the trash next to the toilet."

"Why didn't you say anything?" My chin trembles as I'm caught in his tender, hazel gaze.

"Why didn't you?" There's no anger in his words, only concern, and a desire to understand.

"I…" I shake my head, not having an answer. "I don't know." I've only taken a pregnancy test one other time—and that didn't turn out so well.

He cuddles me on the bed, wrapped in his arms, face to face. He kisses my forehead. "Tell me what's going on in that head of yours."

"I know we're not trying. We decided to wait. But being here with our family and their kids, it's obvious we're the only ones without littles. I caught the baby bug, I think."

His smile is indulgent. "You think?"

"You did too." I swat at his chest.

"Yay." He rolls to his back, tucking me into his side. "It's hard not to. They're all so happy. It's infectious."

"I feel like we're missing out. Life is passing us by." The quiver in my voice has him moving us again till he's on top, looking down at me.

"We've only been married for nine months. You're still recovering, starting your practice. We're not missing out on anything. We fell in love when we were kids—way younger than everyone in this house. Except maybe Gabriel—he fell for Frankie young, but they weren't a couple. *We* were. It took us eight years to get back together. It won't take us that long to have kids, but we've always been on our own timetable, our own journey. It's you and me, Songbird, in this marriage—no one else. When we're ready, I'll gladly impregnate you." He kisses my nose and settles back, watching as his words settle over me.

"Our own time."

"Yeah, I'm on Taylor time. You're on Landon time."

I laugh. He's so corny sometimes.

"Thankfully, we're in sync. It's Tay-don time." He takes it too far.

"Oh, that's bad." I laugh even harder, until it turns into sobs.

"Baby." He rolls to his side, holding me to him, cocooning me, lending me strength. "If you're ready, we'll start now. I have no qualms filling you with my baby-making goodness."

"I love you," I sniff into his chest.

"Love you more, Songbird."

"Not possible."

"I know it's possible because it's true."

"Whatever." There's no winning this silly argument on who loves the other more. I'm just happy he thinks he does. There was a time I thought he couldn't stand to look at me, much less be in the same room with me.

We've come a long way, grown up, learned how to love as adults and not horny teens.

"Maybe we could wait another year. Give us time to ourselves. Finish decorating the house, get Mel's expansion done, and my business more established."

"I'm good with that. I like being able to walk around naked and fuck you wherever and whenever we want."

I run my fingers through his longish hair. My dirty-blond surfer. "You know that's not an incentive, sounds more like a deterrent to having kids if I ever heard one."

He grabs my ass, holding me against his hardening cock. "We'll be kid-free and having a hell of a lot more sex than anyone in this house."

I moan when he moves his hips, rubbing my clit through our clothes.

"At least until I fuck a baby into you." He nuzzles my neck, kissing and sucking.

"Sounds amazing," I gasp when he slips a hand down the back of my pants. "I can't wait."

"Me neither, Songbird."

* * *

CHER

By the time we head to bed, we've meal-prepped for tomorrow, had a wonderfully relaxed Christmas Eve dinner, stuffed the stockings, and played Santa for the kids—after they went to bed, of course. The guys grilled steak and chicken—it was a little cold out, but that didn't stop Cap or our grown boys from doing it. As for the rest of the meal, Reese roasted veggies in the oven, and Taylor and I made bread and salad. We skipped dessert since we had pancakes for breakfast, and we're saving our sweets we spent most of the day baking for tomorrow.

We're having the more traditional meal on Christmas Day of ham and turkey and all the fixings. We've a large brood to feed, but with everyone chipping in, it's manageable, given the large kitchen, double ovens, eight-burner stovetop, and warming drawers.

I think I could live in this beautiful home, surrounded by mountains and the people we love. The whimsical thought of owning this house and spending all our Christmases here, brings a smile to my face, making it hard to keep the toothpaste from dribbling out.

I spit and rinse, patting my face dry. "Did you talk to Taylor?"

"I did." He nuzzles my neck from behind, running his hands round my waist, wrapping me in his strong arms. His green eyes meet my blues in the mirror. "She's okay. She thought there might be a possibility they were pregnant, but she took a test this morning. It was negative. The news of Frankie and Reese being pregnant—"

"Felt like a slap to the face. Our poor girl. Maybe I should go talk to her."

His grip tightens. "No, she's fine. She just got caught up in baby fever." He rubs my abdomen. "I can understand that."

"James, you're not—"

He shrugs. "Aren't I?"

I swivel, needing to look him in the eyes and tell me he wants more babies. "You want more?"

His sigh is soft and dreamy. "I want as many babies as your sweet body will give us, Plum. But, no, I'm not really asking. Just dreaming of one more to round out the number to four."

"I don't know if—"

"Not really asking." He kisses me silent, walking me backward to the bedroom. "But it sure will be fun practicing and making you come again and again as I tell you all the ways I'm going to put a baby in you."

"Cap." My man has a wicked tongue, a salacious mind, and knows how to use both to bring us endless pleasure.

"I can't believe our girls are pregnant at the same time." He stops by the full-length mirror sitting in the corner of the room. "Get naked." He kisses the command down my neck before grabbing a bar stool I hadn't noticed by the closet door and setting it in front of the mirror.

"What are we doing with that?"

He smirks, pulling off his clothes. "Naked, Plum. Now."

If he's going to do what I hope he is, it's the perfect chair. I can grip the back, have cushioning for my knees, and he can adjust the height to the perfect… height for taking me hard or slow and all the ways in between.

I strip.

He chuckles at my enthusiasm as he circles me, assessing my nakedness. I'm no longer self-conscious being naked around him. The love in his eyes and his rock-hard cock show me he likes what he sees.

Ditto.

I could stare at my husband's naked form for eternity and never tire. Some would say we're nearing middle age. But I've never felt so young and alive as I am with him.

He wants more babies.

I've never been able to say no to this man. Actually, I've never *wanted* to.

He pats the chair. "Forearms on the seat, leaning forward."

I do as requested as he continues to circle. On the next pass, he runs the flat of his palm along my backside from one hip to the other. "Beautiful."

He makes one more circuit before stopping behind me, so close but not touching. "You wet for me, Plum?"

Yes. "You better check." I'm feeling sassy and highly aroused. He loves to build me up, make me wait.

The anticipation is the worst… and the *best*.

His chuckle sends goosebumps along my flesh. "Happily."

Surprising me, he lowers to his knees, spreads my cheeks and dives in, tongue first.

"Oh, my g—" I curl forward, his warm tongue, talented and devious, sending spasms and moisture to my core as he laps at the center of my sugarplum.

He grips the back of my neck. "Watch, Cher." He directs me to the mirror as he lifts my foot. "Place your knee on the chair." He helps, holding it in place. "That's it. Now watch me love on your beautiful pussy. No closing your eyes."

I'm shaking, ready to go off. The sight of me spread for his enjoyment is nearly too much. "I won't last."

He kisses the inside of my thigh then runs his nose

along my seam. "Don't hold back. Give me all of those orgasms, Plum."

He gave me my first. He'll have my last and every one in between until our last breaths.

Which might be sooner than I think as he steals my breath with each stroke of his tongue and hungry groans as he feasts upon me like I'm his Christmas dinner.

CHAPTER 12
GABRIEL AND FRANKIE

Gabriel spoons me from behind, sliding in and out of me with lazy strokes. I've already come more times than I can count, and still he's holding out, going too slow to get him there. He has the control of a god—or an avenging angel.

It's early Christmas morning, too early to be awake, but he wanted to get a start on breakfast. Which he did, then slipped back into bed and into me, waking me up in the best of ways. "Love you, Big Man. Merry Christmas."

"Merry Christmas." He rises to his knees, straddles my bottom leg, pushing my top leg up, and thrusts, hard, making me shudder. He leans over, kissing a slow trail to my breast before catching my eyes in a heated embrace. "Love you, baby. Love our kids. Love the life we've made together. Thank you for loving me, my Frankie Angel."

"Don't make me cry, Gabriel." I scowl.

He nudges my nose and kisses my jawline to my mouth. "Call my name."

After all these years, he still loves to hear me say his name as I come, like I could mistake the orgasms he gives me for anyone else's.

There has only ever been one other encounter, and he's not even worth mentioning.

"Always you, Big Man. It was always you."

"Fuck." He scorches my mouth with a life-affirming kiss that has my toes curling and the orgasm I thought for certain I couldn't reach *again*, flame to life.

His stream of cuss words with each pump only gets me hotter. Watching him lose control, his graceful body, huge and ripped, fumbling its rhythm as he pounds into me, sends me over the edge seconds before he groans his release, chanting, "Angel," over and over again.

He gets off on me calling his name. Yeah, well, same.

In his eyes, I'm his savior, his angel.

In my eyes, he's my god.

There's nothing angelic about our love, yet it's heaven-blessed and written in the stars, as I've no doubt he was made for me and I for him.

"Let's get dressed so we can beat the kids to the tree before they rip open all the presents."

"They know better."

Cap put the fear of God in them last night. Told the boys when they woke to stay in the loft until an adult comes and gets them. But that doesn't mean they won't try something.

Dressed, Gabriel kisses my shoulder on his way out. "I'll make coffee and a little something for you to eat to tide you over till breakfast."

He remembers my need to eat first thing to stave off the nausea—at least that's how it was when I was pregnant with Maddyn.

I grip his hand, pulling him back. "You're my forever, always," I breathe across his lips before taking a taste.

"Always, Angel."

* * *

The first time I met Cap, I was an angry kid who thought no *man* could teach me anything I didn't already know. He proved me wrong. But he did it with kindness and compassion and a driving force that taught me how to deal with my anger and a way to vent it in as healthy a way as guys like us can do: being physical in other arenas less destructive but still violent. Fighting.

My Angel showed me how to *love*.

I'm a blessed man as I take in our kids playing with their toys and being kind and gentle with each other. They don't always get along, but they are learning coping mechanisms that will serve them well in life.

All the men in this room have had rough pasts and sharp edges that have been hewn and healed by our women. They in turn let us heal them in our own ways.

Alone we are broken and damaged.

Together we are whole and blessed, not just with our spouses but by our family Cap has amassed—some by blood, all by choice.

"You did good, old man." I pat Cap's shoulder and hand him an eggnog as he thoughtfully soaks in the love contained in this room.

"We've all been blessed, Gabriel. You gave me a larger purpose than just amassing an MMA team. It all started with you and grew into this."

He's being too generous, but it's nice he thinks so.

"Are y'all ready to eat?" Mom slips under his arm. Her happiness is worth any hardship I had to endure to ensure she and Ree had a second chance at life.

"Yeah, I think so." My whistle calls everyone to the table.

Chaos ensues, but I dive in, helping get the kids settled

and food on the table. When every plate is filled, Cap says grace, blessing the food and everyone at this table and those not.

I could die a happy man if every Christmas was like this. Mom, Ree, and I never had happy Christmases. Dad was drunker and more violent. It took time to recover after I kicked him out. Slowly, we made our own traditions. But nothing could have prepared me for the joy of giving until my Angel revitalized my heart—my life. She loves Christmas—her hope, her joy is boundless, especially this time of year.

Kissing my Angel's cheek, I whisper, "Love you," not because she doesn't know, doesn't feel it, but because I do. There was a time the kind of love I feel for her was a foreign concept. The only people I loved were my mom and sister.

Now, I have a room full of people I love and openly admit it.

She leans into me, snuggling my shoulder before laying a sweet kiss on my jaw. "Always," she whispers back.

I believe mercy is granted and not earned.

But I now know love is a gift to be cherished, cultivated, and multiplied.

In our case, we may take multiplying a little too literal by all the children in this room and those yet to be born.

Bring it.

We're ready.

The more the—

"Mer*rier* Christmas, everyone." I raise my glass in toast. "And to many, many more."

THE END

If you picked up A Black Ops Christmas and haven't read the series, you can read about each of the couples in this book in their own full stories. They're Free with Kindle Unlimited, eBook, and paperback.

Check out the Black Ops MMA Series and fall in love for the first time or all over again.

NO MERCY – Gabriel and Frankie
ROWDY – Cameron "Rowdy" and Reese
CAPTAIN – James "Cap" and Cher
COWBOY – Landry "Cowboy" and Taylor
MUSTANG will be Book Five in the *Black Ops MMA* Series

ACKNOWLEDGMENTS

Thank you to the readers who found me and stuck around, my family for their endless support, my Divas who I appreciate more than they'll ever know, and to my editors and PA for making me look like I know what I'm doing. Don't stop reading. I'll keep writing. And don't forget to leave a review.

Blessings, Dana

ABOUT THE AUTHOR

D.M. Davis is a Contemporary and New Adult Romance Author.

She is a Texas native, wife, and mother. Her background is Project Management, technical writing, and application development. D.M. has been a lifelong reader and wrote poetry in her early life, but has found her true passion in writing about love and the intricate relationships between men and women.

She writes of broken hearts and second chances, of dreamers looking for more than they have and daring to reach for it.
D.M. believes it is never too late to make a change in your own life, to become the person you always wanted to be, but were afraid you were not worth the effort.

You are worth it. Take a chance on you. You never know what's possible if you don't try. Believe in yourself as you believe in others, and see what life has to offer.

Please visit her website, https://dmckdavis.com, for more details, and keep in touch by signing up for her newsletter, and joining her on Facebook, Instagram, Twitter, and TikTok.

ADDITIONAL BOOKS BY D.M. DAVIS

UNTIL YOU SERIES

Book 1 - Until You Set Me Free

Book 2 - Until You Are Mine

Book 3 - Until You Say I Do

Book 3.5 - Until You eBook Boxset

Book 4 – Until You Believe

Book 5 – Until You Forgive

Book 6 – Until You Save Me

FINDING GRACE SERIES

Book 1 - The Road to Redemption

BLACK OPS MMA SERIES

Book 1 - No Mercy

Book 2 - Rowdy

Book 3 - Captain

Book 4 - Cowboy

Book 5 - Mustang

Ashford Family Series

WILD Duet

Book 1 - WILDFLOWER

(part of the Heroes with Heat and Heart 2 Charity Anthology)

Book 2- WILDFIRE

STANDALONES

Warm Me Softly

Doctor Heartbreak

Vegas Storm

Wicked Storm

(part of the Wicked Games Anthology)

STALK ME

Visit www.dmckdavis.com for more details about my books.
Keep in touch by signing up for my Newsletter.
Connect on social media: Reader's Group, Facebook, Instagram, Twitter, TikTok
Follow me: Book Bub, Goodreads

A Mountain X-Mas

BODHI AND COCO

BY HARLOW LAYNE

This is a work of fiction. Names, characters, organizations, places, events, and incidents are products of the author's imagination or are used fictitiously. Any resemblance to actual events, locales, or persons, living or dead, is entirely coincidental.

Copyright @2022 by Harlow Layne

No part of this book may be reproduced, stored in a retrieval system, or transmitted in any form or by any means electronic, mechanical, photocopying, recording, or otherwise, without the express written permission of the publisher.

This book is licensed for your personal enjoyment only. This book may not be re-sold or given away to other people.

Cover Design: Ya'll That Graphic

CHAPTER 1
BODHI

"Where are you taking me?" I ask as Coco drives us up the mountain.

Her laugh is music to my ears. She runs one hand up my thigh, coming only inches away from my thickening cock. "It's a surprise. Surely you can be the recipient for once."

I want to take the blindfold off so I can see the smile I know is gracing her beautiful face, but I let her have her fun.

"Do I really need the blindfold, though? What if I was prone to getting carsick?"

"But you're not."

I smile at the laugh I hear in her voice.

"Shit," she mumbles the second I feel the car slow down.

My hands go to the piece of fabric covering my eyes, ready to remove it at any moment. "What's wrong?"

"It's starting to snow."

"Do you want me to drive? I can take over if you want me to." I offer. I'm not sure if Coco's ever driven in snow before.

"I've got this, or at least I think I do," she mumbles the last under her breath. I don't think she meant for me to hear her. "I wanted our first Christmas together to be special."

I take her hand in mine and lace our fingers together, hating to hear the sadness in her voice. "We could have stayed at home, and it would have been special. Every day with you is a gift."

She squeezes my hand before taking it back and doesn't talk for the next thirty minutes. I'm desperate to look out to see the snow and the conditions, but I decide unless she says something, I'll continue this little game of hers.

"Okay, we're here." Her warm fingers caress my cheek before slowly lifting the fabric off my face. For a moment, I wince as I'm blinded from being in the dark for so long, even though the sky is gray and snow falls rapidly around us. When my eyes finally adjust, Coco is hovering in front of me with a small smile on her face. Her blonde hair falls around her face in waves. My fingers itch to run through her hair, but I stop myself.

"It makes sense now why you packed like we were headed to Colorado for Christmas." Leaning forward, I brush my lips to hers. "Thank you for this. Until now, I didn't know how much I missed seeing snow. It's been so long."

"Wait until you see the inside. We have our own winter wonderland for the next week. Now let's get inside before we freeze to death out here." She unclips my seatbelt and jumps out of the car with me following right behind her.

Grabbing our luggage, I watch as Coco talks to the man, I assume is the owner of the two-story cabin where we will be staying. I doubt he'll try anything, but I don't know him, so I keep my eye on them just in case.

As I'm climbing the stairs, Coco shakes the older gentleman's hand and looks back at me with a blinding smile. I give the man a smile of my own as we pass each other on the stairs, and even though Coco and I live in a multimillion-dollar home, I stop in my tracks when I see the inside of the cabin. It looks like a resort you'd see in a magazine. It's all rustic with big wooden pieces scattered throughout, and the view from the windows is awe-inspiring. It makes me wish I had brought my painting supplies to capture the beauty all around me.

Wrapping herself around my side, Coco lays her head on my arm as we look out at the snow-covered mountain and trees. "I brought the camera. I know it's not the same, but there was no way I could have packed up all the art supplies you'd need."

"I brought a sketchbook with me, so it and the camera will have to be enough," I grin down at her. "Although I don't think I'll have much free time."

"I wouldn't plan on it," she purrs.

Once I got the all-clear from my doctor to perform as usual, we've been making up for lost time ever since. Most days, it's a testament that we ever get out of bed long enough for either of us to work. I'm still at the shelter, but I'm also doing everything I can to open the center for children by the summer when they'll all be out of school and more prone to get into trouble.

"Why don't you take the bags to our room while I unpack the food we brought, and then we can sit by the fire?" Taking the cooler from me, I watch as she walks away, swaying her luscious hips. With each step she takes, I think of nothing but taking her from behind. Maybe I'll bend her over the couch or push her up against one of the windows with her full breasts pressed to the cold glass.

I shake myself out of my daydream and head upstairs to find the room where we'll be staying. There are four bedrooms upstairs, and I pick the largest only because it has a fantastic bathroom with a huge tub in front of a big window that looks out at the gorgeous view. This place is amazing. Coco couldn't have surprised me any more than she did with this trip. I know she wants to get away from Oasis since it's her first Christmas without her parents, and I plan to keep her so busy she won't think about them once while we're here.

It has been a long time since I made a fire from scratch, but I manage to start one in only a few short minutes. To my surprise, Coco is sprawled out behind me in all her naked glory when I turn around. Leaning forward, I run my hands up her long, smooth legs. "You look beautiful in firelight." She always looks beautiful to me, but Coco looks more like a Goddess than ever with the orange glow on her.

Leaning forward, she grabs me by the collar of my shirt and pulls me up her body. "I like you in winter wear. It brings out the rugged part of you. We'll have to come up here more often to fulfill all the fantasies I've had playing in my head since you walked out of the closet with those tight as sin jeans and your flannel shirt on." She nips my chin and then smiles devilishly. "Actually, I may confiscate your flannel. I'll wear it and think about how handsome you look today."

"You're more than welcome to it." I'll give this woman everything; all she needs to do is ask.

She slowly starts to unbutton my shirt. With each inch bared, she kisses and licks the exposed skin until my shirt is only a puddle on the floor. I stand to kick off my boots and jeans, giving her a show as I shake my ass to imaginary music.

Sitting up on her knees, Coco grabs my hips as she licks the tip of my cock and then slowly takes it in her warm mouth. Her nails dig into my ass as she hallows out her cheeks and takes me down her throat. My fingers tangle in her hair as I pull it away from her face so I can watch her pretty pink lips move up and down my cock. There's no better sight except for her other set of lips taking me fully into her. One hand moves to massage my balls while the other jacks me off as she treats my tip like a popsicle. It doesn't take long for me to explode. Coco swallows every drop and kisses my tip once she is done.

Not wasting any time, I pick her up and set her on the couch with her ass on the edge so I can suck her pussy lips and fuck her with my tongue and fingers. The moment my tongue swipes through her folds, her fingers are in my hair, holding me to her as if I'd ever want out from between her legs. I could eat her for every meal and still be dying for her taste.

"Bodhi," she moans, grinding her cunt against my face. I love that she takes what she wants and isn't shy about it.

Knowing what we both need, I get up and kneel on the couch. "Get up, my Goddess, and face the back of the couch."

She follows my command and looks over her shoulder at me with her big blue eyes that are begging me to fuck her. Leaning over her, I press her tits into the cushions while nipping and kissing up her neck. Lining my shaft to her entrance, I slowly push inside. This doesn't need to be fast. We have all night. All week, in fact. And I plan to keep Coco in a perpetual state of bliss the entire time we're here.

When I'm fully sheathed, Coco places her hands over mine. Her head falls forward as I start to move inside. Slowly, I pull all the way out until only my tip remains and then slide back in just as agonizingly slow. The feel of her as she stretches to accommodate me. The way her pussy gets wetter and wetter for me with each stroke has my balls tingling and begging for release. When her walls start to flutter, I can't hold back any longer. We're both desperate to come. As she milks my cock of every last ounce of me, my thumb finds her clit causing her to spasm around me again and again.

"Oh my God," she falls forward and pants.

I'm no better as I try to catch my breath against her back. Slipping out of her, I wrap my arms around her waist and drape her over my sweat-soaked body.

Coco's the one for me—not that there's ever been a doubt in my mind—and now that I'm healed, I can't wait to make her my wife and spend the rest of my life with her. I can't wait to see what our future has in store for us. I never thought this would be my life, or I'd ever be this happy when I was living on the streets. Even if I were still homeless, my life would be perfect if I had Coco. She makes everything okay, and with each passing day, she pushes away the demons that have plagued me all my life.

CHAPTER 2
COCO

We, or at least I, must have fallen asleep. Bodhi has been insatiable ever since the doctor cleared him, and I'm perfectly happy letting him take me each and every time. I thought I'd lost him when I had only just found him. Now that I know each day with him is a blessing, I plan to show Bodhi how much he means to me every day.

"You're awake," he whispers into the top of my head. The hand on my hip flexes as he breathes in deep.

Twisting, I prop my head on his chest and look up at him. God, I still can't get over how handsome he is. If he were walking around with a clean-shaven face and his hair short, he wouldn't have been on the streets for more than a night. Someone would have snatched him up and begged him to be a model for a number of things. Hell, he could still be a model, but he doesn't want to follow that career path. Instead, he wants to help all the children in the area, provide a safe place for them to go after school, and teach them art.

No one has a better heart than Bodhi.

"Did you sleep any?"

His eyes flick to the windows and then back to me. "I watched the snow while I had you on top of me." His cheeks pink up as he says his next words. "There's no place else I'd want to be, and I wanted to catalog it all to memory."

Pushing forward, I cup his cheek and brush my thumb over the fading color. "There are going to be plenty more times like this."

"I know," he nods as best as he can while lying down. "But somedays it's harder to remember that than others."

I guess I haven't proved to him that I'm not going anywhere as well as I thought. I'm not sure what I can do to help him except show him each and every day.

"It's been so long since I've been able to enjoy snow. Before, I always dreaded it, wondering how I was going to stay warm."

I can't imagine all he has been through. Our lives have been different in so many ways, but I know Bodhi wouldn't be the amazing man he is today if he hadn't gone through all the hardships he's persevered through.

Brushing my lips to his, I close my eyes and fight back the tears stinging the backs of my eyes. I need to remember Bodhi is here with me now, and nothing is going to take him away from me or put him back where he was before he met me.

"It amazes me that you still have fondness for the snow. I think if it were me, I would dread seeing it. Even now."

"No, you wouldn't." He says so simply. "You're too good, and you'd see the beauty in it."

"How about I show you more of its beauty?"

"What do you have in mind? I have to say it's going to take a lot for me to want to move when I've been sprawled out in front of the fire with you on top of me."

My brows lift. "I have a feeling you're going to like

what I have to suggest." I start to push up, but he pulls me down to place a gentle kiss to my lips before he lets me go. "Come with me."

"You don't have to worry about that. I'll follow you to the ends of the earth to be by your side."

My chest flairs with so much love for him, I am momentarily overwhelmed. Bodhi thinks he's the lucky one, but he's wrong. It's me who's lucky to have found him.

Lacing our fingers together, I take us upstairs and try to find what I'm looking for. I've only seen the place through pictures and the floor plan online. It doesn't take me long to find the master bedroom and the door that leads out to the porch.

"Shouldn't we put on some clothes?" he chuckles from behind me.

"No, but now that I think about it, we should grab the robes on the back of the door in the bathroom."

I've barely said the words before he's back by my side with the robes in hand.

We step outside and are met with chilly temperatures and the most beautiful view. The snow is still falling as it coats the mountain and trees for as far as your eyes can see. There are soft noises as the snow settles onto the world and the animals frolic in the distance. It's absolutely perfect.

Bodhi doesn't say a word as he lets me lead him to the right, where a hot tub sits.

"Can you help me get off the top?"

Before I can even grab one side, he has the top off, and steam spills into the cold air. Off to the side, there's a patio heater that I turn on to help keep what the water doesn't warm.

I watch, fascinated, as Bodhi sets our robes down and steps inside the hot tub. Each movement has his muscles doing the most delicious things. The way each globe of his ass flexes as he steps down before it disappears under the water—he really is utter perfection inside and out.

Leaning forward, he holds out his hand and waits for me to take it. It doesn't take long before I step into the water and relax into my… I'm not even sure what to call him. It seems almost silly to call him my boyfriend when I know I'm going to spend the rest of my life with him. Until his title changes, I guess I'll just call him *mine*.

"I'm not sure how you found this place, but it's perfect. You're perfect." His large hands wrap around my waist and place me in front of him.

Leaning my head back against his shoulder, I let my body float as I watch the snow gently fall to the earth. "It really is perfect." I won't tell him how many hours I spent trying to find this place online. After all Bodhi has gone through, I wanted to do something special for him even though I knew he would say he'd happily just stay at home. I've never met a man as selfless as Bodhi. He's always doing something to show how much he cares for me, all while working to open Oasis Academy.

His hands slowly glide up my ribs with his fingers spread wide before covering each of my breasts. With a soft touch, he massages them, stoking the fire that's been simmering deep in my belly. One thumb grazes over my nipple, sending an electric shock through me.

With each brush of his hand, he hardens underneath me, yet he continues plucking me like a guitar until I'm close to exploding. I rub my thighs together, eager to feel him seated deep inside me. This man makes me insatiable.

"Bodhi," I cry out, needing more.

"I've got you, my Goddess," he whispers huskily into my ear before positioning me until his tip is at my entrance.

Eager to feel all of him, I wrap one arm around his neck

behind me as I sink down on his thick cock. Even after being together earlier, I still need a moment to adjust to his size. Bodhi's cock was made for me, filling me in the most delicious ways. Slowly I start to rock and swivel my hips as I coat him with my juices. It only takes seconds before I increase my pace, greedy to hear his breath pick up and his sexy voice as he comes.

He keeps his hand low on my belly while the other plays with one breast and then the other. I'm so close just from the nipple play that when his lips come into contact with my neck, my walls spasm around his length.

"Fuck," he groans out, shifting his hips and impaling me even further.

I can feel his body trembling as he holds back his release and waits for me to come first. His hand on my stomach slips down between my legs, and my body jolts when his thumb comes into contact with my clit. He presses and circles while thrusting up as I come down to meet him.

Closing my eyes to the outside world, I let myself feel everything, from how the hairs on his chest press against my back to the way his shaft hits my g-spot with each movement. It's all-consuming in the best possible way.

"I need you to come, Coco." His voice shakes as he holds back before pinching my clit between his fingers. And that's all it takes before I soar into the stratosphere and fly.

We lock together as ecstasy floods our bodies and fuses us as one.

I'm still shaking when I start to come down. Turning my head, I arch up and kiss the column of his neck. That fire in my belly is still roaring. Seriously, will I ever be able to get enough of this man?

"That was amazing," I pant, running my free hand

down his muscular thigh while I lightly scratch at his scalp with the other.

"This place is magical."

It is. I try to imagine what it would be like to live in a place like this, but I can't think of anything more perfect for us than the desert. That's not to say I won't try to come here every year at this time to celebrate.

"We should probably get out." His right. Who knows how long we've been out here. With a shift of his hips, he slips out of me, and I instantly feel like a part of me is missing. I know my body will yearn for him until he's deep inside me again.

Pivoting me to the side, Bodhi picks me up bridal style before he stands and steps out of the water and onto the deck. My body shivers as the freezing air hits me. I can't imagine how cold it would be if the heater weren't on. Instead of wrapping me in the robe, he takes long strides to the door before quickly locking us away inside. He moves with purpose toward the bed, pulling the thick comforter back and then carefully depositing me before climbing in behind me and wrapping me in his strong arms.

The warm press of his body against every inch of mine has my eyes drifting closed only a second after resting my head on his bicep.

The last thing I hear before I drift off to sleep is how much he loves me.

CHAPTER 3

BODHI

Coco steps into the kitchen in a pair of flannel pajama pants, a sweatshirt, and bare feet. Her brows are pulled together as she looks at her pink toenails. "Have you seen my socks?"

"They were on the bed when I left to make us some breakfast." I slide the cheesy eggs onto a plate, waiting with bacon for Coco. Even though she watches cooking shows all the time, she still hasn't gotten the hang of cooking and not burning it, so I volunteered to make us breakfast this morning.

"I looked everywhere, and I can't find them. Can I borrow a pair of yours?"

Placing the pan back on the stove, I move to wrap my arms around her waist and hug her to me. "Of course, you can. I'll go grab them and look for yours as well."

"Thank you," she pops up on her toes and kisses my chin.

Heading up the stairs, I'm instantly on alert. I didn't mention it to Coco in case it was nothing, but the shirt I wore yesterday is also missing. Maybe I'm making too much out of our missing items, but I can't help it after everything Coco's been through. I will always remain hyper-vigilant where she's concerned. She doesn't deserve another ounce of pain in her life after what her ex did to her.

I scour the bedroom and bathroom, looking for our missing garments, and find nothing. Well, except for the fact that I can't find my polka dot underwear that Coco loves so much.

Why would anyone be stealing our clothes, though? And who?

My mind instantly goes to the older man who rented the house to us. He does have a key and would know where to hide for us not to see him.

Grabbing a pair of my socks, I go back downstairs to find Coco finishing up the breakfast I made for her. Kneeling down, I turn her chair and slide my socks onto her tiny feet.

"I take it you didn't find my socks." She frowns.

For a brief moment, I think about not telling her, but she needs to know, and I don't want to hide anything from her. For Coco to be safe, she needs to be aware of the situation. "I don't want to alarm you, but I have a couple of items missing as well."

"Well, too late," she laughs nervously, sitting up ramrod straight in her chair and scanning the area.

Pulling her up, I hold her to me, rubbing one hand up and down her back. "I promise I won't let anything happen to you."

"I know you won't, and that's what worries me." I know that I look down at her with a quizzical look on my face. Coco buries her face in my chest and shudders. "I can't bear the thought of losing you."

"I feel the exact same way about you. That's why I'll go to the ends of the earth to protect you."

"If you get shot again, I'll never forgive you," she cries, her hands twisting the fabric of my shirt in the back.

"Just as I'd never forgive myself if you got hurt." I look out into the winter wonderland outside and then down at Coco. "Let's get dressed and go outside to see if we can find any tracks or anything. Maybe we're overreacting." I sure as hell hope we are, but where are our clothes then?

"Yeah," she pulls back and tries to give me a smile but fails. "I'm sure we're just being overly sensitive. No one knows we're here except for that sweet old man."

I sure as hell hope that's the case.

It doesn't take us long to put on our winter gear that Coco had somehow hidden in the back of my SUV. It still feels wrong to call it mine, but Coco insisted I needed my own vehicle. Ever since meeting her, my life has seemed like a dream I never want to wake up from. I'm still in awe every day that Coco looked past everything; the long hair and beard, my dirty clothes, and my homelessness. Instead, she saw what I had always wanted the world to see. Me.

Hand in hand, we descend the stairs into a world of white. The SUV has at least four inches of snow covering it, and there isn't a single track to be found.

"Keep your eyes and ears open. If you even think you've seen or heard something, let me know." My grip on her hand tightens as we walk around to the back of the cabin.

"This place has lost a little bit of its magic, thinking there could be someone else here," she says softly from my side.

She isn't wrong.

We walk down the hill to the back door and deck, only to find untouched snow.

"Do you think the tracks could have been covered?"

Possibly.

"I don't know. Maybe. Let's explore some more and try to enjoy ourselves."

If someone covered their tracks, they probably wouldn't have done so all the way out into the woods. That thought and the amount of work it would take sends chills down my spine.

"Have you ever gone skiing before?" She asks out of the blue.

"I went water skiing a couple of times when I was young, but not snow skiing. That costs money we didn't have. Have you?"

"No, my mom was always scared I'd end up breaking a leg or something. Ski trips were the only thing they ever turned down." She twists her lips so the side. "It seems weird now. They could have gone and not skied." She shrugs, scanning the trees that surround us.

"Maybe she had a traumatic experience before you were born or knew someone who did."

"You're probably right. I was just thinking it would be fun to sled or something while we're here, but there's really no place for it."

The hill the cabin sits on would make a great place to sled if there weren't so many trees around. I'm not sure how we'd avoid them.

Pulling her into my side, I kiss the top of her head. "We can enjoy the hot tub again."

"That was amazing," she smiles and closes her eyes for a moment before they pop back open. "But we've got to figure this out first. There's no way I will be able to relax thinking someone is out here or in the house."

I hadn't thought about someone actually being in the house. It's big enough that someone could easily hide and we wouldn't find them—especially if they know the house extremely well.

"Maybe we should head back. We can always come back out and enjoy the snow once we figure out what's going on." Or at least that's my hope. I'm sure how we'll ever leave the house again if something bad followed us here.

"Bodhi," her voice is shaky. "I'm scared."

Stopping dead in my tracks, I take her face in my hands and rub my thumbs over her cold, pink cheeks. "I'm not going to let anyone hurt you. Not now or ever. Do you believe me?"

She starts to nod but can't with me holding her. "Yes. I know you'll always protect me, but that doesn't mean I won't worry."

"I know." I brush my lips to hers before I rest my forehead on hers. The only thing I can do is let her see the conviction in my eyes. She stares at me. Her blue eyes go from troubled to sparkling in only a few short breaths.

I kiss her one last time before we start back up to the cabin, which takes us longer as we ascend the hill in the snow. It's nearly six inches in some places, making it difficult.

With my hand on the doorknob, I take a deep breath to prepare myself for what we might find. After dealing with Dwayne, I thought we were safe, but now I'm not so certain.

"Stay behind me," I say in a low and even tone.

Pushing open the front door, I head straight to the kitchen and grab the biggest knife I find out of the drawer. Slowly, we search the bottom floor looking for any signs of an intruder or someone else staying here. Really, what would be the odds of Coco having another stalker? Still, I won't rest until I figure out where our belongings are going.

I find nothing, and with each room we search, Coco's

hold on my shirt tightens. Quietly, we head upstairs but halt on the top stair when I hear a scratching noise from the bedroom we're staying in.

Reaching behind me, I squeeze the hand holding onto me. "Stay right here."

I don't wait for her to answer, needing to make sure no harm will come to my Goddess.

As quietly as I can, I open the bedroom door, unsure of what I'll find on the other side. Slipping into the room, my eyes scan every inch of the space but stop on our suitcase sitting on top of the bed. Clothes are hanging out of it, and a few items are on the floor leading into the closet.

I can't decide if I want to tell Coco to get in the car and run, or if I should charge into the closet with my knife raised. The decision is made for me when I hear a noise in the closet. I throw open the door with my knife raised, ready to take on anyone or anything here to hurt us, only to find a gray cat in the corner using our clothes as a bed for what looks like five tiny kittens.

"Coco, you can come in," I shout as I squat down and inspect the make-shift bed.

"Where are you?" Coco calls.

"In the closet. I found who's stealing our things."

"Yeah?" She sounds weary as I hear her get closer.

"You'll never guess who our thief is," I laugh.

"I'm guessing it's not some big, bad dude since you're laughing."

Sitting down on the floor, I turn toward the door as she steps into the opening.

Reaching out, I take Coco's hand and pull her onto my lap. "It's just a mama trying to make her babies a bed with our clothes."

Her body sags against mine. "Oh my god, I can't

believe I thought someone was here to kill us," she laughs, and I join her.

I don't blame her. I thought the same thing. It's going to take a while before we can trust the outside world, and I'm not sure if we'll ever be able to fully have faith that there isn't someone out to get us. Although I hope I'm wrong. I'm drained from just thinking that someone was here for only a couple of hours.

Running her hand along the mama cat's soft fur and not disturbing the babies, she quietly asks, "Can we bring them home?"

"It's your house. If you want a cat or six, that's up to you."

"Bodhi," she sighs and turns in my lap. Her face is soft as she straddles me. "It's just as much your house as it is mine. I've lived there just short of two weeks more than you. Would it make you feel better if your name was on the deed?"

I jolt back, nearly knocking her off my lap. "No, I don't want that."

She smiles at me in the way that, if I were standing, would have brought me to my knees. "Are you planning to end this relationship?"

"Never," is my one-word response. How could she even think such a thing? I'm at the beginning stages of planning how to propose and tie her to me for eternity. It's hard to find the perfect way to show her how much she means to me and appreciate everything she's done for me.

"Okay, I didn't think so. With that out of the way, we're partners. In everything. What's mine is yours and what's yours is mine."

A lump the size of a grapefruit forms in my throat at her words. I try to swallow it down, and my words come out gravelly. "That doesn't seem fair in the grand scheme of things since I have nothing to give you."

Placing her hand on my chest, she rubs her thumb back and forth. "You've given me your heart and soul, and that's more than anyone has ever given me. It means the world to me. I don't need anything else." Her lips turn up at the corners as her eyes shine. "Until we have a baby. Then my life will be complete."

"You want kids?"

"With you, I do. I can't wait to see you as a father."

"And I can't wait to see you round with my child inside of you. To watch it grow and see the two of us in one tiny person finally."

Resting her head on my chest, she slips her arm around my back. "It sounds perfect, and in the meantime, we can have lots and lots of practice."

I couldn't think of a better way to spend our time here than burying myself deep inside the woman I love.

CHAPTER 4
COCO

I watch as Bodhi uses a couple of the sheets from the closet to make a little bed for the mama cat and her babies. He's going to be an amazing father. I knew it before, but after seeing him taking care of them, I have no doubt in my mind. My ovaries are screaming at me to jump him and make a baby with him, stat.

That's not going to happen, of course. Well, not the baby-making part, but I am going to strip him and have my wicked way with him once he's done.

"Are they all settled?" I lean on the closet door frame.

"Yeah, were you serious about bringing them home?" He asks without taking his eyes off them.

"If you want. I don't think we should keep them all, but we could find good homes for the rest." Bodhi's heart amazes me. The amount of love and caring in that one man is more than I could withstand.

"I'd hate to leave them here. Who knows when someone else will rent the place again." He finally turns, holding a kitten against his chest while one finger runs along its soft fur.

"Then we'll take them home." I step back, untie the

robe I have on, and let it slip to the floor. "But for now, I'd like to enjoy the hot tub with you."

Bodhi carefully sets the kitten down before he pounces on me just the way I want. His fingers snake through my hair as his mouth claims mine in the most delicious of ways—his tongue tasting and caressing. My hands go to the buttons on his flannel and quickly undo them. I can't get him naked fast enough.

He smirks down at me loving how I can't seem to ever get enough. "You're so sexy." The way his eyes flair at my admission makes me love him all the more. "I love you." My hands push the fabric from his shoulders, and I watch as it falls to the floor. "So much."

Gripping me by the hips, Bodhi pulls me to him and grinds his erection into my stomach. Dipping down, he brushes a kiss to my forehead, each of my eyes, and the tip of my nose before his lips slowly move against mine. My body melts against his. The hair on his chest rubs against my nipples, causing them to harden.

Unwilling to wait another moment, my fingers quickly undo the button of his jeans and slip into the waistband of his boxer briefs. I push both down past his delectable ass until they fall to the ground.

His large hands drift down my sides and grip my ass cheeks as he hoists me into the air. My legs wrap around his trim waist, my tongue delving deeper into his mouth, wanting all of him.

My back hits the wall, making me smile. No one who meets Bodhi would ever think he's so dominant when it comes to sex. I love how he takes control and his insatiable need for me.

Breaking our kiss with his eyes locked on mine, he lines up at my entrance and slowly pushes inside. I've never felt more whole in my life than when we're connected like this. All the problems in the world disappear, and it's only him and me. The way it should be when you've found your person.

He leans his forehead to mine when he's fully sheathed inside of me. Puffs of air skate across my face as he languidly moves in and out of me. What I thought was going to be hard and fast has changed into gentle lovemaking. It's perfect. He's perfect.

"I love you more than anything in this world," he grunts as he picks up his pace. The tips of his fingers dig into my flesh. The mix of pain and pleasure has my orgasm rushing to the surface faster than I thought possible.

Digging the heels of my feet into his ass, I urge him to move faster as I attach my mouth to his and suck on his tongue. Bodhi doesn't disappoint. His pace quickens to the point that he's slamming into me, the base of his cock hitting my clit in the most delicious of ways.

"Bodhi," I cry out, my walls clenching around him as my entire body lights up with pleasure. Heat shoots down my spine straight to my clit, making my limbs constrict. My nails dig into his back, making him moan.

He pumps once, twice, and a third time before burying himself deep inside of me and groaning into the crook of my neck. After a moment, he starts to pull out, and I whine.

I can feel the smile against my shoulder before he pulls back and looks down at me. "My beautiful Goddess, I am not nearly done with you. You just wait and see."

He steps out of the jeans and underwear around his ankles and then moves us over to the bed. My back has barely touched the comforter when he grips my ankles and turns me on my front. His mouth moves to my ass, and I know I'm in for the ride of my life. Licking and sucking, he spreads me wide, spearing me with his tongue. Lifting my hips, his thumb presses into my clit, and that's all it takes for me to explode all over his face. This time he keeps moving, drawing out my pleasure with soft licks and the caress of his fingers until I'm a pile of goo and about to melt into the bed. I don't even have the energy to turn over. Luckily, Bodhi brings me to his side. Wrapping his arms around me, he pulls the covers over our tangled bodies, and his hands start to wander on their own again.

For the rest of the day, Bodhi worships my body while he whispers sweet words of love and forever.

EPILOGUE
BODHI

I wake up to an empty bed on Christmas morning, which is not what I expected on my first Christmas with Coco.

I quickly dress in a pair of flannel pajama pants that Coco bought for me. She really went all out for our trip with clothes to keep us warm while being stylish at the same time. Not that I care about being fashionable. The only person I care about liking the way I look is her.

It smells like heaven downstairs, which doesn't usually happen when Coco is the one cooking. More like burnt and making the hairs in your nose curl up. Still, I eat whatever she makes because she does it for me.

It's been a struggle with all the new changes in my life since I arrived in Oasis, but I'm adjusting. I want to provide for Coco, not the other way around. I know I'm never going to be rich with money. Not with opening a center for youth in the area, but my heart will be full, and I know I'll be able to help so many.

It isn't the food on the table that catches my attention, though. It's the beautiful blonde laid out in front of the fire, wearing nothing but a red bow tied around her.

"Merry Christmas, Bodhi." She smiles at me, running her hands over her breasts. "Are you going to come over here and untie me or just stand there looking?"

"I haven't decided yet," I husk out. "I think I'm in. shock. This is a pleasant surprise."

She tilts her head to the side and arches her back. "What did you have in mind?"

"I'm not sure," I shake my head as I move toward her. "But don't be fooled; I like what I found."

Her eyes skim down the length of my body and then back up before stopping. "Oh, I can tell by the giant bulge that's threatening to tear through your pants."

Wanting to catch up with the situation at hand, I slip my pajama pants off and leave them on the floor as I stalk toward the most beautiful woman in the world.

Going to my knees, I pull her legs over my forearms and dive my tongue deep into her core. Coco tastes like exotic honey, and I can't get enough. Using my thumbs, I spread her lips, opening her up to me. Her pretty pink pussy is wet and begging for me.

"Are you going to untie me?" She moans as my thumb brushes over her clit.

I peer up at her. "I will, but first, I need to taste you."

"I'll never say no to that." Her hips rise, needing more than the little tease I just gave her.

Lying down between her legs, I can feel the heat from the fireplace on my side as I prepare for a little snack before breakfast.

Rolling my tongue around her bundle of nerves, I plunge two fingers deep inside her and slowly pull them out, making sure to curl them on that spongy spot that drives her wild.

"Bodhi," she breathes out my name, and it sounds like

heaven on her lips. I don't want a single day while I'm on this earth that I don't hear her say my name like that.

Coco's thighs start to quiver against my head, but I keep my pace, wanting to draw out her pleasure. I lick and suck her lips as my fingers pump faster. The sound of her juices and the way her hips swivel to chase her pleasure have me pressing my cock hard into the floor, trying to stave off my release.

"Please, I need more," she begs." Never one to deny her, I add another finger and suck hard on her clit until I feel her walls start to clamp down on my fingers. Only then do I pull out and fill her with my cock. Her walls are still spasming when I sink deep inside. I nearly come undone from their force, but I hold back.

Resting my weight on one arm, I untie her with my other hand. Something shifts inside of me—Coco just gave herself to me. I've already done the same. The moment she brought me home, I was all hers.

"God, you're beautiful spread out before me." Her blonde hair sparkles in the firelight, and her cheeks are pink.

Scrapping her nails up my back, she lazily grins up at me. "You're hot as fuck with your dick inside me, looking at me with so much hunger in your eyes."

That's all I can take before pulling out until just the tip is left inside and then slamming back in. Rising up on my knees, I bring her along with me. My hands dig into the soft flesh of her ass as she bounces up and down on my dick. Her tits jiggle with each movement, begging for my mouth.

I don't deny her, and I never will.

The only sounds in the room are our skin slapping, the crackle of the fire, and our breaths as we chase our pleasure.

When her nails scratch up my back and along the nape

of my neck, I know she's close. Fingers tangling in my hair, she hangs on for dear life as I plow into her. I know I'm not going to last much longer. She feels too good.

"Come for me," I demand, skimming one hand between her legs and pinching her clit between my fingers. Coco's body jolts, riding me harder. Dipping down, I run my tongue along her collarbone and over to one of her pert nipples before taking it in my mouth. I suck and lave it with my tongue before moving on to the other one. Her walls flutter and then grip me like she never wants my dick to leave. I don't want it to either.

I crush my mouth to hers as my cock jerks, stream after stream of my cum spilling deep inside her. I groan into her mouth and press her to me as I bring us both down.

"Merry Christmas, my Goddess. I love you more than I'll ever be able to express."

Lovingly, she places her hand on my cheek as she dips down to kiss me and blinks back happy tears. "I love you, my knight in shining armor."

"I hate to inform you, but I think the breakfast you made has gone cold."

"It was worth it," she yawns and snuggles further into my side.

"How about you take a nap, and I'll make us something to eat when you wake up?"

"And then we can open up our real presents." She yawns again.

"You are my real gift. I couldn't ask for anything more." My gaze goes to the wrapped boxes under the tree, hoping she'll like what I got for her. Nothing will ever be enough, but I sure as hell am going to try.

"I'm going to keep giving you more just as I know you'll do for me."

She's not wrong.

I shift out from under her and scoop her into my arms before standing. "Where would you like me to put you?"

With her cheek pressed against my sternum and her arms wrap around my neck, Coco yawns. "On the couch, so I can watch you."

I don't argue that she won't be awake for long. Instead, I place her on the couch and cover her with a blanket that lays over the back.

After learning firsthand how painful grease splatter can be without any clothes on, I won't make that mistake again, so I put my pants back on.

Examining what all Coco made earlier, I find what looks to be a quiche of some sort. I'm not sure if she cooked it from scratch or pulled it out of the freezer. More than likely, it was already made since her cooking skills haven't improved to this level yet.

Opening the refrigerator door, I lean down and see what's left inside. "What would you like me to make?"

When she doesn't answer, I look over to find her already sound asleep. Wanting to give her some time to rest, I head upstairs to clean up and grab the gift I have hidden inside my suitcase.

The box is small, and I know what she will think when she sees it. I only hope she won't be too disappointed when I don't propose to her today. Not that I'm not planning on it. I am, but I'm still saving for the perfect ring.

The perfect proposal.

Once I've made us each a ham and cheese omelet with toast and fruit, I sit down on the side of the couch. Pushing an errant strand of hair off her forehead, I trace my fingertips along her brows, cheeks, and jaw and then circle her pretty pink lips.

Coco's eyes flutter open, and she smiles at me. "Is

breakfast already done?" I nod, lacing our fingers together. "I guess I fell asleep."

"That's alright. I wanted you to. I plan to keep you very busy today," I smirk down at her.

Her sleepy eyes light up. "I like the sound of that."

Pulling the robe from the end of the sofa, I hold it out to her knowing if she isn't covered, not much will be accomplished. After Coco slips on the robe, I'm suddenly nervous. What if she doesn't like what I got her? What if she's disappointed that I don't propose?

Coco turns to find me still standing by the couch. Her eyebrows rise as the corners of her mouth turn down. "Is everything okay?"

"Yeah, don't worry about me." I clear my throat and take her hand in mine. "Let's eat."

"You can't tell me not to worry. You don't think the cats were a diversion, do you?" Looking at me over her shoulder, she bites her lip.

"No," I practically shouted. "It's nothing like that. It's silly in the grand scheme of things."

Sitting down at the table, Coco doesn't move to pick up her fork. Instead, she stares up at me with hurt in her eyes. "Then why won't you tell me?"

"After seeing all the presents under the tree, I'm second-guessing what I got for you. It's…" I try to swallow the lump in my throat as I sink into the chair next to hers.

Coco is out of her seat and on my lap with her arms wrapped around my neck in a nanosecond. "Whatever it is, I know I'm going to love it because it came from you, and you don't do anything without thought." Resting her forehead on my chin, she's quiet only for a moment before her head pops back up. "Would it make you feel better if we opened presents first?"

Absolutely not.

"You'd think *you* made our breakfast and are trying to get out of eating it."

Coco scoffs and shakes her head. "Why am I such a hopeless cook?"

"I don't know, but I love that you try." I kiss the side of her neck. "Thank you for distracting me for a moment." I nod. "I feel better. I was just… overthinking it, I guess. I want our first Christmas together to be special, and for a brief moment in time, it wasn't."

She smiles up at me and runs her thumb along my jaw. "We haven't had the best luck lately, but nothing and no one is going to stop us if we're a team. It's going to take a little while before we can trust that no one is out to get us."

Closing my eyes, I try to imagine what my life would be like if I hadn't stopped in Oasis or met Coco, but no matter how hard I try, it's impossible. Coco is my soulmate. The person I was always meant to be with, and I would live through every last bad thing I've experienced all over again, knowing Coco Beckett is my end game.

Nuzzling my nose in the crook of her neck, I tighten my arms that hold her on my lap. "I love you. I don't know where I'd be right now if I hadn't spotted you at Tricks. The only thing I know is I would be lost, still trying to find something I didn't know I was missing until you."

I feel Coco take in a deep breath as she hugs me harder. "With words like that, I don't need a present. In truth, I never need anything as long as I have you."

"I feel the exact same way." My voice is barely audible, with all the emotion clogging my throat. I pull her plate in front of us and cut into the omelet. She's been adamant about me eating and regaining my strength, but now that I'm back to one hundred percent, I'm back to taking care of her. I like how her body relaxes into mine as she shifts even closer to me. I will never stop treating the woman on my lap like a Goddess. My everything.

I continue to feed her until we're both full and unable to eat another bite. Only then do I set down the fork before picking her up and placing her on the couch.

With trembling hands, I make my way over to the Christmas tree with its multi-colored lights illuminating the living room and the few ornaments we placed on it on our second day here. Leaning down, I pick up the small box, unable to wait any longer. With the present in my hand, I start to explain. "This isn't what you think. Not that I don't want that with you because I want it more than anything in the world, but as you know, I'm still trying to make something of myself, and my bank account is suffering. But know that it will be the most spectacular day of our lives when I do."

Coco stands and reaches for me. I take her hand and sit beside her before handing her the box. "I have no idea what you're talking about, but I believe you." She laughs, and it's music to my ears. "Can I open it now?"

"Yeah," I choke out. I hate that I'm so nervous, but damn, this is the first time I've ever had to buy a gift for someone I care about.

Her hand covers mine for a long moment before she unwraps her present. I meant for it to be the last gift she opened, but I'm not sure I'll make it until then. Even though she reassured me earlier, I still want it to be perfect.

Coco's hands pause, and I hear her gasp before she looks up at me with tears in her eyes. "Bodhi," she cries. "It's the most perfect gift a girl could ever ask for. Will you put it on me?"

I take the necklace out of the box as she lifts her hair. "Do you really like it?"

Her eyes widen. "Are you kidding me? I'm not sure

how you managed to find a necklace that has the exact same flower you gave me the first time, but…" She clutches the flower to her heart, and a tear slips down her cheek. "This is the most thoughtful gift. Thank you, Bodhi."

"You're welcome," I smile and clasp the hook of the necklace around her neck. "I wanted you to always have a flower with you even if I can't bring you one."

I haven't been able to give her a flower this entire trip. The mountains in December are not ideal when trying to find flowers. If I had known where we were going, I would have planned and brought some to gift her each day.

Lifting the pink flower from her chest, she looks down at it. It's almost an exact replica of the first flower I gave her. I'm not sure how I lucked into finding it, but when I saw it in a shop window one day, I knew I had to get it for Coco. "It's been killing you since we've been here, hasn't it?"

She knows me so well.

"A little bit." Seeing her so happy has my dick hardening in my pants. Even though it's only been a short while, I need to be inside her again. Grabbing her by the hips, I pull her to straddle my thighs. My hands go to the globes of her ass, and I knead the flesh as I pull her bottom lip between my teeth.

I have a feeling it will take us all day and maybe even the next if this is the reaction I get after I watch her open one present—and that's perfectly fine with me. I'm in no rush. I want to treasure every single moment with Coco. Today. Tomorrow. Forever.

Want more Bodhi and Coco? Read their beginning in ***Secret Admirer*** now on Amazon and Kindle Unlimited.

ABOUT HARLOW

Indie Author. Romance Writer. Reader. Mom. Wife. Dog Lover. Addicted to all things Happily Ever After and Amazon.

Harlow Layne is a hopeless romantic who writes sweet and sexy alpha males who will make you swoon.

Harlow wrote fanfiction for years before she decided to try her hand at a story that had been swimming in her head for years.

When Harlow's not writing you'll find her online shopping on Amazon, Facebook, or Instagram, reading, or hanging out with her family and two dogs.

ALSO BY HARLOW

Fairlane Series - Small Town Romance
Hollywood Redemption - Single Parent, Suspense
Unsteady in Love - Second Chance, Military
Kiss Me - Holiday, Insta-Love
Fearless to Love - Insta- Love

Love is Blind Series- Reverse Age Gap Romance
Intern - Office Romance
The Model - Workplace Romance
The Bosun - Military, First Responder
The Doctor - Raine's story - October 14
The Rocker - Coming February 17, 2022

Hidden Oasis Series
Walk the Line - First Responder, Suspense
Secret Admirer - Damsel in Distress, Opposites Attract, Suspense
Til Death Do Us Part - Accidental Marriage, Insta-love

MM Romances
You Make It Easy -Second Chance
My Ex Girlfriend's Brother - MM - November 8
Chance Encounter - Enemies-to-Lovers - December 10

Collaborations
Basic Chemistry - Student/Teacher

Forever - Student/Teacher, Curvy girl, enemies-to-lovers

Worlds

Cocky Suit - RomCom, Office, Interracial

Risk - Forbidden, Sports

Affinity - Part of the Fairlane Series - Accidental Marriage, Enemies-to-Lovers

Until Delilah - Single Parent, Romantic Suspense with The Model tie-in

THE
CHRISTMAS
ONE

BY KATE RANDALL

Copyright ©2022 by Kate Randall

All rights reserved.

No portion of this book may be reproduced in any form without written permission from the publisher or author, except as permitted by U.S. copyright law. This book is a work of fiction.

Names, characters, places and incidents are either products of the author's imagination or are used fictitiously. Any resemblance to actual events, locals or persons, is entirely coincidental.

Editor: Sandy Ebel, Personal Touch Editing

Cover Designer: Y'all. That Graphic.

CHAPTER 1

ABIGAIL

I'm giddy with excitement when I see a text from my best friend, Kasey.

Kasey: We're here.

Me: Be down in a sec.

Finally, the vacation I've been waiting for with my two favorite people on the planet and their significant others. I need this time away like you wouldn't believe. Spending a few days in a cabin celebrating Christmas with my sisters from another mister sounds like heaven. It also gives me the perfect excuse to get out of going home to see my actual family in Charleston, a fact my mother was none too thrilled about.

Kasey: I'll send Donovan up to grab your bags.

I hate to put him out, but then I look at the three bags I packed for a four-day trip.

Me: Sounds good.

I take a quick look around my apartment and go through the mental checklist to make sure I didn't forget anything. When I hear Donovan knock on the door, a wide smile stretches across my face. *Here we go.* I open the door.

"Hey, Don—" I stop mid-sentence when I get a look at who's on the other side, leaning against the frame with a cocky-as-hell grin on his smug face.

"Hey, Red," he drawls in that husky voice he knows all too well is my kryptonite.

It's the Prince of Darkness himself, Jackson Hayes, Donovan's brother—the reason I needed this damn vacation to begin with.

"I thought you weren't coming, Prince. Too busy stocking lube or sex toys," I snark.

Jackson owns a very exclusive sex club in Philadelphia. I went once and had a great time until he made me leave because another man was getting too close for comfort and insisted on driving me home. Yeah, we aren't going into that story. Having him on this trip *does not* change my resolve. Any hanky panky with him is off the table—for good.

"I wasn't, but when my brother told me you were coming, I figured they'd need an extra car for all your luggage." He looks around me and spots the three bags next to the door, then glances back at me, quirking his brow as if he just proved his point.

"Your brother drives a Range Rover, so plenty of room for my bags," I say defensively, propping a fist on my hip.

"Oh, She-Devil." He chuckles. "It's as if you think I don't know how much shit you pack. Donovan's car won't hold everyone's bags."

Wait a second here... "I'm not driving up there with you, Jackson."

"Jeez, Red,"—his hand goes to his chest as if I've wounded his heart—"way to kick a guy in the balls when he's just trying to help."

"Oh, I forgot how magnanimous you are, Prince." I roll my eyes. "Such a giving soul," I drawl.

A wicked gleam shines in Jackson's eyes. "If you've forgotten how giving I am, I'll gladly remind you, Red," he says in a deep, rumbly voice.

Not today, Satan.

"We need to go," I tell him firmly, turning away to grab a bag and hide the blush I feel crawling up my cheeks.

Jackson chuckles again. "Alright, let's get loaded up and get to the cabin."

We take my bags downstairs, and Jackson just has to make a huge production of putting my bags in his trunk. Jeez, they're not *that* heavy. When he slams the trunk shut, he rubs his hands together and looks at me.

"Ready?" he asks.

"Yup." Making my way to Donovan's car, I open the door and find Lindsey and her boyfriend, Aiden, in the backseat.

"Hey, Abs. If you want, we can ride with Jackson." Lindsey is well aware that Jackson and I don't get along. No one knows about the few times we've gotten along *too* well, though.

I consider taking her up on her offer, but that might mean Jackson could catch on to the fact that I don't trust myself to be alone with him. Being in a confined space when it's just the two of us does things to me I'm trying desperately to avoid. I refuse to let him see what he does to me. I have my pride after all.

"No, no, it's fine. See you guys there." I tack on a wide

smile. If I show everyone that everything is fine, it will be... at least that's what I tell myself.

I turn to see Jackson opening the passenger door of his car for me with a knowing smile on his face.

"I guess you're stuck with me for an hour. Whatever shall we do with the time?" he asks with a wink.

With my head held high, I saunter over as if this is totally fine with me. Again, I'm going to fake it 'til I make it, and in the meantime, I won't let the man see me sweat.

"I get to pick the music." Getting into the car, I refuse to acknowledge his comment.

Jackson chuckles and closes the door, then walks around the front of the car to get in. Dammit, the man is beautiful. Even though he's bundled in a warm winter coat and cable-knit sweater, I know what's under those layers, and it's fabulous. Too bad he's a playboy and enjoys the thrill of the chase more than the actual work of a relationship. He may want to continue the secret fling we've indulged in a few times in the last few months, but I'm not interested. Jackson Hayes may be good—even great—for a few orgasms, but he would be hell on the heart, and mine is already scarred enough.

The hour-long drive to the cabin is quiet for the most part. I'm not interested in small talk. I have a difficult enough time keeping it together with his rich cedar scent filling the small space and bringing back memories of when I was wrapped in that scent for hours at a time.

Stop it, Abigail.

There's really only one way to take my mind off the images flashing through my brain.

"You have shit taste in music, Prince." Insults are my go-to. When we're fighting, I'm too annoyed to feel my intense attraction for him. I change the radio station from the slow jam song to something a little more upbeat. "What are you, my eight-nine-year-old grandpa? That shit is boring."

He rolls his eyes. "Actually, Red, it's relaxing. I get enough loud music on the nights I'm at the club. When I'm driving, I enjoy relaxing music, softly playing in the background, which I can form coherent thoughts around."

He moves to change the station, and I slap his hand away.

"Hey, no assaulting the driver while the car is in motion," he complains, shaking out his hand.

"Oh, please, you wuss. That was hardly even a tap. Besides, I told you, I get to pick the music, and grandpa music isn't it." I change it again to a ninety's country station. There, much better. I sit back triumphantly in my seat and ignore Jackson's pout.

It really is a beautiful drive once you get out of the city and look around at the lush greenery. Everything looks so fresh with a light dusting of snow that reminds me of gentle cotton covering the ground. No nasty grey patches out here like you see next to the road in the city.

When we pull up to the cabin, all I can think is, *wow*. I don't know why I was picturing a little cabin by the lake nestled in the woods. This is a damn sprawling estate. My fears of being stuck in a small space with Jackson for a few days have been assuaged. Shit, by the looks of it, I'll be able to successfully avoid him in the house during my entire stay if I want.

"Are you planning on helping me with your twenty-seven bags, or are you just going to stand there gazing at the cabin?" I hear the Prince of Darkness say from behind me as he walks around to open the trunk.

"First off, it's three, not twenty-seven. Stop with the dramatics. Second, you guys need to stop calling it a cabin. That conjures images of a cute little log cabin in the woods.

This,"—I wave my hands toward the mini-mansion—"is the exact opposite of that."

"Red, you should know by now there's nothing small about anything Hayes-related," Jackson smirks.

Cheeky asshole.

Everyone piles out of Donovan's car as Jackson hoists the bags from his trunk. Lindsey and Kasey come over to me with wide, excited smiles, and their good mood is infectious, even after spending an hour in the car with the Son of Satan.

"Damn girl," I exclaim to Kasey. "You've been holding out on us." I look at the house again, and she smiles sweetly.

"I thought the same thing when I came here the first time. If you think this is impressive, wait until you see the inside. It's massive and beautiful. Susan did an amazing job decorating, and nothing has changed since the guys were kids."

Kasey grabs Lindsey and me by the hand and drags us up the front steps and through the front door into the rustic foyer. My family is well off, but the Hayes family is on a whole other level. I look around the massive space. The large kitchen overlooks the living room, where a huge fireplace with brick work stretches to the high ceilings, and large dark wood beams run through the room. Even though the space is enormous, it has a homey feel that's only achieved through someone loving the place and wanting it to be where they can relax with their friends and family. Mrs. Hayes outdid herself, as usual.

"Kasey, show me to my room. I'm utterly spent." I throw my hand over my forehead and feign exhaustion.

"I don't know why you're tired. All you did was harass me about my music choices. I'm the one who had to lug your bags in the house," Jackson calls from the foyer.

I roll my eyes as Kasey and Lindsey laugh.

"Come on, I'll take you up, and you and Lindsey can duke it out over the rooms," Kasey says, leading us toward the staircase.

Lindsey and I peek into each room, and the one at the end of the hall is perfect. It's decorated with a giant four-poster bed with simple white bedding and splashes of dusty pink throughout, and French doors lead out to a small terrace covered in snow. The en suite bathroom looks fit for a queen with a giant clawfoot tub and fluffy towels stacked in a large oak armoire. I love it.

"This one's mine. Finders keepers," I call from the bathroom.

"That's fine. I think Aiden found the room he likes," she yells back. I hear Lindsey laugh and a distinctly male growl from down the hall.

"I like any room with a bed and you in it, Sunshine."

A door slams, then giggles come from the room. Ah, young love. I'm so happy for my sister from another mister. She found her growly bodyguard, and he found peace with the love of his life.

Jackson makes his way to me, carrying one of my bags over his shoulder while rolling the other two.

"Here," he says as he leaves the bags just inside the door to my room.

"Thank you, Jeeves," I say in a haughty British accent.

"I'm not your man servant, Red, but if you need anything in the middle of the night..." He shoots me a suggestive wink, "I'm right across the hall," he says as he opens the door directly across from mine.

Well, shit.

CHAPTER 2

JACKSON

I'm so glad Abigail picked out her room before I came upstairs, and she realized it was across from mine. I know damn well she would have chosen one as far away from me as she could. She likes to fight our insane chemistry, but I know the truth and know why she fights me. She hasn't forgiven me for being a complete tool when we first met over a year ago. *That's okay, Red... challenge accepted.* I'll prove to her I'm not the same guy I was last year.

Lying down on my bed with a wide smile, I think about all the trouble we can get up to this weekend. She's told me we won't be sleeping together again, but my hellcat likes to fight, and fighting turns her on. It's a fine line, though. I don't want to piss her off to where she hates me, just enough to get her fired up and needing somewhere to release that fire. We may look dysfunctional to other people, but we are who we are, and I wouldn't want her to be any other way.

A knock sounds at my door, and Donovan peeks his head in.

"We're going to get dinner started. The girls have already raided the wine, and if we don't get food in them, there will be hell to pay," he tells me with a chuckle.

"I'll be down in a few minutes."

He nods and closes my door.

I have nothing to unpack since this is my room. Running a club in the city, sometimes I need to get away and have some quiet time for myself, so I have plenty of clothes here.

I smile to myself. Of course, they already found the wine. One thing I know for sure about Abigail is she likes a good fight and a good vintage. I may have stocked her favorite label last time I was up here knowing we would be here for Christmas. I'd never dream of telling her that, though. Knowing my girl, she'd insist she actually hates it and wouldn't drink it on principle.

When I go downstairs to the living room, Aiden already has a fire started. He's such a Boy Scout. Probably knows how to rub a couple of sticks together to build a fire in no time. We've come a long way, Aiden and me, especially considering he punched me in the face just a couple months ago for putting his girlfriend and my best friend, Lindsey, in what he deemed a dangerous situation. Not to mention all the times he's had to clean up after me in my wilder days. I used to give him shit because I didn't like him, but now it's because it's fun as hell to watch that vein in his head thumping in time with his heartbeat. He's a good guy, and Lindsey loves him, so I can't ask for anything more.

The girls have made themselves comfortable on the stools in front of the bar separating the kitchen from the living room.

"What have you ladies gotten into?" I ask as I spy the open bottle of wine.

"Whoever stocks your wine rack has excellent taste," Abigail says as she takes a sip.

"You don't say." Grabbing the glass from her hand, I take a sip. "Mmm, delicious." I stare at her and watch her eyes flare with desire, then quickly shut down. She doesn't want me to see how much I affect her. That's fine. I already caught it.

I smile and look at Lindsey, whose gaze darts between Abigail and me. If I've said it once, I've said it a hundred times. Sometimes, it sucks to have a best friend who was an investigative journalist in her former life.

"So, what's for dinner, Donovan?" I change the subject before Lindsey has time to formulate any ideas about what she just saw between Abigail and me.

"Lasagna, Kasey's mother's recipe," Donovan replies as he slides two large pans into the oven.

I look at my brother's girlfriend, who is probably one of the worst cooks known to man, aside from her sister, Lindsey.

"Did you make it?" I ask nervously.

"No, Donovan did." Kasey laughs at my obvious trepidation at eating anything she *tried* to cook. Abigail snickers next to her, and Kasey smacks her arm. "What? I've gotten better. Tell them, Donovan."

"Yes, beautiful. You've become very adept at chopping veggies." He winks in her direction, and she shoots him a dirty look, sticking out her tongue at him.

"You're going to be in trouble for that later, mister," she tells him with an exaggerated pout.

"Do your worst." He sends her a smoldering look, and she looks away, blushing into her wine glass.

Those two went through the wringer when they first started dating—dealing with my stalker, both Kasey and Lindsey being held captive by said stalker, and having major trust issues with each other as a result of everything surrounding the kidnapping—but their relationship survived, and they've grown stronger for it.

If I'm right, my brother has a little surprise for Kasey in his overnight bag.

When we came out here as kids, my parents often threw large dinner parties for various businessmen and politicians. My mother wanted to make sure there was room for everyone and that it felt like a big family dinner on vacation. We still have the giant table, though not nearly as many people come here. When my father suggested we get a smaller one, she told him she keeps it, hoping it would be filled with grandchildren one day. She's subtle like that.

Sitting down for dinner at our large dining table, I'm next to my brother, with Abigail sitting directly across from me.

Well, well, can't escape me now.

"So, what do you girls have planned for the weekend?" Aidan asks as he dishes a large portion of the savory lasagna for him and a slightly smaller portion for Lindsey.

"Well," Kasey begins. "I thought today and tomorrow we could hang around the house and relax, and I made massage appointments for us the day before Christmas Eve."

"Oh, I could use a good massage," Abigail groans, taking a long sip of her wine and leaning back into her chair.

Finding Abigail's foot under the table, I nudge it with mine. Her questioning gaze meets mine, and I wiggle my brows in her direction. Feeling a sharp kick to my shin, I choke on the beer I'm sipping while Abigail looks on with a triumphant gleam in her eye.

Wench.

"Was your family disappointed you weren't going back to Charleston for Christmas?" Lindsey asks Abigail.

Abigail clears her throat, clearly uncomfortable with the direction of the conversation. "There isn't much that doesn't disappoint my family about me these days," she replies flatly.

Abigail doesn't talk about her family much, but from what I've gathered, they aren't very close. We don't discuss those kinds of feelings during our moments together. It's mostly her telling me harder and not to stop. Seeing her stony expression when Lindsey mentions her parents makes me wonder if I should bring it up to her later. Or if she'd kick me in the balls for trying to get personal. Probably the latter.

Dinner wraps up, and we're sufficiently stuffed from the lasagna Donovan made and the salad that Kasey chopped the vegetables for. Everyone makes sure to tell her what a good job she did, but she just smirks and laughs at us trying to placate her. Gotta love a woman who has a good sense of humor about her lack of culinary skills.

Abigail offers to do the dishes while everyone heads to the living room in a food coma, so of course, I volunteer to give her a hand.

"What are you doing in here, Prince?" Her eyes narrow, and suspicion laces her tone.

"What does it look like?" Pretending to be confused by her question, I scrape the plates into the trashcan.

She turns her body toward me and watches as I work. "Well, it looks like you're doing manual labor, which really isn't your style, now is it?" She's not buying it for a second.

"Maybe I just wanted to harass you for a few minutes while we're alone," I reply, a faint smile playing on my lips. No use trying to deny it at this point.

She snorts out a laugh. "Yup, that sounds more like it."

Abigail looks at the pile of dirty dishes and back at me. "I can do this. Why don't you go hang out with everyone in the living room?" She nods her head at our friends, who are sitting in front of the fire and enjoying an after-dinner cocktail.

"Nah, I'm good here."

"Suit yourself." She shrugs her shoulders and goes back to rinsing the plates.

We work side by side quietly. I scrape the plates as she rinses and loads the dishwasher. Being this close to her and smelling her light, citrus perfume conjures memories of being in her apartment, wrapped in her sheets. Fuck, that was a good night.

Abigail does her best not to look me in the eye and concentrate on her task at hand. I've decided it's my mission to get her a little flustered and see if I can get her claws to come out. I brush her hair from her shoulder, and her body goes rigid at my touch.

"What are you doing?" she asks through clenched teeth.

Giving her a heated look, I trail my fingers down her spine. "You have no idea how hard it is for me to be this close to you and not touch you," I whisper.

She whips her head toward me, fire in her glare. "Everyone is right there in the living room, Jackson. You can't touch me like this where everyone can see," she hisses.

"No one is paying us any attention, Red." I look toward the living room, where Donovan, Kasey, Lindsey, and Aiden are setting up a game of cards on the table in front of the fire. "If you don't want our friends to see me touching you, then come to my room tonight," I murmur in her ear.

Her jaw clenches as she inhales a deep breath through her nose, then slowly lets it out of her mouth. "I told you we aren't doing that again, Jackson."

Dammit, I see we're still at the obstinate stage of the evening.

"Red, I don't know why you fight this attraction so hard." She opens her mouth to argue, but I hold up a hand, effectively cutting her off. Her eyes narrow, obviously not appreciating me stopping what I'm sure was going to be an empty denial of our chemistry. "But if that's how you want to play it, just know my door will be unlocked if you change your mind." I give Abigail her personal space back, and we finish doing the dishes in silence.

Joining the others in the living room, we decide to play gin rummy, my personal favorite. Donovan and I have played this game with our dad since we were kids and are pretty good. Of course, I should have known Abigail would have us all beat hands down.

"Where did you learn to play cards like a shark?" I ask Abigail.

"Growing up, I spent a lot of time at a bar just outside of Charleston. After our homework was done, my best friend and I would play cards with the regulars."

"What were you doing at a bar—underage—after school?" I'm shocked her parents would let her hang out in a bar. The few times Abigail's talked about them, I've always had the impression her parents were image-obsessed stiffs.

She giggles at my reaction. "It was my best friend Julie's uncle and aunt's bar. We would go there after school to do our homework, then get sodas and snacks for free. It wasn't like we were hanging out and drinking underage."

"Your parents didn't care?" I ask her.

"No, my mom was usually at some board meeting for a charity event or something she was a part of. As long as I was home for dinner by six and stayed out of trouble, they didn't really care where I spent my afternoons after school." Sadness clouds Abigail's eyes for a moment but she Okay quickly shakes it off and deals another game.

I can tell there's a lot more to the story than she's letting on. She's a tough nut to crack. Good thing I have all weekend to work on it.

CHAPTER 3

ABIGAIL

It's three in the morning, and I'm lying in this huge comfortable bed, but all I can do is think about sneaking across the hall to Jackson's room. His warm breath against my neck when we were in the kitchen was almost my undoing. I was so close to turning my head and pressing my lips against his. Goddamn him, why does he have to be so tempting?

Hanging out with everyone was a blast, even when I was trying not to let it show how much Jackson was affecting me. Keeping it together around our friends is definitely going to be a chore this weekend, but I'm not ready to tell Kasey or Lindsey about what's been going on between Jackson and me. Not that anything *is* going on, but I never divulged to my two best friends that he and I slept together after the club or any time after that. It's not that I want to keep secrets from my friends, but I've been burned in the past with a relationship not working out and my blood family taking the side of my ex. I don't want to put Kasey and Lindsey in the position where they'd have to choose between Jackson and me, so not talking about it seems like the best idea. Maybe. I'm not sure.

God, why did I let him in my bed in the first place?

Unfortunately, that doesn't change the fact that I'm lying here, arguing with myself not to sneak over to Jackson's room. I told him we weren't going to have sex again, and I meant it, but when the wine is flowing and Jackson is being his damn charming self, the reasons for not wanting to continue whatever it is we're doing get hazy.

No, the best thing for me to do is just to go to sleep, then tomorrow, I can pretend my resolve hadn't wavered. Problem solved.

Hopefully.

Not bothering to get dressed, I opt for the fluffy robe hanging in the bathroom for guests. I make my way downstairs in the morning after a fitful night's sleep. My long red hair is tied up in a messy bun, and the only thing on my mind is how much caffeine I can get into my system before the rest of the house wakes. Unfortunately, a six-foot, blonde hair, blue-eyed sex god is in front of the coffee pot. *Sex god?* I must be exhausted.

"Morning, Red. How did you sleep?" Jackson gives me a knowing look, surely noticing the exhaustion in my eyes.

I'm not a morning person by any stretch of the imagination, but I'll be damned if I let him see how much he's already messed with my head this weekend. "I slept great in one of the most comfortable beds I've ever been in. How about you?" Plastering a wide smile on my face, I try to hide how irritated and tired I really am.

"Huh, that's weird. I could've sworn I heard you tossing and turning all night."

I would love nothing more than to slap the smirk off his face.

"Jackson, don't be creepy to our guests," Donovan says as he walks into the kitchen with Kasey under his arm.

"It's not creepy, brother. I just wanted to make sure Abigail was comfortable in her room."

"If you think standing outside my door and listening is being a good host, you have a lot to learn, Prince," I scoff.

"Are you two ever going to stop bickering?" Kasey laughs out.

"No," we reply at the same time, which makes Kasey laugh harder.

Jackson hands me a cup of coffee, and I take a sip—a little sweet and a little creamy, just how I like it. I offer him a small smile in thanks, and he nods as if it's no big deal. Kasey looks between the two of us, and I can see the dots connecting in her mind. I need to shut that shit down quick.

"So, what should we do today?" I ask Kasey.

A wide smile stretches across her face, her previous train of thought momentarily derailed. "I thought it would be fun to take a walk around the property and enjoy the snow, maybe build a snowman. You know, like we used to do when we were kids."

"Growing up in the south didn't lead to many winters with enough snow to build a snowman, but I'm up for it." I sip my coffee. Damn, it's perfect.

Aiden makes his way into the kitchen, followed by a zombie Lindsey, who plops down on a barstool at the counter. He makes her coffee, then sets it down in front of her, and she gives him a grateful smile. Taking a sip from the cup, Lindsey breathes out a sigh of satisfaction.

"Ah, liquid gold," she says, admiring her cup of coffee.

If I thought I had a caffeine addiction, it's nothing compared to Lindsey's. The girl can't be bothered with life before her first cup. Good thing Aiden knows and always has coffee waiting for her when she wakes up in the morning. *That's a good man right there.* My eyes wander to Jackson, then down to the cup of coffee in my hands.

Son of a bitch.

"What's the plan for today?" Lindsey asks the room.

We fill her in on our ideas, and she gets a big smile on her face.

"Kasey, do you remember all the snowmen we used to build with Dad? We would have a whole family put together in a matter of an hour or so."

"Yeah." Kasey laughs. "I remember the pipe we found to put on our daddy snowman. Mom asked where we got it from, and when we said Dad's office, she was so pissed he had a pipe." Both of them laugh with tears in their eyes.

It's nice to see them remembering their dad. They lost him at such a young age. For a long time, Lindsey was afraid to love another man because she was scared to lose him like she had lost her dad. Then Aiden came along and broke down all her defenses. Now my honorary little sister is happier than I've ever seen her.

"All right, Sunshine, bring your coffee upstairs, and we'll get you all bundled up and ready to go out in the cold," Aiden tells Lindsey, then kisses her on the top of her head. She giggles and grabs her coffee before they make their way back into the room.

"Come on, beautiful, let's get you ready for the day, too," Donovan tells Kasey. She gives him a questioning look before a knowing smile stretches across her face.

"Sure, yeah... I need to finish getting ready," she replies a little too quickly. Kasey grabs Donovan's hand, and they make their way back upstairs.

I look at Jackson and let out a sigh. "It looks like it's going to be a while before we leave the cabin."

Jackson shrugs. "Well, they say if you can't beat them, join them, Red." He shoots me a sinful smile, and I roll my eyes.

"Dream on, Prince."

My estimation is correct, and it's about two hours before we all head outside. We decide to make it into a competition between the guys and girls who can build the best snowman. Kasey insists that we girls have this in the bag, considering all the snowmen she and her sister built growing up.

"And who will be judging this contest?" Aidan asks suspiciously.

"We'll put it to a vote," Lindsey suggests.

"I don't think that's fair. You'll just vote for your own snowman," Aiden replies, eyeing the work she's started on her snowman.

"It's cute that you think you have a chance to begin with. We're totally going to kick your asses." Lindsey winks and gets back to building the base of her snowman.

She isn't wrong. Our snowman, or rather snowlady, is fabulous. The boys do a decent job, but ours totally Blows theirs out of the water—or snow. We even went so far as to find a stick that could hold a wine glass, and I donated my Chanel scarf and a pair of gorgeous earrings to complete her look. She's wearing one of my wrap cardigans. I brought plenty, so getting one wet is no big deal. The boys barely have the globes of snow on straight, and all they found was a carrot for his nose and a couple of small rocks for his eyes.

The girls and I take a step back and admire our work when suddenly, a cold ball of snow hits me in the back. When it explodes, some of it goes into my jacket, and it's freezing against my neck. I turn around on a screech and catch a proud smile on Jackson's face.

"What's wrong, She-Devil? Afraid you're going to melt from a little water?" Jackson quips.

"Oh, you're in for it now, Prince." Reaching down, I grab a hand full of snow and quickly pack it into a loose ball. When I throw it at him, it goes wide and hits Aiden square in the chest. He looks over at a laughing Lindsey, and a smile lifts the corner of his lips.

"Do you think that's funny, Sunshine?" Aidan bends down and picks up more snow. "You know what this means, right?" he asks menacingly.

Lindsey backs away from him with wide eyes and a warning in her expression.

"This means war!" Aiden takes it off after Lindsey's retreating form.

Just then, a snowball comes flying and hits Kasey in the stomach. When she looks down, a pile of snow smacks her right in the face, the remnants sliding into her jacket. She shakes it out and screeches, "Donovan!"

"All is fair in love and war, Beautiful."

"Not feeling the love right now, Babe." Quickly bending down to pick up a handful of snow, she throws it, and the ball glances off his arm.

I laugh as snow flies between Donovan and Kasey. Neither of them takes the time to form a proper ball, so they're falling apart mid-flight. Lindsey is still running from Aiden, trying to bend down and pick up as much snow as she can to throw back at him as he chases her.

Looking around, I notice Jackson has disappeared. Oh, that sneaky bastard. There aren't a lot of places to hide, but I spot an outbuilding not too far from where we built our snow people. Acting as though I'm going back into the house, I bypass the stairs to the porch and make a wide loop toward the back of the outbuilding. When no snow comes flying at me, I hazard a guess that Jackson is on the other side, watching the melee unfold.

Walking quietly through snow isn't as easy as you would think. It looks so fluffy and soft, but every time I take a step, it crunches beneath my feet. The outbuilding is surrounded by icy pavement, but at least it's not as noisy to walk on. Carefully making my way to the back of the building, I spot Jackson peeking his head around the corner opposite me. Molding a ball of snow in my hand, I sneak up behind him. He's getting it down the back of his shirt. I'm right behind him, but when I move to yank his shirt back, I lose my footing and fall backward. I'm about to eat shit on the icy pavement, and it's going to hurt like a bitch. Before a yelp has time to leave my lips, Jackson turns around and grabs me around the waist, flipping us so when we fall, his back hits the snow, and I land on top of him.

"Oh my God, are you okay?" I exclaim as I try to scramble off of him. His arms band tighter around me as his bright blue eyes look up at me, laughter dancing in them.

"I'm perfect." He squeezes me closer.

Remembering the other times we were in this exact position, those unwanted butterflies make an appearance low in my belly. His hand swipes my hair behind my face, and I'm so damn tempted to lean down and kiss his cold lips. Suddenly, he flips us over, so my back is to the ground, and before I know it, freezing snow is shoved down my pants.

"You son of a bitch!" I screech as he bolts up and runs away.

"You heard my brother… all's fair."

I don't know about the love part, but the war is on.

CHAPTER 4

JACKSON

The girls may have won the snowman-building contest, but we definitely won the snowball fight. Lindsey, Kasey, and Abigail trudge up the stairs to the house, their cheeks rosy from the cold and hair sticking to their heads from the melted snow they were pummeled with.

"I'm going to go soak in a hot bath while you guys make dinner," Abigail declares as she makes her way up the stairs.

That was the deal we made at the end of our epic battle. The guys would cook dinner if the girls stopped trying to shove snow down our pants. All of us agreed we would rather not get frostbite on body parts we planned to need later... I hope. I saw the way Abigail looked at me when we were on the ground. I would have done something about it, but I need her to come to me—then *with* me.

We all decide it's probably a good idea to take our wet, messy selves upstairs to take showers and get ready for dinner. Donovan is already prepping the steaks when I walk into the kitchen, with Aidan trailing behind me.

"Ah, good choice. My girl enjoys her meat." Donovan

and I chuckle at Aidan's accidental innuendo, and Aiden looks at us with confusion in his eyes. "A bunch of bloody wankers you two are," he drawls when he catches on to what we're snickering about.

"Hey, I wasn't the one talking about my girl and her meat," I retort.

"What are you boys giggling about?" Kasey asks as she wanders into the kitchen.

"Nothing, Beautiful. Why don't you grab the potatoes and wash them for me?" Donovan says.

"Oh, I would, but…" Kasey looks at him as she grabs a wine glass and an unopened bottle of wine. "The deal for our surrender was you guys would make dinner, and we get to relax." She blows my brother a kiss, grabs the wine opener, and makes her way into the living room just as Lindsey and Abigail come down the stairs.

"Ladies, I grabbed us a bottle," Kasey calls. "The boys are going to be busy making dinner while we're busy drinking this fantastic wine."

"Another one of my favorites." Abigail eyes the bottle Kasey is opening.

I turn around with a small smile tipping up the corners of my mouth. Knowing it was one of her favorites, I stocked it the last time I was here. My brother notices my smile and looks at me questioningly.

"That's not a label Mom usually stocks here, is it?" Donovan asks.

"I don't know. Maybe she's broadening her taste in wine." I try to pretend like I had nothing to do with it and that his suspicion isn't warranted. He scrutinizes me a bit longer, then shakes his head and points to the potatoes on the counter.

"If you're going to stand there and spout some bullshit, you can do it while you're peeling potatoes."

"Sure thing, brother."

This whole pretending for Abigail's benefit is getting harder and harder around my nosy brother and reporter friends.

Dinner is delicious, as usual when my brother is the one cooking, and we're all stuffed as we make our way into the living room. Exhausted from playing in the snow, none of us can muster the energy to get out a deck of cards and play a round like we did last night. We're all content to stare into the fire and unwind.

"I'm beat. I think I'm going to head up to bed to relax," Abigail announces on a yawn. Standing, she grabs her wine glass and makes her way to the stairs. "Good night, love muffins," she calls as she heads up to her room.

"I think Abigail has the right idea." Kasey looks at Donovan, then bends and gives him a light kiss on the lips. "Don't be long," she tells him before retreating up to their room. Lindsey heads up as well, and it's just the three of us left.

"Jackson, want to tell the class what the hell is going on with you and Abigail?" Donovan turns his attention to me as soon as the girls leave.

Aiden raises his eyebrows, interested in my explanation as well.

"I don't know what you mean," I say, trying to deflect his question.

"Bullocks. Don't think we haven't caught on to the glances you've been giving each other. Not to mention the little things you've been doing for her that are completely out of character for you," Aiden chimes in.

I could lie and tell them it's really nothing, but they'll find out sooner or later—preferably sooner if Abigail stops being so damn stubborn.

"We've had a few nights when we've enjoyed each

other's company," I tell them non-committedly. "That's all."

"That's not all. If it was, you wouldn't have bothered switching around your schedule so you could make it here. In fact, you didn't even plan on coming until you knew Abigail would be here this weekend," Donovan says, pursing his lips, obviously not believing me.

It's true. When I thought it was only going to be the two couples, I had no interest in coming. But when he told me a few days later that Abigail was going to be joining them, I rearranged my schedule to be here.

Taking a deep breath, I blow it out and lean farther into the plush sofa.

"Fine, you're right. I hoped spending time together would soften her up, and we could finally get past whatever hang-ups she has about making sure no one knows we've been sleeping together. That woman is stubborn as hell and still insists that no one find out."

"Would that have anything to do with how you two met or your not-so-stellar reputation?" Aiden asks.

"I don't know... maybe. She insists she doesn't want it to be awkward if we don't work out, but I think there's more to the story." What, I have no idea, but I'm determined to get her past it.

"Whatever you do, brother, be careful," Donovan warns. "That's Kasey and Lindsey's best friend. Shit, she's more than that to them. If you hurt her in any way, those two will have your balls."

I nod in agreement. Like he needed to tell me that.

"Listen to your brother," Aiden tells me. "I would hate to have to dispose of your body once Lindsey was done with you. I've just started to like you." He gives me a small smile and slaps my knee before standing. "I'm knackered myself. Good night." Turning, he heads to his room.

"Well, that wasn't ominous or anything," I mumble, turning toward my brother.

"Trust me when I tell you, you should be more concerned about what those girls will do to you if you hurt their honorary sister than anything Aiden would do." He chuckles and stands. "I'm going to bed."

I wave him off, then close my eyes and lean my head back to rest on the couch. Remembering the nights Abigail and I spent together, I smile. Yeah, I'm willing to take my chances.

It's late, but I haven't been able to sleep. There's a light knock at my door, and Abigail peeks her head in.

"Did I wake you?" she asks softly.

I sit up in bed and shake my head. "No, come in."

She carefully makes her way inside the room as the door shuts with a soft click behind her. Gliding over to me, she sits on the edge of my bed as I scoot over to make room for her. Her eyes trace the smooth lines of my naked chest before she subtly shakes her head, and her gaze meets mine.

"I need to ask you a question. I've noticed some of my favorite things on this trip." She quirks a brow. "Same as I noticed when we went to Club Noir last month."

I smile as the memories of that night dance through my head—not about her at the club but what happened when I took her home.

"Jackson?" she prompts.

"I wanted you to have things around you that make you happy," I reply softly as my fingers graze the ends of her soft red locks.

Energy crackles between us, and before I have a chance to ask her what she's thinking about, her lips slam into mine. When she pulls away from the kiss, I see the decision in her eyes.

"Fuck it," she breathes out.

Leaning up and grabbing her by the back of the neck, I pull her to my mouth and taste the wine she drank at dinner.

"What are you doing to me?" she whispers against my lips.

I lay back as Abigail throws one of her thighs over me and straddles my hips. I quickly relieve her of her soft, button-down shirt before pulling her back to my mouth. The feel of her hard nipples against the smooth skin of my chest has my entire body on fire. Tracing my lips down her neck to her collarbone, I nip her sensitive flesh.

"Red, I need to be inside you," I growl into her throat.

Her sensual moans fill the otherwise silent room, and I take it to mean she's on board with my plan. Reaching over to my nightstand, I grab the strip of condoms I brought from home, hoping this is where we ended up. The movement gives her the opportunity to shuck out of her pajama bottoms, then she drags my pajamas and underwear down my legs and throws them to the floor before straddling my hips again. We're a naked, writhing mess, and it's perfect.

"Jackson, you have to be quiet. No one can know I'm in here," she says between hard kisses and soft pants.

I would like to say her hesitance is a huge turnoff, but I'm not about to look a gift horse in the mouth.

Quickly sheathing myself, I grab Abigail's hips and slowly guide her down my hard length.

"Fuck," she lets out on a long exhale.

"Shh, baby, you said we have to be quiet." I chuckle softly as her face screws up in pleasure. I'll be damned if I make it easy for her.

I grasp her by the back of her head and slam her mouth against mine, and our tongues duel for dominance. The motion causes her to lift off my hips slightly, and I take the opportunity to grab and hold her steady as a slam up into her. She whimpers, but that's not enough for me. I want her to lose control—the control I've tried so hard to break in her, which is already broken in me.

"Oh my God, Jackson, I'm about to come," she whispers against my lips.

Doubling my efforts, I pump into her faster as sweat drips down my forehead. My jaw clenches in determination to get her there because I'm almost there myself.

I flip us over, and Abigail's copper hair fans across my pillow. Damn, that's a beautiful sight. Grabbing her leg, I throw it over my shoulder as I thrust into her deeper than I could go before. With her eyes squeezed shut and her lips slightly parted, she grabs the headboard to prevent it from slamming against the wall. I know that face—the face of someone trying to quiet their explosion. That simply won't work for me.

As I rub her clit in fast, tight circles, she arches her back as her body aches for release. Moments later, she stills, her back bowed as a silent scream falls from her open mouth. The feel of her tight pussy strangling my cock is enough to throw me over the edge, and I spill myself into the condom with a long groan.

Dropping her leg to the bed, I flop over on my back next to her, sweaty and satisfied. My eyes caress the curves of the body lying next to me. A sheen of sweat covers her naked form, and her eyes are still closed, but a small smile plays on her lips—the smile I've come to know well during our time together. My girl has been thoroughly fucked and is thoroughly satisfied.

Abigail turns her head and squints her eyes at me. "Oh, don't look at me like that."

My eyes widen in surprise. "Like what? I'm just lying here, trying to catch my breath."

"You know the look. It's akin to watching you pound your chest with male pride," she tells me with a hard eyeroll.

A laugh escapes me at her ridiculous analogy. Leaning over, I softly press my lips to hers.

"What can I say, Red? You bring out the beast in me."

"I wouldn't go so far as to say you're a beast, Prince." She chuckles.

I grab her hip and yank her against me, our bodies touching chest to chest.

"Give me about five minutes, and I'll show you how savage I can be."

CHAPTER 5
ABIGAIL

I sneak out of Jackson's room at about three o'clock in the morning. He's still asleep after round two, so I quietly dress and go back to my room. Had I woke him, he would have latched onto me, and things would've heated quickly, but I'm still convinced that no one knowing about whatever we have going on is the best course of action.

He's his usual charming self over breakfast, even making me a cup of coffee just the way I like it again. I'm a mess of nerves that he'll let it slip how we spent our night. As far as I know, he's said nothing to anyone about our "relationship," but we've never tried to hide it while sneaking around under the same roof as our friends. I brush off the few heated glasses he sends my way and quickly look at Kasey and Lindsey to make sure they didn't catch anything. They're too enraptured with their own men to notice the awkward tension between Jackson and me. Well, mainly me.

It's early afternoon, the three of us girls are lying on massage tables set up in the living room, having all the knots gloriously rubbed out of our sore muscles. The guys are in the rec room in the converted basement, complete with a small theater, four full-size arcade games, and a pool table. Everything you would need to entertain two teenage boys and their friends, or in this case, three adult men.

"Hey, Abigail, I noticed you and Jackson have been getting along pretty well on this trip. Are you two finally burying the hatchet?" Lindsey asks.

Oh shit, I hope she hasn't worked out what's going on. This is what happens when your two best friends are reporters. They'll ask the right questions to get you to spill your guts. My mind is screaming deflect, deflect, but at the same time, I *want* to confide in my friends about my conflicting feelings about my relationship with Jackson. It's that witchy reporter magic… I just know it.

"It's my Christmas gift to you two, not to have to referee between us." Hopefully, that throws her off the trail. I'm just not ready to talk about something when *I* don't even know what's going on.

"Well, I appreciate the new dynamic you two have going," Kasey says. "It's a nice change of pace. I was worried we would have to put you two on separate sides of the house." She chuckles at her joke, but her assessment isn't that far off.

I almost wish we were on separate sides of the house. Having him right across the hall is definitely more temptation than I could withstand last night.

"We're all adults here, ladies. Jackson and I can play nice for a few days." I need a new conversation… stat. "Kasey, you and Donovan have been living together for a few months now. Any chance you're going to be tying the knot soon?" Let's put her under the spotlight and see how she likes it.

"I don't know, but I don't need to rush anything. He's it for me."

If I could see her face right now, I know there would be a wide smile stretched across it. She gets like that every time she talks about Donovan. I'm so unbelievably happy for my sister from another mister, it *almost* wipes away my irritation from talking about Jackson… or trying *not* to talk about Jackson.

It's ridiculous that I'm afraid to confide in my two best friends about the shit storm of emotions floating through my mind every time the subject of Jackson and me comes up. I wouldn't mind talking to them about my feelings or anything else having to do with us, but the idea of what will happen when we don't work out… Jackson is family, and I'm not. Doesn't take a rocket scientist to figure out how that would go down. I know they would mean well, but eventually, I would be shut out of their lives since Jackson is Donovan's brother. That's what happened between my sister and me, and we were blood. I broke up with her boyfriend's brother and refused to give him a second chance, which was enough for her to decide our relationship wasn't worth it. I would be devastated if that happened with Kasey and Lindsey.

These thoughts are not helping me relax as my strong-handed male masseuse tries to work out the kinks in my neck. When he touches a particularly tender spot, I let out a loud groan. The sound of a cabinet door slamming comes from the kitchen, and I look up, catching Jackson glaring darts between me and my masseuse, Christopher. The man doesn't look happy. I cock a brow and lift the side of my lips up in a small smile before putting my head back down on the massage table. What Jackson doesn't know is the woman doing Kasey's massage is Christopher's fiancé. Let him sweat for a second.

I already know he doesn't like seeing other men's hands on me from his reaction when I was dancing with the couple at his club. Personally, I like that he's a little jealous. My ex never gave two shits if another guy flirted with me. He was too busy getting a blow job from whatever sorority sister showed him the time of day.

A notification chimes from my phone with an incoming text. I look up again to see Jackson's eyes dart to my phone, then back at me.

"Who is it?" I ask.

"Your mom."

I'm not dealing with her right now. Rolling my eyes, I lay my head down again, frustrated with the turn this supposedly relaxing massage has taken. Why can't I just have an hour to decompress and have the tension rubbed out of my body? I don't want to think about relationships, my mother, or that I haven't RSVP'd to my sister's wedding because I don't want to deal with my family's matchmaking schemes to get me back together with my ex. And I certainly don't want to have to think about where this thing between Jackson and I could go, if anywhere. The only thing I need right now are these considerable knots rubbed out, a shower, and later, a copious amount of wine.

Since no one has the energy to cook tonight, we order pizza from a local pizzeria. Sometimes, carb loading with a delicious glass of wine is about as close to heaven as one can get.

Of course, Lindsey eats half a pie herself. I swear I don't know where that girl puts it all. Aiden watches her proudly as she inhales another large, meaty slice. Is it weird that he's so impressed by her eating skills? Whatever works for them, I guess.

We decide to take advantage of the home theater and have a relaxing night vegging out and watching a movie in the basement rec room. Witnessing the Albright sisters debate over which cheesy action movie to watch is hilarious. Growing up, this never happened in my house. Besides, my sister only likes anything with a sappy romantic ending. Personally, I like the shoot 'em up scenes. Watching people getting blown up is therapeutic. Don't judge. They finally settle on an old eighties action movie.

Donovan and Kasey are on one reclining loveseat, and Lindsey and Aiden are on the other. Naturally, that sticks me with Jackson on the remaining loveseat. The guys had gone to the store this afternoon while Kasey, Lindsey, and I were taking a nap after our massages. I didn't sleep well last night—Jackson and me together doesn't lend itself to a good night's sleep. Not that I'm complaining. The nap was heavenly, and my brain finally turned off for a while. After a shower and pizza, we're all settled in the loveseats, watching the movie and gorging ourselves on the popcorn and candy the guys brought home.

Midway through the scene, when the villain declares his intentions for world domination, I feel something rubbing the side of my thigh and glance down. Jackson's pinky is moving in slow circles over my yoga pants. I shoot him a tightlipped glare and shake my head, mouthing, "Knock it off."

He looks back with innocent eyes, shrugs his shoulders, and mouths, "What?"

My eyes pointedly dart to the heads of the two couples sitting in front of us, then back to him. His hand retreats, but an irreverent smirk dances on his lips as he watches the movie and shovels popcorn into his mouth. Not even thirty minutes later, he pulls the good old yawn move, stretching his arm behind the back of my seat. Who does this guy think he's fooling?

I glance back in his direction, and he's watching the movie as though he isn't trying to pull a fast one on me.

When I feel his fingers trail through my hair, I smack his hand away, glaring daggers in his direction again.

"Stop it," I hiss at him quietly.

Jackson turns and shushes me. Me! This guy is trying to get frisky where any of our friends could turn around and see, but somehow, I'm the one with the issue. Absolutely ridiculous.

Maneuvering my body as far away from him as I can, I put my back against the armrest. Jackson takes it as his opportunity to grab me by the calves and throw my legs over his lap. This guy just won't quit. For the sake of not drawing attention to ourselves, I keep my legs in his lap and throw a blanket over us, so if anyone turns around, they won't be able to tell where my legs are.

Absentmindedly, he begins rubbing the arches of my feet. God, that feels good. Even though I had a massage a few hours ago, there's nothing better than having someone dig there. A deep ache flares to life low in my belly, and I rub my thighs together to alleviate the pressure building between my legs. I spot a small smirk on Jackson's lips, his only acknowledgment that he knows what his touch is doing to me. Damn him.

When the movie ends, I realize I spaced out for the last half of it. Jackson's strong fingers had created a riot of emotions throughout my body. I spent most of the movie hoping he wouldn't move his hand farther up but at the same time, wishing he would. His touch never strayed past my knee, and I'd be lying if I said I wasn't slightly disappointed.

Our friends catching us wasn't something I was prepared to deal with, but I was willing to risk it at that moment. My mind kept going back and forth with the idea that we're all adults, and if they knew Jackson and I were seeing each other, so what? Too bad that nasty voice of self-doubt crept in, telling me if anything went wrong, I'd be out, and Jackson would stay in.

As the credits roll, I remove my legs from Jackson's lap and curl them to the side as if I'd been laying like this the whole time. When Donovan turns the lights on, washing the theater in a warm glow, Kasey turns to face me, concern etched across her brow.

"Are you feeling okay, Abs? Your cheeks look a little rosy."

"I'm fine, just a little hot." Hot and bothered is more like it. I throw the blanket off and fan myself.

"Maybe you should head upstairs and get some rest. I hate to think you're coming down with something," Jackson tells me.

"That's a great idea. We should all get some sleep." Aiden stands and grabs Lindsey's hand, hauling her off the loveseat. "Come on, Sunshine."

Lindsey yawns and allows him to drag her up the stairs as Donovan and Kasey follow.

"It's just us now, Red," Jackson whispers, leaning into me.

"I'm tired." Putting a hand on his chest, I push him back. "I'd hate to be coming down with a cold and get you sick."

"You know damn well that's not what has your checks blushing." A smirk plays on his lips.

"Can't be too safe." I shrug and stand. "Night, Prince."

Walking past him, I refuse to look down at his handsome face. I was already faltering while the movie was playing. No need to look temptation in the eye again.

An hour later, a knock sounds on my bedroom door, and I roll my eyes, not surprised. When Jackson pokes his head and sees I'm still awake, he enters the room and closes the door behind him.

"Jackson, what was that during the movie?" I ask, still irritated he was so brazen and that I let him.

"Red, you can't seriously expect me to watch some beefy guy with his hands all over you, then have you sit next to me in a dark room and not replace his touch with mine." Prowling to the edge of the bed, then up my body, he brings his face over mine.

"So, that was a show of possession? He touched me, so now you have to stake a claim? We're not on the playground, Jackson," I reply irritably. I want to push him away, but the weight of his body on mine has my legs instinctively wrapping around his waist, like a Pavlovian response or something. I couldn't control it if I tried.

Yeah, that sounds like a perfectly reasonable explanation.

He trails light, wet kisses down my neck to the swells of my breasts. Lifting my nightshirt over my hips, he continues his sensual descent.

"Maybe not, but you know the old saying…" He stops when he reaches the top of my panties and locks his eyes on mine. "If I lick it, it's mine." He quickly pulls my panties down my legs, spreads my thighs, and takes a long lick up my drenched center.

Shuddering with pleasure, I decide I would be an idiot to argue at this point. We're on vacation. Enjoying a few nights of orgasms never hurt anyone.

CHAPTER 6

JACKSON

Three in the morning on Christmas Eve, and just as I expected, Abigail kicked me out of her bed. I'm getting really tired of not having a full night's sleep while I'm on vacation, but that woman is still insisting we keep our activities a secret. I'm not sure what her hang-ups are when it comes to pursuing a relationship with me... well, except that I fucked up a year ago. She has no problem sleeping with me but refuses for it to go any further.

My brother comes down the stairs, still in his pajamas, and goes about making a cup of coffee for himself and Kasey.

"I'm going to do it tonight," he says quietly with a nervous lilt to his words. He doesn't have to elaborate; I know exactly what he's talking about.

Turning to him, I clasp his shoulder, excited I get to witness such a monumental occasion in his life. There were a few years there when Donovan and I weren't close—to put it mildly—but after dealing with my stalker and me staying with him while he was recovering from a gunshot wound, our relationship turned a corner. He even asked me to go ring shopping with him when he decided to propose on this trip. To say I was honored is an understatement. I've always loved and respected my brother, but recently, we have the closeness we shared as young men. I'll never take that for granted again.

"Why do you seem nervous? It's not as if you think she's going to say no, is it?" He can't possibly be worried about that. I've never seen a woman more in love than Kasey. Not that I have much experience in that particular department, but she looks at Donovan the way my mother has always looked at my father, and they've been together nearly forty years.

"A little? I don't know." He turns and pours himself a cup of coffee, then leans against the counter as he takes a sip. "When the subject came up before the trip, she said it's hard for her to imagine walking down the aisle without her father. I want to marry the woman more than I want to take my next breath, but the idea that she'll be sad on her wedding day guts me." Donovan runs a hand down his face, obviously pained at the thought of causing Kasey any sort of heartbreak.

"You can have a small wedding, brother. Make it about what she's comfortable with, not what she's missing on her wedding day. She loves you and wants to marry you. If she didn't, she would have told you." If there's one thing I know about my future sister-in-law, it's that she has no problem speaking her mind.

"That's very true." Smiling wryly, Donovan chuckles. "Then the only person I'll have to convince to keep it a small affair is our mother."

We both wince. Susan Hayes is an event planner extraordinaire. Asking her to keep her oldest son's wedding low-key is like asking the Pope not to pray on Sunday.

Leaning against the counter opposite him, I tilt my head to the ceiling, wondering what to say to make him feel better about her involvement.

"She might surprise you." It's a weak attempt at best. Honestly, we both know it will be an uphill battle.

"Have you met our mother?" Donovan looks at me as if I'd just said the most preposterous thing he's ever heard.

"Fair enough," I say in agreement. "But don't let anything deter you on this, Donovan. When all is said and done, Kasey will be married to you, regardless of whether it's a ceremony with just the two of you or a lavish wedding with five hundred people."

"Thanks, Jackson." He nods and tips his lips up in a small smile of appreciation. Making Kasey a cup of coffee, he turns toward the stairs, then stops as though he suddenly remembered something.

"Any headway on the Abigail front?"

"Nope." Letting out a frustrated sigh, I push off the counter and grab my own cup of coffee. "She still insists it's nothing more than sex. I need to figure out a way to make her see this for what it really is or move on. I can't keep banging my head on the proverbial wall." The thought of giving up on our fiery chemistry leaves a hollow feeling in my chest.

"And what is really going on?" Donovan asks, raising a surprised brow.

He's never known me to take this much interest in a woman. I've had plenty in my life, don't get me wrong, but this is different, deeper, and he sees it plain as day on my face. Too bad a certain redhead doesn't.

"She's not like anyone else, brother. She doesn't care about the Hayes' name or the money. In fact, I would go so far as to say the idea of being with someone in my position is a turn-*off* for her. She challenges me at every turn and has never put up with any bullshit from me. I fucking love that she knows her worth and refuses to settle for anything or anyone who doesn't fully appreciate it." I smile at the thought of her tough-as-nails outer shell and the soft gooey center I know is in there—somewhere.

"She has me by the balls, and I don't even care." I shrug.

"I've never heard you talk about a woman like this, Jackson. It's refreshing to see this side of you." Donovan looks at me with a contemplative expression.

We both know he's referring to the side I showed the world for many years—the rich playboy who didn't have a care in the world. The one that Abigail first met and still has her doubting me and my intentions.

"I haven't been him in a long time, brother." Not since I realized that actions have consequences, and sometimes, the people we love pay them.

"True, and if anyone can come up with a way to make Abigail see that, it's you. I have faith in you." Donovan turns and heads upstairs to deliver his woman's coffee as I stand motionless in the kitchen.

My brother hasn't had faith in me—about anything—for many years, let alone anything to do with a woman's heart.

After breakfast and coffee, Donovan and Aiden start dinner, the whole traditional Christmas spread—turkey, stuffing, mashed potatoes, green bean casserole, and figgy pudding, a recipe from Aiden's mother.

We spend the day relaxing around the house. The girls have a bit of a spa day, giving each other pedicures and manicures while the guys handle something in the kitchen or play pool in the rec room.

When we sit down to eat, I sense some trepidation from my brother and notice a ring box-shaped bulge in his pocket. Kasey is filling her plate and raving about how delicious everything smells, completely oblivious to Donovan's discomfort.

Once everyone is settled with a plate in front of them, Donovan clinks his wine glass, signaling a toast. Standing, he looks around the table with affection. Kasey looks up at him with her glass raised and a broad smile on her face.

"I just wanted to say a few words before we start eating." He nervously clears his throat. It's amusing to see my stoic, big brother nervous for once in his life. "I'm so glad we could be here, out of the city, celebrating Christmas together. This place holds so many memories from our childhood, and it's one of my favorite places, so it's fitting that Kasey and I are here, celebrating with our favorite people."

Abigail, who is sitting next to Lindsey, leans her head on Lindsey's shoulder, smiling at Donovan's kind words.

"It's also fitting that our favorite people are gathered for what I have to say… or rather ask." Donovan sets his glass on the table as he lowers himself to one knee in front of Kasey.

She looks at him, surprise etched in her features, as he gently takes the glass from her hand and sets it next to his. Reaching into his pocket, Donovan pulls out a light blue box and opens it, revealing a solitaire diamond nestled in a rose gold setting. Kasey's hand immediately goes to her mouth in shock as she looks from the box to Donovan's misty eyes.

"Beautiful, I have been utterly bewitched by you since the moment I laid eyes on you at my press conference. My infatuation quickly turned into a deep, all-consuming love, I can't live without. You turned my world sideways the first time I tasted your sweet skin and felt your soft lips touch mine. There was no turning back after that moment. I knew then, just as surely as I know now, you're the woman I'm meant to spend my life with." Taking the ring out of the box, he holds it out in front of her.

"Will you marry me?"

Kasey nods as tears stream down her face. "Of course, I will!" she exclaims as she almost knocks him over with the force of her kiss. They're both laughing when Donovan pulls away from Kasey's lips to slide the ring onto her finger. He cups her face in his hands and whispers, "I love you," before crashing his mouth against hers in a very inappropriate-for-company kiss.

Looking around the table, I see Lindsey nestled into Aiden's side, tears streaming down her face. Abigail is wiping her napkin under her eyes, trying to gain her composure. I want to go to her and hold and kiss her. I want to celebrate my brother and her best friend with her. I want her to lean into me like Lindsey is leaning into Aiden.

Abigail's phone, sitting next to her on the table, lights up with an incoming call. Glancing down, she declines whoever is trying to reach her, and the only visible sign of irritation is the slight clenching of her jaw. If I hadn't been watching her so intently, I would have missed it. She quickly wipes any annoyance from her features as she and Lindsey stand and envelop Kasey in a teary hug. The girls are busy oohing and aahing over the beautiful engagement ring as I pull my brother in for a hard hug.

"Congratulations, brother. I couldn't be more excited for you."

"Aye, mate. Congratulations," Aiden says, pulling Donovan in for a back-slapping hug. "Well deserved."

When the girls have had their fill of crying over their newly engaged sister, we all sit down to eat. Of course, the conversation quickly turns to wedding ideas while the future bride and groom exchange happy, loving glances.

Abigail's phone lights up again, this time with a text notification. The screen flashes 'Mom,' and Abigail flips the phone over.

Huh. I'm not sure what that's about, but I intend to find out.

CHAPTER 7
ABIGAIL

He finally did it. Donovan proposed to Kasey. Honestly, I thought it would have happened right after they moved in together. Donovan has never been the type to not go full force, stopping at nothing to get what he wants. It wouldn't surprise me if the idea of marriage has been floating in his mind since the first time he kissed her. That's how far gone he's been for her since day one.

The celebration continues well into the evening, drinking champagne and dancing until we're winded and have to take a break, then do it all again. The only thing that mars the perfect evening is the phone call and text from my mother. Both started, 'Merry Christmas,' then quickly delved into questioning if I ever planned to respond to Cesily's RSVP. Same as the other voicemails she's been leaving me for the last week.

I'm not about to let my mother's interruption dampen this amazing moment, so I simply turn my phone over and put it out of my mind.

Floating on cloud nine, I make my way upstairs. I'm so damn happy for my friends. We're all exhausted from the excitement and copious amounts of champagne. I caught a few heated glances Jackson threw my way, so I figure I won't be alone in my room for long. There's something magical about this place. I usually never miss an opportunity to verbally spar with the Prince of Darkness, but we've kept it tame these last few days. That certainly doesn't mean I'm about to tell the whole world—or our friends—what we've been getting up to, but it's made for a relaxing trip.

There's a soft knock at my door, and I feel those excited butterflies flutter in my stomach... and lower. For all of our issues outside the bedroom, Jackson and I are pure fire between the sheets. Too bad it can't go any further. Fire this hot is sure to burn out in spectacular fashion, and I don't want to be turned to ash when it happens. Unfortunately, the temptation to touch the fire overrules my determination to stay far away from the handsome devil.

Not waiting for me to answer the soft knock at my door, Jackson quietly slips in and locks the door behind him. We've both had a lot to drink tonight, as evidenced by his lazy, seductive smile as he prowls to my bed.

"Hey, Red," he purrs as he slowly slips the blankets down my waist and over my legs, revealing my naked form. I figured why waste time putting on pajamas when I knew he planned on taking them off tonight.

"Hey, Prince. Fancy meeting you here,"

His eyes peruse my body, and he bites his lower lip as a sinful chuckle escapes him.

"Were you expecting me?" His brow lifts as he watches my thighs rub together in anticipation of his touch.

Instead of answering, I crook my finger, beckoning him.

"I seem to be a bit overdressed for this little meeting." His hands go to his shirt, and he tries to undo the small buttons. His attempt is amusing as he sways on his feet, the alcohol affecting his balance.

I rise to my knees and undo the buttons, giggling at his obvious difficulties. He stops me when I'm halfway done, taking my face in his hands and bringing his lips to mine. When he pulls back, he gazes solemnly into my eyes.

"You're so fucking beautiful, Red. I'm addicted to your mouth."

He kisses me again, and I feel it straight to my toes. This sweet side of him isn't something I'm ever prepared for. I need us in more comfortable territory.

"Gee, Jackson, are you sure you're even going to get it up right now? Whiskey dick is a real thing." I snicker.

His deep chuckle sends a thrill tingling down my spine as he grabs my hand and places it on his long erection.

"Please, She-Devil. Seeing you naked would make even a coma patient hard." He rubs my hand over his length for good measure. "Goddamn, you have the most perfect tits." His hand plumps my breast as his forefinger and thumb twist my nipple. "So responsive," he groans out as he plays, watching my nipple go hard between his fingers.

"You know, coma patients can't open their eyes to see anything," I tell him.

"That fucking mouth, Abigail. Always giving me a hard time." He twists my nipple harder.

I yelp, then let out a soft moan, loving the way he perfectly plays my body.

Distracted by his movements and the erection I'm rubbing, I've stopped unbuttoning his shirt. Growing impatient at his own lack of nakedness, he removes his hand from my breast and rips his shirt open, sending the remaining buttons flying.

"Dramatic much?" A laugh escapes me when I hear a button ting off the lamp on the bedside table.

"You were taking too long." He lifts his shoulder in a small shrug and pushes me back onto the mattress. Crawling over me, he latches onto my nipple, sucking deeply.

"Oh God," I breathe out as my fingers tangle in his hair, holding him to me.

"You can call me Jackson... no need to be formal." His fingers find my drenched clit and softly rub back and forth, but not enough to get me to come. No, that wouldn't be his style. He likes me to beg.

"I'll show you heaven tonight, though," he says between small bites on my breast.

"Seriously, Hayes?" I burst out laughing. "I'm about to revoke your man card with these cheesy as hell lines. Where do you come up with this shit? And who have they ever worked on because I'd like to have a serious conversation with that woman."

Jackson removes his mouth from my breast and laughs with me.

"There she is," he says as he works my clit in slow, torturous circles.

"What do you mean?" I ask as I arch my hips trying to coax him into doing something *more* with his fingers.

"You were tense at dinner. I wanted to make you laugh."

"So, you thought you would do that with your dick?" I look at the ceiling as if pondering the idea. "Seems reasonable," I reply as I nod.

"Wench." He pinches my clit, and I let out a sharp gasp.

"It's rude to play with your food before you eat it, Prince. I'm surprised your mother never taught you that."

"Can we not talk about my mother when I'm about to be balls deep in your perfect pussy."

"You're awfully confident for—"

Plunging two fingers into my drenched channel, he finds that spot inside that curls my toes.

Jackson lifts up and sees the look of pure ecstasy across my face.

"You were saying?" he says in that cocky as hell voice that irritates yet turns me to mush.

Damn him.

His heated gaze goes to where he's pumping in and out of me. His eyes move to mine once again with a wicked gleam in them.

"Time for dessert." He moves down, and his lips latch onto my clit. His tongue lashes furiously as he holds my gaze for a moment before my eyes roll to the back of my head. Riding the wave of pure bliss, I come all over his hand. Holy shit, the man's mouth is lethal in the best way imaginable.

Jackson stands from the bed and strips off his torn shirt and his pants, then bends down to grab a condom from his pocket.

I lean up and take his impressive erection in my hand. "Not bad for a guy with whiskey dick," I quip as I stroke him.

"Why don't you do something else with your mouth instead of giving me shit."

Glancing up, I watch his eyes glaze over as I take him in my mouth and swirl my tongue over the head. He pumps in and out gently a few times before ripping away from me.

"Enough," he hisses. "I need to come in your pussy, not your mouth." He flips me around and pushes my chest to the mattress before smacking my ass.

"Hey," I protest.

"That's what you get for all your shit talk… and this," he says before slamming into me.

I let out a loud moan, so loud that if our friends weren't

asleep, they would have surely heard me down the hall. The sheets are wrapped tightly in my fist as Jackson rails into me at a punishing pace.

"What were you saying about whiskey dick, She-Devil," he pants out.

"Nothing... just fuck me," I cry out.

His knowing chuckle tells me he's well aware of what he does to me and that he can fuck me into silence better than any man before him.

"I need you to come, Red." His hand comes around to play with my sensitive clit again. "I'm so close. Fuck, you feel too good," he moans out.

Between feeling his cock thicken inside me and his magical fingers, I fall apart for the second time tonight, moaning into the mattress. Tightening his hand in my hair, he stills, then I feel his cock jerk inside me as he follows me over the edge.

He leans down and kisses the crown of my head before pulling out and walking to the bathroom. When he returns, I'm lying face down on the mattress, still trying to catch my breath. Lying next to me, he pulls me over him, so I'm partially covering his sweaty chest.

I look up and see his eyes are closed. "What are you doing? You're not sleeping in here, Jackson."

"Relax, Red." He peeks at me through a slightly open eyelid. "I'm just going to lay here for a minute before I fuck you speechless again."

Nodding, I lay my head on his chest, and the sound of his soft breaths and rhythmic heartbeat soon pull me under.

The shrill sound of my phone wakes me from a deep sleep. I'm completely disoriented when I reach for it and answer, not checking the caller ID.

"Hello, Abigail," my mother says.

Shit.

"Hello, Mother, why are you calling so early? Is everything alright?" I ask groggily.

"I thought I would try to reach you before you get busy. It seems you're too busy to talk to me these days, so I figured if I got ahold of you early enough, you would have time to chat."

Wow, not even—I look at the clock—six a.m., and she's already starting in with the guilt trip.

"Yeah, sorry." I rub a hand over my puffy face. "It's been busy around here."

She lets out a noncommittal hum. "I'm calling because I need your answer on whether you can fit your sister's wedding into your busy schedule."

Damn, she's really going for it.

"Mom, I still have to talk to my boss about it. I promise to do that when I get back to the city, okay?" I so do not have the energy to deal with this right now.

"Fine. I expect to hear from you tomorrow then." Before I can tell her I won't be back in the office until next week, she hangs up.

Well, Merry Christmas to you, too.

An arm bands around my middle and I tense. Shit. We fell asleep after round two, and Jackson's still in my bed.

"Good morning," he mumbles sleepily, kissing my bare shoulder.

"You shouldn't be in here," I tell him as I throw my phone back on the nightstand.

"Why was your mom calling so fucking early?" He groans, ignoring my reprimand. Not that it was particularly stern. I think he fucked the fight out of me last night.

"My sister's getting married on Valentine's Day, and I haven't RSVP'd to her wedding," I explain as I lie back down. My head aches something fierce from all the champagne I drank last night.

"Why?" he asks, resting his head on his propped-up hand.

Closing my eyes, I let out a long sigh. "We don't get along." I look at Jackson, and he motions with his hand for me to continue.

"Fine," I huff out. "Cesily is marrying my ex's brother. It was a bad breakup. He cheated, I told him to fuck off, and my family took his side. Every time we were all at the same event, my family would do little things like have us sit next to each other or call him over to include him in conversations, and invite him to all our family functions… little things like that. They wanted us back together. My sister and mother told me that's what men in his position do sometimes and that it was no big deal. He would never actually *be* with those other women, and I should be happy to be the one wearing his ring."

Jackson looks at me with a curious expression, then shakes his head in disgust. "What the actual fuck?"

"Yup," I say, answering his rhetorical question. "The failed matchmaking attempts got so annoying, I told them if they didn't stop, I would leave Charleston. They didn't, so I left."

Laying his head back on his pillow, he looks at the ceiling, trying to process this insight into the unharmonious relationship I have with my family.

"Do you think they'll try again at the wedding?"

"Undoubtedly."

He stares at the ceiling for a moment before a wide smile stretches across his face. Turning his head to me, he says, "Take me."

I draw my brows down, looking into his smiling eyes. "Uh, say what?"

"Take me as your boyfriend." His arm moves to my waist again, and his smile widens. "Show them you're beyond their bullshit matchmaking since you have an amazing boyfriend who dotes on you every chance he gets." He nods. "I'll play the perfect boyfriend for the week, and they'll forget all about the loser who was stupid enough to cheat."

I must still be drunk if I'm considering this, but maybe Jackson is onto something. It would certainly keep my ex away from me, and my mother would never be rude or unwelcoming to someone with Jackson's last name. It would also mean I would have to spend the week with him alone. Lines could get pretty blurry between us without our friends there as buffers.

"I don't know, Prince. Family stuff can be intense. Are you sure you want to put yourself in that situation?"

"I want to keep the smile on your face from last night." He looks at me with kind eyes. "The one that dimmed every time your mother called. She may think your ex was hot shit, but she's never met a Hayes." He gives me a confident smile, followed by that sexy-as-sin signature smirk of his—the one that got me in this mess with him, to begin with.

It would be amazing to have someone in my corner at the wedding. Someone who can serve as a reminder of how far I've come and what an amazing life I've built away from my family and their bullshit.

"Okay then." I cautiously nod, not entirely believing I'm agreeing to this. "Let's do it. You can be my amazing boyfriend for a week."

His smile gets even wider, and he smacks a quick kiss on my mouth before moving down my body.

"What are you doing? You need to leave before everyone wakes up," I hiss.

"I will, but first, I'm going to show how I like to wake up my girlfriends." He shoots me a wicked smile, then throws my leg over his shoulder and takes a long lick up my center.

My back arches at the delicious sensation.

Oh, shit. What have I gotten myself into?

* * *

Thank you for reading Jackson and Abigail's story. I hope you had as much fun reading them as I did writing them. If you want to read their full story, you can check out my website at www.katerandallauthor.com for the link to their book, The Other One, as well as The Good One (Kasey and Donovan) and The Fragile One (Lindsey and Aiden).

Happy Reading!
Xoxo,
Kate

THE CHRISTMAS
PLAYBOOK
KATIE RAE

This is a work of fiction. Names, characters, organizations, places, events, and incidents are products of the author's imagination or are used fictitiously. Any resemblance to actual events, locales, or persons, living or dead, is entirely coincidental.

Copyright @2022 by Katie Rae

No part of this book may be reproduced, stored in a retrieval system, or transmitted in any form or by any means electronic, mechanical, photocopying, recording, or otherwise, without the express written permission of the publisher.

This book is licensed for your personal enjoyment only. This book may not be re-sold or given away to other people.

Cover Design: Ya'll That Graphic

CHAPTER 1

ALI

It had been roughly two months since I stood in front of the world and gave my one and only press conference about my relationship with Cam and Kace. I never wanted to do that again.

After putting on a brave face and all but yelling to the world that I was in love with two men, I crashed. It took days to recover from the adrenaline and the front I had exuded during what should have been a private moment.

I guess that was the price I paid for falling in love with the best athletes the world had ever seen. Cam and Kace were Gods in their sports, and the media focus on their lives was nonstop. That made me a media target as well, since I had captured both of their hearts.

So many articles about me laced the newspaper stands, magazine stands, and all of social media. The words *whore* and *slut* were tossed around so often that it was a miracle I had stayed in one piece.

The guys tried to shield me from it as much as possible.

Sure, we didn't come outright and say, "We are together," but we indicated our truth and despite the backlash, I still had no regrets. Because when it came down to it, no one knew us better than we knew ourselves. We were not a kink or a fetish. We were three people who couldn't live without one another, and chose to love each other despite what people thought was the *correct* way to love.

"Earth to Ali," Kace whispered in my ear from behind me as his soapy hands cupped my breasts. We had decided to run a hot bath after watching Cam's football game on TV, and remained there as we waited for him to join us.

"Cam should be home soon," I moaned as I pushed myself into Kace's hands.

"You miss him?" Kace bit my ear gently and pushed his growing erection into my lower back.

"I always miss him. I feel guilty when I'm not there. I should have just gone to the game. You should have gone to the game."

"Baby, Cam didn't want us to go. Monday night football against New England? The media was everywhere. We aren't going to let them bombard you and trust me, he would rather have me stay with you."

I sighed and leaned my head back on his shoulder, knowing he was right. I had gone to just a few games since Cam was reinstated with the team. When I did go, it was a circus, trying to get Kace and I to a suite without someone wanting us to answer questions.

The guys were still overly protective of me, as well. Not just where the media was concerned, but where my ex —Alan—was concerned. He had been arrested and was in jail, but I still had nightmares and got scared when I was alone. It was like my subconscious would never let go of what he did to me.

"You know what I think?" Kace had humor in his tone, and it made me smile in anticipation of what he was going to say. "I think, when we hear the alarm turn off, and know for sure Cam is home, I should spread you open and make him watch me fuck you just like this."

His fingers dipped between my legs and into my pussy, showing me what he meant. Thoughts of Alan, and guilt from missing Cam's game, quickly washed away, and I giggled at the thought of Cam walking in on us.

He would love it.

As far as our relationship went, we were still testing boundaries where the guys were concerned. I spent a lot of time alone with each of them, but we indulged in us all being together when we could. There were so many times I wanted to ask them for more, but our relationship was still so new. Not to mention, we had battled so much that it didn't feel like it was time to push anymore limits.

However, both guys slept with me every night they were both home. They both kissed me and touched me freely. They took turns with my body, and both got off on watching me with the other. So when I heard the sound of the alarm being turned off, I knew Cam was home and I opened my legs wider for Kace.

He quickly started using two fingers to bring me on the cusp of an orgasm before he slowed down. He was racing Cam, seeing if he could bring me to the brink before Cam ascended the stairs. "Shhh, not yet. Right when he gets upstairs and finds us in his bathtub, then I'll let you come."

He kept strumming me gently, keeping me on edge and close to exploding in his talented hands. His hard cock was still pressing into me, and his mouth was on my ear–his tongue drawing an outline around my helix.

Just as the door to the bathroom eased open, and my eyes locked onto Cam, Kace curled his fingers inside of me and let me fall over the edge. I never closed my eyes, keeping them on Cam so he knew what Kace and I were doing was for him.

Cam quietly walked closer to the bathtub and sat on the edge, leaning down to kiss me as my orgasm started to wane. "I should be able to come home to that every fucking night."

I reached my wet hand up and cupped his jean covered cock. "Get in with us."

Cam's eyebrows shot up and he looked behind me to Kace. They often spoke without saying words, but I had caught on to their thoughts. Cam was asking Kace if that was okay.

Whatever Kace's face said, made Cam stand up and start unbuckling his jeans. He watched us as he shed his clothes and took his watch and shoes off. I knew he had showered after his game but getting clean wasn't what this was about. This bath was about getting dirty, and I wanted both of my guys with me for the night.

CHAPTER 2

CAM

We beat the shit out of New England on Monday Night Football. It should have been a statement game for me, but the interest in my personal life seemed to overshadow every one's care for how I played. Not that I cared what anyone thought, but anything said about Ali sent me into a rage that I didn't know I was capable of before I met her.

She brought out a beast inside of me that had laid dormant until he had something to fight for. It was hard enough trying to navigate a normal relationship, but add in the fact that there were three of us, in the spotlight, and it was a never ending battle.

The three of us had been bouncing between our three homes, but always stayed together. Kace wasn't playing baseball at the moment since it was the offseason, so he and Ali spent a lot of time at his place or hers. But when I was in town, they would come out to my place so I could spend time at home and see them.

That was where I found them after my game–in my home, in my bathtub–and life was damn near perfect. Kace making her come as I walked in was like getting an early Christmas present. He knew exactly what made me happy.

We had been best friends since we were young, but sharing Ali was new territory for us. Through the months of our still fairly new relationship, we got more and more comfortable being intimate with all three of us present. We worked together to make sure her nights were always filled with passion, and took turns filling her body up the way we knew she liked it best.

Kace and I always said to her–and to each other–that whatever she wanted, she could have. She led the way and set the pace between the three of us. All we wanted was her and her happiness.

Which was why I was shedding my jeans and flashing them both with my very hard cock as I got ready to slide into the opposite side of my bathtub. The tub was big enough for three, though I didn't think that was its intention since it was oval shaped. Still, what Ali wanted, Ali got. And after Kace smirked at me with a little nod of approval, I decided that sharing a bathtub with my best friend was worth it if I got to have Ali between my legs.

We had shared everything else, why not bath water?

The only thing I hadn't accounted for was how large Kace and I both were. So as I stepped into the hot water and eased my way down, I realized I would have Kace's feet on either side of my hips.

Ali eyed me with appreciation as I positioned myself in front of them. When I was trying to find a place for my feet, Ali grabbed them and lifted them onto Kace's thighs, leaving my legs open for her to slide between.

Kace didn't move or protest, just leaned back and watched as Ali turned around and leaned back on my chest so that she was facing Kace as well.

"Mmm," she moaned a little, pushing her feet onto Kace's chest. "I think I just found heaven."

Kace eyed me over her shoulder and smiled, not giving a shit that we both were using him as our ottoman. He grabbed Ali's feet and started rubbing them, making her move slightly against my hard dick.

"Miss me?" I whispered into her ear as I reached around to grab her tits into the palm of my hand.

"Always," she purred.

"What did you two do today?" I directed the question to Ali, but my eyes were on Kace's as he smiled, waiting for her answer.

"We discussed your Christmas present." That was an unexpected answer, so I paused all of my movements as I thought about what she said. "It's our first Christmas together, but I'm not really sure what to get the man who has everything."

"Honestly," I huffed. "I assumed that the orgasm Kace just gave you was my present."

I could hear Kace chuckle as I ran my nose along Ali's jaw. "I will think of something special," she continued. "I want our first Christmas to be perfect."

"I have a game on Christmas in Cincinnati, sweetheart. Or did you forget?" Ali didn't go to the away games because of the media attention she got and my lack of ability to make sure she had a safe place to watch the game. I didn't trust anyone in any stadium but our own.

"I know," she sighed, "but you'll come home that night and even though it will be late, I want to share a little Christmas with you two."

"Don't get me anything," I urged. "All I need is you." I then looked up at Kace, who had his head leaned back and his eyes closed while he continued to rub Ali's feet. "Or just be naked in my bed, wearing a bow on each of these tits."

Kace laughed but didn't look up or open his eyes. "I said the same thing. All I need for Christmas are those babies in my mouth."

A shudder ran through Ali at Kace's words, and I eased my hand down her stomach to cup her pussy. "I don't get jealous of Kace very often," I told her. "But the fact that he will always be home for Christmas and I won't be, makes me want to hang my cleats up and live the rest of my life inside your bed, your bath, and your body."

She sat up, her back leaving my chest, and a coolness settled between us as she turned around to face me on her knees. "But I promise to make our Christmas special."

I lifted my hand to her cheek and ran my thumb along her lower lip. "As long as I get to spend it with you two, it will be perfect no matter what."

The glint in her eyes showed me she accepted my words—for now—but that she still wanted to do presents. Kace and I had already decided on what we were getting her, but I was kind of surprised that Kace spent an evening helping her decide what to get me. He and I both didn't expect anything from her.

I looked over her shoulder at Kace, who had lifted his head and was watching Ali and I. The nerves I had felt in the beginning of our relationship still crept up sometimes when he watched us. I think sharing a bath, and my legs being on top of his, was adding to my new level of apprehension.

As if Ali could sense my unease, she grabbed onto my cock and started stroking. Her touch took my mind off Kace immediately, and I tilted my head back to soak in the feeling of her playing with me in the warm water. She gave me solo attention for a few minutes before she shifted a little, drawing my attention back to her movements. She settled in between mine and Kace's legs and reached out to grab his cock as well. He and I both started grunting at the sensation.

I never planned to fall in love with the same woman as Kace, much less share such intimate moments—but they were now my favorite moments. His moans at her hands added to how good it felt–how dirty it felt–and I was lost to the sensation.

CHAPTER 3
KACE

Cam's heels dug into my thighs as he moved his hips under the hot water. He was chasing his orgasm in Ali's hand, and I was going to come right behind him, despite the fact that I may have bruises on my legs when it was all over with.

"Fuck, Ali," he seethed through gritted teeth, making me start jerking my hips in her hand as well.

Our voices were bouncing off the walls of the bathroom, making it feel as though we were creating our own porn video. Even Ali had started moaning despite the fact that we weren't touching her.

I reached up to grab one of her nipples and pinched while Cam simultaneously moved his right leg off of me and in between her legs. She used his calf for friction, rubbing her pussy on him as she stroked us. It was dirty and brazen, and completely sexy since she had no idea what the hell she was doing–just so lost to the need.

There was no way I could hold on any longer. I pushed into her hand, trying to chase as much friction as I could in her tiny hand as I came in the bathwater I shared with them both. I almost lost consciousness as the steam billowed around my face and I sucked in hard to catch my breath.

Then I leaned up and put my hand between her and Cam's leg, letting her concentrate more on his dick and less on her own release. I pushed two fingers inside of her, and I wasn't sure what she did to Cam, but he hissed at the same time.

"Work his cock, babygirl, and let me be the one who takes care of you."

Her pussy clamped around my fingers as I spoke, and my thumb pressed into her clit to help her chase her imminent release. I looked up to Cam, who had wrapped his hand around hers, both holding his dick and stroking together.

As soon as his head tilted back, he took his hand from hers and let her finish him alone as he came in the bathwater the way I had just done. Ali started coming as well, keeping her hand on Cam to ground her as she moved against mine.

It took us a few minutes, but eventually, we all caught our breaths and took stock of the cum floating around the water. "I think we need a shower," I teased, making Ali giggle.

Cam stood first, lifting Ali into his arms and walking toward the shower that sat at the end of the tub. It was glass, and I could see right through it. On more than one occasion, I had sat there in that exact spot and watched Cam and Ali fuck against the tile under the five showerheads that Cam felt like he needed in that extra-large shower.

I usually ended up working my own dick until Ali came to the bath to finish with me. She would bounce on me as the water sloshed around and we were both coming from our connection.

This time, I climbed from our bath and joined her and Cam in the shower. Ali was too spent to fuck around some more, but Cam and I both had our dicks at half-mast by the time we got cleaned and exited the shower.

Ali had made her way from the bathroom first, telling us she needed to head downstairs and get water, but Cam held me back in the bathroom for a minute. He had a sour look on his face and for a second, I thought maybe he was upset about what we all had just done. But that didn't seem likely since we both loved being with Ali, even when the other was around.

"You let her shop for a Christmas present for me?" He pushed my shoulder while I grabbed the toothpaste from the drawer.

"Ow, motherfucker," I smirked. "She wants to do something for you and asked for my help. What did you want me to do, say no? It's her way, Cam. What Ali wants, Ali gets."

"I just don't want her spending money on us. She gave everything she had to Mary's cancer bills, stopped working at the bar, and hasn't written much freelance stuff because she's been so messed up about what happened with Alan. I just don't want her to feel any more pressure."

"I agree." I nodded at him through the mirror. We were both wrapped in towels, and he was standing behind me with his hands on his hips. Our eyes locked and I fought the urge to tell him Ali's secrets. "But it's not like that. She knows you aren't going to be here and has a small gift up her sleeve. No money involved."

"Fuck," Cam breathed a sigh of relief. "I have been so worried about her. I hate that I had to go right back to playing football and haven't been able to be with her as much as I need to be."

"I'm here," I assured him. "And when spring training starts, you will be the one here with her more. And in between those moments, we can all be together. We've got this. We are better together, both being with her, just like you set into motion when this all started."

"I know." He walked up to the second sink and got his own toothbrush ready. We stood in silence, brushing our teeth and casually glancing at each other in the mirror. I tried not to look, but my eyes went down to where his towel was tented. Even talking about Ali made us both so fucking hard.

Cam caught me looking and laughed while he spit into the sink. "I'm going in there and fucking her again. I missed her last night."

I nodded, understanding completely. The night before games, Cam had to stay at the team hotel downtown and couldn't be home. So Ali and I were in his bed alone, curled up and enjoying each other. He wanted that same time with her before he headed right back to practicing all week, and I couldn't say I blamed him.

"You go spend time with her," I agreed. "I'm gonna go eat and then make good on a promise I made to her before you got home."

Cam pulled me a little so I was facing him. "You know I don't care if you're with us."

"I know," I laughed. "But this is all part of our plan. She is going to distract you while I work on some things."

Cam groaned, knowing I was talking about his elusive Christmas present. Then he opened the bathroom door and we both walked toward the bed. Ali walked in from the hallway with a bottle of water in her hand and stopped dead in her tracks.

"You okay?" I tilted my head and asked her, while also looking around at what had her startled.

"I still have to pinch myself when you are both standing naked in front of me."

Cam had dropped his towel and was climbing into bed while I pulled some shorts on and walked toward Ali, who was still in the doorway. "Can you distract him for me? I'm going to make sure that *thing* is done."

I kissed her nose instead of her mouth just so I didn't ruin her bright and beautiful smile. She let me pass her and I shut the door as I headed downstairs, letting them catch up while I took care of business.

CHAPTER 4
ALI

"I made the rest of the calls today," Kace said as he handed me a cup of coffee.

"I love you," I sighed, although I wasn't sure if I was talking to Kace or the coffee. We had spent another day at Cam's house before driving back into the city where Kace and I both lived. Kace checked in at his place before we walked across the park to mine. It was cold out, and all I wanted was a cup of coffee on my couch.

"Cam just texted me and said he was leaving practice early, so he should be here soon."

I took a sip of the coffee he had made for me and then turned my head in his direction. "My dad wants us to come visit for a Christmas dinner. I told him I would definitely go, but I wasn't sure if you and Cam would want to."

"Fuck yeah, we want to go."

My dad had been all too accepting of my two-boyfriend situation, but I'm not sure he realized it wasn't two individual relationships. The three of us were one whole relationship, and I guess Christmas dinner seemed like a good time to tell him that.

"Mary will be there," I added. "She has been staying at Dad's a lot."

Kace smiled over his own coffee and waggled his eyebrows. "I bet she has."

"Ugh," I threw a pillow at him, and he batted it down, laughing. "I do not want to think of my dad and Mary like that."

Mary was once my mother's best friend, before my mom passed away. She was the reason I met Kace and Cam, and I loved her dearly. I was happy that she and my dad found comfort in one another, but that didn't mean I wanted to think about what they may be doing.

"Hey, do you ever think that he may wonder about us?" Kace teased. "Think he knows you practically humped Cam's leg while holding on to both of our dicks?"

I flushed beet red and rolled my eyes. Kace loved pressing my buttons and pushing my limits. He lived for getting me to turn red, telling me it was a sexy shade on my cheeks, even at the expense of my sanity.

"Kaaaace," I groaned. "Please don't make me think of my dad, and what happened the other night, at the same time."

His laugh made it all worth it, though. He threw his head back and I could see his body shaking from how hard he was laughing. That was something we all did more and more of–laugh.

The key in the door made me turn my head and Cam started walking in with a big smile on his face. He dropped his bag and took his shoes off, then locked the door up tight. Even though Alan was in jail, we still locked my apartment every time we were there. We never wanted to run the risk of him getting out and coming back.

I didn't move, since I had my coffee in my hand, but

Cam walked in and sat behind me, circling me in his arms. "How was your day?"

"Better now." I leaned back to kiss his jaw as he nodded at Kace.

"You?"

"Good," Kace lifted his own coffee to his lips. "Got a workout in…"

I zoned out as they talked about their practices and workouts. Kace always told Cam what he worked on and with who, and Cam always told Kace how his practice went. I listened sometimes, but I mostly just basked in being between them. Their friendship was stronger than ever, and never waned. It was magic watching them together. It still amazed me that I had been brought into their circle and loved as much as they loved each other.

"What are you thinking, Babygirl?" Kace squeezed my calf that was resting next to his leg on the couch.

"Just how lucky I am," I sighed.

"Did you hear what Cam said?" He nodded behind me to look at Cam.

"No, what?"

"I don't have practice the rest of the week." Cam smiled. "I fly out Saturday, so aside from having to study the playbook for this week, we have two days to do whatever you want."

"Playbook?"

"The book that has all our plays in it. Everything we have done in the past that worked, plays we want to run in the future, and when would be a good time to utilize those plays."

"Geez, I thought you just showed up and threw the ball," I joked.

Cam grabbed my cheeks and shook my head playfully.

"Ha, ha! Okay, focus. What do you want to do for the next two days?"

"All three of us?"

"Of course," they both said at the same time.

I knew exactly what I wanted to do, but I didn't know if the guys would be on board. I bit my lip and leaned up so I could turn and look back and forth at both of them.

After a minute, they both laughed, and Cam pulled me back into his chest. "What is that sexy brain thinking?"

"I want to decorate for Christmas," I blurted. "I know you both mentioned that you never bothered because you spent Christmas with your families, but I feel like I want the joy of Christmas wherever we are."

"I'm on board with that," Kace nodded. "At Cam's, since his house is all picturesque and perfect?"

We had already decided we would be spending Christmas night at Cam's. He wasn't going to be there because of his game but we wanted to be there when he got home.

"All of our places, that way no matter where we are at, there are lights and Christmas cheer."

Both guys just stared at me with blank faces, but their smiles slowly formed. I knew I sounded like a kid with sparkles in her eyes, but they made me want to paint the town in red and green. They made me want to celebrate in a large way.

Like a family.

Maybe that was what it was all about. I had found my own family with them, and it was natural to want to start new traditions with the ones you loved.

"That's a good idea," Kace confirmed. "Tomorrow we can go get decorations and use Cam's truck to go from place to place."

"Or," Cam's voice was serious and I could feel him

tense behind me. "We could all just live together in one place."

It had crossed my mind on more than one occasion that the way we bounced from each of our places wasn't sustainable. But moving in together seemed too soon, didn't it?

My eyes widened at his words, but only Kace could see me. His smile told me he was on board, and all I had to do was say the word.

"I don't want to give up my grandma's apartment," I blurted my first worry. Grandma left me my tiny apartment and it was a sacred place for me.

"We don't have to get rid of any of our places," Kace pulled me across the couch and into his arms. "This apartment isn't big enough for us all, but we could always turn it into your office. Or a crash pad for after our games here in the city."

"You're serious?"

"Of course I am." Kace nodded toward Cam and added, "He is too."

"Do you ever see this ending?" Cam asked me as I looked into his eyes.

"No," I said quickly. I never saw an end to what we had. I would die without them in my life.

"You planned a Christmas surprise for Cam," Kace whispered. "Let this be *my* present. You, me, and Cam...all together."

"Oh my God," I breathed while also nodding. "Let's do it."

"My place," Cam confirmed. "It has everything we need to be a family together. We will keep yours and Kace's apartments too."

Tears sprang in my eyes as reality was hitting me. We were forever.

CHAPTER 5

CAM

Just like that, we spent my two days off decorating my house full of Christmas and moving most of Kace and Ali's things into my house. The big things stayed where they were, but between them both, I was going to need more closet space.

We..we were going to need more closet space.

My house was no longer *my* house, it was ours. I bought that house hoping to one day have a family to share it with, and while my family may not look the way I imagined, it was better.

Excitement and peace ran through me as I imagined them always being home with me, never having to worry whose house to go to or where they would be when I got home from games.

Ali was dragging us through a store for Christmas stockings, something we forgot on our first trip to get decorations. The store she chose was a busy department store in the mall, and on a Friday night, a couple weeks before Christmas, the mall was the last place I wanted to be.

She told us she knew which ones she wanted and could just run in and get them, but we would never let her go in alone. So we donned our hoodies and a hat, and followed her into the large store.

Ali went straight to the stockings and started looking for one labeled with an A, a K, and a C. She was moving quickly, and I felt good about getting what we needed and leaving.

"An A," she squealed with excitement and handed it to Kace before turning back to the stack for more.

Normally, we would have ordered most of this to avoid the stores, but Ali wanted it done before I left, and I caved, knowing how important it was to her to make me happy. She knew traveling away from them, especially when we were making so many major decisions, was hard on me.

"K!" she squealed again and handed another stocking to Kace.

His face mirrored mine—a huge smile because of her excitement. But we were distracted and let our guard down for just a minute. That was when all hell broke loose.

"Cam Nichols?" I heard a woman scream.

Before I could look up, I had a strange woman in my arms hugging me and begging me for a picture with her. Kace tried slipping away to keep from being noticed as well, but when I looked at him, so did the fan, and she screamed his name as well. "Kace Jackson?"

Everyone in the store probably heard her scream and we were immediately surrounded by people asking for pictures and autographs. My eyes scanned for Ali, wanting to make sure she was okay, but she was nowhere to be found.

Panic settled into my stomach. Had she not been kidnapped a few months ago, maybe I would have been more at ease, but it was still ingrained in me to worry about her and protect her. I yelled for Kace to get his attention, but it was pointless since he was being mobbed as well. He couldn't hear me, nor could he move, but I could tell he was also looking around for her.

I wanted to yell for her, but calling her name out loud seemed like a bad idea. Maybe she had snuck off to avoid what Kace and I were being bombarded with. We both signed autographs for a minute, smiled, and took pictures. We talked about how we were there to shop for Christmas just like they were, and people gasped at the idea of us doing our own shopping.

Fair enough.

When I looked up again, I saw Ali waving her hands to get our attention. Kace noticed her as well and she pointed toward the exit with a huge smile on her face. Did she think this was funny?

I guess in a way, it was, now that we knew she was safe.

A few more autographs were signed, and I grabbed Kace away from a woman who was rubbing her tits on his arm. Kace used to love that kind of attention from fans, but I could see the clear discomfort on his face now that he had found Ali. Ali's tits were the only ones he wanted that close to him.

"We gotta go," I said loud enough that everyone could hear.

Kace turned into me, and I wrapped my arm over his shoulder, guiding him to the door. Once he got away from the lady with the tits, he stood straighter and took the lead. He pulled my arm and together we ran toward the exit.

When we pushed through the doors, my truck magically appeared and we dove into the backseat like Olympians on the high dive. Thank God I had asked Ali to hold my keys in her bag.

"You two are always causing a scene," she laughed as she drove my truck out of the parking lot.

"I was just thankful you snatched those stockings from my hands and bailed." Kace was breathing hard, still catching his breath from our sudden sprint. How were we world class athletes and that out of breath?

Adrenaline?

"I found the C right when I heard your name being yelled, so I went to the checkout counter while it was all clear."

"You…?" I started laughing and couldn't even finish my thought. "You took the time to check out?"

"We went through a lot of effort to get these stockings before you left." She lifted the bag that was in the front seat to show us her purchase. "I wasn't leaving until I had them. Plus, you two made the long lines disappear and I checked out in a snap, so thank you for that."

My phone started buzzing in my pocket and I pulled it out to see that I was being tagged in several pictures. Kace was looking at his phone as well, so I knew he was getting the same notifications.

I rarely looked at the pictures I was tagged in, but since Ali was driving and I was content, I scrolled to see the pictures we had just taken. I sat up quickly and started laughing, pushing my phone to Kace for him to look at what had me rolling.

"Oh shit," Kace laughed and put my phone in front of Ali for her to see. Ali just nodded, like she knew exactly what we were looking at and smiled, satisfied with herself.

When I got my phone back, I looked once again at the picture of me and the first fan that called my name. In the background was Ali, intentionally photobombing the picture. She was holding the stocking with the C on it high in the air and covering her face just enough that no one else would know who she was.

Her face had become well known since our united press

conference, and even though we knew she would be in the media more, as time went on, we still all agreed to block her face when able—especially until Alan was sentenced.

The original poster of the picture didn't even mention her in the background, but to Kace and I, it was obvious she was there and happy with her stockings.

"I cannot believe you photobombed that poor woman," I laughed again.

"She bombarded my shopping trip with my boyfriends. Fair is fair."

"But next time, let's just order those online."

CHAPTER 6
KACE

Ali jumped around the room, happy her plan was coming together. I winked at her while she checked something off in her red, glittery book with the Christmas tree on it. Somehow, I was both helping her with this project, and being hidden from it as well.

Ali closed her book with a snap and jumped into my arms. "Cam is going to be so excited."

"I just think it's amazing that you are arranging all this for him."

"It's our first Christmas together, and even though I know he is being all 'tough football player man', I know he's bummed he'll be out of town."

I nodded as I ran my fingers through her hair. We had a fire in the fireplace as we waited for Cam to come in from his game. It was an out-of-town game, two weeks before Christmas, so it was going to be late. But that was what Ali and I did, we waited for Cam.

We must have fallen asleep because before I knew it, Cam was reaching down and picking Ali up into his arms while kicking my leg. "Let's go to bed."

I mumbled and looked for the clock, wondering how

long I had been out. The fire had burnt down, and the only light was the lamp next to the couch. Cam was walking toward the stairs with Ali cradled against him. He kissed her head and whispered something to her before stopping five steps up and looking over the railing down where I sat.

"Bed. Now," he demanded.

I shook the remaining cobwebs from my tired brain and turned the lamp off before climbing up the stairs behind them. Cam laid Ali down in the center of our bed and I immediately pulled myself into the covers behind her.

Cam looked down at us as he started to undress. It wasn't sexual, but it was intense. Cam had no intention of fooling around with a sleeping Ali, but he was anxious for us all to be in bed together. His eyes locked with mine after he pulled his shirt over his head and tossed it to the ground.

He didn't have to say anything, but I knew something had happened. He climbed into bed in front of Ali and kissed her forehead again. Ali had been going a million miles per hour, trying to make sure Christmas was perfect, so she was exhausted. She didn't even budge when I lifted my head up and rested my chin into my hand.

"You okay?"

"No," Cam admitted freely. "Every time we lose, people ask if I'm distracted by my personal life. I'm assuming you and Ali didn't watch the post-game interviews."

"No, we turned it off." I winced.

"Good," he sighed. "She doesn't need to hear all that bullshit."

Taking my hand from my chin, I reached over the top of where Ali's head rested on the pillow and squeezed Cam's shoulder. His eyes were closed, and he was taking deep breaths, trying to cool his anger. I laid my head onto my bicep and closed my eyes as well, keeping my hand on

Cam and hoping he could get some rest. He was safe now—home with us—and he would feel better once he had some sleep.

* * *

I woke up to moaning and grunting. Before I even opened my eyes, I knew Cam and Ali were making up for lost time next to me.

Reaching out, I cupped Ali's breast to let her know I was awake, but kept my eyes closed and listened to them as I attempted to drift back to sleep. Her hand came up to squeeze mine and held onto me as Cam thrust himself in and out of her body. It was still dark outside, so I knew it was early—too early to be awake.

I also knew once Ali stirred enough to realize Cam was home, she probably pulled him on top of her and begged for his dick. She hated when he was away for games, and my stomach twisted, thinking of how much more often I would be away when baseball season started.

We had to make the most of the times we had together.

As if sensing my thoughts, her hand left mine and came to my chest. Her nails scraped down my pecs and caused me to groan. I kept one hand on her tit and took my free hand down into my shorts to grasp my cock. I stroked myself a few times before I allowed myself to fully give in and lower my shorts.

Ali's nails sunk deeper, leaving marks across the tattoos on my chest. I knew she wanted me to turn over and kiss her, maybe even allow her to stroke my cock for me. But there was a part of me that enjoyed getting myself off to them fucking next to me.

I didn't waste time or let the feelings linger. Cum

poured from my dick, coating my chest as well as Ali's hand.

"He couldn't resist," I heard Cam grunt into Ali's ear. "He loves seeing you like this."

I grabbed Ali's hand, that still rested on my chest, and squeezed her fingers as Cam pushed her over the edge. She screamed his name and he came right behind her, while I slid out of the bed and snuck to the bathroom.

As I washed my hands, I could hear them settling into the afterglow. Whispered words, small moans, and Ali's satisfied giggle made me smile as I looked at my reflection. I looked happy, content, and nothing like the man I was at Christmas the year before.

I skipped out on festivities last year, not even making it to my parents' house for Christmas dinner. Nor did I visit with Cam's family, even though I had been invited. Cam had a game out of town, much like this year, and I was too busy chasing random pussy in a warm climate to care about celebrating the holidays.

Now I was helping the girl of my dreams create the perfect Christmas for my best friend–and me. And to top it off, I was excited about the whole thing.

After getting a warm rag ready, I walked into the bedroom again and tossed it to Cam, who I knew made a mess of our fucking sheets. He caught it in the air while Ali nuzzled her nose on his cheek.

"Where you going?" Cam barked at me as I opened the bedroom door.

"Water," I yelled back without looking at him.

"Bring me some."

"Lazy ass motherfucker," I mumbled, loud enough for him to hear. I could hear his laugh and I smiled as I made my way down the stairs.

Grabbing a bottle from the cabinet, I placed it under the

water reservoir on the fridge and let it fill while I grabbed my phone from my pocket. Curiosity was getting to me, so I pulled up Cam's interview from after the game and watched while I had a second to myself.

"Would you say your personal life is too complicated for you to concentrate on football?" he was asked.

"My personal life has nothing to do with football," Cam scoffed at the interviewer.

"But it is safe to say that since you and Kace Jackson…"

"My personal life has nothing to do with football," Cam repeated, cutting the interviewer off after he said my name.

Another interviewer popped up with a question and Cam looked her way. *"So Cam Nichols is off the market?"*

His eyes squinted and he tilted his head to look at her. She was behind the camera that pointed at his face, so I had no idea what she looked like, but I knew the face Cam gave her. It was the look he gave me when he got home that night.

Utter astonishment.

"And so is Kace Jackson," he finally replied, making my eyebrows shoot up to my forehead.

CHAPTER 7

CAM

Kace jumped when he heard the words I said in my interview, causing water to spill out over the top of the bottle he was filling.

"Fuck," he whispered, grabbing a towel and throwing it on the small puddle on the ground.

"So either I just admitted we are both with Ali, or I insinuated you and I are a couple." I spoke to let him know I was there.

"Damnit," he whispered again, moving the towel with his foot to a new spill. "I was just kidding about you being lazy, I was gonna bring you water."

I leaned on the counter behind me, propping my hands on the edge, and leaned back. "You took too long."

That wasn't true. Ali fell asleep the second I took the warm cloth to her body, so I decided to check on Kace.

"Sorry," he grimaced, knowing I came in while he was watching the interview. "I got curious."

"How bad did I fuck up?"

"You didn't." Kace shook his head and leaned on the counter next to me. "I don't give a fuck."

"I don't either." I defended myself even though I didn't

have to. Kace knew we only cared about how any of this affected Ali.

"She's okay," he whispered. "She's just about ready to face the world. Let's get through Christmas and give her that before we turn her world upside down with ours."

Two more games, I thought to myself. Two more games and Christmas would be over, and we could start our new year together. At least I was home until the day before Christmas. We were going to go see Ali's dad, Philip, and Mary. Philip lived about two hours away, so it was going to be an all-day event on my only day off. That meant I wouldn't see my own family for our Christmas party, but my mom seemed understanding.

In fact, my parents seemed way too understanding when it came to my relationship with Ali and Kace. Mom was wary at first, but she took to Ali quickly—and she already loved Kace. She thought what we had was unorthodox, and I guess it was, but she also saw how happy it made me.

I wished I could share my family Christmas with Ali, but it seemed like something that would never happen. Not when there were three of us, with three different families. We would always be forced to choose, and that was if I even got to be around at all. Next year could be totally different.

A twinge of jealousy shook my body as I stood quietly in the kitchen. Kace was lost in his own thoughts, but he noticed my change and nudged me.

"What's up?"

I had never been jealous of Kace and Ali, because I always knew I got to share the same things with her as well. I knew she loved me just as much as she loved him, but for the first time, it almost didn't feel like enough.

"I'm jealous," I admitted. "I found something I love

more than football and I'm jealous I can't spend our first Christmas with her the same way you can."

"Man," Kace sighed, "I get it, because I think of all the things I'll miss all summer while I'm playing ball. I'll be off in Milwaukee and you two will be laying on a beach somewhere in Aruba."

"She won't vacation without you."

"She won't have Christmas without you," he responded back adamantly.

"Fuck," I laughed and shoved off the counter. "I sound like a pussy."

"You are," Kace laughed with me. "We both are. Ali has turned us into two fucking pussies... I fucking love it."

When the laughter died down, we caught each other's eye. We faced one another for a beat, straight faced and serious. It was intimate in a way, with the lights dim and the sounds of our heavy breathing being the only noise.

I had never been sexually attracted to Kace, or any man for that matter. But the intimacy he and I shared with Ali had caused us to care for one another on a deeper level than we ever had before.

We didn't talk about it, but we knew it was there.

Maybe not the same love we had for Ali, but something more than just friends. It was undefinable, and made me feel both weak and strong at the same time.

"Back to bed?" Kace's husky voice broke the silence.

I nodded and turned around to head back toward the stairs, feeling Kace behind me the whole time. When we got to the top and I started to open the bedroom door, Kace stopped me and turned me around to face him again.

There was no light and I could barely see him, but I felt his arms come around me and pull me into a hug. "Remember when you told me to tell them whatever I wanted?"

"Yeah." I could barely get the word out because the reminder of the time Kace was the one facing the media was still too fresh. It hurt, remembering Ali being gone and the world wanting to know more and more about us. I told him to say whatever he wanted, that I would have his back.

"It's your turn," he said so low I barely heard him. "Say whatever you need to, you know I will have your back."

"Thanks, brother." I squeezed him in a bear hug, letting him know I understood.

He didn't want me coming home worried about what I said, he wanted me to say whatever I needed to say to survive. Media storms were relentless, and I couldn't just hide away. The second I was back with my team, nearly two months ago, it had been nonstop for me. And if we won on Christmas Day, we would clinch a spot in the playoffs, and that meant it would go on even longer.

A part of me wanted to throw the game and make it all end for a while, but I knew I would never do that. I wouldn't do that to my team or my coach. I wouldn't even do that to myself.

"Christmas Day," I whispered as we broke our hug. "It will be better after Christmas Day."

By then, I wouldn't be so pissed about not being home. I would be past the family Christmas party that I am missing and past the pressure to make the playoffs. Not to mention, the moments I spent at home were like a recharging process. I would soak them in and be ready for another day.

Our house was decorated with silver and gold. We had stockings hanging over the fireplace and a tree with bright white lights. Presents scattered the blanket that was wrapped around the base of the tree and the smell of fresh cookies were in the air.

I was dressed in slacks and a button up shirt that I kept open at the collar. I stood with a glass of whiskey dangling from my hand as I looked at everything in the living room. It was daylight out, so the ambiance was subdued, but my thoughts were drifting to the night before when Kace and I took turns making love to Ali while the fire burned and the lights twinkled.

All week, I had been practicing, but with a home game on Sunday, we got Friday off. As soon as Ali was ready, we were going to head to her dad's house to have our first family Christmas gathering. Some part of me was glad it was with Ali's dad, because he had been more than welcoming of Kace and I into Ali's life.

All he cared about was that Ali was loved, and he knew we both loved her. I knew his home would be a safe place for us to be ourselves and I was looking forward to doing something outside of our bubble we had created in our home.

"Ali said the two green ones are for her dad and Mary," Kace mumbled as he passed by me and headed to the kitchen.

I squatted down and retrieved the green presents from the tree and placed them next to the box of cookies Ali had made. Kace quickly returned from the kitchen holding clear tape and scissors as he once again passed by me.

He quickly made his way up the stairs and yelled, "Pour me one," as he got to the top. I did as he asked and within minutes, I heard his footsteps coming down the stairs again.

"You okay?" I laughed.

Grabbing the scotch I poured for him, he took a sip and smirked. "Just doing my lady's bidding."

"What is she doing up there?"

He shrugged. "She's not letting me in on all her secrets."

"I'm ready!" Ali bounced down the stairs with excitement and looked at us dressed up for the day with her dad. "You guys look good in everything. It's not fair."

Settling my empty glass down on the coffee table, I walked toward her and grabbed her into my arms. "What's not fair is that you are wearing that dress and we can't even take it off of you."

"Yet," Kace interjected.

He had a point–we couldn't take it off of her *yet*–but we would. It wasn't the fanciest dress, as her dad wanted to keep things casual, but it hugged her body, showed her legs, and gave me a peek at just enough of her tits that my mouth was salivating. She had a sweater on, and would need a bigger jacket when she was outside, but the thought of the cold air making her nipples pebble under the thin fabric was making the plan to go to her father's house seem like the dumbest idea in the world.

For Philip, that dress may be casual and innocent, but to me—and probably Kace—it was enticing and sexual. Fuck, I wanted her so bad. It was like I was never going to get my fill of Ali Hansen. I was going to burn for her for as long as I lived.

CHAPTER 8

ALI

So many things to do and so little time.

I knew I was trying too hard to make it all perfect, that my sanity was close to faltering, but I couldn't help myself. It had been way too long since I had looked forward to Christmas.

"Fucking hell," I heard Mary shouting from behind the door. We stood on the porch to my dad's house, which was also my childhood home. The guys had yet to go there and see where I was from and how I grew up, and a part of me was nervous just because of what their opinions would be.

Not that Dad's house was a dump, but it was meager, and a lot of the work that needed to be done to keep up with a home was no longer something Dad bothered with—although the poinsettias that sat on either side of the front door were a nice touch.

"Why did you knock?" Mary asked as she opened the door wide. She didn't bother with pleasantries and didn't try being someone she wasn't. Mary was a hard-nosed woman, with a mouth that would put a sailor to shame. Her and Dad were like night and day, so it made me giggle every time I thought about how close they had become.

"The door was locked." I moved to hug her and she gave in, wrapping an arm around me and swaying me back and forth.

"I fucking know that," she spoke into my ear as she continued to hug me. "But don't you have a key?"

Pulling back, I looked down at her and shrugged. "Kace drove, so I left my keys at home."

Hearing his name was just enough to make her look behind me and see my guys standing there watching us. Mary's eyes started to twinkle, and she moved around me to get to them.

"My babies! My lying, good for nothing, can't-throw-the-ball-to-the-wide-receiver-if-his-life-depended-on-it babies!"

"Mary," Cam leaned in for a hug that Mary returned with no problem. "I see you have been watching me play. Thanks for the support."

I could hear the teasing tone in Cam's voice and the smile in his eyes. He knew Mary never minced words. and he was professional enough to know there was truth behind what she was saying.

"Hey," Kace called out. "I'll have you know, I haven't missed one throw to a wide receiver yet this year."

"Your time is coming." Mary let go of Cam and turned to hug Kace. "Once baseball season starts, I'm sure you'll find something to suck at too."

"Aw Mary," Kace laughed. "You sure do make the holidays a warm and special time of year."

Her laughter was infectious as she led us into the kitchen, where my dad was stationed over a huge turkey.

"Dad!" I squealed. I kissed his cheek and settled for a side hug, since his hands were covered in seasoning. "You need a hand?"

"Nonsense," he huffed, and looked behind me. "Good to see you boys."

"Good to see you too, Philip," Kace said at the same time Cam replied with, "Glad to be here."

"Go ahead to the table. Mary and I will serve up dinner. It's ready and warm."

Dinner ended up being amazing. I had almost forgotten how good of a cook my dad was. He didn't make the effort much, but I wondered if that had changed now that Mary was with him. Having someone to cook for was much better than preparing a meal for one. I knew exactly how that felt.

Afterward, we sat in the living room with coffee and the cookies I had brought, admiring the tree that Mary and Dad had put up. It was a mixture of old ornaments and ones I had never seen before. It suited them and made me smile.

We also exchanged gifts, giving each other simple and meaningful gifts like we did all the years before. Dad looked relieved and I assumed he thought with Cam and Kace's money, I would be more extravagant. But that wasn't who he was, and I didn't want to change our special traditions.

Then we broke down and told Dad and Mary how we all three moved in together. Neither of them were surprised since they knew we were all practically together every night anyway. I would even go as far as to say Dad looked relieved. Cam's house was safer than my apartment and just like I did, Dad often thought about what happened to me with Alan.

The night ended before I was ready, but we still had a two-hour drive back to Atlanta. Hugging my dad tightly, I promised to visit again after the new year, and he promised to come into town before Kace had to report to spring training. That way, we could host them for dinner and show them our house.

* * *

I sat in the backseat on the way home, wanting to rest while Cam and Kace talked about sports and whatever else they talked about. It wasn't long before my eyes started to close, and their voices started to fade. But before I fell asleep completely, I heard Kace in the passenger seat speaking to Cam, who opted to drive home.

"She's out," he whispered.

"Good," Cam spoke softly back.

"She wants to go to the game on Sunday."

"I'll call Benny and let him know." Benny was Cam's contact with the front offices ,who helped him arrange a suite for us when we came.

There was a small beat of silence before I heard Cam speak again. "Love you," he whispered.

"Love you too, bro."

I was no longer able to doze completely off, but I kept my eyes closed as tears leaked and ran down my cheek.

For some reason, they rarely let me see those moments between them. When I was around, they told me how much they loved me, but hardly ever each other. I knew they were feeling it more and more with the holidays close and us moving in together. Hearing them made me emotional, though. Not with fear, but happiness.

Cam and Kace were both so complex. Protective, strong, and fierce while also vulnerable, passionate, and tender. I knew a lot of that began when I joined the picture. They started feeling things and doing things they never had before, and it's all been a whirlwind.

I knew deep down that I had only added to their lives,

but hearing that their bond was still strong for myself was something I needed every once in a while. It didn't always have to be about just me and one of them. Our relationship was also about the two of them and what they meant to one another.

"Baby? You okay?" I heard Kace ask, then felt his hand rub my knee.

I opened my eyes, letting the pool of tears that were behind my lids flow freely. Kace was turned around, reaching as far as he could to keep his hand on me from his seat. "I just love you two."

Kace smiled sheepishly, realizing I had heard him and Cam. "We love you, too. Almost home, babygirl."

I nodded and took Kace's hand, stroking his index figure gently as if it was his cock. His eyes widened and he licked his lips, catching on to my need for him. "Step on it," he grunted to Cam.

Cam's laugh was the only indication that he heard Kace or even knew why he said it. But he did as he was told and hurried through town to get us home as soon as possible.

Once we were through the gate, Cam pulled into the garage and hopped out of the car quickly. He opened my door and pulled me into his arms, carrying me as Kace opened the doors ahead of us.

Instead of heading to the bedroom, he placed me gently on the floor near the Christmas tree that sat right next to the fireplace. Kace started a fire with the click of a button, while Cam made sure the Christmas lights were turned on the tree.

The ambiance was romantic, and I was once again on the verge of tears from pure happiness. I leaned back on my hands with my knees up, waiting for them to join me and thinking of how lucky I was.

Cam finally sat next to me and started opening a bottle

of champagne as Kace crawled from the fireplace to where I was sitting. With his hands on my knees, he spread my legs and inched his way between them, getting as close as he possibly could to me.

We all held onto the flute of champagne that Cam poured us and even though I felt kind of silly doing so, I lifted my glass to make a small toast. "To us," I blushed. "To the love we all share, to the holidays for making these moments extra special, and to a future where we no longer care or worry about what others may think."

I could hear Cam grunt his appreciation to the last part since he was the one facing "everyone". Kace smiled and winked at me as we all three brought our glasses together. Cam lifted the remote that practically controlled the whole house and hit a button that started soft Christmas music. Not traditional songs, but a symphony that created a sensual holiday tune.

When my champagne was half gone, Kace took the glass from my hand and set it aside with his. He gently found my lips and pulled me onto his lap. The heat from the fireplace was more prominent on my arms as I wrapped them around his neck. But that heat paled in comparison to the burn I felt when Cam's lips found my neck from behind me.

In the beginning, the three of us navigated these moments differently, unsure of how to be intimate when there were three of us. But in the last few weeks, it seemed to be coming more and more natural, no longer hesitating or questioning where we should be or what we should be doing.

Cam's hands crept around to the front of my dress and tugged my breasts free from the top. He started kneading and rubbing, making me moan into Kace's mouth.

"Suck her tits," Cam commanded.

Kace pulled back and took his direction, lowering his mouth to my nipples and biting gently before taking me all the way in his mouth. He sucked hard, going from one to the other as Cam held them up for him. Kace's hands rubbed up and down my legs at the same time, causing goosebumps to form on my skin.

I started to shake, almost sure I was going to come without them even touching my pussy. I started unconsciously humping the air between Kace and I, hoping I could find his body for friction. Instead, he held my hips in place and forced me to be still as they both continued to pleasure my body.

My hand went behind me, searching for Cam's neck. I needed something to hold on to, and some way to bring him even closer to my body.

"I'm right here." He dropped my breasts, causing Kace's mouth to pop off and wrapped me into a hug from behind. "I got you."

Kace widened my legs and hooked his finger into the lace of my underwear. "So wet."

"Let me watch him make you come again," Cam whispered. "Let him…"

CHAPTER 9

KACE

Cam was holding Ali between his legs as we all three sat on the floor by the fire. Her back was against his chest, and I could see both of them staring at me.

Cam nodded at me slightly, and I knew what he wanted before he even said the words.

"Let me watch him make you come again," Cam whispered. "Let him…"

The phone rang, startling Ali from her lustful daze. Her head started swiveling around, as if she wasn't even sure where the noise was coming from or what it was. I started to tell her to ignore it, that whoever it was didn't matter. I could tell Cam was thinking the same thing. But I also realized it was almost midnight, and that no one called that late unless it was important.

Cam helped Ali up and they went in search of her ringing phone while I waited in place, hoping she returned quickly.

"I forgot to call my dad when we got home, you know he worries," she spoke frantically as she pulled her bag from the floor and started pulling out the phone.

"Hello?" She answered, without even looking at the screen. "I was gonna…"

Cam was casually walking back to where I was when he stopped and turned to face Ali again. She had stopped speaking mid-sentence and her face was pale. Her mouth was hung open, her eyes were huge, and right when I started to stand up so I could go to her, the phone dropped from her hand and shattered on the floor.

Cam was closer, so he got to her before I could, but I joined them and we both stood in front of her, willing her to tell us what had just happened. Just like we always did, we built a wall with our bodies, shielding her, and making her feel safe.

"Who was that?" Cam asked.

"Is your dad all right?" I pressed, needing to know.

"It was Alan," she croaked. "He called to wish me a Merry Christmas."

Just hearing her abusive ex's name made my fists clench, and a need to destroy something took over my body. Cam grabbed my wrist, grounding me, while also taking his other hand to Ali's face.

"Where was he calling from?"

"I don't know." Her face was pale, and it looked like she had seen a ghost.

"He's still in jail," I promised her. "I'll call Rick right now and make him make sure of it, but he would have told us if he was released."

Cam let my arm go, knowing that once I had a mission, I was safe from destroying the walls. I grabbed my phone from the coffee table in the living room and pressed Rick's name. Within minutes, he was able to confirm that Alan Berkman was still in jail, and had been given three phone calls for Christmas.

Ali was his first and only call.

"He won't call you again," I guaranteed. Rick was now making all the moves he needed to make to get Alan's phone privileges revoked–and a higher penalty for calling his victim.

"I'm okay," Ali nodded, almost to assure Cam and I more than herself. While I had been on the phone, Cam had moved her to the couch and was holding her in his lap. I sat beside them and took her hand.

"What did he say?" It was entirely selfish, asking her to repeat his words, but I wanted to know how much of his face I was going to tear off once I saw him again.

"He said 'Merry Christmas, you little whore'. I dropped the phone after that." Tears were in her eyes, and I took my thumb to the top of her cheek to catch them when they fell.

Cam and I both stayed quiet, unsure of what to say. We all knew it was a stab at not only his hatred toward her–and us–but also the fact that he knew she was with us both. In his eyes, that made her a whore, and it was that general consensus that kept Cam's lips sealed when he faced the media.

There was no way to explain how much love we all shared to the world. To an outsider, our relationship would be deemed nothing more than depravity.

Not to mention, Cam and I both knew the amount of female attention we created. We were "Atlanta's Most Eligible Bachelors" and women flocked to us, craving our attention and interest. There were already blogs and articles posted about Ali. How unfair it was, how it made her a piece of trash, and what a slut it made her, were just some of the articles I saw.

She said they didn't bother her, and I believed her. But it bothered Cam and I. We were defensive of her, wanting everyone to understand what we were and knowing that would never happen.

"Can you guys give me a minute?" she asked, standing from Cam's lap and walking toward the stairs.

"Of course."

"We'll be up in a minute."

Once we heard the door shut, I looked back toward Cam, who was shaking his knee, trying to keep his anger in check.

"I want to kill him," he murmured, his eyes staring at the fire. "I would literally spend the rest of my life in jail to keep that bastard out of her life."

"Yeah, me too," I crossed my arms and leaned back on the couch, also staring at the fire.

"I say we send him a Christmas present. Maybe a list of all the ways we can kick his ass."

I huffed a little, wanting to laugh, but also too far gone to see Cam's idea as anything but efficient.

"Let Rick take care of it this time, but if he so much as breathes her name again and we catch wind of it, I say we pay him a visit."

"Deal." Cam wiped a hand over his face and sat up a little. "Let's get upstairs."

"She asked for a minute alone."

"She's had a minute," he stood and waited for me to stand with him. "Now let's go make her forget the name *Alan*."

CHAPTER 10

CAM

I glanced up at the suite I had Kace and Ali in, and saw my sister waving down at me like a lunatic. Becca was one of my older sisters but only by a year. Sometimes I felt lightyears older than her.

She never seemed to have any problems, always smiling, and happy. She took to Ali more than anyone else in my family had and they had become pretty good friends. So when she found out Kace and Ali were going to my home game before Christmas, she asked to come too.

"Boss?" I heard Tyson Black, one of my favorite tight ends, call me.

"What's up?" I threw him the ball as we continued our pregame warmup.

"The best way to get that anger out is on the field." He threw the ball back to me and then ran out a little farther for another pass. I started to throw it but paused at his simple, yet very true words.

Ty was one of those players who would have spent his life fighting, surrounded by drugs, and possibly dead before he was twenty-one if it hadn't been for football. He was the definition of using his anger on the football field. He was known for his aggression and lack of fucks. Always willing to throw a punch if the situation called for it.

He also had a point.

Ty may not have known what was up my ass, but he knew my body was pulsing and my fingers were constantly curling into fists. He saw my eyes and how they cut every time someone spoke my name.

"Or in the bed," he flipped me the ball again and added his last two cents before he headed to the locker room.

In the bed was the only place I didn't feel the tension in my shoulders and the rage in my heart. The bed was where I felt safest, and escaping inside my girl was therapeutic all on its own.

By the time Kace and I joined her upstairs the other night, she was anxious to find her escape in us as well. The romance that had started that night was long gone and was replaced with a basic and feral need.

"Got that head on straight today?" my head coach came up next to me and asked. Levi Peyton wasn't even forty years old and was already the most successful head coach in the league. He got that way because he was smart, headstrong, and didn't take anyone's shit. Not even mine.

"Yep." I tossed him the ball that Ty had left me with, playfully starting a game of catch. He tossed the ball back but eyed me skeptically. "Gonna take Black's advice and take it out on the field."

"Black gave good advice?" Coach smirked.

"I hope so," I shrugged. "Because I'm gonna take it."

"Look." Coach approached me, getting closer so we weren't forced to speak loud enough for anyone else to hear. "I know you have been through hell and back. I know you are dealing with feelings and shit that you never have before. And I know we didn't give you any time off to decompress and find your new normal. We pushed you right back in front of those cameras and all you want to do is play your game and go home."

I was about to say something, but Coach held a hand up and cut me off. "I don't know the details, and it really isn't any of my business, but if you need to, you can walk off this field limping right now, and I will have the big wigs up there put you on the IR list."

I cocked my head at his offer. Coach was willing to put me on the injured reserve list to spare me? I didn't know if I was touched or pissed. I must have looked even worse than I felt.

"Nah," I laughed him off as if his offer was a joke, even though it wasn't. "But can I play defensive end tonight?"

His laugh was loud, causing people near us to look back at him. I knew there wasn't a chance in hell he would let me play defense. "I bet that would get the attention off your personal life."

"And let me hurt someone," I reasoned.

"I was gonna pretend to put you on the IR, not actually have to because you're dead."

"Yeah, yeah." I rolled my eyes and moved away, then took one last glance to the suite before jogging toward the locker room, giving myself one more minute before the game started.

* * *

Ty was right.

Play the game angry and you're almost untouchable. I guess a lot of credit could go to my offensive line. Or the fact that Ali and Kace were there with me. Either way, I played great, and the media somehow laid off me for the day.

A Christmas miracle.

The last week before our Christmas game in Cincinnati went well. We practiced hard, because that game was going to determine if we made the playoffs. The entire team was buzzing with excitement.

Kace cooked a special dinner for the three of us on Friday, the night before I had to fly out. I had gotten in late, so it was almost ten at night by the time we all finished and made our way to the living room.

Kace and I sat down in front of the Christmas tree and Ali followed, a questioning smile on her face.

"What are we doing down here?"

I knew that tone in her voice. She was both intrigued and hoping we were planning on taking her clothes off like we did the other night.

And we would.

But first, Kace and I wanted to give her our Christmas gift.

"Since I won't be here Sunday, we wanted to give you your Christmas present."

"But you will be back Sunday night and we can exchange gifts then. Mine isn't ready!"

I took her hand and pulled her closer to me. "We thought about that, but I want you to have it before I go."

"It's not a car, is it?" She looked panicked. Ali didn't have a car. Kace and I joked that we would buy her one, but she refused to accept something so extravagant from us. Especially so early in our relationship.

"The fifth anniversary is the car anniversary," she had argued, making us laugh.

We respected her wishes, and did not buy her a car. Instead, we got her something we thought would mean a lot to her. She knew we could afford everything and anything, so we wanted it to be special.

"No car," I laughed again. Reaching to the back of the Christmas tree, I pulled a small gift that Kace had wrapped for us and handed it to Ali.

Kace had gotten closer to us, his leg leaning against mine as his smile got wide. "Open it."

Ali's eyes glassed over, crying before she even knew what it was. "You guys…"

"Open it." I repeated Kace's words, excited for her to see what it was.

She started tearing at the paper, and made it to the small black box. Lifting the top off, her gasp was all I needed to make it through the rest of the holiday with a smile on my face.

"Cam?" She moaned. "Kace?" She drew his name out, turning to him and then back to me. The tears finally fell from her face and her hands started shaking.

I gently took the box from her hands and pulled the bracelet from where it was nestled in satin and velvet. Kace took the empty box and set it back under the tree, then took her hand and held it up for me. I clasped it onto her wrist and watched as she held each charm and looked at them closely.

"A #20," she sniffed. "For you two."

She grabbed the next one, a lock, and Kace explained to her. "For the one I broke when I kicked in your door." She smiled up at him, remembering the sore memory but knowing it was vital in how we became *us*.

"A cocktail glass, for the ones you spilled everywhere the night we knew we were going to fall in love with you." She laughed as I recalled the memory of her being pushed with a tray full of drinks. I had caught her while Kace had stood in front of her to protect her. Somehow, we all began our unbreakable bond that night.

"Oh my God," she cried, no longer laughing.

I looked down and realized she had made it to the next one and I stopped breathing, worrying what she thought.

CHAPTER 11

ALI

The charm bracelet was more than I ever could have imagined. It wasn't the kind you got from a chain store jeweler, it was the kind that came from somewhere exclusive, and probably cost more than three cars would have.

I knew they had all the money in the world and would want to get me something, but this made the gift I had been working on for them seem ridiculous.

I couldn't take my eyes off the fourth charm, and I could tell the guys were worried about what I thought.

"A diamond?"

"It's real," Kace said quickly, fear in his voice. "Just something for the future."

The diamond was huge. I didn't even want to guess how many carats it was. "You guys…"

Cam turned me around to face him. "We added that one because all these others represent our past, but this one," he gently lifted it with one finger. "This one represents our future. And every time you start to overthink what we are, or think that you will ever have to choose between us, or whatever else that crazy brain of your thinks… you can look down and know that we have promised you forever."

"And when the time comes," Kace took over, so I turned to the sound of his voice. "We can move that diamond to a setting on your finger."

That was impossible, because from the moment I chose them both, I knew we would be limited. But that wasn't something I wanted to mention at that moment. It was also something neither of them were ignorant to, so my words would have been wasted.

Instead, I chose to focus on how much they loved me.

"I don't even have the right words," I choked on more tears.

There were a few more charms and I fingered each one. One was a microphone that looked similar to the one I had in front of me the first time I spoke publicly about being with Cam and Kace. There were also grapes, noting the time we picnicked together–the day I learned their real names and who they really were. The last one was a simple silver square, but engraved were the numbers 678, representing the place we all met.

As more tears came down my cheeks, I was pulled into the air and gently moved to the middle of the couch by Kace. He backed away and Cam stood next to him, shoulder to shoulder. *Their protective wall,* that I always thought of when they stood like that.

We all stayed still, watching one another and waiting for the moment the tension finally snapped. They were both in jeans and t-shirts, while I was in a comfortable dress that almost met the floor when I was standing.

With their eyes on me, it reminded me of the first time we were intimate together. My apartment, my bed, as they told me to get undressed for them. I was timid, but they both helped my nerves along by undressing as well.

This time, I didn't need the help or the push in the right direction. I knew what I wanted and more importantly, I knew what they wanted.

"Don't move," I whispered, my voice still too scratchy from crying to speak any louder.

As they watched on, I opened my legs and pulled my dress up to my waist, showing them my red panties and the wet spot I undoubtedly had in the middle. My breasts nearly spilled out of the dress from the thin straps, but more so when I squeezed my tits together for them.

I could see Kace's hands starting to shake and Cam's fist clenching and unclenching. They wanted to touch me, to help me, but they also wanted to wait for me to ask for it.

I used my right hand to slide my fingers into my underwear and swirled my finger into the wetness that had built up. Then I pulled my hand up to show the guys how turned on I was.

"Fucking hell," Kace whispered.

With a quick smirk their way, I held up the bracelet on my left wrist and stalled. "This is the most beautiful bracelet I have ever seen."

"It's not just a bracelet," Cam said, remaining still. "It's a playbook."

My intake of breath was loud, making them almost leave their positions and head toward me. It was just a brief statement, but I remembered everything he told me about a playbook.

Past plays that worked, plays for the future, and the most important parts of the game.

I guess it was a playbook.

Our playbook.

I fell in love with them a little more at that moment and my body started, once again, buzzing with need for them.

"Kace?" I asked coyly, barely able to look him in the

eye. I opened my legs wider and invited him in, wanting him to kneel in front of me and taste how wet I was for him.

He moved at the sound of his name and fell right where he knew I needed him. His hands pushed my knees apart, and he licked his lips as his gaze went from my eyes to between my legs.

"You are so fucking wet, baby. These panties are ruined." He lowered his mouth over the lacy center and sucked at the fabric, making a sound so erotic, I started pulsing.

Cam was still in the spot he had been standing in, watching Kace as he started pulling my panties down my legs. Once they were off, he wrapped my legs around his neck and took his mouth back to me, licking gently before roughly pushing his tongue inside of me.

I tried suppressing my moans, keeping my eyes on Cam. Through his jeans, I could see how hard his cock was, but he wasn't so much as twitching a muscle. A few months ago, they had promised me that if I told them not to touch me, they wouldn't, and I was going to have to invite him before he would even dream of caving.

Those circumstances were different, but Cam was strong-willed, and used every chance he got to play games with me. That was why I called Kace first, because he was less likely to keep still, and one of them watching me with the other had been a turn on for me since the first time I asked for it.

"He feels so good," I said to Cam, as Kace continued moving his mouth over my core. Cam's eyes darkened a little, the only sign he gave me that I was making him crazy. "I love you," I added, hoping it eased his pain.

His eyes only darkened more, his mouth never even coming close to moving so he could return the words back to me. He was a statue, watching his best friend bring me to the brink of coming and waiting his turn.

"What are you thinking?" I asked, urging him to talk to me.

"How I hope he's skimming his teeth along your clit because I know you love it so much," he said quickly.

I cried out as Kace heeded Cam's words and took his teeth to the nerves of my clit but withdrew before he let me come. Cam smirked, knowing what Kace had just done, and started wiggling his fingers, more anxious than ever to join us.

Kace had moved to kissing my inner thigh and I reached down to run my fingers through his hair. The motion caused the straps of my dress to fall, and my nipples caught the cool air that surrounded us.

"Ali," Cam warned, his strength beginning to wane. Cam was always so delicate and sensual, but not when he was driven to the brink. That was exactly where I wanted him, and he was so close.

"Lose your clothes, Cam."

I had never seen a man undress as quickly as he did, and when he was done, he started moving forward to me before stopping himself.

"What were you gonna do?" I asked with a smile.

"Fuck your mouth," he said matter of fact.

I nodded, "That is exactly what I want."

He grabbed his cock while closing the gap between us. Before I could blink, his feet were pressing into the couch on either side of me as he held my head still and forced my jaw open. He pushed himself into my mouth, almost too hard, showing me how unhinged I made him.

Kace had backed away and from my peripheral, I could see him taking his clothes off as well. He started stroking himself as he watched Cam pump himself in and out of my mouth.

Tears sprang to my eyes every time Cam hit the back of my throat, but he never let up and I never stopped him. For as hard as it was to take all of him, it also made me feel like a fucking queen.

Just when I thought he was going to come, he pulled back and jumped from the couch, pulling me with him.

I stood between him and Kace as both quietly eyed me and each other. Something was about to happen, and I wasn't sure I was ready for it.

CHAPTER 12

ALI

"I love you too," Cam finally spoke, responding to my earlier words. "But you make me a monster and you do it so intentionally."

I nodded, trying to hide my smile.

"Why don't you do that to him?" he asked, nodding his head toward Kace.

"He's already a monster," I argued.

Cam was already shaking his head, disagreeing with me. Neither of them were monsters, but when it came to me, as I had said before, Kace was easier to trigger. Watching Cam squirm was euphoric. And they were the ones that started the games we played.

Cam's arms came out to grab my hips and he turned me, so I was bent over the arm of the couch. He took his fingers to where Kace had left a mess between my legs and inserted two of them inside of me.

"Suck his dick," Cam grunted as Kace lined himself up in front of me.

Kace grabbed my hair and lifted my face up to look at him while he eased himself into my mouth. Then his eyes shot up to look at Cam, and I knew he wanted to watch Cam fuck me.

Cam withdrew his fingers and replaced them with his cock. I couldn't see Cam, but I could see Kace bite his lip as he watched Cam find his pace inside of me. Then his eyes were back on me, and he caressed my cheek with his thumb as he held me steady.

Together, they found a rhythm, moving in and out of me at the same pace. My arms were holding me up, but they started to shake as I felt my orgasm getting closer and closer. Kace had already teased my body so much that it wasn't going to take anything to make me come, but I wanted to wait for them. I wanted us all to come together.

As if sensing my thoughts, Kace's thumb made its way under his cock and to my bottom lip, tugging on me to make sure I was paying attention. "We aren't stopping at one. I want to hear you screaming so much that we scare the reindeer away."

He must have known what his words were going to do to me, because he withdrew himself from my mouth right as Cam's cock hit so deep inside of me that I started to scream.

"Fuck," he grunted. "I love it when you're loud."

Before my body could rest, the guys changed positions and Kace flipped me over again. My pelvis was on the arm of the couch, lifted to just his height. He was using the head of his cock to swirl my juices around while Cam knelt down on the couch behind me.

He pulled my chin into the air and pushed his cock into my mouth where Kace had just vacated. The evidence of my orgasm was coating my own tongue as his balls hit the tip of my nose.

"I can't decide if I want to come in your mouth or all over your face," he grunted.

Kace was easing his way inside of my pussy and just like before, they found a rhythm that kept my body pulsing and my legs shaking with need. That time, my clit was hypersensitive and just a few pumps of Kace's wide cock had me squeezing him with an orgasm.

Cam didn't pull out of my mouth, though. He muffled my screams with his cock and rode out the vibrations my throat made for his own pleasure.

Kace was fighting with himself, slowing down and trying not to come before he was ready. He leaned forward and started to kiss me, but with my mouth being occupied with Cam, he settled for nipping at my neck and speaking into my ear.

"I almost messed up and kissed Cam's cock, baby girl. Think he would have enjoyed that?"

I nodded, not sure Cam could even hear Kace's words. I also wasn't sure Cam would have been into Kace's lips on his dick. My guys were never too interested in each other sexually, but emotionally, they were as connected as any two humans I had ever known. Sometimes I wondered how that would translate when they lost control in the bedroom–or on the couch–but it was something I always kept to myself.

Kace's laugh made his body shake and it felt good with his cock inside of me. I moved my hips, hoping he understood that I was ready for more, and I wanted him to go with me.

"Maybe I'll surprise him one day and see what he does," Kace whispered before pulling away from my ear with one last nip.

His words were the secret, and before he could even set his rhythm again, I was coming around him for a third time. Cam pulled from my mouth that time, letting me scream and catch my breath, but I reached up to hold him over me and pumped my hand along his shaft.

His balls hung close to my mouth and with just a few strokes of my hand, he was spilling over me, coating my chin and chest. Kace didn't stay inside my pussy either, he pulled out and closed my legs, using my thighs clenched together to finish himself off.

The tip of his cock peaked out and started pouring his cum onto the neatly trimmed hair of my pussy. It was like they were marking me when they did that. If one of them came on my body, the other wanted to as well, to make sure when I cleaned myself up, I had them both on my skin.

It made me feel desired in a way that was so base, I could have come again from my thoughts alone.

The guys pulled away from me and Cam lowered my head to the couch. Despite the fact that his come was on my chin, his lips found mine and he smothered me with feelings that made me want to cry.

"Upstairs," Kace said sternly, as if we had forgotten I was a mess.

Cam pulled me into his arms, and I wrapped my legs around his waist, causing the evidence of all our love making to get trapped between our skin. He continued to kiss me as we followed Kace into the bathroom and directly into the warm shower he had started.

When he set me down, Cam looked into my eyes, and it felt like all I saw behind the clear blue was a war he battled. One he felt he fought alone, and one he would continue to fight alone.

"You don't want to leave," I guessed, as I continued to look into his eyes.

"Of course I don't," he swallowed around a lump in his throat. "But I am, and I am going to kick some major Cincinnati ass, then I am going to come home and, like

Kace said, we will make sure Santa skips our house. He won't be needed, nor will he be welcome. Poor Santa can't handle the things we are going to do to your body."

I was both proud and turned on, seeing Cam so fierce. Not only about us, but about his career. I knew he had been having a hard time, but seeing him fight through and still being the best was sexy. His mental strength was just as sexy as everything I saw in him physically.

Kace pulled me into his arms, and once again placed his mouth to my ear. "I can't wait for him to see our surprise."

Cam could hear him, and he smirked as he grabbed the soap from the shelf. He lathered himself first, but quickly started on me as Kace licked the water from the back of my neck. There wasn't a chance in hell I could keep going, exhaustion was seeping into me so fast that I was surprised I could even keep myself on my own two feet.

We made it to bed, and I twisted my bracelet around in awe as the guys climbed in on either side of me. They both pushed their bodies up against me and held me tightly as they figured out where their arms and heads were going to rest so that we were all comfortable.

"I love you," I whispered into the dark room to both of them.

"Love you too," Cam said at the same time Kace said, "Love you babe."

With their arms laying over my stomach, and their heads both close to my neck, I reached behind me to see where their other arms were.

Interlocked above my head, both holding each other's biceps as they created a cocoon for me. A safe place that held more warmth and love than I ever thought possible. A place where no one judged, and we could be whatever and whoever we wanted to be. Where it wasn't about jealousy, discontent, or even sex. Just three people who loved each other in ways no one else could understand.

We didn't need anyone else to understand.

We knew.

And it made me even more excited to surprise Cam with a gift of my own.

CHAPTER 13

KACE

"Ready?" I squeezed Ali's knee as the private plane I had hired started rolling down the runway for takeoff.

"Yes!" she squealed and looked out the window as we lifted off, Atlanta quickly becoming a blur.

As requested, I helped Ali arrange a Christmas present for Cam, and now we were seeing it through.

It was Christmas morning, and we were headed to Cincinnati to watch Cam take the Jets to the playoffs. He had no idea we were coming, and no idea I had arranged everything with the help of the Jets' staff. Even his head coach knew we were coming and had arranged for us to be able to head down to the field in the last few minutes of the game. That way, we could be with him to either celebrate or console him, depending on the outcome of the game.

It was trickier to arrange those kinds of things without Cam being involved, but it paid to be me sometimes, and everyone jumped when I asked.

"The private jet is overkill though," Ali eyed me.

"We couldn't risk commercial flight delays." She felt

guilty that a flight team had to work on Christmas just because of us, but I knew how much I was paying them, and it was enough to change Christmas to any day they wanted. "And we couldn't risk someone recognizing us and flashing random pictures on the internet. The whole surprise would be wasted."

"True," she agreed as she pursed her lips and turned back to the window.

It only took an hour and a half from wheels up to wheels down, and Ali and I were exiting the plane. I stopped before we headed down the steps and thanked the small crew for working on the holiday.

"No problem, Mr. Jackson. Our pleasure," the Captain said as we shook hands.

"But it looks like snow here in Cincinnati later. We may need to head out earlier than you requested."

"Y'all go ahead back and enjoy the rest of the day with your families. We'll stay in Cincinnati tonight and have you grab us tomorrow if the skies are clear."

"Sure thing, boss," he nodded.

With one last salute, I guided Ali off the plane and toward a car I had arranged to drive us to the stadium.

"As much as I'm glad you let them fly back to their families today, we didn't bring any clothes for an overnight trip."

"We won't need clothes," I teased, speaking loud enough that our driver smiled and turned a little red around the ears.

As predicted, the snow started falling the minute we made our way to the suite that we shared with the owner of the Jets and his wife. They both gave me the creeps for reasons I could never explain, but since I was Kace Jackson, they were all too inviting to give Ali and I a safe place to watch the game.

By the time the fourth quarter started, Cam had played like he knew we were there. Atlanta was up by four touchdowns, Cam was being taken out of the game to save his arm for the playoffs, and Ali and I started putting on our jackets to face the snowy field together.

We said our goodbyes and headed down, the process being smooth since I set everything up ahead of time. When we emerged from the corridor, a few fans recognized me and I turned to Ali, silently asking her if she was sure about her gift.

She nodded and smiled, squeezing my hand tightly. So we pushed past everyone and lined ourselves up behind the players that stood along the sideline.

After just a few minutes, the clock ticked down to zero and the players all ran to the center of the field to celebrate their playoff berth. I took Ali's hand and together we joined the team, letting our presence be known and not hiding or shying away from anyone.

The cameras caught us as we congratulated the players we passed, but I pulled Ali toward midfield where I knew Cam would be for his post-game interviews.

"Ready?" I asked one more time. I needed to be sure she understood that her gift was going to cause chaos.

"He isn't going to do this alone," she assured me. "Not anymore. Never again."

I was so damn proud of her. Not that I wanted her in the face of the entire world, but she was publicly choosing to be our equal. Cam and I may be the ones who faced the microphones in our faces, but she was telling the world to go fuck themselves.

She dropped my hand when she spotted Cam and started running. Even with the camera in his face, she didn't hesitate. She wanted to congratulate him and celebrate, give Cam his Christmas present in front of the world.

I stopped walking and slid my hands into my pockets, ready to watch the show. My two favorite people in the entire world.

And the look on Cam's face, when he saw Ali, was worth everything.

CHAPTER 14

CAM

I was happy, don't get me wrong. But I wanted to hop on that plane home more than I wanted to talk to anyone.

Unfortunately, my job description entailed speaking after the game. It was literally in my contract—speak to the press after clinching a playoff spot. Plus, the plane wasn't going to take off until we were all on there.

If we even took off. It had been snowing since the start of the game and my gut told me that we would be grounded until it stopped. But at the very least, I could get back to my hotel room and Facetime Kace and Ali.

I was already planning on telling Kace to make Ali come so I could watch, over and over again. It wasn't my favorite way to be with them, but it had its appeal when I had to be away.

"Cam," the interviewer grabbed my attention as my teammates hugged me in the middle of the field. "Cam, over here."

She placed a hand on my shoulder and angled me toward the bright light at the top of the camera. I knew Kace and Ali were watching. They turned the TV off after some of the games but Christmas Day and a playoff berth? They would be watching for sure.

Somehow, peace had been surrounding me since I got to the stadium that day. It was almost as if Kace and Ali were there, and I didn't have to miss them. My fight or flight was protecting me, giving me the tranquility I needed to be the best I could for my team.

"Cam?" the interviewer began. "The Jets head to the playoffs again. How does it feel?"

"I never really doubted this team," I explained. "This season was completely unorthodox but as a team, we rose above the trials and used that to fuel our desire to win."

"Last week, you played like a man possessed. Somehow, you came right back out here today and did it again. How do you keep that level of competitiveness without wearing yourself down?"

"Oh I am exhausted," I replied, being careful to keep the profanity I wanted to use a bay. "But Ty told me something last week that I have held close to my chest and used to push through these last couple of games."

"Can you share what he told you?" she asked excitedly, thinking I would reveal a secret code that no one else had ever heard before.

"He told me to play angry," I smirked.

She was about to ask another question but before she could, I was being pushed backward. The scent of my girl was invading my senses and I wrapped my arms around her, knowing she was somehow there with me.

"I love you," she cried. "I am so proud of you!"

"Fuck," I breathed quietly. "What are you doing here?"

"There was no way I was spending Christmas without you."

I started backing away from the camera, the interviewer too stunned to do anything but smile. As if he were Santa,

Ty walked in front of her microphone and started talking about how Atlanta was unbeatable, and we were taking the Super Bowl again.

He was full of shit, extra loud, and I knew it was all to distract them from me.

With Ali in my arms, we slid out of the light of the live feed, and I placed her down so I could hold her face and look at her. Her nose was red, her lips were blue, but she was smiling and satisfied with herself at how she managed to crash my interview.

"Where's Kace?" I asked, looking behind her.

"He's here! We flew in this morning."

"Are you two crazy?" I laughed. "This is going to be a circus."

"But it will be our circus, not just yours. We will never spend a Christmas apart, Cam. I know you two want to protect me from the limelight, but this is me showing you that I am okay. My present to you both. I can handle it. I don't care what anyone else thinks. Their opinions will never keep us apart—especially on holidays."

She lifted onto her toes and kissed me, for everyone on the field—and the world—to see. I wrapped my arms around her waist and lifted her from the ground so I could swing her a little.

"Congrats on the win," she winked.

"Mmm," I kissed her again before I added, "I should have known you were here. I felt good this entire game."

When our mouths reconnected, I felt another hand come down on my shoulder. I knew it was Kace without even looking, so I continued to kiss my girl for a few more seconds.

"Don't I get credit?" Kace laughed. I pulled away and faked like I was going to kiss him too, since he wanted credit and all. "Fucker!"

The three of us stood in the middle of the field, knowing we were being watched. The snow was coming down harder, the stadium was playing Christmas music, and if I tuned everything else out, I could almost imagine we were in one of those snow globes.

"I love you two," Ali said loud enough for anyone to hear. "Merry Christmas."

Kace grabbed her hand and pulled her into him, kissing her lips. "Love you too."

I pulled her to me and kissed her where Kace had just been, tasting his gum on her lips as I tried to get her as close as possible to me. "I love you. Merry Christmas."

* * *

We were able to walk off the field with Ali holding each of our hands. No one asked and we didn't stop to do anymore interviews. Coach had cleared the rest of my night for me, and I barely got changed out of my uniform before I was running toward the car service Kace had hired.

Thanks to the snow, we weren't going to head back to Atlanta, but that didn't seem to matter anymore. They were in Cincinnati with me and even a night in my small hotel room seemed like Christmas magic.

Once we were closed in and warm, Ali pulled two wrapped gifts from her bag and waved them at us. "I got you guys something."

I immediately turned to Kace, who looked just as shocked as I was. "Was this trip not your gift?"

"Yeah," she nodded in his direction. "But I did something else. It's kind of lame, especially since you two gave me this." She held her wrist up that had her bracelet on it and looked nervous.

I wanted to argue with her and let her know that it didn't matter. But she took a deep breath and continued to speak.

"I guess you could say it's a playbook." Her eyes were cutting from me and Kace then back again. "Just like you guys, I wanted to give you something that spoke to everything that led us here and everything we have to look forward to. Open it."

Kace and I both started opening the Christmas wrapping at the same time, and within seconds, we each had a book in our hands. I opened it and thumbed through it, realizing it was written like a novel with pictures taped inside.

"It's a journal, but you guys relate better to the word 'playbook'. They are just small entries that I had started writing, replaying moments that meant a lot to me. I cannot play sports or afford major things, but I can write, and I couldn't think of a better gift than to give you two my version of our story. My words. Not just the past, but the future."

There was a lot of room to add pages and memories.

"Ali," Kace spoke first. "This is the perfect gift."

I nodded but couldn't look up yet. How did this woman turn me from a big, bad football player, to a pile of emotions—on the same fucking day?

"If you look inside," she spoke to Kace, who had moved to stand next to her. "It has dates and things we have done. But there is also a schedule of sorts. You helped me make some of this possible to surprise Cam, but here is the final product."

I finally looked up and walked to where they were standing. Ali's smile was bright, and she turned Kace's book to show me.

"You will never miss Christmas, Cam. Tomorrow, your family is doing their Christmas Day and we will be there. The next day, Kace's parents are hosting us. Every year, we will make this work so that not only do we get to see all of our families, but we also get to be together."

"Then maybe one day," Kace added, moving to where we made a circle. He took Ali's hand and kissed her fingers, while resting his other hand on my shoulder, squeezing tight. "One day," he continued, "we can combine our families and make Christmas a day to remember."

"Just as memorable as this one," I agreed. "Our first Christmas."

ALSO BY KATIE RAE

The GAMES Series

The Games We Play

The Lies We Tell

The Love We Make

The Way We Dance

The Way We Fight

Men of the Military

Ranger

Raptor

RECON

The Boys of Summer Novella

Pretty Boy

Man of the Month Club Novella

Love Bites

Silverbell Shore Series

Now & Then

Co-Write with Zoey Drake

Dirty Monsters

Christmas Freebie (Manny from The Lies We Tell)

Manny Christmas

ABOUT KATIE RAE

Katie loves hot heroes, strong women, and happily ever afters.
She lives in South Florida, married, and has two girls.

Apart from family time and writing, her true loves ironically all start with B's: baseball, beaches, baked goods, baking shows, baseball pants, books, bargains, vodka, and her Roomba.
Well, 7 out of 9 isn't bad!!

Join the fun in Katie Rae Reader Group and sign up for Katie Rae's Newsletter!

Also, www.katieraebooks.com is now LIVE. Check out extras, events, book information, signed paperbacks, and MORE!

TRAVELING
THE SNOWY
ROAD HOME

INTERNATIONAL BESTSELLING AUTHOR
K.B. BARRETT

Copyright © 2022 by K.B. Barrett and Woman of Words Publishing

Edited by Mackenzie at Nice girl Naughty Edits

All rights reserved. No part of this publication may be reproduced, distributed, stored, or transmitted in any form or by any means, including photocopying, recording, electronic, scanning, screenshots, or other electronic or mechanical methods. It is illegal to copy this book, post it to a website, or distribute it by any other means without prior permission of the author, except in the case of brief quotations embodied in critical reviews and certain other noncommercial uses permitted by copyright law.

This book is a work of fiction. Names, characters, places, and incidents are the product of the author's imagination. Any resemblance to actual events, locales, or persons, living or dead, is coincidental.

Send Inquiries to:

Po Box 762 Ada, MI 49301

ALSO BY K.B. BARRETTT

'I FOUND YOU SERIES' NOVELS
Everything I Need
Anything For You
Nothing Without You
Something About You

'MOUNTIAN ROADS' NOVELS
Saved by the Mountain Man (prequel)
The Twisted Roads Home
What Drives Us Home
Traveling the Snowy Roads Home
The Road to Finding Home
The Place that I Call Home

STANDALONE NOVELS
Home Across the Endless Waters
At A Dreamwalkers Mercy

CHAPTER 1
MELANIE

She really needed another bag.

Looking down at the remaining pile of notebooks, containers from lunch, and her coat that she still needed to manage to stuff in, she was second guessing her choice of picking one of her smaller purses this morning.

It never ceased to surprise her how much stuff she ended up going home with at the end of the day.

Or maybe it was that it was unorganized. Whereas her job was keeping the office in order and running smoothly, she never seemed to be able to do it for herself and her own stuff.

It didn't really matter, she guessed.

Nothing really mattered lately.

Her stomach churned as her thoughts turned dark.

She had been fighting her tears and thoughts all day.

Four Years.

That was how long she and James had been married.

The number didn't seem real, though, because over the last four years that he had been deployed, they had spent less than six months together.

Six months.

Four years of high school together, practically attached at the hip, and then when they got married and were supposed to be starting a life together, they got six months.

For four years she had been carrying this and this year she figured that it just might break her.

This year brought a new worry.

With one more glance around the office where she worked, she grabbed her bag and what she could hold in her hands. The rest would have to wait till tomorrow.

After locking the door, she threw everything in the front seat of her truck. Granted, it wasn't actually her truck. As she climbed inside, she had to use the side railing to help her up, and immediately turned on the heater.

When James had left for deployment, he had demanded that she drive his truck. Saying that her little car wasn't safe to be driving in the mountains. They both knew he was talking out of his ass, though, since her car was less than two years old, and her Pop had gone with her to buy it. But he had seemed desperate, and she hated to admit it, but she did feel closer to him when she was driving it.

Especially when it had been months since she had even talked to him.

She rubbed at her chest where the ever-present ache shot through her and reminded herself to breathe. Wearily, she looked down the main street of the little town, Savage Valley, that she lived in, and wondered if she should splurge for a takeout from Tracey's Diner.

It would be the second time this week, so she probably shouldn't, but cooking had no appeal when it was just for her. And at the moment, a microwave meal was sounding even less appealing.

Not to mention that her father owned the only grocery

store within an hour's distance. If she showed up there to try and find something for dinner, it would be nonstop questions.

She just couldn't deal with that today.

Her phone rang, and she blindly reached for it. "Hello?"

"Hey, sweetheart." She clenched her eyes shut.

"Hey, Dad." Just the sound of her dad's voices often made everything better, but today was not an average day.

"You doing okay?" Why did people ask her that when they knew she was far from okay.

"Yeah," she replied, even though she was far from it.

"Any word?"

The same question.

Every day.

And like every day, it was the same answer.

"I'm sorry, hun," her father said gently, taking her silence for an answer, and she wiped at the tear that escaped.

When everyone had said that marrying James young would be hard, she hadn't cared. Neither of them had cared. They had been madly in love, and nothing was going to change their minds.

But time was a monster to young love.

It played tricks on your mind.

And when your husband was deployed a mere three weeks after you were married, and had only been home once in four years, it started to wear on you in a way that not even that long-ago warning could help.

"Maybe tomorrow," her dad said, but he knew, like her, that it wasn't coming then either.

"I'm really worried." She whispered the words that she had been too afraid to say.

"I know. Have you tried calling anyone?" She had to

remind herself that he was just trying to help, as a flash of annoyance and anger filled her. Leaning forward, she rested her forehead against the steering wheel.

"Yeah. It's the same answer. It's a no-contact, high-priority mission. It's just that, the longest we have ever gone without contact is, like, two weeks at most."

It had been three months.

And any military wife could see the signs.

But James was her high school love.

The only man that she had ever loved and the only man she ever would.

She refused to accept the signs.

"Maybe you should come stay with me for a bit. I don't like you being in that big house all alone."

The big house he was referring to was James's family's place. It was a big house on over fifty acres. When James's parents had passed in his senior year of high school, it had gone to him. It was way more than the two of them needed, with five bedrooms and several barns. But when he had told her that it would make him feel closer to his family if they lived there, she had willingly packed up her little room she had been renting and moved out there with him.

That was five years ago.

That had been when he was home.

She couldn't tell her Pop that being without him in that big house was starting to wear on her, because the truth was, she couldn't leave. It was the only thing of James that she had left.

"Thanks, Dad, but I'm okay."

"Honey..." her dad started to object.

"It's all I have left of him," she choked out, the words hitting to close to home.

"It's going to be all right," he whispered, even though

they both knew it did little to ease the pain that she was trying to fight off.

Because it would never be okay.

This couldn't be happening!

"You going to the tree lighting tomorrow?"

Savage Valley may have been a small town, but when it came to holidays, they sure didn't act like it. Tree lightings, decorations, town outings, the whole thing was done up with style. Always being way more festive than any other town close to them. She probably should go, get out of the house and spend time with her friends and family. But she already knew she wouldn't.

"Probably not, Dad." She didn't give any excuse. Christmas was hard. Bar none. And she was not in the mood to celebrate.

"I'm going to pick up some dinner from Tracey's," she muttered, sitting back, exhaustion and unease pulling at her.

"Okay, hon. Love ya." Her father sounded like he wasn't ready to get off the phone, probably worried about her, but she wasn't giving him a choice.

She needed to get her food and get home, so she could break down.

"Love ya too," she replied automatically, but her mind was already gone.

If she blocked it out, she could pretend that life was perfect. That she was getting off work and picking up dinner for both of them, and that when she drove down that long road to their house, he would be standing out on the front porch, waiting for her.

Stupid.

She put the phone down and drove off.

You can do this!

She just had to keep pushing, and everything would be okay.

Pushing through work.

Pushing through life.

Praying that everything would work out, even if she was starting to realize that it never would.

CHAPTER 2
MELANIE
THE PAST

"I can't believe you are getting married!" her sister, Margaret, squealed.

That was Margaret. High-pitched or nothing.

She smiled, still staring in the mirror, not believing that the girl in front of her was actually... well, her.

"I never thought this day would come," she whispered, feeling like it wasn't real.

Was she really going to marry James?

Was she really going to get to spend the rest of her life with him?

"Oh, posh. You two have been together since freshman year in high school. Everyone knew it would happen."

That was true.

Still didn't mean that she hadn't been dreaming of this day.

"Daddy is going to flip when he sees you." She smiled again.

"I wish Mom was here," she whispered, and Margaret smiled sadly, reaching up to adjust one of the flowers in her hair.

"I know. Me too. She would have loved James for you."

Yes, she would have.

A knock on the door had them both pausing, before a familiar head of dark hair quickly peeked around it and he snuck in.

"James! You cannot be in here!" Margaret screeched, trying to block his view.

"You really think you can stop me, runt?" he poked at her, and she could only imagine the scowl Margaret was giving him. For a woman that claimed to love James for her, the two bickered a lot.

"Ugh, whatever." Margaret stomped off, and she heard the door slam as she turned around and got her first look at her future husband.

In the four years that they had been together, she had seen James in a lot of different ways. Anything from jeans and a t-shirt to the suit that he had worn to their prom. Her favorite had always been when he first got up in the morning, with sleep tousled hair, his sleep shorts riding low on his hips and no shirt on.

That had, and always would be, her favorite.

But seeing him all decked out, with the small wildflower corsage pinned on his jacket, that look would always stick with her.

"God, baby, you look soo…." He stopped and swallowed, then seemed to pull himself together. "You look beautiful."

The way those words washed over her was like any other time, but more.

"Thank you."

"I had to come steal a kiss, but now seeing you… in that dress… God, baby." He groaned and reached up to mess with his tie.

She stepped forward and swatted his hand away,

straightening the plain black tie and smoothing it out for him.

"It's crooked," she said softly, gazing up at him.

He was staring into her eyes with a look on his face that she had only seen a couple of times. Once was the first time they had ever made love.

The next was the day that she had said she loved him.

The last time was the day she had said she would marry him.

"I love you, you know that?" he murmured huskily, his hand sliding around her waist and fisting like it always did. As if he was holding on till he got the answer that he wanted.

He may be her high school sweetheart, but he was also the other half of her soul.

"I love you too." She reached up, intent on kissing his chin, when he shifted and claimed her lips instead.

Pressing in deep and accepting nothing less than total surrender, that's how he kissed her. His lips caressing, teeth nibbling, and his tongue sweeping in to play with hers.

A quick tap on the door had them pulling apart, leaving her dazed, right before Margaret slid back inside.

"It's a good thing that we haven't done her lipstick yet. But if we don't finish, she isn't going to be at the altar."

James rolled his eyes, but still didn't make a move to step back.

Instead, he leaned forward and grabbed her chin, rubbing his nose against hers before leaving a kiss on it.

"You ready to do this, baby."

God, yes, she was.

CHAPTER 3
JAMES
PRESENT

The picture was worn and faded. As if it had been held too many times. The edges were worn and frayed, but the smiling face in the photograph was still the same.

And holding it, he still felt the same familiar ache.

God, how could one person miss someone so fucking badly?

"Yo, James! Cap wants you!" his partner and best friend, Dean, shouted, and he quickly tucked the photo back into his hat and slid it on.

Dean gave him a look as he walked by, but didn't say anything.

Honestly, if it wasn't for Dean, he didn't think he would have made it this far. Being away from home was hard enough. Being in a third world country, fighting some war, was worse.

Missing his Melanie.

That was just about killing him.

When he had been young and faced with a decision of college or building a life in Savage Valley, it had seemed simple. His family had lived there and died there, and Melanie was there too.

A no brainer.

But his prospects had been short and all he knew was that he'd had to support the life that he wanted with her.

When the marine recruiter had come to their high school, it had been like all his prayers had been answered. Little did he know that the recruiter was looking for numbers and would have told him just about anything to get him to sign.

That left him here walking across the desert sand, wishing like hell he was back at home.

"Cap. You wanted to see me," he said, pushing the flap aside and walking into the captain's tent, ignoring the plume of dust that rose and seemed to linger everywhere.

Being in the desert, you had to push aside some things to mentally make it, and the fucking sand dust was one of them.

Fuck, he missed the mountains.

"Sit, son," Captain said, pointing to the chair across from his makeshift desk. They may be in the fucking marines, but they had been on this godforsaken mission for months, and protocol with each other had slid away somewhere around week one or two.

"Your papers came in. I need to know what you want to do."

It wasn't even a question.

"I'm done, Cap," he answered almost immediately, and his captain nodded like he knew that had been coming.

"I understand. I'm sad to lose you, but I get it. You will need to fill these out, but you should be out of here in a couple of weeks."

A couple of weeks? Shit!

"What about the mission, sir?"

"There will always be someone to fight, son. Now or later doesn't matter. We haven't had any new intel in weeks, and the brass knows we are stalled out. Nothing to do but wait and no sense in you waiting here if I can get you home."

He hated to leave his team in a lurch while in the middle of a mission, but Cap was right. They had literally been sitting on their asses for weeks now, and he wanted to lay eyes on his girl.

He leaned forward and signed his name on the line, then set the pen down.

That was it.

His stomach churned as he sat back in his chair. A feeling that he wasn't sure he was able to label.

He was officially done with the marines.

Cap nodded to him, and he got up, leaving just a quickly as he had gotten in. Cap never had been one for long, drawn-out conversations.

Their mission was supposed to be simple. A look-out spot trying to gain new intel. Watching a back road that insurgents had been using more and more. But pretty quickly, they had figured out that something else was going on, and *more* had turned into almost four months of not talking to his Melanie.

Not hearing her voice.

Fuck.

He didn't even know if the marines had let her know he was all right.

Sometimes protocol sucked balls.

He walked back into his own tent that he shared with Dean and two other men, as Dean gave him a look.

"You signed."

A statement. Not a question. If there was anyone that understood him and his reasonings it was Dean.

But leaving his team, and Dean, would be hard.

"We'll be fine, man. Your girl needs you," Dean said, reading him well.

"I'm telling you, in a couple of months when your papers come through, my couch is open, man," he reiterated, and Dean just smiled, not committing.

James knew where he was from, what he wanted, and where his home was, but Dean was the opposite. Foster homes and homelessness, that was Dean's past.

He just hoped that someday Dean could find what he had.

"So what's the first thing you are going to do besides kiss your girl?" He smirked and Dean chuckled. "Yeah, never mind. I don't need to hear that shit."

Four months of no calls, and nine months of not seeing her, and he wasn't sure what ached more.

His heart or his hand from yanking it off to her picture in his head.

Her pretty sapphire blue eyes and curly brown hair.

God, he missed his girl.

Just then, a screeching sound filled the air, and he froze.

Fuck.

His eyes shot to Dean a moment before he heard yelling outside the tents.

Dean's eyes held the same terror that he knew was reflected in his own.

"Get down!" he roared, right before the explosion rocked the ground.

He was tossed to the side, the image of dust and fire before him, and the memory of his Melanie filling his mind before it all went black.

CHAPTER 4
MELANIE

"Here you go," Tracey said, plopping another container down on the table and taking the twenty that she held out. "You hear anything?"

"Nope," she snipped. Everyone was constantly asking her that, and she was sick of it. But worse than that, she was sick of the pitying looks she'd receive after they asked. It was a look that said that they knew, and they were waiting for her to catch up.

"Hey, honey," Mac said as he walked in and took a seat next to her.

"Hey," she replied, turning and looking into the same familiar blue eyes that they had gotten from their father.

"Was hoping to catch you and see if you wanted to do dinner." He thought he was being sneaky, but she knew exactly what he was doing.

"Thanks, but I'm headed home."

"Want company?" She frowned, biting back her words and trying not to snap.

"I don't need pity."

"It isn't pity, honey. You'd be doing me a favor. If I

have to hear one more time from Pop that I need to be spending my nights with a girl to settle down with, I'm going to lose it. At least if I'm with you, he can't harp on me."

"I don't understand why you still live with him." She loved her father, but even she knew that space was the best thing for their relationship.

She needed her own life.

And Mac did too.

And it wasn't as if he didn't have the space. He owned several acres of bare land outside of town and his auto shop, and even had an apartment above it, for Pete's sake.

"I've actually been thinking of redoing the apartment above the garage," Mac muttered, picking up the cup of coffee that Tracey set down.

Even this late at night, Mac could drink a gallon of it, and then turn right around and pass out.

"Really? That could be cool."

"Yeah. This year has been great, and I've got the capital. It would be nice to just wake up and walk downstairs." She chuckled.

That was Mac.

Simple was best.

"I'm going to go. Love you." He gave her a look, as if he wanted to say something more, but then thought better of it. Standing, he wrapped his arms around her and gave her a squeezing hug.

"Love ya," he whispered against her hair, and she nodded, fighting to keep her tears at bay as she grabbed her bag of food and headed out.

The road in front of her wavered, her tears threatening to blind her, as she drove out of town. By the time she reached the gravel road to the house, her chest was aching, and she was breathing heavily, trying to keep it together.

She reached up and wiped at her tears angrily. How was it that she had gotten herself into this situation? When she had been younger, she had never thought that her and James's life would have been like this.

Looking forward to a future without him, that was the horrifying truth that she was going to have to admit.

That at this point, he might not be coming home.

"No!" she sobbed out. Slamming on the brakes, James's truck jerked to a stop, and she pulled over to the side of the road and threw it in park before banging her hands on the steering wheel.

"NO! AHHH!" she screamed, her lungs burning, as heartache like nothing she had ever known filled her. Starting deep in her heart, and leeching out to every part of her soul till she thought she wasn't going to be able to breathe.

Gasping for air, she sobbed uncontrollably, clenching the steering wheel till her knuckles were white.

God, please no!

She didn't want this to be happening!

She wanted to be able to blink and when she opened her eyes, have James sitting next to her. His beautiful slate grey eyes smiling back at her.

But life wasn't always what you wanted, and fate often proved that it wasn't fair.

After a moment, she sighed and wiped at her cheeks again. Smearing away the tears as exhaustion took hold of her.

Then she pulled herself together the best she could, put the truck into drive, and headed home.

Home to a house that was supposed to signify the start of her life with James.

Home to a house filled with nothing but memories of him.

* * *

MELANIE

Past

James smiled across the table at her as her Pop and Mac went at it about some engine part.

"Pop, love ya, man, but you own a grocery store," Mac growled, crossing his arms over his chest.

"You saying I don't know shit?" Pop challenged.

James choked around the bite of food in his mouth, trying to contain his laughter.

"Yeah, I am." She shook her head. Mac was the only one that would talk to their Pop like that. Both she and Margaret would be shaking in their boots from the glare that Pop was giving him, but not Mac.

Secretly, she thought that Mac just liked to rile him.

"Boy! Where the hell do you think you learned it all from?" Pop tossed his napkin on the table and stood.

"Pop, you never did step foot in that garage."

Mac was right. Pop hated cars.

"Well, I…" They kept going, and James gave her a look while jerking his head toward the front door, silently telling her to meet him out on their front porch.

They both quietly excused themselves, neither Pop nor Mac seeming to notice they were gone as James shut the door behind them.

Even through the closed door, you could still hear them going at it.

"Well, I think that was a successful first time hosting dinner," James said with a laugh as they walked to the far corner of the porch where it looked out over the field and hills.

It was her favorite spot to sit at night and about a month

ago, James had splurged and bought her a pair of nice wooden chairs for them.

But she was too antsy to sit, so she stood at the railing.

She didn't want to sit because that meant the night was coming to an end.

"Yeah," she said quietly with a forced smile, as he came up behind her and wrapped his arms around her, resting his chin on the top of her head.

"Dinner was really good, sweetheart." She nodded, not answering. James wasn't a good judge of her food. She could burn it to a crisp, and he would still sing her praises, but she had to admit that the pasta bake had turned out pretty good.

But that wasn't what was on her mind.

"It's going to be okay," he whispered, knowing something was on her mind.

"I know. I'm just going to miss you," she voiced as her heart clenched.

They had always been together. Ever since high school, she could count the number of days they had spent apart on one hand.

What if, once they were apart, he found out he liked it better?

She didn't admit that fear, but James had always been able to read her like a book. He turned her, pinning her against their porch railing as he slid up to her. Pressing his body into hers, he grabbed her chin, bringing her gaze up to his.

"I've loved you since I first saw you, Melanie sweetheart, and I'll love you till the day I die." Tears tipped over the edges of her eyes and rolled down her cheeks.

"I'm coming home, sweetheart."

"Promise?" she whispered shakily.

"I promise," he whispered against her lips before he kissed her gently.

The cicadas in the background filled the night air as he continued to lick and nip at her lips, and for just the moment, she let go and soaked in everything he had to give her.

Late into the night, once her brother and Pop had left and there was nothing but just them in their bed, she soaked it all in.

Soaked in every moment until the next morning, when he boarded a plane and left.

CHAPTER 5
MELANIE

K*nock.*
Knock.
Knock.

The knocking at the door had been happening for a while, but she was hoping that whoever it was went away.

It could be anyone.

Mac, Margaret, Tracey, but it was most likely Pop.

And she did not want to deal with anyone, let alone her Pop.

Over the last two weeks, it had been nonstop drop-ins from her family and friends. She appreciated it, really, she did, but it was now Christmas Eve morning and although James and her had been together for a host of holidays, they had never had a Christmas together.

Never had a Christmas morning waking up in each other's arms.

Now it was looking like they never would.

She hated Christmas.

When five minutes slid into ten, she finally got up and walked to the door. Ignoring her hair and day-old pajamas, she flung it open to see that it was indeed her father.

"Honey." That look of pity burned her guts, and she flicked the switch inside of her to turn everything off.

She didn't mean to do it. It wasn't a conscious decision, but she'd had enough.

"Listen, I know you mean well. I know everyone does. But I can't do this right now. I need you guys to leave me alone." Her words were harsh and bordering on mean, but she couldn't bring herself to care.

"That's not what family does, honey," Pop murmured softly, and she hated it.

Hated it with every fiber of her being.

"I don't need family right now. What I need, I can't have." Then she shut the door in his face and collapsed to the ground. Her chest ached as she tried to hold in her sobs, knowing that they wouldn't do anything but leave her worse than she'd been before.

As Pop's footsteps faded away and the tears started up again, she wondered if there would ever come a day that she would stop crying.

Somehow, she found the strength to get up and walk back to her bedroom. Ignoring that it was morning and that she really shouldn't be getting back in bed, she climbed back in anyway and pulled James's pillow against her chest. Then she reached over to the nightstand drawer. Pulling it open, she grabbed the folded-up piece of lined paper and sat back, leaning against the headboard, her strength leaving her.

She opened the piece of paper, knowing that reading the words again would leave her raw and in pain, but not being able to stop herself.

When she and James had decided to write their own vows, she had been so nervous. Nervous of not only making a fool of herself, but also not knowing how to put her feelings into a little paragraph. She'd managed, of course, with Margaret's help, but James hadn't had that issue.

He'd written his vows months before the wedding and when he had stood up next to her, he hadn't needed a piece of paper to remember them. It wasn't until months later, when he had been gone, that she had gotten a letter from him, one that included those very vows.

Sweetheart,

Right about now, you're missing me something terrible. I know because I miss you even more. But I wanted you to have this. I wanted you to know that from the day we got married, I've carried this with me. Carried you with me.

I love you, Melanie.

Vows....

Melanie sweetheart, I've loved you since I saw you the first day of sixth grade, and I will love you till the day I die. I could go on about how you make me stronger, or how you make me want to be a better man, and it would all be true. But the real truth is that when I look into the future, there is nothing there but you. I can't picture my life without you, and I don't want to. So thank you for loving me, thank you for being here for me, and thank you for being my bride.

Her sobs turned to wails as she clutched the letter to her chest and gave in to her heartache.

How was she supposed to go on if James was gone?

CHAPTER 6
MAC

Mac sighed and stopped knocking. Pulling his coat closer to him, he thought about what he should do as he looked around, eyeing the snow piles that were glistening in the evening light.

Honestly, even though it was Christmas Eve, and even though he knew that Melanie shutting herself inside and not letting anyone in was bad, he had to admit he understood.

Pop and everyone in town wanted to help her, to the point that he knew they were dropping by unannounced. His Pop had been by just that morning, but if it was him, he wouldn't want people in his face. Even if they were worried.

More than worried.

They had all known that today would hit her hard, as it did every year. But she was shutting them out to where they couldn't help her. He wanted to remind her of who James was and that he wouldn't have wanted this for her, but it seemed almost cruel to bring James into it, so he settled instead.

"Melanie honey, I'll leave, and I'll let you be, but

please, honey… Remember, you aren't alone," he murmured to the door, hoping that she heard him.

Ever since he was fifteen years old, and he had come to live with his dad, he had seen it as a job to help take care of his sisters.

He had personally seen what happened when a person didn't have a family surrounding them and caring for them. And when a teenage boy is suddenly thrust into a world where nobody has secrets and family is everything, it does more than just throw you for a loop.

It changes the way you see the world.

He just whished there was something he could do to help Melanie.

He climbed into his truck and headed down the hill, feeling like he had failed.

God, James…. We need you, man.
She needs you.

CHAPTER 7
JAMES
PAST

"Where are we going?" she whined, trying to lift the edge of the cloth he had tied around her head. He reached out and swatted at her hands for what had to be the hundredth time.

The next time he decided to surprise her, he wasn't going to tell her beforehand. She did not handle surprises that well.

It was fucking cute, though.

"I told you, it's a surprise."

"Well, you said that, yes, but I figured..." She left it hanging, and he smirked at her.

He knew that tone. She was thinking she could use that cute little look and get her way. Or get him to give into her, but it wasn't going to work.

Mostly because he was having too much fun.

"James," she whined again.

"You know you are too cute when you do that." She huffed and sat back.

"If you pout like that a little more, you may just get something else." She knew what her pouting did to him.

Her lips stuck out, just waiting for him to bite. Hell, she did it on purpose all the time.

She got off on the fact that what he really liked was when she wrapped those lips around his cock.

He had to stifle a groan just thinking about it, and looking over at her now flushed cheeks, it was a good fucking bet that she was thinking the same thing.

"Mind out of the gutter, sweetheart."

"You're the one that put me there."

Couldn't argue with that.

He pulled into the campground where he had rented a cabin for them to celebrate their one-year anniversary and chuckled as she practically jumped up and down in her seat by the time he stopped.

"Hold your butt."

"I want to know!" she screeched.

"Yeah, yeah," he muttered, then got out and went around the front of the truck, opening the door and helping her out.

"Watch your step." He couldn't explain the feeling that filled him when she reached for his hand and blindly trusted him to help her get down.

A simple thing.

But also, something that was very heaving in its meaning.

He loved that about her.

He loved everything about her.

"Okay, sweetheart," he whispered as he stepped behind her, wrapping one of his arms around her waist and pulling her body into his, her sweet curves fitting to him like she was made to. Then, with his other hand, he reached up and lifted the cloth off of her face.

"What is this?" she whispered.

"I rented it for us. Things have been so crazy with Mac

opening his shop and your Pop needing your help and me being gone a lot, so I wanted us to have this time just us."

"Just us," she whispered, her voice shaking.

"Yes, sweetheart. Just us. Just us and three days of remembering just how much I love you."

She turned then, her face tipping back, her hands clenching in his shirt as her blue eyes that were glistening with unshed tears shot straight through him.

It didn't matter if she was going to say something. He was helpless but to kiss her.

"Inside," he growled as her hands fisted in his shirt and she leaned into him. She moaned but didn't make any move to actually go inside, so he took matters into his own hands by fisting her jacket at the back of her waist and forcing her to move.

"Inside," he growled out again and fuck him if she didn't moan once more to match it.

He barely had the door closed when one of her hands slipped into his pants, and the other fisted the collar of his shirt, trying to pull him down. Then she was meeting him halfway on her tiptoes, sticking her tongue out to lick at his bottom lip.

"Sweetheart, I'm trying to be good here," he muttered as her hand in his pants wiggled around enough that she could wrap her fingers around his dick, and his head fell back on contact.

"I don't want good," she whispered, biting at his chin.

No, she didn't.

She never had.

She only wanted him, and fuck, it did something to him that she got off on giving him everything she had.

Wrapping his fingers around her wrist, he pulled her hand out of his now undone pants, twisted her body till she was leaning over the counter at the entryway. He stood flush behind her, and her ass rubbed against his dick as she wiggled around in front of him.

"You wore this to fucking torture me, didn't you?" he muttered while holding one of her hands behind her back and using the other to reach up under her dress.

"Fuck." He stilled as his fingers met her wet heat and nothing else.

Fucking nothing.

He pulled her back quickly, his heart and dick pounding in rhythm, lined himself up, and entered her in one thrust. Her back arched as she moaned long and long, and his balls ached with the sound.

Leaning forward, placing one hand on the wall for support, he nibbled at her ear, her breathy little pants doing more for him than the sweet squeeze of her warmth as he held himself still inside of her.

"No panties, sweetheart?"

"Mhmm." He nearly chuckled at her incoherent moan.

"You know I don't like you without something covering *my* pussy, right?" He jerked inside of her as her pussy spasmed.

Fuck, his girl was wild.

"It was for you," she husked out, her chest heaving with her words, her breasts moving with it. Fuck, he wanted them in his mouth, but as her pussy spasmed again, he knew it would have to wait till another time. He wasn't fucking pulling out.

"You like tempting me, don't you, sweetheart?" Her keening moan got higher as he continued talking in her ear, nipping and sucking on the sensitive flesh of her neck.

"Like knowing that you drive me wild."

"James."

Almost there.

"Like knowing that I'm the only man that will ever know what this sweet pussy feels like."

"Ahhh!"

Yes, that was it.

He leaned back and grabbed her hips, letting her hand go, and started a punishing pace. Thrusting in and out, using deep, hard thrusts, and praying he could hold on long enough for her to go over the edge with him.

"You need to come, sweetheart," he gritted out, knowing he was quickly losing the battle.

"James." Her high-pitched moan said that she was almost there.

"Now, Melanie," he warned her.

"James!" Her pussy tightened even more, the little ripples giving away that she was almost there.

"Fuck," he groaned as his balls drew up tight and that fire along his spine let loose. He couldn't hold it anymore as he came, continuing to thrust, a shot of pride hitting him when her back arched a bit more and a long, keening cry of pleasure fell from her lips as her body started to shake beneath him.

Fucking finally.

"James," she moaned again, softer this time, moments later.

"Yeah, sweetheart?" he whispered, leaning forward and wrapping his arms around her, taking some of her weight.

"Can I see the rest of the cabin now?" she asked innocently, and he threw his head back, laughing.

CHAPTER 8
MELANIE
PRESENT

This was heaven.

Sitting in the warm sun overlooking their property on their front porch, the fields and hills seeming to surround them with peace, the porch swing slowly moving back and forth, a warm breeze in the air.

His arms were around her, their fingers latched together as if he didn't want to let go of her any more than she wanted to let go of him.

"Love you, sweetheart," James murmured as his head dropped, and she felt his breath against the skin of her neck.

"I love you..."

Knock.

Knock.

Knock.

She jerked awake, her hand flying out automatically to his side like it had since the day he had left.

It was the same every morning.

There was just a moment between when sleep left her, and reality intruded, that she forgot that she was alone. That he wasn't here holding her, his arms wrapped around her, and in that moment, she could breathe.

Then that feeling of unimaginable agony would fill her chest and her lungs would seize.

She rolled her head into the pillow, the one that was supposed to be his, but no longer smelled like him, and let go of the sob in her heart.

"Ahh!" she cried out, the pillow muffling the sound as the knock on the door sounded again, and she flinched.

God! Couldn't people just leave her alone!

She threw back the covers with an angry wave, swiping at her tears and quickly slipping on her slippers, the floor being too cold without them, then stomped through the house toward the front door.

The house was dark, with only a single light on in the living room to guide her way, nothing bright and colorful to reflect that it was Christmas morning.

Nothing cheerful.

No Christmas tree.

No lights and presents.

The room was a direct reflection of how she felt.

If she couldn't have James, then she didn't want any of it.

The chill of the room swept over her, giving her goosebumps through the nightshirt she was wearing as she reached out, and with a flick, unlocked the door and threw it open.

"Why can't—" The words died on her lips at the sight before her.

Snow had crept up the porch from the night's storm, leaving a peaceful, pristine setting, except for one set of boot prints that led right up to the man standing in front of her.

"James," she whispered raggedly, the words like water over rocks in her throat.

He looked the same, but different. He had a full beard now, his head of normally short hair was a little longer, and his shoulders looked a bit wider than she remembered.

"Hey, sweetheart."

His voice.

God, his voice.

For too long, she had only dreamed about that voice.

Prayed that she would someday get to hear it again.

She blinked, wondering if she was still dreaming, but when she opened her eyes, he was still there.

Her James.

That was when she lost it.

Throwing herself forward, violent sobs that she had been trying to hold back for weeks came rushing forward. Deep, healing, soulful sobs wracking her body as her knees collapsed under her and then she was in his arms.

"You're here!" she sobbed out, her arms clenching around his neck and shoulders. The feeling of him, of his skin pressed against her, the hair at the back of his neck twisted in her fingers, was like nothing else.

She was never letting go.

CHAPTER 9
JAMES

Pulling up to his house, the soft blanket of snow covering all the fields and trees was the best sight he had seen in nine long months.

That was, until she opened that door.

It was early, only four in the morning, but the sight of her in her pajamas, her face bare of makeup, just *her*, he almost couldn't speak.

She started to say something as she flung open the door, a look of anger and hurt on her face, but the words died as her eyes widened and her mouth slid open as she blinked.

"James."

God, her voice.

"Hey, sweetheart," he murmured, and he got to watch that wash over her before she leapt forward, her body slamming into his right before she started sobbing.

God, he missed her in his arms.

He tightened his arms around her and breathed her in, her familiar scent of vanilla and *home* filling him and making everything that had happened in the last two weeks worth it.

"You're here." There was a wealth of pain in her voice

in those two simple words, and it cut him to the quick. He knew that not being able to call would have been hard on her, it had been hard on him too, but that pain—that was something else.

"It's okay." He said the only thing he could think of and knew it fell flat when she pulled back and cupped his cheek, looking up at him in amazement and yearning, the tears on her lashes glistening in the morning light.

"I thought you were dead," she choked out as something flashed in her eyes.

That made him pause.

Dead?

What the fuck!

"Sweetheart. Didn't you call…" He stopped as that something in her eyes filled her whole face, and his world right then and there spun faster, knowing that what she was about to say would rock him.

"I called everyone I knew!" she sobbed. "I tried everything. Nobody would tell me anything except that you were on a mission. That they wouldn't be able to contact you. I thought it was a ploy. Something to appease me till they brought your body home." She finished on a yelling sob, then wrapped her arms around him again and shoved her head in the crook of his neck, her shaking hands grasping at the collar of his shirt as if she was hanging on with everything she had.

Brought his body home.

Her words rolled over him.

Holy fuck!

"I'm so sorry." That feeling deep in his chest that weighed on him started crushing him as he realized what he had left behind and the lasting pain that had followed her because of it.

"I can't lose you!" She was past incoherent now, her

arms tightening around him as if she was never going to let go, and he knew that if he didn't get her settled down soon that she was going to make herself sick.

"Hey, sweetheart. I'm not going anywhere, okay?" he said as he hefted her up, her legs wrapping around his waist, and moved in the door. Dropping his bag next to them and shutting the door behind them with his foot, he started into the house.

Was she always this light?

He reached the couch and sat down, intent on calming her, but she surprised him when she twisted around. Her sleep shirt, or his shirt rather, rode up on her thigh, showing her bare and uncovered ass, and he lost his train of thought.

She didn't seem to have the same issue as she fisted her hands in his hair and slammed her mouth down on his.

Quickly, their kiss became heated as she nipped and sucked at his lips, her hips rubbing against his dick, her thighs wrapped around him as she sat in his lap, and he was content to just soak it in.

God, she felt good.

Before long, their hands started roaming, and he'd had enough of sitting back and kissing her.

He wanted all of her.

Now.

He leaned sideways, settling her so she was under him, reveling in the feel of her thighs wrapped around him as she opened them wider, as if welcoming him home.

"I missed you," she choked out as he fumbled with his zipper before she reached down and took over.

"I missed you too, sweetheart." Sliding his fingers through her folds, he flicked at her clit before sliding them deep inside her wet heat. He clenched his eyes shut, his head falling forward to her chest, as it hit him that she was there in his arms.

Fuck.

"I don't want your hand. I want you. Please, James, it's been too long," she whispered against his ear, her tongue coming out to lick at the shell.

Nine months too long.

Nine months without feeling her skin.

Nine months without tasting her.

Nine months without falling asleep after having her pussy wrapped around him.

Nine months of waiting in hell.

Her hand slid up and cupped his cheek, and he opened his eyes to find her tear-stained ones staring back at him.

"I love you." She whispered the words that for weeks he had longed to hear.

Words that broke him.

He surged up, fisting the shirt she was wearing and shoving it up as he slid inside of her with a groan to match her gasp.

He didn't take his time.

He didn't even remember to breathe. He simply started thrusting into her sweet heat and let her take him home.

* * *

MELANIE

His gaze was distant as she rubbed her hands over his sculpted chest, cupping the water and letting it wash away the soap. He was definitely more muscular now, and adding that to the new full beard, the teenager that she fell in love with was almost nowhere to be found.

In front of her was a man.

"Hey," she whispered, and he flinched, his troubled eyes finally coming back to her.

In the last few months, something had aged him. Not physically, but mentally. She could feel the heavy weight of it surrounding them.

"You know I'm here if you want to talk, right?" He nodded.

"I know, but honestly, sweetheart, I just want to enjoy being home." She nodded back, but knew that she would have to keep pushing. He had never been good at sharing his problems, too intent on providing everything for her rather than focusing on himself.

She drew her finger over a red puckered scar on his side and her stomach dropped at the implication. It wasn't the first scar that he'd come home with, but this one was new, and she hated every one of them. She hated them because each one took something from her man.

"You're' not going to let it go, are you?" He chuckled, pinching her chin and tilting her head back as he backed her into the cold tile wall. She didn't care, though. His wet body was pressed against hers and she could feel everything.

"No," she husked out, answering his question, hoping that look in his eyes meant that she was going to be getting round three right here in the shower, but he only shook his head.

"Sweetheart, you wore me out. Give a man a sec to recuperate." Leaning forward, he nipped her nose. "Let's get out, and we can talk," he whispered before leaning down and giving her a soft and gentle kiss.

As he pulled back the covers on the bed and laid down, she fought her tears. It had been too long since she had done something so ordinary with him, and her chest began to ache. He laid on his back and wrapped one of his arms around her, pulling her into him, the blankets on the bed draped over both of them as he heaved a big sigh.

"Fuck, I missed our bed," he muttered and kissed the top of her head as they lay there in the silence.

"What happened?" she whispered, breaking the silence and fingering the scar again.

His arm tightened around her before he gave her what she needed to help make him heal.

"We were gathering intel on a new route into an insurgent camp. It was supposed to be routine, but we quickly learned that it was a chemical base."

"Chemical base?" she asked, her brow furrowing.

"Bombs, sweetheart," he said softly, and her heart jumped.

"Is that…" She sat up quickly, looking at him in horror, her mind instantly spinning about what she almost lost.

"No. Hey. It's okay," he quickly reassured. "They bombed our camp, but nobody died." He reached up and brushed his finger over her cheek, leaving a warm trail in its place before pulling her down till she was resting on his chest again. "It's all right."

"Are you going to be okay?" she asked, fighting tears again.

"Yep. No lasting damage."

"How's Dean?" Tilting her head back, she looked up at him.

"He's okay. He had some shrapnel in his leg, so he is still in recovery, but he will be discharged in a few more weeks."

"He's coming here, right?" she asked, already knowing how close the two were.

He gave her his soft look, the one that said that he loved her and didn't know how to tell her just how much.

That look made her melt.

"Yeah, sweetheart, he is." She nodded and laid her head

back down on his chest, letting the feel of his hot skin soothe her aching soul.

For months, she had been sleeping in their bed by herself. The coldness of the blankets was the hardest part to get used to, but with James there snuggled in next to her, she found that she couldn't keep her eyes open, and before she knew it, she was out.

CHAPTER 10
JAMES

She was lying on her side, her arm thrown up over her head, her naked ass curled into his semi hard cock, her bare breasts only slightly visible from under the curve of the blankets wrapped around them, and he was satisfied in a way that he hadn't been in months.

And that wasn't just his dick talking.

That feeling that he had carried with him the last few years, the emptiness that seemed to pull at him in his darkest moments, it was gone.

He was home.

But he couldn't sleep.

Because he was looking at her and he knew that this last deployment had taken its toll on her too. She had lost weight, her face leaner than before, with dark circles under her eyes that he knew came from too many sleepless nights.

Too many nights without them together.

And based on the state of the house, she hadn't been taking care of any part of her life.

The house was dark.

The fireplace cold, and there wasn't a single Christmas decoration in sight.

That was *not* his girl.

His girl loved Christmas.

Ironic that they hadn't gotten to spend one together.

But she had always sent him videos of herself in front of the Christmas tree on Christmas morning. Her mug of hot chocolate in hand, her adorable Christmas pjs with the silly reindeer on them curving her body. She would open her gifts and he would watch a smile cross her face every time.

She always made it magical, even from thousands of miles away, and he'd been looking forward to seeing it all in person.

But now, knowing what she had been going through, knowing that she had thought he was dead, he couldn't blame her.

But he could do something about it.

Slowly sliding out from behind her, he tucked the blanket around her before pulling on his pants and going to get some firewood.

Then he had calls to make.

* * *

MELANIE

When he had cuddled behind her late in the morning, his big body cold to the touch, quickly heating them both as he slid his cock deep inside of her, groaning as if he would die without it, that was when she had slowly woken up.

Her hand had reached out, grasping his tightly, a breath of relief leaving her, clenching her eyes shut, as she'd realized it hadn't been a dream.

He was here.

Then he started thrusting, and she lost all thought as he

quickly brought her to a body-shaking release and then quickly followed after. Holding her tightly to him.

"You want to go on a walk with me?" he murmured, kissing down the slope of her neck and to the swell of her breast.

Honestly, she wanted to stay here in bed and pretend the world didn't exist. That it was just her and him in their own little world, but she knew she wasn't going to get her way when he pulled away.

"Let's get you out for just a few minutes." He gave her a look, and she didn't argue. She wasn't ready to admit that she had started to spiral down a hole without him, but somehow, with that one look, she suspected that he already knew.

It didn't take him long to have her dressed and out the door, and although she wouldn't admit it, it was nice to go on a small walk. The birds were about the only noise as the snow on the ground muffled anything else, making the whole walk seem even more peaceful. What made it the best walk she had ever been on, though, was his hand clasped in hers.

"You haven't been taking care of yourself," he said, broaching a subject that she would rather he not have brought up. But he was stubborn, and she knew that he wasn't going to leave it alone.

"I missed you." She whispered her only defense.

"I missed you too, sweetheart, but I thought you would have…" He stopped and sighed.

"I'll do better next time. It was just the not knowing that got to me. I was doing okay, but then that last mission had you gone for so long, and I didn't even know if you were okay." She looked away and sighed, feeling his eyes boring into her with so much intensity that she could hardly stand it. "It was harder than I thought. But

I'm prepared now. I know what's going to happen this time..."

"I'm not going back."

His words threw her, and she blinked, gaping up at him. "What?"

"I signed my release papers when I was overseas. I'm done. "

"You're done?" She couldn't help the hopeful lilt in her voice.

"Yes." His beautiful eyes were searing into her.

"Done." The tears in her eyes trailed over her cheeks.

"Sweetheart..." His face softened.

"I love you," she whispered and watched as it washed over him.

"I love you too, sweetheart. Just you and me, okay?" He finally took the step forward that brought his body to hers and wrapped his arm around her.

"Now let's get you a Christmas tree."

* * *

"How about you get up in the attic and bring the Christmas stuff while I clean this tree off," he said while pulling the small tree that she had picked out behind him.

What did it say that he had dragged the whole thing home and wasn't even out of breath?

She stomped up the back porch steps, making sure to knock the snow off her boots.

"You want me to start breakfast after that?" she asked, leaning down to unlace her boots, hoping that she had enough food to actually make something.

She was regretting not going shopping, especially since she knew she would get that look from James again when he found out.

"Sure, sweetheart," he replied distractedly as he leaned the tree against the back porch, then followed the same routine as her, stomping his boots before unlacing them and making his way into the laundry room.

Weird that he was taking off his shoes, only to have to go back out and get the tree.

"You need something?" she asked, wondering if maybe he had forgotten something, but when she looked back, he only smirked at her.

Okay, something was up.

She was just about to turn around, when the light in the living room caught her attention.

Holy crap!

All her Christmas decorations were up.

From the holly above the fireplace, to the snowman pillows on the couch, to the tall, fake candles she liked to use in the windows.

It was all there.

"What—"

"I love you, sweetheart," he whispered, coming up behind her and wrapping his arms around her. "I had your Pop, Mac, and Tracey come up. It's not the full thing, but…"

He's right, it wasn't the full thing. There weren't cookies on the table, or her special Christmas cake stand, and there wasn't the scent of Christmas dinner coming from the kitchen.

The tree wasn't up yet, and the fire wasn't lit, but with him behind her, pressed in tightly, and his arms around her… "It's perfect."

"Tracey is having Christmas dinner at the diner, and I told them we would meet them there, but I wanted us to have Christmas morning together." She twisted so she could look up into his eyes, reaching up to cup his bearded cheek.

"I love you," she whispered before he leaned down and kissed her, his lounge sweeping out to lick at the seam of her lips before pushing her backwards till the back of her knees hit the couch. Pushing her down, he followed her, so that he was lying over her, their legs twisted. She could feel his hardness pressed against her and it took everything she had to not arch up and grind into him as he placed his weight onto his elbows on either side of her head, surrounding her.

"I love you more than anything. You know that, right, Melanie?" There was something in his eyes, something new, something that she knew she wanted more of.

"I know."

"You know I would do anything for you."

"Yes."

"And you would do anything for me, right?" he whispered, his thumb playing with the edge of her jaw, sending shivers along her spine as his hips rolled slightly into her.

"Yes," she barely managed.

"Then can my Christmas gift next year be a baby?" he asked softly, and her heart leapt in her chest.

Holy...

"I want a beautiful little girl that looks just like her mama," he husked out, running his nose along hers, his eyes staring deep into hers, and just like that, any freakout that she might have thought about having slid away, and she knew that she would give him anything.

Especially this.

"Yes."

His smile was worth it.

But then again, he made it worth her while too.

EPILOGUE
JAMES

Christmas Eve - One year later

He leaned back against the counter and smiled, watching his wife as she chatted with Emma and Eleanor about some new book that Eleanor had published. Based on the pink cheeks of all three of them, he was guessing that it was another one of her spicy romances that they loved to read.

Henry, Eleanor's man, was standing behind her with a proud smile on his face as he watched his wife as well. It was the look of a man that knew his wife was happy and therefore he was happy too. He should know. He suspected that he had that same look a lot these days.

Branson chuckled from beside him, before shaking his head, probably thinking the same thing he had been. Then he walked off to get his wife, Emma, and drag her to the food bar, again.

"That man can eat," Mac grumped from next to him. The guy had been extra off lately, and he knew that Melanie, along with Pop, had both been on his case, but unlike them, he knew what was going on with the man, or rather, *who* was bothering him.

Just like Branson, Connor, and himself, it looked like Mac was the next to take the plunge.

He smirked and shook his own head before walking over to his wife and wrapping his arms around her, his hand coming to rest on her big belly out in front of her.

Yes, best Christmas ever.

Follow Up

f @KBBarrettRomanceAuthor

in @kbbarrettauthor

t @kbbarrettauthor

www.authorkbbarrett.com

Make sure to follow K.B. Barrett
for up-to-date information on all her upcoming books
Find all her links at
www.authorkbbarrett.com/links

ABOUT K.B. BARRETT

K.B. Barrett lives in western Michigan with her wonderful husband and three kids. Her love of books started early, thanks to her grandmother, an avid reader who encouraged her to love all books. Eventually she had too many ideas and decided to start writing her own books. What started out as a small hobby led to her first book, *Everything I Need*, being published in March. She likes writing romantic books that are full of suspense and complicated, but they always come with a happily ever after.

Originally from Oregon, she and her husband have had the pleasure of living all over the United States. While she enjoys traveling to new destinations, it is the feeling that you get from living in a new place that she loves the best. For her there is nothing quite like having a life full of adventure. She feels blessed that she has had the opportunity to go wherever the wind decides to take her, whether that is traveling and exploring new places, following her kids around, or simply sitting out on the deck enjoying coffee in one of her colorful mugs.

KB Barrett

www.authorkbbarrett.com

THE *Surprise* WITHIN

LISAMARIE KADE

Copyright 2022 by Lisamarie Kade

Edits and proofreading by Magnolia Author Services

2022 Kade Publishing LLC

CHAPTER 1
FALLON

It's quiet here. Almost too quiet. The only sounds are the waves crashing along the shoreline and the palm trees dancing in the wind. Taking a sip of my Malibu Bay Breeze, complete with an umbrella in it, I glance around. There are not many people out here on the beach on Christmas Eve.

Then again, I wonder how many people vacation in the Bahamas for Christmas. Probably not many. Christmas typically means snow while sipping hot cocoa by the fireplace.

I'm all for a white Christmas. However, Trent got called to do some sort of training for the Marine Corp Reserves. That left me with zero plans for Christmas and since his parents, Vivian and Tom Maxwell, had already booked a trip to the Bahamas for the holidays, they insisted I tag along. I'm not really tagging along. I have my own oceanfront suite on Paradise Island. I haven't even seen his parents yet today. We'll do Christmas Eve dinner later at a local steak and seafood restaurant.

Just thinking about being here for the next few days without Trent makes me miss him. I wish he was here, though I understand it is his duty. I know all too well how military life goes. We've been friends forever and I was there when he went off to the Marines, having different assignments all over. It's kind of how our relationship formed in the first place. Me here in the states with him far away in Japan. That's military life.

So, while he is in North Carolina, here I am, in a white bikini, sipping a cocktail by the ocean. I guess it's not all that bad.

After laying in the sun for a while, I decide to head back to my suite to relax in the bath. Lucky for me, the bathroom has a huge jacuzzi jet tub. I downloaded an Abbi Glines novel on my e-reader before climbing in. Nice and relaxing before getting ready for dinner.

As soon as I got out of the tub and wrapped myself in a fluffy towel, I sent Trent a text wishing him a Merry Christmas Eve, but he hasn't responded. Again, it's just something I've grown used to. A lot of the time, he can't be on his phone. Another part of military life.

I stare at myself in the mirror as I finish applying lip gloss. My dark hair is curled. I went light on the smoky eye look. I hope I'm not overdressed. The silver sequin dress stops just above my knees. Thin straps and low cut down the front, but not super low cut. Like my boobs aren't popping out. It's tasteful. Vivian told me to pack a nice dress for tonight's dinner. I just hope it's not overkill for where we are going.

Heading out to the front lobby of the resort, I send a text to the Maxwells letting them know I'll grab us a cab. As soon as I hit send, another text comes through.

Trent.

Hey babe miss you. How is your day?

It was good, leaving for dinner with your parents now.

Enjoy dinner. I miss you.

Miss you more

Sliding my phone in my clutch purse, I wave down a cab and climb into the first one that stops.

"Just a moment, two more are coming down now."

The driver nods at the same time my phone dings. Pulling it out of my clutch, Vivian's name flashes across the screen. I slide open the message.

Go on ahead dear, we are running a few minutes behind. We'll meet you there.

She sends a follow-up text with the address to the restaurant, and I quickly rattle it off to the driver. I sigh while staring out the window. Tall buildings light up the night sky. Signs for casinos and nightclubs pass by in a blur as the cab driver takes me to our well my destination.

Vivian told me to be ready by seven. I double check our texts to make sure I didn't misunderstand. Nope, didn't read it wrong. I hope everything is okay with them.

Tom and Vivian are like my second parents. Well, they might as well be. Even growing up, my parents couldn't be bothered with me, their only child. Instead, I spent my time in the Maxwell house with the boys. Connor and Trent. Connor was my best friend. God, just thinking about him makes my heart ache. I miss him so damn much it hurts.

The driver pulls into Moon Beach Cove, pulling me out of my dark thoughts. I pass the driver a tip as I climb out and adjust my dress.

The tall white building is lit up in twinkling lights.

From the looks of it, there may be a resort or casino here as well.

Walking in, the hallway is lined with blue twinkling lights. It's got a nightclub vibe. I continue on my way, my silver heels clicking with each step I take.

Once I reach the podium, the hostess smiles brightly at me. "Good evening."

"Hi, I have reservations for Maxwell."

The hostess, whose tan skin glows under the lights perfectly, smiles while tapping away on the tablet in front of her. She looks up a moment later. "Your table is ready if you'll follow me."

Once seated, I glance around, a little nervous to be here alone. Vivian and Tom said they would be right behind me. I would think they would be here by now.

To ease my nerves, I distract myself by looking over the menu. Everything sounds so good that I'm going to have trouble deciding what to order.

"Good evening, ma'am, may I start you off with something to drink?" The server's deep voice almost startles me.

"Yes, a Malibu Bay Breeze."

"You got it. Are you still waiting on others to join you?" He takes a glance at the other menus laid out before looking at me once again.

"Yes."

"Very well, I'll be back shortly with your drink."

I watch as he walks away, lost in thought. Why do I feel so anxious?

It's because you're waiting on Trent's parents.

Suddenly, I feel someone's breath on my ear, and I stiffen. "Tell me you love me."

That voice! I push my chair out so fast, that he has to catch it to keep it from falling to the ground.

Trent.

I throw my arms around his neck as he wraps his around my waist tightly. Trent's lips find mine as he kisses me hard, letting me know just how much he has missed me.

Reluctantly, I pull back. The realization that Trent is actually here hits hard.

"You're here! You're really here."

"What? Did you honestly think I'd miss our first Christmas together?"

"Well, I knew you had training, that was out of your control."

"Surprise." He winks. "I flew in this morning."

"This morning?" I ask as he guides me to sit back down in my chair. I had completely forgotten that we were in a restaurant full of people.

I watch as he pulls out the chair next to me. The veins in his hands are thick as he grips the back of the chair. It makes my mouth water, and just like that, I am no longer hungry anymore. Well, for food anyway. I can only think of those hands roaming my body while Trent devours me.

"Don't worry, Fal, they'll be plenty of room for dessert." Trent taps the menu with a smirk. "For now, let's focus on dinner."

I give him my best pouty face. The fact that he reads me so well says a lot. He's always been able to read my thoughts, even when I didn't think he noticed me at all.

The server comes back returns with my drink and asks Trent what he would like before leaving us alone again. It dawns on me; his parents are still not here.

"Wait, what about your parents? They should be here by now."

Trent laughs while I glance around looking for them. A smirk forms on his face when I bring my attention back to him.

"What's so funny?"

"Nothing, they will not be joining us tonight."

"What?! Were they in on this?"

Trent nods like he just pulled off the world's greatest prank. Ass.

"But it's Christmas Eve."

"Yeah, and I've been away from you. I wanted time with you alone. We'll see them tomorrow."

I pull him by the collar of his shirt. The urge to kiss him is strong. The second our lips connect, everything else falls away. The chatter, the sound of glasses clinking. Nothing else matters.

Trent is here.

All too soon, I feel Trent pulling back. He grabs my hand, bringing it over to his lap, rubbing it over his erection.

"If you keep it up, we will not make it through dinner. I prefer you to eat something so you have energy for all I have planned later."

Hot damn.

His words alone have me squeezing my thighs together while I gape at him in shock.

"See, look. I got you all hot and bothered. Now, let's order."

As if he didn't just have me rubbing his hard-on, he winks once and waves his hand, getting the server's attention.

"I'm on the first floor," I say as we walk through the entrance of the resort.

"I know."

"Huh? How do you know?"

With his hand on my lower back, he guides me through the lobby toward the rooms. "I told you, I arrived this morning. I watched you lay out by the beach and then head in."

"Oh my god! And you never came down?"

"Believe me, I wanted to. I wanted to march my ass out on that beach to cover you and that skimpy bikini right up so no one could look at my girl."

I swat at Trent, shaking my head. "You never cared before about my swim attire." We've spent years in his parent's pool. Numerous pool parties. Back then, though, he never even looked my way.

When I pull my key card out, Trent snatches and opens the door. He drags me in quickly before I can even get my feet to move, nearly causing me to trip. He shuts the door in a rush, locking it. He turns around and looks at me with a heated stare. I feel his dark eyes undressing me. The fact that he wants me so bad has me reaching behind to unzip my dress.

"Don't. Do not undress, Fallon. I'll be the one doing the undressing." Trent walks up slowly while unbuttoning his shirt. The anticipation is killing me as he removes it and tosses it on the dresser.

CHAPTER 2
TRENT

Merry Christmas Eve to me. Fallon looks so fucking hot. I've been dying to sink my dick into her since I saw her laying on the beach this morning. It took everything in me and a few reminders from my parents not to march out there and fuck her right there on the beach. They kept reminding me that I would ruin her surprise.

Fallon sits on the edge of the bed, waiting for my next move. Walking over, I lean over her, putting one arm on each side of her. I trail kisses from just below her ear to down her neck and collarbone. She leans back, giving me access, moaning in return.

Sliding one hand under her dress, I run my fingers up the inside of her thigh. Reaching under the lace, I feel she is already wet for me. It makes my dick throb more just knowing how badly she wants me.

Standing back up, I push her dress up so it bunches at her hips. Pink lace stares back at me, begging to be ripped off. That's exactly what I do. I yank Fallon's thong off so fast she yelps. Squatting, I run my tongue along her wet slit, teasing her. God, I've missed this. Missed her, the way she tastes. I've missed everything about her.

Her moans fill the room as I continue licking and sucking, pushing her closer to the edge. Her hands grab the back of my head holding me in place. She's close now. Flicking my tongue over her clit, she comes undone, screaming out my name.

That's right.

Let the entire hotel know who you belong to. My cock swells knowing she is mine.

As Fallon's shaking slows, I stand up and remove the rest of my clothing. I want nothing more than to sink into her pussy.

"Unzip your dress," I demand.

She does so without question. As soon as it is unzipped, I help her pull it over her head. I want to see my girl naked. I stare at her while throwing the dress behind me, not giving a shit where it lands.

Leaning on her elbows, Fallon is naked. She wasn't wearing a bra tonight. Fuck me.

She is a fucking sight too.

Her dark hair is already messy, some of it falling over her shoulder. Her perfect tits rise and fall with each breath she takes.

She is all mine.

Fallon O'Neil is mine.

Coming in close, I spread her legs further apart. Lining my dick up at her entrance, she arches slightly, pushing against my erection. She wants me inside of her now, but I want to drag this out.

"You are mine."

Fallon nods. Nope, that won't do.

"I need to hear you say it. You are mine."

"I am yours." She bites her lip nervously.

Rubbing my thumb across her lip, I pull it out and lean down to kiss her. Fallon kisses me back with such passion, I thrust into her slowly. She moans into my mouth, and I swear it's the hottest thing. The way she moans at my touch, it makes me want to shout, *"She's mine!"* From the rooftops. I want every guy to know they'll never have her.

Never, and I plan to make sure of that.

I continue with slow movements, wanting this to last. Making love to my girl. Our bodies moving together as one is some kind of perfect.

"Trent," Fallon breathes out.

"Yeah, babe."

"I love you."

Those three words. Every time I hear them, I'm reminded of how lucky I am to even have her. I nearly threw our relationship, and friendship for that matter, out the window, but somehow this woman picked us up and put us back together.

"I love you."

I speed up my movements, feeling myself getting close. Her nails drag down my back as her moans grow louder.

It doesn't take long before we climb that mountain and fall over the edge together, as one.

CHAPTER 3
FALLON

Sipping my coffee, I stare out at the clear blue waters. My body is sore in the best way. Trent made love to me and then he fucked me like there was no tomorrow. I guess sore is an understatement. I regret nothing though. I'm just so glad he is here and that we get to spend Christmas together.

I glance back at him, still sleeping. He's tangled in the sheets. I should have stayed in bed with him, but I couldn't sleep. I don't know why; usually, when Trent is home, I sleep well. He calms me. It's when he is gone that I don't sleep well and sometimes nightmares of the past come back to haunt me. Not as often now, but they still pop up every once in a while.

"Merry Christmas, Connor," I whisper, staring up at the sky. Another holiday without him. It makes my heart hurt.

"Fal." I hear him yawn. "Come back to bed."

Shaking my thoughts, I stand and head toward the bed. Trent looks to be passed back out. I giggle. An idea comes to mind. A naughty one.

I pull the sheets back a little. He's semi-hard. Perfect.

Climbing on all fours, I move across the king-size bed and wrap my hands around his cock.

I stroke him slowly, feeling him swell in my hand. He rolls slightly so that he's completely on his back now, but otherwise I think he's still asleep. Or he's playing that he's asleep. I really don't care. I'm on a mission.

Bringing my lips to the tip, I lick ever so slowly down his base. Repeating my movements, I do this several times before finally taking him into my mouth. My free hand moves to his balls as I suck his cock slowly.

Deep moans leave Trent's mouth. Moans that having me growing wet. Keeping a slow yet steady motion, I taste a little pre-cum. I swipe my tongue over his tip, needing more.

"Fal, fuck," Trent moans as he fists my hair. He forces me to take him deeper, faster.

I love what I do to him. His cock swells even more, letting me know he's getting close. I continue my aggressive movements even while my eyes water from how deep I am taking him.

"Fuck!" Trent growls as he grips my hair, keeping me in place. His cock pulsates in my mouth as warm liquid coats the back of my throat.

"Swallow," he demands, and I do. I milk every ounce of cum from his cock and swallow.

Once his cock stops thrusting, I pull back slowly and look up at Trent. I wipe the corner of my lip and wink.

"Good morning."

"Oh, it's a good morning, all right." He pulls me up on top of him, kissing me once on the lips before pushing his tongue in to kiss me deeper.

He reaches between us. "So wet for me."

I can only moan into his mouth as he teases me with his finger, rubbing it in circles.

I feel his erection and pull back, breaking our kiss. I grab him, lining him up at my entrance, and sink down.

He hisses out a string of curse words as his hands move to grip my hips, guiding me up and down. It doesn't take long for the sweet feeling to build back up and the moment Trent moves a hand from my hip to my clit, I know I'm done for. He rubs and applies pressure, sending me over the edge. Uncontrollable waves roll through me as I ride him harder.

"That's it baby, fuck."

Trent squeezes my hips tightly, holding me still as he fills me. I'm weak as I collapse on top of him. Both of us are covered in a sheen of sweat. I don't even care because there's nothing quite like Christmas morning sex.

* * *

"Come on, Fal, we are going to be late!" Trent shouts from the front of the room. I'm still in the bathroom, putting the finishing touches on my makeup. After a mind-blowing morning, I went back to sleep, only to be woken up by Trent saying we needed to hurry. Apparently, I missed the memo that we are having Christmas breakfast with his parents.

I wish I had known; I would have never gone back to bed. I look like hell. No makeup is covering my tired eyes. None that I packed anyway.

"Fallon, get your ass out here!"

Sighing, I hit the light switch and walk out. Trent is leaning up against the door, feet crossed at his ankles. His dark hair is a little shorter than I would like, but I get it, he has to keep it short when he reports. He's wearing a grey shirt and black jeans that hug his hips and muscular thighs just right. A sexy smile plays on his lips. He knows I'm checking him out, and damn if he doesn't look good.

"We are late. You know what my parents will think we were doing that caused us to be late?"

"Shut up!" I walk up and go to swat at his chest, but he catches my wrist pulling me to him.

Trent kisses my forehead, then trails down the side of my face, peppering kisses along the way until he reaches my neck. He nips me once before pulling back.

"Trent," I warn. If he keeps this up, we will definitely be late.

"Okay, fine let's go." He smirks, pulling me out the door.

"I'm stuffed," I say as the four of us walk down the sidewalk to head back to the resort. Trent leans over. "I'll be stuffing you later." I nearly gasp and push him away. God, I hope his parents didn't hear him. We are adults and all, but still.

"Vivian wants to go back to the room for a little while to relax before this evening's festivities."

We are having dinner at the resort later. Vivian and Tom said they made the reservation about eight months in advance because it is Christmas after all.

"Okay, I was thinking of hitting the beach with Fallon for a bit so that works."

I smile at Trent's words. I'm kind of tired and want to rest, but the thought of being in the water with him has me rethinking that plan. There's just something about us and being in the water together. It has gone from sitting on the edge of the pool as a teenager that crushed on him from a distance to getting to touch his half-naked wet body now.

After getting changed and gathering up towels and sunscreen, we head out through the French doors that open up to the beautiful blue waters. The ocean at home sure doesn't look like this. Not one bit. And while it seems odd to be spending Christmas on the beach, I would probably be doing the same thing back home in Florida. Either that or I'd be in the Maxwells' pool. Florida doesn't participate in winter.

I set everything down and apply a little sunscreen. It may be December, but according to my weather app, it's eighty degrees out and slightly cloudy.

"Will you apply some on my shoulders?" I ask Trent.

He nods and walks up to me, taking the bottle from my hand. Moving my hair to the side, he starts applying the sunscreen.

"You know I could take you right here, right now."

"Trent." I try to keep my voice firm, but it fails me. His words make me weak.

"I won't, though, I don't think I could handle anyone else seeing you melt at my touch. I wouldn't want anyone to catch a glimpse of--" He pauses to grab my pussy.

Fuck. Him and his words. I'm nearly ready to pull the string on my bikini. He can have me wherever he would like. People seeing us is the farthest thing from my mind currently.

"I really don't want anyone seeing you in this either." He waves a hand at my swimsuit. It's not like it is super revealing. A simple black bikini.

Shaking my head at him, I saunter toward the crystal blue water, shaking my ass as I go, teasing.

"Fallon."

Peeking back over my shoulder, I wink. "Come on, lover, let's cool you down."

He jogs down to catch up with me just as my feet hit the water. He grabs me around my waist and runs into the water. Surprisingly the water is somewhat warm even with the cloud coverage.

"God, I've missed this," Trent says as he spins me around before letting me go. My feet hit the sand, the water is only waist deep.

"Missed what?"

"Us, being together, being carefree."

"Like this?" I splash at him.

He's not wrong. We have been through some rough patches. We've been through a lot of heartache over the past few years, and somewhere along the way, we lost the ability to just be together and have a good time.

Slowly though, I think we are finding our way back to happiness. Back to before things went to shit.

Trent grabs my wrist, preventing me from splashing him more. One swift pull and I'm wrapped back in his arms.

"I love you, Fal."

"And I love you."

He drops one hand from my waist. Lowering it underwater, he drags it down my skin until he comes to my bikini bottoms. The minute his fingers skim under them, my eyes shoot to his.

"Trent..." I trail off before looking around. It's pretty dead out here, considering it is Christmas Day, but still.

"Shh," he replies as he dips a finger inside of me.

He leans down, kissing me. His kiss is almost desperate, as if he can't get enough. Hell, at this point, I can't get enough of him. His movements turn carnal as he adds a second finger. His kiss turns rough. I can't help but moan into his mouth. What's happening between us is raw, too raw. Yet, I welcome it.

Trent releases my mouth, trailing kisses along my jaw down to my neck. The sensation of it plus what he's doing under the water has me on the brink of losing all control.

"Let go for me."

His words go straight to my core as his finger sweeps over my clit, applying just the right amount of pressure. Waves break around us as I lose control, calling out his name over and over.

"Mine, forever."

I'm too lost in pleasure to respond to that statement. Forever? Everything is still too foggy, there's no way he said it. Trent and I have only just begun dating seriously. Well, for the past six months anyway, even though we go back farther than that. Trent couldn't commit, didn't know how to. I guess I really didn't either, not until I jumped on a plane and flew across the world to see him.

Maybe that's why I'm having trouble understanding what I think I heard. That is until Trent tips my chin up to look him square in his dark eyes.

"Did you hear me, Fallon? You are mine. Forever."

I swallow slowly, I can only nod in response. No words come. Not a single one.

CHAPTER 4
TRENT

Telling Fallon that she was mine forever felt good. It felt real. She looked shocked, or maybe she is confused by my words. She has a right to be, after all. I've put her through hell and back more than once, but she's it for me. She's going to know it too. Soon.

We wade in the water quietly for a few more minutes before I nod. "Ready to go in and relax before dinner?"

"In a minute, I'm kind of enjoying being out here."

"Whenever you are ready."

I won't rush her. I love seeing her out here like this, completely relaxed. She's always loved being in the water. She would spend all summer in my pool.

She dips underwater and comes up, brushing her dark hair out of her face. She's so fucking perfect. Water beads off her chest. I have to resist the urge to reach out and wipe it away. I want to. I want to fuck her right now. The erection in my swim trunks agrees. However, I need her rested for later. If I take her now, I won't be easy, and she may be too sore later for what I have planned.

Fuck, just thinking of what I have planned has me stroking myself through the wet fabric. I really should drag her out of the water and take her back to the room because I'm not sure I trust myself to keep control for much longer. Especially watching the way her tits bounce each time a wave passes.

Fallon clears her throat, eyebrow raised. She caught me staring. She swims over to me, throwing her arms around my neck. The second she steps in close, I know she can feel my hard-on.

Her eyes widen, confirming.

What's more, is she grinds into me. She's fucking teasing me.

"Fallon," I warn.

She doesn't reply with words. Instead, she wraps her legs around me, rubbing her pussy against me. If only there wasn't material in the way. Not that it has stopped me in the past.

Fuck.

She has no idea what she is doing to me. My resistance is like a rubber band being pulled. I'm about to snap. I try to keep it at bay by sliding a finger into her. Like that will keep me from wanting to stick my dick into her.

Who am I kidding?

I sink into the water a little more. I don't want to risk anyone seeing us like this.

"Trent, please," Fallon breathes into my ear as she continues rubbing against me.

Her words are my weakness. The rubber band snaps and without another thought, I yank the string on one side of her bikini. I watch with hooded eyes as it floats away from her smooth skin. Holding her tight with one arm, I make quick work of freeing my dick from my trunks. I thrust into her so hard that she screams out. I quickly cover her mouth with my hand.

"You gotta be quiet, babe."

She doesn't listen because she continues moaning and biting into my hand each time I thrust into her. The water slaps around us. It would definitely be obvious to the naked eye as to what we are doing but I don't care.

Nothing compares to fucking Fallon in these crystal blues waters and one thing is certain, she'll be sore later.

Oh well.

* * *

I glance over at the bed. There, wrapped in the white sheets, is my girl. She's become my whole world. What took me so long to realize that?

Connor.

Shaking my head at the thoughts of my brother, I walk into the bathroom to get ready. Grabbing my toothbrush, I let the memories of earlier on the beach rush back.

Fucking Fallon in the ocean wasn't in my plans, but boy am I glad I did. It was damn amazing and one of the hottest moments with her. Comes in second to the night we were together in the hotel.

Afterward, I carried her out of the ocean and back into the room where I ran her a shower and washed her body. I put her to bed naked with her hair still wet. She'll probably hate me for that, but it is what it is. She needed sleep for later.

Fuck, just thinking about later makes me nervous and horny. I knew I was in deep a few years ago. I just chose to deny it. Hurt us both more than once. Made us suffer more than once. Fucked with her head more than once. God, I was a piece of shit to her.

Not anymore though. Not after tonight if I can help it.

I'm damn lucky she is still here by my side. That she

didn't give up. She fought for us even when I thought she was stupid for doing such a thing.

Spitting the toothpaste into the sink, I rinse out my mouth and continue getting ready. I want tonight to be perfect.

I can't believe I planned all this; well, with the help of my parents. A tropical island holiday that will consist of Christmas dinner at the resort, followed by dessert on the beach. Surprising Fallon with my arrival was one thing, but tonight will be an even bigger surprise.

I hope.

Walking back into the room, I go over to Fallon. Her back is to me, exposed with her dark hair all over. I hate the thought of having to wake her, but if I wait any longer, we will most likely be late for dinner.

"Fal, babe." I lean down, gently nudging her. "Come on, it is time to wake up. You need to get ready."

She stirs, rolling toward me. The sheets drop just low enough that her perfect tits are now on display.

Hell, if I'm not being tested right now.

I step back, having to adjust myself. I'm too tempted to take one in my mouth and if I do that, we will not be leaving this room. Fuck.

"Fallon."

"Mmhm."

She rolls again, this time away from me. Thank fuck. My erection is begging to sink into her pussy which I'm sure is wet and ready. She's always wet, always ready. When it comes to Fallon, I'm never satisfied. I can never get enough of her.

"Come on, babe, we need to be getting ready. My parents will be meeting us in an hour."

She sits up fast, the sheets now gathered at her waist. Her sun-kissed skin is taunting me. From her breasts down to her toned stomach. God, I need something else to focus on and fast.

"Time to get ready." I tap the silver watch on my wrist and turn away quickly to gather my socks and shoes.

"I know it's Christmas and all, but can't we just skip dinner and stay here? We are on vacation together after all."

Technically our first vacation as a couple. I don't tell her that. Instead, I smile and turn back to her. Fallon's green eyes sparkle with desire. Desire I know all too well. She makes it so dam hard not to give in.

"After dinner, I promise we'll come back up here and not leave for the next twenty-four hours."

That's something I can guarantee. After dessert, we will be coming back here, and I will be devouring Fallon to the point she won't be getting out of bed tomorrow.

That promise alone has my dick straining against my zipper again. Dammit. The second I move my hand to adjust myself, Fallon's eyes follow. She swallows hard before her eyes find mine again. I smirk, shaking my head.

"Get dressed, now."

And then I walk out of the room before I fuck her right then and there.

CHAPTER 5
FALLON

My hair took forever. It was full of knots. I shouldn't have let Trent put me to bed with wet hair. At the time, it sounded like a great idea. He had thoroughly consumed me and my body. The end result was, I needed sleep.

Giving myself one last glance in the mirror, I'm glad I got to sleep some, even if my hair was a pain in the ass to do. I've pinned sections back and curled them. My dress is hunter green, velvet. It's trendy and festive. My dress stops at my knees and makes my boobs look good. I hope Trent likes it.

Speaking of Trent, I have no idea where he went. He rushed out after he caught me watching him. He wanted me. I wanted him and yet he denied us both, leaving me with a slight ache between my legs. I'm still sore, but it will never stop me from wanting more. Trent Maxwell is someone I can never get enough of. Never.

After sliding my gold sandals on my feet, I send Trent a text letting him know I'm ready. I sort of feel terrible. His gift is back home. Left under our artificial Christmas tree. The one we decorated in a beach theme before he left for training. When I decided to go on this trip, I only snagged Tom and Vivian's gifts, throwing them in my luggage just before I walked out the door. He'll understand, I'm sure. It just makes me feel bad.

I hear the key card unlocking the door and turn in that direction. Trent walks through the door. He takes my breath away. His muscular build takes up the entire doorway. His black button-down shirt is undone at the top. The silver chain around his neck is barely visible. The khaki's he's wearing sit low on his hips. I picture how hard his dick strained against them earlier. My mouth nearly waters thinking about springing him free and wrapping my mouth around his thick cock.

Trent doesn't come in any further. I wish he would though, but I know he won't. From his rigid stance to the tic in his jaw, I know he is resisting the urge to attack me. Instead, I'll be anxious all night, and in a hurry to get back to this room where he promised we would stay and not leave.

"Fallon, we need to go."

Trent's words drag me from my dirty thoughts. His hooded eyes burn my skin.

Right.

Christmas dinner.

With his parents.

We arrive at the restaurant to find Tom and Vivian already seated. Shit. I was so distracted that I left their gifts.

"Crap, I need to go back to the room, I left the gifts."

"Nonsense, we can do them later, sit." Vivian waves a hand at me while the other hand brings a glass of wine to her lips.

Trent nudges me forward, holding out a chair for me. He sits down next to me, immediately placing a hand on my thigh. Goosebumps layer my skin. I'm not cold, no, his touch does that to me.

"So have you two been enjoying yourselves?"

I smile at Tom, nodding. Trent goes on to tell him about our morning swimming. His hand slides higher up my thigh, causing me to shift slightly in my chair. If he goes much further, he'll realize I am lacking panties. I wanted to surprise Trent later, but he just might get a sneak peek.

As he continues talking about our swimming adventure, he leaves out the part where he fucked me in the turquoise waters. I'm glad for that because how awkward would that be? I can never be sure with Trent because sometimes he has no shame in blurting things out.

Our dinner seems to come and go quickly. The four of us were so caught up talking and just enjoying the time together that when I glance at the time on my phone, I see it's almost nine pm.

"Should we order dessert?" I'm nowhere near hungry, just having ate what was probably hands down the best dinner I have ever had in my life. And that says a lot because Tom is a hell of a cook back home.

"No!" Trent nearly snaps, causing me to flinch slightly.

"Trent!" His mom eyes him in warning before looking over at me. "Fallon, dear, raincheck on dessert. Tom and I are getting old. We need our sleep."

Without another word, they both stand and come around to hug and kiss us goodbye.

"Merry Christmas, you two."

I smile. "Merry Christmas, good night."

I sit there, slightly confused, as Trent takes care of the bill. I feel deflated. That's not how I expected dinner to go. Not with his parents rushing off after eating. It's Christmas, I wanted to spend more time with them. I mean, yeah, I want to be alone with Trent, but it's still Christmas and they are family. Those two people are so important to me. More important than my own parents, whom I've yet to receive a text or call from today.

I turn toward the wing our room is down, but Trent catches my wrist. "Let's take a walk on the beach."

"Okay."

Suddenly, he pulls me into him, his dark eyes searching mine. For what, I don't know. It's enough to make me worry.

"What's wrong?" His voice is laced with nothing but concern, and it makes me feel guilty.

"Nothing, I just, it's just you snapped about dessert and your parents rushed off. I worry you hurt their feelings or something."

My words are rushed. I'm feeling all sorts of emotions and can't seem to sort it all out to explain.

"Babe, I didn't hurt their feelings. Look, I just have different desert plans for us."

"Oh."

"Are you okay, seriously, Fal?"

"I'm fine, you could have warned me though, you know?" I shove at his chest.

"What, and ruin the surprise? No way."

He releases my wrist, moving his hand back to where it rests on my lower back, guiding us out of the sliding doors. Salty air fills my lungs instantly. It's dark but the moon casts its glow, allowing us to see all it touches. The ocean waves crash quietly as we continue walking.

Not far ahead, the moonlight beams off of something, catching my eye. There's something on the beach, but I can't quite make out what the object is.

Trent's hand moves to mine, squeezing it tightly. I look up at him and he gives me a quick glance before staring straight ahead. The way he swallows causes that worried feeling to resurface.

As we walk closer, I can finally make out what it is. It's a circular table, covered in a white tablecloth. Two chairs. Red poinsettias are placed in the center. We seem to be heading to it.

There's also a small globe glowing on the table. Two glasses of what I can only guess to be champagne. Based on the bubbles anyway. There are also two small dessert plates with some sort of chocolate on them.

"Trent, what is this?" I ask as we walk up to the table.

"Dessert."

Trent doesn't say anything else as he guides me to my chair before walking to his and sitting down. I study him. The light bounces off his face just right. In this moment, I don't think Trent could look any hotter. Strong jaw lines, light stubble. Dark eyes that bore into mine. He looks confident. Never in a million years did I think I would ever date this man in front of me. A silly crush once upon a time that faded only to come back to life years later.

"It's chocolate truffle."

Trent pulls me from my head as he lifts the small piece of chocolate from the plate. I do the same and take a bite.

It's good, so good.

"Mmm," I moan, finishing my piece. Grabbing the flute, I take a sip. Yup, champagne.

"I take it you like it?" Trent smiles slyly at me while waiting for me to respond.

"Uh, yeah."

He's silent for a moment while continuing to look at me. His gaze makes me shift nervously.

"We've come a long way, wouldn't you say?"

His question comes as a surprise. I'm not expecting it.

Trent's a guy, he doesn't think about these types of things. He's not wrong. It's just strange that he is bringing it up.

"I'd like to think so."

"Thank you for fighting for us when I was too stupid to realize." Trent stands, coming around to me. He turns me to face him and then grabs both my hands, holding them. His hands tremble slightly. I can just barely feel it. Something is up, and alarm bells start going off. My heart starts pounding nervously in my chest. Blood rushes in my ears.

"Trent." My words are barely a whisper.

"I love you, Fal."

Before I can repeat the words to him, he drops to his knees.

Oh. My. God.

My mouth drops open and I go to cover it. However, Trent refuses to let go of my hands. His grip is firm.

"I know I was a complete ass, and I probably don't deserve you some days, but the thought of you with anyone but me is not acceptable. I will spend the rest of my life proving that to you." He pauses, and I watch in complete shock as he swallows. He finally removes my left hand and reaches into his pocket. Trent pulls out a silver box with a tiny red Christmas bow on it.

"Fallon, will you marry me?"

He removes the lid and holds out the box. A huge round diamond is displayed on the silver velvet. This time, my hand does fly to cover my mouth. Tears threaten to spill. This cannot be real.

"Fal, tell me you'll marry me." Trent's words are strained.

My eyes shoot to his. He's waiting for my answer.

Holy shit. Did he just ask me to marry him?

"Fallon--"

Shit. Yes, I nod, unable to form words. My lip quivers as the first tear falls. Trent catches it, wiping it away.

"I need words, Fal."

Still nodding, I somehow find my voice. "Yes." It comes out weak, but it's all I've got. I'm so caught off guard that I'm left speechless.

"Yes?" Trent's voice cracks. He asks the question as if he's not sure he heard me right.

I grab his face as my brain finally catches up. "Yes! A thousand times, yes!"

I lean in to kiss him, and he grabs the back of my neck, pulling me to him. He kisses me deeply. As if he cannot get enough of me. I can taste the champagne mixed with truffle on his tongue. Everything in this moment is so surreal. We can't seem to kiss each other enough. It's intoxicating, and I suddenly wish we were already back in the room.

Trent Maxwell asked me to marry him. Marriage wasn't even a blip on my radar. We said we would take things slow. This is the opposite of slow and somehow it feels right. It feels perfect.

Trent starts to pull back, biting my bottom lip as he goes. We're both out of breath as he rests his forehead against mine.

"Thank fuck," he whispers.

I giggle. "Why do you say that?" I lean back slightly to gauge his reaction.

"A part of me didn't think you would say yes, considering all I've put you through."

I smile and rub his jawline before gripping his chin to kiss him again. I need his lips on mine. He kisses me back. This time slowly, passionately. Trent pours everything he is feeling into it. I can feel how nervous he was. I can feel how much he loves me.

This time when we part, I am the first to speak. "I love you, Trent. Nothing else matters."

I swear he lets out a breath like he was waiting for my confirmation.

"I love you. You're mine. Forever."

His words are confident. Like he has never been so sure of anything in his life. It makes my heart swell knowing just how much he loves me.

He leans back and pulls the ring from the box. I can't take my eyes off the white gold ring. I'm still in shock over the size of the diamond. This must have cost Trent a small fortune.

He grabs my left hand and slides the ring on. He kisses my hand once before letting it go for me to examine the ring. I hold it up. It fits perfectly. How he knew my ring size is a question for another day. Right now I don't care. I study the single diamond as it shimmers in the moonlight.

"Merry Christmas, Fal."

I can't contain the tears as I smile back. "Merry Christmas, Trent."

The ring is perfect. Tonight has been perfect. Absolutely perfect, I think as another tear falls. I can't help it. So many emotions.

"Well!" I hear a cheerful voice.

Vivian.

I look up from staring at the diamond on my finger to see both of Trent's parents standing there. Their faces are lit up in excitement. They knew!

"She said yes!"

Happiness radiates from Trent as he stands, pulling me up with him. His arm snakes around me tightly as they come up.

"Wait! Did you know?" I don't know why, but I need to know. I just have to.

"We did. Congratulations!" Tom says as he claps Trent on the shoulder.

Meanwhile, Vivian grabs my left hand. She nods, saying nothing, but I can see the silent tears stream down her face. It makes my heart constrict. She is full of emotions, like me. This must be hard, yet exciting for her. In a way it almost makes me feel guilty. She's clearly torn, and it breaks my heart.

"Vivian." My voice breaks, whispering her name.

Trent goes still next to me. He grabs my right hand, holding it tightly. Too tightly.

She shakes her head. "I'm fine. Don't you worry about me. I'm just so happy for the two of you." She pulls me in, placing a quick kiss on my cheek.

When she steps back, my eyes find Trent's. His dark eyes narrow. He's worried I'll change my mind. That the guilt will override what we've built. I can feel it pouring off of him.

While the guilt may creep in from time to time, the love I have for Trent is always there. It never wavers. We both deserve to be happy, even on the days I don't feel I deserve to.

Squeezing his hand, hoping to reassure him, I turn my attention back to his parents. They are standing there, wrapped up in each other. They are happy for us, that much is evident.

"I can't believe you two knew this entire time!"

Tom laughs. "It was all Trent. He planned everything. The trip and all."

My mouth gapes once again. He did all of this? Before I can begin to process, he interrupts my thoughts.

"I think it's time I take my bride-to-be back to our room." Trent's words are strained, and I can't tell if it's because he is still worried or if it's because he's dying to get me in bed.

"Right, yes, good idea." Tom winks. "Merry Christmas, you two."

"Good night."

We stand there in silence, watching them retreat toward the resort. Trent's uncertainty vibrates off of him in waves. He's tense. I want to do nothing but reassure him.

"Trent, I love you."

His dark eyes shoot down at me. "You loved him first."

His haunting words hang there like a knife to my gut. It nearly kills me. He was so sure not even thirty minutes ago, and now he is second guessing.

I reach up, grabbing his face. "I love you now. Do you understand me?"

His mouth is on mine in an instant. I feel the tension fall away as our tongues collide.

CHAPTER 6
TRENT

Walking back to the resort, I feel like I need to clear the voice in the back of my head that has been nagging me. I know Fallon loves me. I don't doubt that for a second. However, since seeing my mom and her reaction, it's been bugging me. I never thought it would hurt her. She assured me a thousand times that she was over the moon for us. She was even with me when I chose the ring. I guess I just didn't think about...

Connor.

"I need to ask you something."

Her eyes find mine; a seriousness falls across her face. She knows what's coming and that makes me almost feel bad for asking.

"Go on."

"Do you ever feel guilty for loving me?"

Fallon closes her eyes, stopping right in her tracks. "I feel guilty for arguing with Connor. I feel guilty about what happened. But no, I don't feel guilty for loving you." A lone tear falls as she opens her eyes to look at me.

It's there, the hurt, the guilt, the love. It's all there. She feels everything I feel. It gives me reassurance that I am not alone in this. We are in this together. That war within my mind isn't just my battle, but both of ours to fight together.

I grab the back of her neck, pulling her in. I kiss her with everything I have in me so she'll never doubt my love. Never. Her hands grip the back of my neck, holding me tightly too. She matches me.

That voice in the back of my head quiets, allowing me to be happy.

* * *

I practically drag Fallon through the lobby. I'm in a hurry to get her alone. I couldn't wait for my parents to retreat. Don't get me wrong, I'm glad they were there and that they witnessed my proposal from a distance. But right now, I just want to bury myself in my girl. I need to feel her.

"Trent!" Fallon laughs as I all but push her into the room. Grabbing the *do not disturb* sign, I slap it on the doorknob and slam the door closed, locking it.

When I turn to look at her, all the air leaves my lungs. Fallon's back is to me as she is opening the double doors that open to the ocean. It reminds me of when I surprised her at Emma's wedding, and she invited me to stay the night with her in her hotel room. So much has changed since that night. We were just two friends. Best friends and then I crossed a line. A line I'm now grateful for crossing.

I continue taking her in while she stares out into the darkness. The thin straps on her dress reveal her tan back. I can't see the freckles that are painted across her shoulders, but I know they are there. It makes my mouth water. I know every detail of her body. To know Fallon is mine and that she's not going anywhere. My dick strains in my pants, reminding me that I am a man on a mission.

I start unbuttoning my shirt as I make my way to her.

Stepping into her back, I brush her dark hair aside and pepper kisses along the back of her neck and shoulders.

"Mine," I whisper as I continue kissing her.

"Yours."

That one word does me in. Grabbing her wrist, I pull her toward the bed.

"Take off your sandals," I demand as I make quick work at removing the rest of my clothes.

When Fallon reaches to remove her dress, an idea comes to mind. I snatch her hand away. "No, leave it on."

She cocks an eyebrow at me but does as she is told. I pull her to stand back up and turn her around to face the bed. My hands roam her entire body. Little moans escape her mouth.

After torturing myself for a minute, I finally reach for the zipper of her dress.

"Do you remember that night in the hotel?"

She sucks in a breath. She does.

Very slowly, I pull the zipper down.

She had asked me to help her unzip her dress. It was like she was taunting me. I can remember it so vividly. The way she licked her lips. It was at that moment that the air shifted between us. Everything changed.

"Yes."

Fuck if I don't nearly lose it hearing her answer. I want to rush and strip her out of her dress however, I want to savor this moment more.

With the zipper of her dress now fully unzipped, I reach up and grab the right strap. I slide it down, kissing her shoulder, and arm as it goes. Once it falls to her wrist, I reach up, grabbing her breast. Her head falls back, and she wiggles against my cock.

I repeat the process with the opposite strap except when

the strap hits her wrist, I remove it and bring her hand up so that I can examine the ring on her finger.

Fuck.

Fallon O'Neil is mine.

Mine.

I kiss her hand once before dropping it back down to her side. Fallon's breath picks up as my hand skims her side. I grab the material of her dress and yank it down. It bunches at her waist. Spinning her around, I take her in. From her silky skin to her perfect tits. Her nipples are pebbled, begging to be touched.

Taking one in my mouth, I swirl my tongue and nip. Whimpers leave Fallon's mouth as her hands find the top of my head. My hair is still too short for her to grab, even still, the way she touches me, holding me in place. I fucking love it.

She's breathing heavily when I finally pull back.

"Are you wet for me?"

"Why don't you find out for yourself?"

My dick twitches at her words. She holds her head high. When she is feisty, it makes me want her ten times more. She used to be so shy and quiet so when she gets smart, all I can think about is bending her over and spanking her.

So, without wasting any more time, I shove the rest of her festive dress down her hips, allowing her to step out of it.

Holy fuck.

Fallon is not wearing anything under her dress. Her bare pussy is on display for me. My eyes shoot to hers. All I see is desire. She smirks at me before her eyes drop to my erection.

"Well, are you going to touch me?"

"Such a smart mouth." I lean in, biting her bottom lip.

At the same time, I slide a finger up her thigh and between her folds easily.

She's soaked.

She moans into my mouth as she reaches for my cock. "Trent…"

"I know, baby."

I gently guide her down on her back on the bed. Her naked body has never looked so good. Maybe it's because she's now my fiancé.

Hovering above her, I line my cock at her entrance and tease her, only giving her the tip. She bucks her hips up to try to get more. I pull back, not letting her have it. Fallon groans and reaches out to run her nails down my chest. It's enough to almost cave and sink in. I resist though, wanting to tease us both a little more. Now I won't lie, it is pure hell not giving in. It's almost painful. But knowing I'm driving her crazy underneath me is worth it.

"Tell me you love me."

"You know I love you."

"Tell me." I leave the words hanging in the air.

"I—"

Slowly I push the tip in, pausing.

"Love—"

I push in a little further.

"You."

I push all the way in until I'm fully seated in her. Hell, she feels amazing. I decide to go slow. As much as I want to go hard and claim her over and over, I fucked her hard earlier and want to give her a little reprieve.

We find a slow rhythm as our mouths and hands explore each other like it's our first time. In a way, I guess you can say it is, as an engaged couple anyway.

When Fallon moans my name in my neck, I know she's close. I can feel her tightening around me. Picking up the pace a little. I capture her nipple in my mouth. She arches off the bed, grabbing my back. I bite down, adding a little pressure, and she digs her nails in, clawing at me. It stings, but I don't care. She can fucking mark me any day. I release her nipple from my teeth and swirl my tongue around it. That's all it takes. Fallon screams out my name as her pussy clamps down on my cock. It feels too good and before I know it, I'm thrusting hard, spilling into her. Her pussy continues milking my cock. Taking every last drop of me.

We're both panting, covered in sweat. I roll, taking her with me to snuggle her into my side. Soon, she'll have my last name. Just that thought alone has me wanting to sink back into her.

"I can't wait to make you my wife. For you to have my last name."

Fallon leans over, kissing my neck. "I can't wait to be your wife."

"Fallon Maxwell."

We both suck in a breath, hearing it out loud for the first time. I've said it in my head a million times since I started planning this. There's nothing quite like hearing it out loud.

"I love you," she whispers.

"I love you, Fallon."

I swear I could stay like this forever, but another idea comes to mind. One that I hope she'll be okay with.

"Want to fly home tomorrow?"

She sits up and studies me. "What? Why?" Worry lines her features.

I lean up on my elbows and plant a kiss on her lips, trying to reassure her. "I was just thinking how much better it would be to fuck my fiancé in our home, under our Christmas tree."

Heat floods her face and I can only laugh. Something

I'll never get sick of is making Fallon blush. She's quiet though, not giving me an answer.

"Well, what do you say?"

She tucks a stray hair behind her ear, "I think I would like that very much." She reaches across me, running her fingers down my abs to my cock. It grows hard the second her fingers grip it.

I suck in a breath as I pull her on top of me, positioning her exactly where I want her. Fallon takes the lead, guiding herself down on top of me.

Fuck, it feels good.

It always feels good.

I watch as my woman fucks me. She throws her head back, her raven-colored hair falling around her shoulders as her tits bounce. It's the perfect image of her. One I can get lost in.

And I do just that. I get lost in everything that is Fallon Raine O'Neil, the woman that agreed to be my wife on Christmas Day.

ABOUT THE AUTHOR

Lisamarie Kade is a romance author living in the sunshine state with her husband and small army of children.

When not writing, she can be found chasing the kids around or volunteering for one of their many activities.

Lisamarie enjoys chocolate peanut butter cups, music, and reading something steamy while sipping sweet wine.

OTHER BOOKS BY LISAMARIE KADE

The Secrets We Keep

Mended Hearts

The Christmas Breakdown

The War Within

Shattered Illusion

the christmas PLAY

BY L.M. REID

This is a work of fiction. Names, characters, organizations, places, events, and incidents are products of the author's imagination or are used fictitiously. Any resemblance to actual events, locales, or persons, living or dead, is entirely coincidental.

Copyright @2022 by L.M. Reid

No part of this book may be reproduced, stored in a retrieval system, or transmitted in any form or by any means electronic, mechanical, photocopying, recording, or otherwise, without the express written permission of the publisher.

This book is licensed for your personal enjoyment only. This book may not be re-sold or given away to other people.

Cover Design: Ya'll That Graphic

Editing: Sandy Ebel, Personal Touch Editing

CHAPTER 1

HUNTER

It's gorgeous outside. The sun is shining, and the temperature is in the low seventies. It's the perfect day for a road trip into the mountains.

If only it wasn't for the massive snowstorm in Aspen holding up our plans and ruining any hope of making Christmas with our families.

Yesterday, Quinn had a photo shoot that deterred us from leaving with everyone else. His plan was to leave first thing this morning, but Mother Nature had other ideas. She seemed to think it was the perfect time for an unexpected middle-of-the-night snowstorm. Not the roads are a little slippery kind, either—a massive, the roads are impassable, and there is no way in or out kind. At least not before Christmas.

"Can't you pull some strings?" Quinn whines as she pouts on the couch. Her arms are crossed over her chest, and her eyes are red, threatening tears.

"Baby, I wish I could, but I can't make the snow disappear or the roads safe. I'm sorry."

It's our first Christmas together and Quinn's first "traditional" Christmas—ever.

She and Mason, her brother and my best friend, grew up with absent parents who only cared about themselves and their drug addiction. Their entire lives, they only had each other. There was no Santa, no gifts or family meals. Just the two of them in front of the television, watching Christmas movies and wishing they were in them.

This year was supposed to be different. We were going to spend it with my family in Aspen. Mason and Avery were joining us. I had plans to make the perfect Christmas for Quinn. I knew it was important to her, but I hadn't realized just how much until now.

Seeing her like this breaks my heart. I wish I could fix it, somehow make it better for her. The blue strands of hair she had when we first met are gone, replaced with red for the holiday season, and she's wearing an ugly Christmas sweater, one of many she bought for the trip.

I sit next to her on the couch and put my arm around her. "I know this isn't the Christmas we planned, but—"

"There are no buts, Hunter. It's ruined. They're all there, and we're here." She blows out a breath. "I know I'm being a baby… it's just… I was really excited."

"I know." I press my lips to her temple. "I'm sorry. I promise we'll still have an amazing Christmas."

She glances around our home. "We don't have a single decoration."

"We can fix that. We can go to the store, and—"

"Just stop, Hunter. It's over." Quinn pushes her hands into the couch and rises to her feet.

"Where are you going?"

"I'm going to bed. I'm sad, tired, and just want to sleep."

Watching as Quinn disappears into our bedroom, frustration seeps in, knowing I can't fix this for her, can't make her dream come true. Running a hand through my hair, I pace our living room. Money may not buy happiness, but it sure as hell can help me give her a special Christmas, even if we can't spend it with our families.

Operation Save Quinn's Christmas is in full effect.

CHAPTER 2

QUINN

Sinking into bed, I pull the covers high up around my neck.

Grateful Hunter didn't follow me, I allow the tears I've been fighting back to flow. Not only is this our first Christmas together as a couple, but it's also the first time I would be celebrating Christmas with a real family. Well, more than just Mason. As much as I hate that I'm acting like a petulant child, upset because she didn't get her way, I can't seem to help it.

Mason and I, we never had much growing up. I remember all the years of Christmases Mason and I spent alone. Hungry. Sad. Still, through the worst of times, we always had each other. Even if it was just the two of us huddled in front of a television, praying Santa didn't forget us. Side note—he always did.

It was the one constant that never changed. Not when Mason got signed by the Red Devils. Not when we—he—had money. We never celebrated Christmas, not really. We stuck to what we knew—our tradition of crappy television and crappy food. The magic of the holiday season never existed for us, so it never felt as though we were missing out on anything.

Until now.

Until Hunter.

He changed everything, him and his childlike holiday spirit. So, reluctant as I was, when he mentioned going to his parents' home in Aspen for the holiday, I got swept up in the idea, in all of it.

Now, it's gone.

No chance of celebrating a traditional Christmas. No spending the holiday with Mason.

Every ounce of Christmas spirit I felt drains out of me as I tug the covers further over my head.

* * *

Hunter's voice rings out through the bedroom, "Rise and shine, gorgeous."

"Go away," I grumble from beneath the covers.

"No can do," he says as he yanks the covers off me.

"Hunter," I scold him.

"Tomorrow is Christmas Eve, and if we want to salvage the holiday, you have to get your sexy ass out of bed."

The curtains that had been drawn are now wide open, sunlight streaming through the floor-to-ceiling windows and blinding me.

"I appreciate the effort, but I'd rather just skip the holiday if you don't mind," I say, shielding my eyes with my arm. I can feel his hands on my ankles as he pulls me to the edge of the bed.

"Actually, I do mind. This is our first Christmas together. No way in hell am I missing out on that."

"Ugh, fine," I grumble as I sit up. As soon as I do,

Hunter's hands are on my shoulders, pushing me back down. "You just said that I need to get ready."

"You do, but first… I need to put you in a good mood."

"And how do you intend to do that?"

He rips off his shirt and tosses it onto the floor, exposing his toned, bare chest. It's enough to make any woman smile, and I'm no exception.

"Okay, you win. I'm smiling."

"Good." He reaches for his shirt.

"What are you doing?"

With a wicked smile on his handsome face, he covers my body with his.

"Got ya."

I giggle and squirm beneath him as he peppers my neck with kisses.

"You are nothing but trouble, you know that?"

Rolling us over so I'm on top, straddling him, Hunter laughs.

"I'm trouble?"

A visceral reaction has me grinding against the strained mound in his jeans, the erection begging to be inside me.

"We're never getting out of here, are we?" he asks.

I toss my head back in laughter. "Not until you make me happy."

Hunter flips me off him. "I accept your challenge and promise you two orgasms."

"Just two?"

"We have things to do. Two will have to suffice." He pauses. "For now."

CHAPTER 3

HUNTER

After ensuring Quinn was in a good mood, we quickly dressed and got ready for the day. First stop, Quinn's favorite coffee shop for some caffeine.

Holding the steaming cup of coffee between her hands, Quinn takes a sip of coffee. She emits a satisfied sigh that has me wanting to take her back home and have a repeat of what we just did.

"So, what's on the agenda?"

"For starters, we need a tree. Can't celebrate Christmas without a tree."

"We could just not celebrate Christmas."

"Not happening. After the tree, we should probably get some decorations. Food, too."

"Neither of us cooks," she reminds me.

"Doesn't mean we can't. How hard can it be?"

"You and your never-ending optimism. Have you never heard people complaining about cooking holiday dinners and what a pain it is?"

"First of all, you love how positive and optimistic I am.

Second, they're cooking for the masses. We just need enough for us."

"Love is a strong word for how I feel, especially today. And cooking for you is like cooking for the masses."

I'm a six-foot-four football player. Of course, I like to eat. And yeah, it takes a lot to fill me up.

Her shoulders slump. "I appreciate what you're trying to do, but—"

"No buts, Quinn. We can still make this work. You just have to trust me."

She sets her coffee on the table. "I do trust you."

"Then let me do this for you." Taking her hands, I give them a squeeze. "For us." My eyes lock on hers, pleading with her. "Please, Quinn?"

The smile on her lips is faint, but it's there. "How can I say no to you?"

"You can't. I was kind of banking on that."

She groans and gives her head a quick shake as though resetting. After she squares her shoulders, there's a legit smile on her face.

"Okay. Let's do this."

"Yeah?"

"Yeah."

After breakfast, we head to our first stop, a nearby Christmas tree lot. When I drove by it the other day, it was filled with gorgeous evergreen trees. Today, we pull into the parking lot, and there are—none.

"Sorry, we just sold the last one about fifteen minutes ago," the guy says.

He doesn't intend for me to hear him, but under his breath, he mumbles something about people waiting until the last minute. We might not be the only ones in this predicament, and putting together a perfect last-minute Christmas might not be as easy as I thought.

Quinn looks a little dejected, but I keep my positive attitude.

"There's another one just a few miles away."

We make our way to the second lot to find it just as empty as the first.

"This isn't over yet." Wrapping my arm around her shoulders, I pull her close. "Third time's a charm."

We head out to yet another lot, and I was right. We pull into the lot, and low and behold, this one has trees, although even from our seats in the car, we can tell not one of them is worth a damn. They all look like they are in worse shape than Charlie Brown's Christmas tree. Only, I don't think we could salvage any of them.

Lot number four was another disappointment. We are running out of tree lots—and out of time.

"Ugh, just forget it," she says, throwing her hands up in the air, exasperated.

"There's one more place," I tell her.

The trust that Quinn had instilled in me is long gone, though. "Let's just go home."

I grab her by the waist and turn her around. Her back is pressed up against the car, my hands framing her face. "Don't give up on me, baby."

"I'm not giving up on you. I'm giving up on Christmas."

"Come on, Quinn. Do you think Santa wants to hit billions of houses in one night? No. But does he give up? Also, no."

Even she can't help but break a smile at my sheer enthusiasm.

"Besides," I tell her. "You'll love this part."

"Fine. What's next?"

"Shopping."

CHAPTER 4

QUINN

"Merry Christmas, Hunter," a group of young women say as we pass them.

It's the third group today to ogle my boyfriend. Most of the time, I couldn't care less. In fact, I almost find it amusing. But today, in my current mood, I want nothing more than to tear them limb from limb.

"Merry Christmas, ladies," he says, giving them a wave before turning his attention back to me earning him a scowl. "That's not my fault."

"You could quit being so damn handsome and sweet," I reply. Draping his arm over my shoulder, he pulls me close.

"You prefer when I'm naughty, don't you?"

As he nuzzles my neck, I pretend to shoo him away, but we both know it's a weak attempt. "Oh, yeah, you're real naughty, mister Boy Scout."

"Is that a challenge?" He raises his eyebrows in question. "Because if it is… I will rise to the occasion." The dirty double entendre earns him a smile.

"I'd like to see you try."

"Right here? Right now?"

"You wouldn't."

"Wouldn't what?" Claire asks.

I whip around when I hear the sound of my best friend's voice behind me.

"Claire? Oh my God, what are you doing here?"

"Hunter invited us for shopping and lunch."

Grateful to see my bestie, I do a little happy dance and pull her in for a hug, then turn to Hunter.

"Had to call in reinforcements, huh?"

"A smart man knows when he needs help." Hunter presses a kiss to my temple. "Besides, after lunch, Ashton and I have some things to do, so I figured you could use the company."

"Wait, you mean you're ditching me? After all this rah-rah-sis-boom-bah Christmas cheerleader crap?" My hands are on my hips.

Hunter mirrors my stance. "Who would you rather shop with? Me or Claire?"

I don't respond because we both know my answer.

"That's what I thought," he says before grabbing and tossing me over his shoulder. "Let's get some lunch."

The Mexican restaurant we decide on is my favorite. It's also packed. Luckily, the host recognized Hunter and Ashton from the Red Devils and sat us right away. One of the perks of having such a famous boyfriend. Though I am pretty sure his sweet smile and charming ways alone would have gotten us seated. The guy has a way with women. How else could he have nabbed a proverbial party girl like me?

"Really pulling out all the stops today, huh?" I give Hunter a soft nudge with my shoulder.

"Nothing but the best for my baby."

I don't even need to look at the menu to know what I want.

"Two steak tacos and a forty-six-ounce margarita," I tell the waitress when she appears at our table.

Hunter's eyes widen.

"What? It's been a rough day."

CHAPTER 5

HUNTER

Talking to Ashton, my attention is on Quinn, the most relaxed I've seen her all day.

The tree search had been a struggle, and poor Quinn looked so dejected. Maybe her partaking in the set-up of my little plan wasn't for the best. Especially after I realized just what a struggle it might be. That's when I called Ashton and Claire. The plan is for Ashton to help me put together my little Christmas wonderland while Claire keeps Quinn occupied.

So far, it seems to be working. Though as lunch ends and we're about to part ways, Quinn looks at me suspiciously.

"You're up to something," she says, pointing her finger in my direction.

"Who me?" I ask, feigning innocence.

"Thank you, Hunter." Her smile is enough to make all the effort worthwhile, but the kiss she pulls me in for? That makes me want to go to the ends of the earth for this woman.

"I would do anything for you, Quinn. You know that."

Another peck of a kiss because I just can't get enough. "Go, have fun shopping."

She nods happily. "I will. Remember, no gifts."

I roll my eyes at her ridiculous request. Just because she never got gifts before doesn't mean she shouldn't now. Listening to her talk, though, she was very adamant. So, this year, I'll agree to her request. Beyond that, I make no promises.

Ashton and I watch the girls walk away, a little longer than we should.

"So, what's the plan?" Ashton asks when we can't enjoy the visual anymore.

"To give Quinn the Christmas of her dreams."

"What exactly does that entail?"

"A tree. Decorations. A sleigh. Santa."

"Santa? That's a pretty tall order. On really short notice."

"I know, but… I would do anything for her. I just want to give her the Christmas she envisioned or as close as I can get. She needs this. She deserves it."

"I get it, but how?"

I pat him on the back. "That's where you come in."

"Of course, it is," Ashton says with a laugh.

Connections and good friends help my afternoon with Ashton go a lot smoother than my morning with Quinn.

Candy canes, a snow globe, lights, the sleigh—it all quickly comes together. Before long, Ashton and I are elbow-deep in fake snow, putting the whole thing together to surprise Quinn tomorrow.

"All we have left is the sleigh," I tell Ashton.

We both look over the edge of the building at the massive item sitting on the sidewalk.

"And just how do you plan on getting that up here?" Without giving me time to respond, Ashton says, "And don't you even say that's where I come in. No way in hell are we getting that up here."

The sound of a helicopter overhead grabs our attention. Looking up, I wave.

"What's that?" Ashton asks.

"*That* is how we're getting that sleigh up here.

"Claire says she doesn't know how much longer she can keep Quinn entertained," Ashton says as I nudge the sleigh into place.

"Fuck."

Sure, the rooftop is all set, but I still haven't managed to do the most important thing.

"Relax, man, we'll get it done. What do we have left?"

"The most impossible thing—a fucking tree."

"How hard can it be?"

Thirty minutes later, Ashton feels my pain.

"This is crazy. No trees? Anywhere?"

I rest my head against the back of the car seat, my optimistic attitude gone.

"Let's meet the girls," Ashton says. "You and Quinn finish off the rest of your day, and I'll take care of the rest."

"How in the hell are you going to find a tree? We've been looking all day and came up empty-handed."

"Don't worry. I have a plan. Just stall Quinn as long as you can."

Easier said than done.

CHAPTER 6
QUINN

I couldn't have been happier to see Claire. As much as I love Hunter and what he's trying to do, I'm just not in the mood. It's a valiant effort on his part, but I'm over the holiday season and would just like to move on.

"That's really sweet of him," Claire says when I tell her what Hunter's been trying to do.

"I know. I've just never cared much about Christmas. The only thing I wanted was to spend it with our families. With that off the table, I just don't feel like celebrating it at all."

"I get it, but you have to remember. Hunter is a Christmas guy, and this is your first Christmas together. He wants to make it special. He also has a weak spot for you. One pout and the guy would turn the world upside down to make it right."

I'm well aware of the lengths that Hunter would go for me. That isn't the issue. The issue is that I don't want him to.

"Well, he's not giving me a choice, so it doesn't even matter."

"Good for him." Claire takes my arm as we walk.

"Now, let's talk about the important stuff—what are you going to get Hunter for Christmas?"

We make our way through the crowded store arm in arm so we don't lose each other.

"We decided not to exchange gifts."

"We?" Claire probes.

"Okay, I decided we aren't exchanging gifts, but Hunter agreed."

"Reluctantly, I'm sure. Why in the world would you want that?"

"You know I don't care about material things. Besides, what more could I want? I have a man that loves me, an amazing home..."

"And a wardrobe to die for."

"Exactly." I twirl around in the form-fitting skinny jeans and cropped red sweater. "Like I said, no gifts needed, so I'm not really sure what we're shopping for."

We reach the lingerie section.

"You could give him this," Claire suggests as she picks up a hanger, holding the skimpiest lingerie I have ever seen, and that's really saying something.

I pull on some of the strings, trying to figure out what it is, let alone how it would go on. She might be onto something, though. Technically, the lingerie isn't for him, but it's his eyes that will bug out of his head when he sees me in it, which would make *me* his gift.

"Not a bad idea."

The shop has everything you can imagine—sweet and sexy, leather and lace, hard-core built-in bondage lingerie. Turning my head, I eye the leather-and-metal outfit, which includes handcuffs. I make my way through the aisles of lingerie, looking for something Hunter might like.

Swept up in the naughty little outfit, I almost miss

Claire calling out to me. She says my name again, and I turn.

"I bet Santa would love to see Mrs. Claus in this."

Essentially, the outfit is a red lace bra and panties with red fur trim, like you would see Santa wearing, though I don't think his suit is quite this skimpy. Between the bra and panties is a strap of satin fabric. It's simple but sexy and full of holiday cheer. While I might not be, Hunter certainly is, and I'm pretty sure he would love it.

Grabbing the item from her hand, I inspect it further and a giggle.

"I could be his ho, ho, ho."

This little number might just be what helps salvage our first Christmas.

CHAPTER 7

QUINN

Today has been one for the books. A whirlwind of emotions mixed with non-stop shopping has left me exhausted.

The "one last stop" Hunter promised turned into a two-hour excursion.

"I'm tired, and I'm hungry," I whine. "I just want to go home."

"What about this one?" He's holding a glass ornament.

"Fine, yes. If it will get us out of the store, buy it."

"You're no fun," he tells me as we stand in line to pay for the Christmas decorations we were able to find.

"I'll show you how fun I can be," I tell him.

He laughs, blowing off the comment, which I have every intention of following through.

In the car, driving down the highway, I decide exactly how to show him just how much fun I am. Sitting in the passenger seat, I stare at Hunter, taking in every gorgeous piece of him—blonde hair, handsome face, biceps that stretch the material of his shirt to the max.

When he catches me watching him, he gives me a quizzical look, trying to figure me out.

"You have that look in your eyes."

"What look is that?" I ask coyly.

"The one that says you're up to something."

"You know me so well." Shifting in my seat to face him, my hand glides down his toned arm before dropping to his thigh. His Adam's apple bobs up and down as he swallows the desire that threatens to consume him… and potentially crash us. My fingers make their way to the button and zipper on his jeans. Undoing them, my hand slides inside and releases his dick.

"Quinn…"

Not long ago, I would have thought Hunter would push my hand away and scold me for my actions. He's the quintessential good guy—a real boy scout—except when it comes to sex.

He adjusts in the seat of his luxury SUV to make himself more comfortable—and more available.

I lower my head, my lips hovering right above his engorged cock. The mere thought of what was about to happen was more than enough to rile him up.

He says my name again, his tone less forgiving and more demanding. My tongue flicks over the head of his cock, and he groans.

"Yes, Hunter?"

I'm toying with him but now isn't the time. His cock throbs against my cheek as he fists my hair.

"You're killing me, baby." He gently lowers my head, not giving me a choice to do exactly what I was teasing. My mouth swallows him whole until he hits the back of my throat. "Oh, Christ."

Hearing the satisfaction in his voice is more than enough to encourage me to keep going—not that I had any intention of stopping. I love pleasing him almost as much as I love being with him. And the reciprocation? It's off the charts.

As we drive down the road, my head bobs up and down, mouth and tongue stroking his cock. Every groan, every word he utters is a complete turn-on. I can feel my panties soak from the sound, and I can't wait to see what he'll have in store for me later. I suck him hard and deep, taking satisfaction in the sounds and words it elicits—another throb, an involuntary buck of his hips, the words, "Fuck, baby, I'm close," falling from his lips. A few more moments and I can taste him as the remnants of his orgasm fill my mouth.

That's when I hear it—sirens.

"Oh, shit."

"Stay down," he tells me.

"What?"

"Put it away, then pretend like you're sleeping," he instructs me as he pulls off to the side of the road.

"You're kidding, right?"

"Do it, Quinn."

I do as he asks because the last thing I ever want is to be a source of contention. It's what initially drove me away from him to begin with—the fear of past mistakes haunting him. Now, it would be us—something we did—that could destroy him. And I would know it was all my fault because, let's face it, no way in hell would Hunter have done this stuff before.

"Hello, Officer," Hunter says after he rolls down the window.

"Hunter Adams?" the cop exclaims.

Hunter shushes the officer. "My girlfriend's sleeping. She's not feeling well."

I can't believe what I'm hearing. Hunter Adams just lied to a cop. For me. Because of me.

"Sorry to hear that. Anything I can do?"

"Thanks, no. Just trying to get her home so she can rest."

"Just be careful. You were weaving a bit back there."

I stifle the giggle that threatens.

"Sorry about that. I almost spilled my coffee."

They chat a moment longer, and when the cop leaves, Hunter lets out a sigh of relief.

"See, being the good guy pays off."

"You just got road head and lied to a police officer," I say, still curled up in my seat. Only now, I'm smiling at the man I love. "I'm starting to think the whole nice guy routine was just a ruse."

"You keep doing what you just did, and it might be a thing of the past."

CHAPTER 8

HUNTER

Quinn Ford—trouble with a capital T.

Thank God for her and her wild ways. Not only was the blow job outstanding, but it also bought Ashton the time he asked for.

"As much as I want to get home to finish what you started," I say as I pull into the grocery store parking lot, "we need food."

"Please tell me we're buying frozen pizza and that you don't seriously want me to cook Christmas dinner."

"I'm trying to make Christmas better, not end it." My jab earns me a punch to the shoulder. "I intend on cooking."

"I'm not sure that's much better."

Grabbing a cart, I push myself on it like a scooter. "You have no idea what kind of talents I possess in the kitchen."

"Oh, no, I know all about your talents. You're great at counter sex. Or kitchen table sex. Cooking though… that's not one of them."

I hop off the cart and grab a ham. "It's already cooked, just have to warm it up," I say, placing it in the cart.

"Fine, what else?"

"No Christmas is complete without mashed potatoes." I lift a bag of potatoes off the pile.

"Do you know how to make them?" Quinn asks with a raised eyebrow.

"I'll google it."

"Or… we could get these." She holds up a container of already mashed potatoes. "All we have to do is microwave them."

I glance between the bag of potatoes and the container she holds in her hand. It's not how Mom would do it, but then again, I'm not Mom, and I'm pretty sure edible food is preferable to homemade food. Dropping the bag of potatoes where I got it from, I reach for the container in Quinn's hand.

"Next… cookies."

Making our way down the baking aisle, I try to decipher what we'll need to make cookies, but there's such a variety, I'm at a loss.

"I've got this part," Quinn says as she tosses some stuff in the cart. "Chocolate chip, okay?"

"Perfect."

"Looks like we're not the only ones shopping for the holidays." The cart is full, and the lines are long.

"Astute observation, Captain Obvious," Quinn says with a giggle.

"You're really asking for it today," I tease.

She leans in close, her lips against my ear. "After what I did on the way here, I better get it… and good."

Her breath against my skin, the sound of her voice, the words filled with promise.

"Fuck, Quinn, I'm hard again."

Biting her bottom lip, she smiles, pleased with herself and the uncomfortable state she's left me.

CHAPTER 9

QUINN

When we arrive home, Hunter opens the door to our condo, holding it open and allowing me to step through first. The bags fall from my hands when I see the Christmas tree in the corner of our living room.

"Where? How?" I'm practically speechless.

So is he. Where I expect him to be beaming with pride, he isn't. Seems he's stunned by the tree in the living room, too.

"I'll be damned."

"Where did it come from?" Making my way to it, my fingers gently brush against the needles, careful not to make them fall.

Hunter picks up a note from the mantle.

Merry Christmas!
Ashton

He hands the note to me. "I can't believe he did that for us."

"The kid can be a pain in the ass, but he's good people."

"I know we've had a few bumps in the road, but I hope you're enjoying the holiday so far."

"Enjoying it? Are you kidding?" I wrap my arms around his neck and pull him close. "It's amazing."

"I know it's not what we had planned, but I wanted to make it as special for you as possible. You know I would do anything for you, right?" He brushes a strand of hair away from my face. "I'll fight any battle, right any wrong. I'll do whatever I can to make your dreams come true."

If only he knew just how far I had fallen before him and how his mere presence lifted me back up. He's already made all my dreams come true—the moment he set his sights on me.

"You are my dream come true." I press a kiss to his lips. "And this is the most perfect Christmas, better than I could have imagined." Wrapped in his arms, I glance around the room, surveying the tree, the bags, and the decorations. It's all a bit overwhelming. "So, where do we start?"

Hunter doesn't seem the slightest bit overwhelmed. "

I thought we could decorate and save the tree for last. Really make this place look festive." Sheer happiness and complete optimism radiate off him.

"Sounds good to me." Sifting through the bags, I pull out the garland and head to the mantle, weaving it through the items we have up there.

"Already looks more festive in here," Hunter says as he sets a Christmas snow globe on the coffee table.

I pick up the globe and shake it. "Do you know I've never seen snow?"

"Seriously?"

I nod. "It was one of the reasons I was looking forward to going to Aspen. But then the snow had to go and ruin everything."

"We'll get there someday, I promise."

I don't doubt that he'll make sure to make good on that promise.

Hunter grabs something out of one of the bags and hands it to me—a Christmas stocking with a Q on it, holding another with an H.

Smiling, I run my fingers running over the letter. "Okay, maybe it didn't ruin everything."

Each piece of Christmas décor lightens my mood. It might not be the Christmas I envisioned, but being here with Hunter is still more than I could have ever hoped for. After the room is set, we work on the tree, Hunter stringing the lights and working on the garland.

"I got you a little something," Hunter says as he hands me a box.

"We said no gifts."

"You said no gifts. Besides, this isn't a gift, just another decoration."

I give him a sideways look before tearing into the box. Inside is a delicate glass ornament in the shape of a heart, with the words "Our First Christmas - Hunter and Quinn - 2021" etched into it.

"Oh, Hunter." I trace my fingers over the words. "It's beautiful."

"I wanted to make sure it was the first ornament we put on our first tree."

"First of many."

His hand caresses my cheek. "First of many." His lips press against mine.

"Thank you, Hunter, for today and the ornament. I'm sorry for how I acted. This, being here with you, is the perfect Christmas."

His arms wrap around me, holding me close. "I'm glad you're enjoying it. And I promise, it only gets better."

"What do you mean? How is that even possible?" There's a mischievous smile on his lips. "Hunter, what did you do?"

"Nothing." His face turns serious, trying to hide the smile he can't stop from reaching his eyes.

"Hunter Adams, if you don't tell me what you're up to…."

"You'll what?" he taunts me.

"I won't finish what we started earlier."

Hunter laughs. "That's your loss as much as it is mine."

He's got me there.

"Come on, let's finish this tree. Then we can have some fun under it."

CHAPTER 10

HUNTER

Snow.

How did I not know she had never seen snow? All she had to do was say the word, and I could have rectified that.

The question is—how can I make it happen now?

Money may not buy happiness, but it sure as hell can buy something to make her happy.

"Where are you going?" she asks as I grab my phone and head toward my office.

"I have to make a call. I'll be right back." Closing the door behind me, I dial Zack, a friend from college. He was the guy who knew everyone and could get you whatever you wanted. A great guy to have in your corner. Still is.

"Hey, Hunt, what's up?"

"Merry Christmas, man. How are you? How's the family?"

"Right as rain. Couldn't be happier."

"Listen, I hate to bother you with it so close to Christmas, but I need a favor."

"Name it."

I tell him my dilemma—the trip, Quinn, the snow.

He laughs. "You're not going to believe this—"

With Zack? Just about anything is possible.

"I probably will."

"I actually have one. Needed it for my daughter's play last weekend."

It's like a Christmas miracle—something I truly believe in.

"Can I borrow it?"

"I'll do you one better. I'll personally deliver and run it. That way, you can enjoy the snow with your girl."

"I can't ask you to do that. Tomorrow's Christmas Eve. You should be with your family."

"It's going to be pandemonium at my house. Believe me, you'd be doing me a favor."

Just as I hang up the phone, Quinn enters the office.

"Everything okay?"

"Yeah, sorry about that." I walk over to her, wrapping my arms around her. "I had a message from an old friend. Just wanted to check in and see if everything was okay with it being the holidays."

"You are such a good guy."

"I try."

"Look what I found." Quinn holds mistletoe above her head.

"Looks like I owe you a kiss." Our lips meet softly.

She lowers the mistletoe to her lower belly, a sexy smile on her face.

"I think you owe me a few more."

"Happy to oblige."

Hoisting her up, I set her on the desk, her ass on the edge. With her help, I slide the denim off her silky thighs, her green panties following suit.

"Perfection," I say as I appreciate my view, the smooth, glistening skin of her center. "Are you wet for me?"

"Soaked," she pants.

My tongue runs along her opening, flicking her clit.

"So good."

"More, Hunter. Please."

I love it when she begs.

I cover her with my mouth, my tongue toying with her clit. She writhes beneath me, her fingers gripping the edge of the desk. The sounds she's emitting are sexy as hell. Sliding my finger into her, I work it in and out. Withdrawing my finger, I replace it with two.

"Oh, God, Hunter."

Her body moves, fucking my fingers, taking what she needs from me.

"That's it, baby. Come for me."

My mouth covers her clit, sucking the already sensitive bud until she tumbles over the edge. She cries out in ecstasy as she rides out the pleasure of her orgasm. Her body collapses, relaxing on the desk.

"I think this should be one of our Christmas traditions."

"I agree," I say, pressing a kiss to her stomach.

CHAPTER 11
QUINN

"Hunter?" I call out when I wake up lonely in bed. No answer. "Hunter? Where are you?" Still nothing.

Something catches my eye—a piece of paper taped on the mirror above my dresser. Sliding out of bed, I make my way to it and pull it down.

Merry Christmas Eve, Quinn.

This is just the beginning for us and for our first Christmas together. I can't wait to spend it with you.

All you have to do is follow the clues to find me.

Clue 1 - Go to the place where we first made love in our home.

"Where we first made love," I repeat. My feet carry me out of the bedroom into the living room. I remember the day I moved in. I didn't have much and didn't live far, so we brought in the few boxes of my stuff. As we were bringing in the last of it, Hunter welcomed me to our home. I swooned. I kissed him. We barely made it through the door.

"The front door."

I go to the door, but there's nothing there. This is it, I'm sure of it. I close my eyes, recalling the night. I'm right. I know I am. Except it wasn't the interior part of the door.

I pull the front door open, and there is the next clue.

Clue 2—The night our lives changed, we bumped into each other. I had no idea then that we would end here, but I am so glad we did. Your next clue is there.

My first thought is the hotel. That's where we ran into each other. The first time we had sex, but I don't think that's what he's referring to. Still, it looks like I'm leaving the condo, so I better get dressed.

Rushing back to the bedroom, I toss the silky pajamas I'm wearing to the side and reach for the gift I picked up at the store yesterday—the two-piece lingerie set, red lace with white fur trimming the edges. Between the small amount of fabric and the see-through lace, it leaves little to the imagination. I toss on one of Hunter's zip-up hooded sweatshirts over it and head down to the lobby.

"Merry Christmas, Ms. Quinn," the doorman, Freddie, says.

"Merry Christmas, Freddie. Do you by any chance have something for me?"

As I was changing, I remembered before we saw each other at the hotel, I bumped into him in the lobby. He had been upset and bolted out of the building into the street.

"As a matter of fact, I do." He smiles as he hands me the envelope.

"Thanks, Freddie. Tell Letti and the kids Merry Christmas." I rush off with a wave to read the next clue.

Clue 3—It's raining, it's pouring….
Finish the song to figure out where your next clue is.

I laugh just thinking about it.

It's raining, it's pouring—the old man is snoring.

The old man he's referring to is none other than our building maintenance manager, Jerome, who we found asleep on our couch after we asked him to check the air conditioning last summer. The poor guy was so embarrassed. After he left, Hunter began to sing the children's rhyme, and we burst out laughing.

Heading down to the lower level of the building, I knock on Jerome's office door.

"Merry Christmas, Quinn," Jerome greets me.

"Merry Christmas, Jerome. Do you have something for me?"

He nods his head. "Sure do."

Only this time, it's not a note but a box—a gift-wrapped box. He gives me a wink before closing the door. I tear open the paper and lift the lid off the box. A key.

A key to what?

The building operates on access cards and codes, not keys, so what in the hell does this mean? Where is the next clue? I examine the box looking for something—anything—another piece of the puzzle. This key can't be all of it. If it is, I have no idea where it could lead me. I stand outside the door and try to piece together what I have.

Jerome.

The key.

The sleeping incident.

The night he gave us uninterrupted access to the rooftop, which is supposed to be off-limits.

That's it. The rooftop.

I get giddy when I realize where the clue leads. Rushing to the elevator, I punch the bright red R for the rooftop.

The elevator doors open, and when I step onto the rooftop, it's like a Christmas paradise. My mouth falls open, my eyes wide with wonder. Christmas trees, gift boxes, reindeer. Amid all of it, Hunter is perched on a sleigh so big, I can't even fathom how he got it up here. He's wearing a pair of red pants with a Christmas shirt. Some might say it's silly. I say it's perfect.

"Hunter."

"You figured it out."

"I can't believe you did all this," I say, trying to take everything in. As much as I love my surroundings, I love this man even more, and I'm finding it hard to take my eyes off him. "How did you do all this?"

He runs his hand over his jaw. "I called in a lot of favors. It's all worth it to see that smile on your face."

The sleigh. The fake snow. The Christmas tree. It's like a winter wonderland.

"I love it." I make my way closer and press my lips against his. "I love you. You are the most incredible man in the world."

CHAPTER 12

HUNTER

Overcome with joy, Quinn kisses me, but not just any kiss. The earth-shattering, ball-tightening kind of kiss. Unfortunately, it ends just as quickly as it began. Soon, she's out of my arms, her body turning in every direction, taking in her surroundings.

"I still can't believe you did all this."

"I told you I would do anything for you, Quinn."

"You've done more for me than you know, Hunter." She glances around the rooftop. "Are we… alone?"

"We are."

"Good. Because I have a little something for you, too." Slowly, she slides the zipper on my hoodie down, and beneath the cotton material lies lace—barely any of it, but lace, nonetheless. The hoodie slides down her body, off her arms, and onto the ground. Quinn is in the hands-down sexiest Mrs. Claus outfit I have ever seen.

"You know, if Mrs. Claus dressed like this, Santa would never leave the house to deliver gifts."

"The poor children."

"Happy Santa." I run my hand over my jaw as I take her in. "Christ, you're breathtaking."

"Breathtaking, huh?" She hops up on the edge of the sleigh and spreads her legs, baring everything.

I need her. Now. As I take a step toward her, she waves her finger at me.

"Not yet."

"You're killing me, baby."

"Sweet way to go, though, isn't it?" Sliding her hand down her body, her fingers find their way between her thighs, the place I'm dying to be. She runs her finger over her center, and her head falls back, exposing her breasts even more.

Unable to control myself any longer, I reach beneath my red sleep pants and take out my throbbing cock. As I watch her finger herself, I move my hand up and down my shaft, trying to ease some of the tension she's building in me. When she moans with pleasure, my balls tighten.

"Please, Quinn." I might be begging, but when it comes to her, I don't care. She's worth it. Every glorious inch of her is worth it.

She removes her fingers and extends them to me. "Want a taste?"

I want so much more than a taste, but I'll take what she's offering—for now.

Moving closer, I wrap my hand around her wrist and guide her fingers to my lips. Slowly, I slide them into my mouth, tasting her on my tongue.

"So good," I murmur when I've licked them clean.

"More?" Her hands are on her knees as she pushes them further apart.

"I want it all." I lower myself to the ground before her. "I want to taste every inch. I want to feel all of you. I want to own you the way you own me."

She lies back on the sleigh spread wide before me.

"Take me, Hunter. I'm yours."

"All of you?" I ask, my tongue lapping her center.

"All of me."

As I slide my tongue inside her wet center, my finger traces the rim of her ass. The sensation sends her soaring, her hips bucking up. Patience wears thin as I watch her writhe and wriggle beneath my touch as her orgasm washes over her in waves.

"Get up." Settling myself on the seat of the sleigh, I pat my knee.

Quinn takes her lip between her teeth as she straddles me.

"Like this?"

"No, like this."

My hands fall to her hips and guide her down onto me with one hard push. A strangled cry falls from her lips as I fill her. She's right where I want her. As she adjusts to me, she begins to move. My hands leave her hips and pull at the lace covering her breasts. The material tears with little effort, and her breasts spill into my hands. Dipping my head, I take her right nipple between my teeth while I knead her other breast. Her fingers grip my shoulders as she quickens her pace.

"That's it, baby. Just like that." She is fucking perfection as her pussy grips my cock.

"I'm going to come."

"Not yet." My tongue flicks over her sensitive nipple.

"I can't hold on," she cries out.

"Fuck me, Quinn," I growl. "Fuck me... hard."

She bounces on my cock, hard and deep. "Hunter!" There isn't a doubt in my mind the people on the street below us can hear when she screams out in pleasure. Her fingernails dig into my skin, my name a curse on her lips.

Losing control, I buck into her aggressively until my

orgasm is on the verge of hitting. At the last second, I pull out, coating her body in cum.

CHAPTER 13

QUINN

Hunter and I lay wrapped in each other's arms as day turns to evening. We spent the whole day on the rooftop, basking in the sun and making love.

"I know this isn't exactly the Christmas we had planned, but is it okay so far?"

"So far? Please tell me you don't have anything else crazy planned."

"Nothing crazy, just waking up with you in our bed, sitting in front of the tree with our coffee, then trying to not destroy Christmas dinner."

"Speaking of… We're supposed to make the cookies tonight."

"You ready to head back?"

I nod. As amazing as all this is, I just want to be home —our home—with him.

When we get home, I retreat to the kitchen to send a text to Hunter's mom. When we were at the grocery store, I knew he was clueless, so I bought items to make chocolate chip cookies and hopefully, his mother's sugar cookies. I even snuck in a Christmas tree cookie cutter.

Armed with her recipe, I turn on Christmas music and start baking. The kitchen might look like a disaster, but the cookies seem to turn out okay.

With my surprise in hand, I head off in search of Hunter. When I find him, he's standing on the balcony, his hands pressed on the railing, very reminiscent of our time in the Bahamas.

"What are you doing out here?" I ask, joining him on the balcony.

"Checking out the Christmas lights." He turns and sees the plate. "What's this?"

"Your mom's sugar cookies. I asked her for the recipe."

He takes a cookie from the plate and bites into it. "These came out great."

I bite into one, nervous I had messed up his mother's recipe.

"They're not as good as your mom's, but they're not half bad."

"They're better."

I shake my head, doubting the truth of his words. I've had her cookies, and these aren't nearly as good, but I appreciate his unwavering support. "It's a beautiful night."

The sky is slightly overcast, but between the clouds, you can see the stars. Balconies, building tops, and even the football stadium are decorated in beautiful Christmas lights. The whole city looks like it's twinkling.

Hunter takes the plate and sets it down, then wraps me in a blanket before pulling me into his arm, my back resting against his chest. As we take in the view, something lands on my face. I brush it away, but a moment later, it happens again.

"What the heck is this stuff?"

"Ashes, maybe."

"Ashes? Why in the hell would…"

Suddenly, tons of the "ashes" fall, only not the dingy color of ash. They're white, bright white—some might say snow white.

I recall what I told Hunter earlier about never seeing snow and his quick retreat into the office to make a call.

The man is unreal in the best way.

"It's snow. You got me snow."

"I would give you the world if I could."

"You are my world, Hunter."

I twirl around under the falling snow, my arms extended out as Hunter's laughter fills the air.

CHAPTER 14

QUINN

Barely eight on Christmas morning, Hunter's phone is already ringing.

"Hey, Mase. Merry Christmas." There's a pause as Mason speaks. "Yeah, okay." Another pause only piques my curiosity. "Okay, we'll check." He hangs up the phone.

"What did Mason want?"

"He said there's a delivery for us."

"Who delivers on Christmas?" I ask as Hunter helps me to my feet.

"Uh… Santa." I roll my eyes. "Well, he does." His hands grip my waist. "Just look at what he brought me for being such a good boy." Hunter winks at me before kissing the tip of my nose.

"Seriously, though."

He shrugs. "Guess we should go find out."

We toss on some clothes before heading to check the door. When we step out of the bedroom, the stockings are still hung by the chimney with care, but it's not Saint Nicholas standing there. It's Mason and Avery, Hunter's parents, and Hudson and Hayley.

"What are you guys doing here?" I ask excitedly before turning to Hunter. "Did you do this?"

"No, but whoever did is lucky we got dressed before we came out here," Hunter says.

"Hey," Mason interjects. "He's not the only one with connections." A proud smile covers his face. "This was all me."

"It included a lot of phone calls and a very scary plane ride," Avery adds. "But it was so worth it."

Avery wraps her arms around me in a hug, and I never want to let her go. I'm so beside myself with joy, I don't know what to do except let shine the one emotion I try not to experience. I cry. Big crocodile tears stream down my face as I make my way through the room, hugging the only family I've ever had and the only one I'd ever want.

"Looks like you two made the most of things," Hunter's mom says as she looks around our home at the scattered Christmas decorations, the tree, and the packages beneath the tree.

"It was all Hunter."

"I had some help," he admits.

"You can say that again," Ashton boasts when he enters the room, Claire following behind.

"The gang's all here," I shout excitedly.

"Where's my gift?" Mason asks, looking point-blank at Hunter. "I let you date my sister. You better have gotten me something good."

Like two kids, Hunter and Mason fall to the ground and wrestle. I shake my head at the scene, but I love every minute.

The Christmas I thought was destroyed turned out to be more than I ever could have imagined.

Later that night, after all is said and done, Hunter joins me out on the patio.

"Penny for your thoughts," he says as he hands me a glass of champagne.

"I am just thinking about how perfect today was. Heck, how perfect my life is. And it's all because of you."

"I can't take all the credit. You make things pretty incredible around here." He lets out a small laugh. "Sometimes, I think about where we were a year ago."

"Separate towns?"

"Separate lives. When I really think about it, I can't even picture it. I can't envision a life without you, Quinn."

"Lucky for you, you don't have to. I'm not going anywhere. Not now. Not ever."

"Merry Christmas, Quinn."

"Merry Christmas, Hunter."

He raises his glass and clinks it against mine.

"To the first... of many."

ALSO WRITTEN BY L.M. REID

Hard to Love Series

Hard to Hate

Hard to Trust

Hard to Forgive

Playing the Game Series

Playing the Game

Playing the Field

Playing to Win

Played Out

The Knights Football Series

Whatever She's Got

Whatever it Takes

Whatever Happens – Available January 2023

Worlds Books

Heated – KB Worlds

Acceptance – The Salvation Society

ABOUT L.M. REID

L.M. Reid writes contemporary romance filled with emotion and a whole lot of steam. Her heroines are strong and feisty, and her heroes are sweet and sexy.

L.M. loved reading as a child and really fell in love with books while reading the Babysitter's Club. The series spurred her love of writing, leading her to create her own series as a kid, "Best Friend's Forever."

Growing up watching soap operas, L.M. has always had a flair for the dramatic and a love of all things romance.

She's just a Midwest girl with simple tastes and dirty thoughts.

She lives in the state, where they swear there is more than corn, with her husband and son. She's an iced coffee addict and loves Swedish Fish. While her heart belongs to romance, she loves curling up on the couch with a good—or bad—horror movie.

Website: www.lmreidauthor.com

Book Bub: http://scarlet.pub/LMBB
Facebook (Page): https://scarlet.pub/LMFB
Reader Group: https://bit.ly/lmreidRG

Instagram: https://scarlet.pub/LMIG
Goodreads: https://scarlet.pub/LMGR

Hijacked Holiday
A RACING HEARTS CHRISTMAS STORY

A RACING HEARTS CHRISTMAS STORY

BY MAY GORDON

This is a work of fiction. Names, characters, organizations, places, events, and incidents are products of the author's imagination or are used fictitiously. Any resemblance to actual events, locales, or persons, living or dead, is entirely coincidental.

Copyright @2022 by May Gordon

No part of this book may be reproduced, stored in a retrieval system, or transmitted in any form or by any means electronic, mechanical, photocopying, recording, or otherwise, without the express written permission of the publisher.

This book is licensed for your personal enjoyment only. This book may not be re-sold or given away to other people.

CHAPTER 1
PENELOPE

Louisville is stunning in the winter. Snow piles up, covering all the surfaces and trees of Stone Legacy Ranch. It looks like a winter fairy tale. The dark red, white, and oak barns stand out among the vast whiteness. Having the Christmas season on us makes last year feel like a lifetime ago. So much has happened. It all started with me breaking into Conrad's office, then we started our adventure of training Opus and winning the triple crown. Then, of course, my accident and my temporary memory loss. I still can't believe everything that has happened.

We were just married this past fall, and I thought the stables couldn't look any more beautiful with the autumn colours, yet here we are. Winter may be my favourite season, yet.

"Penny dear, what are you doing up this early." Donna, our house manager and friend, walks into the kitchen, turning on the lights.

I was cuddled up in one of the bay windows benches, looking towards the barns.

"I couldn't sleep. It started snowing again early this morning."

"Good gosh, more? It's going to be extra work in the barn." She comments, going to the coffeemaker.

"Conrad and I already talked. We are going to hire a company to come out and plow the property and any areas we use a lot."

"That's very thoughtful, dear. I'm sure Burt will appreciate it."

Burt is our Barn manager and Donna's boyfriend, though they hate the term. "Anything to make the stables run more smoothly. It's been chaos these last few months."

"Well, winning the triple crown will do that to a farm. But it's exactly what was needed."

She's right. Before, Conrad struggled to keep this place something his father would have been proud of. And now? Opus is the most considerable stud fee and in high demand. Owners want to send their horses here to train and myself to race them. But this holiday, I want us to slow down. We've been through so much and so busy that I want this Christmas to be remarkable. I want to give Conrad the most amazing Christmas, our first one as a married couple.

I unfold myself from the bench seat and walk over to Donna, grabbing myself a cup of coffee. "I need a perfect Christmas gift for Conrad."

"Anything you get him, he'll love," Donna assures me.

I shake my head. "No. It needs to be perfect; this whole holiday needs to be perfect. He deserves it."

"You both do." She chimes in. "But I agree, anything you need dear, I'll help." She grins.

I instantly feel much better. "First thing we need to do is decorate. It's already December, and we have nothing up."

"I know exactly who to call. There is a company who decorates houses and barns." Donna says with excitement.

"And I'll get the in-door decorations. Tonight, we will have a Christmas tree party." I feel giddy just thinking about it.

I chug my coffee, then pour a cup for Conrad, leaving the kitchen to head to our room. Being farm people, we are both early risers, but even I'm up earlier than usual. I quietly open the bedroom door.

Conrad is still passed out. I shuffle over to his side of the bed and sit down. I place his coffee on the bedside table. He always looks so peaceful sleeping and not the firm, cranky, amazing man I'm used to. I lean down to kiss him, trying to wake him up sweetly. He groans, tossing a bit before his eyes flutter open. His smile is soft and still sleepy.

"Good morning, beautiful." He reaches up to stroke my face. "You're up early this morning."

"I couldn't sleep; the snow outside is so beautiful." I reach over and pass him his coffee. "I was thinking after we do the walk-through of the barns we could go shopping."

He looks at me oddly; I understand why, I'm not a shopper unless it's for a horse. "For Christmas decorations." I clarify.

"The farm hasn't been decorated since my father died. My mother always loved Christmas."

My heart sinks at the mention of his mother. Sophie was so loved and such a spirit. I wish I could have met her.

"Then lets bring it back. This Christmas will be the first of many Christmases, full of holiday spirit and love.

Conrad looks at me for a long minute, his face softening. He pulls me in for a tight hug before placing a kiss on my lips.

"Alright. Let's have the best first holiday together."

And it will be, I'll make sure of it.

CHAPTER 2
CONRAD

The property looks like a winter wonderland. The barns and house are decorated with lights, red ribbons and wreaths with music playing in the background. It's all exquisite and festive, just like my mother had it. I'd thought I'd feel sad. The memories of my mother and how she loved Christmas, or how Christmas was always a tragic time for us once she died because we missed her. But this makes my heart full of love and joy. My spirits are lighter, and I'm looking forward to the holidays. Even if we are busy, this will be a quiet and romantic month with my new wife.

"Looks great. It reminds me of the old days when you were just a child." Burt smiles. "Even the workers are in better spirits."

"It's great. Penny will take photos of the horses with wreaths around their necks for the website and social media."

"Brilliant idea."

I have to agree with him. Usually, I can be a big grinch this time of year, but with all the changes and effort Penny is putting into this winter season, I love everything about it.

"There is still a mountain of paperwork in the office," I mutter, feeling my holiday buzz winding away. "Where is Penny?" I ask, feeling the need to see her.

"She took Opus to the back pasture," Burt tells me.

I head that way. Opus. Or Lu, as I first called him when I was stuck with the beast. I remember how defeated I was with that horse. He was untrainable, and I thought my family's legacy was gone. Then Penny came into my life and made everything better. She trained Opus, won the triple crown, and became the love of my life. I don't know what power she has, but I'm glad she's using it for us.

I spot Penny sitting on the fence, watching Opus frolic and play in the snow. I walk up behind them and wrap my arm around her waist.

"Hey, how's the paperwork? Caught up with all the breeding requests?"

I let out a huff. "Are you kidding me? There are so many; it's becoming a bidding war."

"That's a good thing, hun. It means more money." I explain the obvious.

I watch the pure black stallion move along the snow, his dark coat looking even darker against the white. Watching him like this, he looks like some beautiful creature, not the beast I know him to be.

"I saw the tree got delivered this morning," I tell her. "Could you pick a bigger one?" I joke.

She grins. "It's the perfect size. We have a big house; having a small tree would be pathetic."

I guess she's right. "So, what did you have planned for tonight?" I know she has something.

She turns to me, her face bright with excitement. "We have a tree trimming party tonight. Just the two of us. I even have these fun Christmas-themed drinks planned, and Donna and I are making a ton of appetizers."

"What, no meal?"

"Nope! Just all our favourite appetizers. And we will be making our ornaments too, to celebrate our first Christmas together."

I grin at her excitement; it's contagious. "And will this night end with us relaxing in the hot tub together?"

She leans down and kisses me. "Of course."

I groan almost painfully. "How many more hours till this day is done?"

She looks at her watch. "10. Work harder it will go by faster."

"That's not how time works." But I wish it did.

Penny and I spend the rest of the day working. From tedious farm paperwork to training horses. We work side by side all day, just like my parents used to do. The whole time Penny can't stop chatting about everything we will be going through over the holidays. She sounds super excited about it. I know what she's doing, and I had the same plan. After everything we've been through, having a holiday we can look back on and remember as the best first Christmas as a married couple. I want that too.

When the day finally finishes, we're both so tired and ache we decide to hit the hot tub first before dinner and decorating the tree. When I first settle into the warm water, I moan in relief; it is just what I need.

"Great idea, baby. Now we can eat and decorate feeling relaxed." Penny says, coming to sit next to me. I wrap an arm over her shoulder, pulling her closer, leaning down to kiss the top of her head.

"I could stay like this forever." Something about a hot tub in cold weather makes it feel so much better.

"We would look like wrinkly old raisins." She laughs, looking up at me. "Would you still love me?"

"Nothing in this world would make me stop loving you." I kiss her again, but this time with other intentions in mind.

I reach over and grab her hip, pulling her onto my lap. Her body pressed up against mine feels fantastic. It turns my skin on fire; she always makes me burn. I don't think I can wait till tonight; I need her now.

"Let's do it right here," I growl against her lips.

"Yes." She breathes out. "Right here." She kisses me deeper.

I reach up to pull the string on her top when voices stop my action. It's not Donna, and I can't place the rest. Some of the barn men came up to the house for some reason.

"Oh god." Penny moans in disbelief and rests her head on mine. "Please, no. Not now, not my holiday."

"Darling, what is it?" I pull back to look at her.

A knock from the side door catches my attention, and to my shock, I see Penny's brother Oscar waving like an idiot at me. But not just him, my in-laws too.

What the hell? So much for our peaceful holiday.

CHAPTER 3
PENNY

My holiday has officially been highjacked.

I look around the breakfast table. My family decided to surprise us for the holidays. Usually, I would be all for it, happy and excited about their visit. We just saw them at Thanksgiving, but I know they have been busy with the training farm back home in England. I didn't mind that; I've spent every Christmas with my family since I was born. Is it selfish of me to want one quiet one with my husband?

I look around the dining room table to see our whole house. My mom, dad, brother, Donna, and Burt are all busy chatting and having a good time. I should feel happy; some people would kill to have a house full of family for the holidays. I can't shake the dark cloud that's formed over my head. It is selfish and stupid, but I can't help how I feel.

Last night was a disaster. After Conrad and I got out of the hot tub, the whole night was the opposite of what I wanted. My mother insisted that Donna and Burt join us; together, the women got out of hand and decorated the tree themselves. Burt and my father got drunk and were loud and obnoxious the whole night. Oscar and Conrad may be civil, but they still have some tension. Conrad did assume he stole millions of dollars from him and put him in jail. But I would hope that would be smoothed other by now. They spent the night taking jabs at each other. I spent most of my time trying to referee them both. To say the night was exhausting was an understatement, and nothing I had planned.

"Oh, and dear, we need to go into town for some shopping and to the market." My mother suggests. "Donna, you need to come with us."

I plaster on a smile, nodding my head at her. I wouldn't say I like shopping. Unless it's for horses, I don't care for shopping for much else.

"Conrad, you need to show me what horses you have in training. I would love to take a look." My dad calls out. Always the horse trainer himself.

Great. Now I'm not the only casualty. Poor Conrad is being pulled into this chaos too. I need to find a way to make this a terrific holiday still. I focus on my breakfast brainstorming when there is a knock on the side door from one of our farm hands. From the looks on his face, it's nothing good. Just when I thought our holidays couldn't get any more chaotic.

* * *

Two hours later, we are helping Donna and Burt move into the only guestroom. A part of the roof of their cabin collapsed, causing their place to become unlivable. So, our quiet holiday of two has now turned into a house packed with seven. Selfishly I curse how many extra rooms this house has.

But of course, if they need a place to stay, they are more than welcome to the spare room; I only wish it had happened after the holidays.

As I set up the guest bathroom, Donna walks in, a sympathetic look on her face.

"I'm so sorry, dear. I know this isn't what you wanted. This was supposed to be a quiet holiday for the two of you, now it's the opposite of that."

I let out a long sigh. "It's not your fault Donna; these things just happen." I shrug. "I'm just trying to find a way to make the best of it. It's just so hard to do that with everything." I wave to the house. "I'm sorry about the cabin."

Donna pulls me in for a long hug. "I know, dear." She pulls away and smiles at me. "Now, lets not stay up here feeling sorry for ourselves. Your mother said she wanted to finish decorating the house."

Great. I love my mother, but she can be overbearing on her best day. And here I was, hoping to finally have my own Christmas for once, something I designed and made with my husband. Well, not anymore. I need to make peace with it; maybe I can carve out some quiet time with Conrad.

The rest of the day is busy; nothing new there. But instead of dealing with horses, it is family members. By the time the day was over, we were all sitting in the living room enjoying an after-dinner hot apple cider. I'm exhausted. And saw Conrad for a total of five minutes alone today. I look across the room to see my father and Burt occupying his time.

Burt breaks off from the group and stands in the middle of the room.

"If I could have your attention." He says, seeming nervous. That's not like him; he's never scared of anything. He opens his hand, gesturing for Donna to come to stand beside him. "I did have this plan to do this in private and more romantic in our home, but our roof had other plans."

Donna giggles, still not getting the hint where this is heading, but I knew. And I couldn't be more excited about it.

"But being with friends and family seems like the perfect place to do it." He pulls the ring box out of his pocket and then, with shaking legs, kneels. "Donna Smith, will you do us the honour of being my wife?" he asks the question.

Donna bursts out in tears, nodding her head yes. With the ring slipped on and a kiss, they hug. I wipe happy tears of my own, then go to congratulate them. My mother is just as excited; she and Donna have become close friends.

"This is so exciting and perfect timing Donna. You always said you wanted a winter wedding." My mother chimes in.

"Oh, we can't possibly do it this winter. Next is well enough."

"Why wait? We're all here; it doesn't need to be big; we can make it happen with all of us here." Burt says, looking around at us all.

"Of course, whatever you guys want," Conrad says with a smile.

"Then it's settled. The wedding will be on Christmas Eve." She claps.

"That's only a week away," Donna says in shock.

My mom pulls me to her side, squeezing me. "It will be a lot of work, but we will get it done between us all." She beams.

"Donna, don't worry. This will be a fairy tale wedding." I smile at her. I can see the concern in her eyes. But I don't want her to feel guilty about this. Besides, I've all but given up on my low-key Christmas.

CHAPTER 4
CONRAD

I don't think this house has ever been so busy. My whole life, it's been my father and me, and this big house has open rooms. A part of me likes it, even hoped for it. But I can feel sadness in Penny. We were hit with many surprises as of late, and I know she was looking forward to a small and intimate holiday. The last few days have been a clusterfuck; between our busy regular farm work, add-on in-laws and a wedding to be planned, it's not much of a holiday when you think about it.

I don't think I've seen Penny very much these last few days. By the time she comes to bed, I'm asleep or vice versa. Whenever I've seen them here, she's been busy with either her mother or Donna. Zero alone time. None. And it's starting to wear thin.

I stare at the stack of paperwork sitting on my desk. I feel like it's grown just by me ignoring it. Another obstacle is getting in the way of my alone time with Penny.

"Gosh, look at that pile. More breeding requests for Opus." Burt comes into the office.

"If he weren't making us millions, I would complain, but I can't," I mutter.

"No, you can't, son. This is what you wanted." Burt pats my shoulder. "Penny just finished on one of the yearlings if you wanted to have a minute with her."

That sound like a great idea; I need a break from doing nothing. "She's in the training barn?" I ask him.

"No, her mother had to drag her away for some wedding planning help."

I'm sure she loved that; the wedding planning was nonstop. Add entertaining family plus our regular barn work. It's been chaos. I pull on my jacket and walk back to the house. The dining room is a mess of magazines, laptops, and papers. Donna and Penny were in deep discussion with her mother about something.

"Red roses in winter will be stunning." My mother-in-law suggests.

"I agree; they would look perfect," Penny says.

"Ladies," I interrupt.

The look on Penny's face screams thank you. She looks like she wants to get out of here.

"Conrad, how are you." Donna smiles.

"Good, I just wanted to steal Penny for a few minutes. You can spare her?"

Penny instantly stands. "Be back in a second." She says before walking towards my office. I follow close behind her.

As soon as the door closes, I push her up against it and give her a long kiss. I just wanted a moment, some private time. But after this kiss, I feel like I will need a few hours with her.

"Lets go out for dinner, just the two of us. We can go into town and get a hotel. Hell, lets stay the week." It was an impulsive suggestion, but one that now feels like a brilliant idea.

She lets out a long sigh, defeated. "I can't. I promised

Mom and Donna I would run into town with them to finish picking flowers, cake, and god knows what."

I rest my head against hers. "How did it end up like this," I mutter more to myself. Penny tenses for a second, and I look down to see what's wrong. Before I can ask, the office door opens, and Oscar and his father push their way in.

"Conrad, there you are. We planned a big poker game with Burt and a few other barn hands." My father-in-law says.

"Right now?" I ask in disbelief. I still have so much work to do, and Penny and I haven't even discussed when we can carve out some alone time together yet.

"Not now, tonight. It's going to run late. We need a ton of supplies." Oscar says. "I'll need your help. Can we set up in the den?" He fired out about twenty more questions before he was done. By then, Penny had left to leave with Donna and her mom. I felt like shit. Something was bothering her.

After helping Oscar set up a plan for tonight, I head back to the barn. Two of our barn hands greeted me in the middle of a brawl. It took three of us to break them up. Then they up and quit. So on top of everything that's going on, we are now down two employees.

"How will we fill two jobs this time of year?" I complain to Burt.

"We can get some greenhorns temporarily." He suggests.

Having amateurs in my barn makes me uneasy. We have million-dollar racehorses here; it just takes one mistake to ruin a horse.

"I don't want a bunch of green people here."

"I can reach out to some of the local race barns. See who wants some extra work over the holidays."

"But till then, we will need to pick up the slack," I mutter.

"When was the last time you mucked out any stalls? It's good for the soul." Burt says.

I can't help but roll my eyes. Growing up he would say that about every chore.

"Fine. What's more work added to our plate." How can I fit anything more into it? I have no idea, but what choice do I have?

CHAPTER 5
PENNY

Running the brush over Opus, I finish polishing his coat before moving to his mane. I gave him a light ride today, it's pretty cold and I didn't want him to sweat too much. Even if the indoor riding is heated, I feel like he should get something like a holiday, even if I'm not.

I still have a few horses to get through today; keeping up with the regular training schedule has been challenging. I almost feel like I'm going to fall behind altogether.

"Why so glum, Penny?" Burt asks to lean on the stall door.

I smile at him, not wanting to confess my worry, frustration, and guilt about how the last week or so has been going. My mind wanders back to what Conrad said: "How did it end up this way?". He sounded disappointed and sad —the opposite of how I wanted him to feel.

But beyond my holiday wish is Burt and Donna's wedding. Something I'm happy about.

"Just thinking about your wedding, and why you haven't asked me to be your best woman?" I grin.

He laughs, shaking his head. "I'm having none of that; having you guy there is enough for me. You're family."

My heart warms from his words. He's right. We are family. "I guess it won't be long till you are promoted to grandpa, huh?" I say it off handily as a joke, but it's true. One day Conrad and I will have children, and Donna and Burt will be grandparents.

Burt's eyes shine with happy tears. I didn't mean to make him emotional, but damnit, if he isn't making me emotional too. "Don't you start crying now, Burt or I'm going to, and this will be a whole mess," I warn him.

He nods his head in agreement. "We have way too much work to do, and I'm only running on half-engine days. That poker party took it out of me last night."

I don't recall precisely when Conrad came to bed, but it was late. I don't think he got more than a few hours of sleep. "Where is Conrad anyways?"

"He needed to meet with the hay distributor." I nod my head recalling his plans. When did he even mention that to me? Or did I just read it off his calendar? I finish brushing Opus and then help Burt with lunch feed. In my head, I start planning an evening for just the two of us, no matter what.

That plan lasted about an hour, when my mother and Donna come racing into the barn. Almost in tears about cancelled catering, late decorations, and God knows what. We spent the rest of the day trying to figure out this stuff. With the wedding only a few days away and on Christmas Eve, we don't have much time.

"Where is Oscar?" I ask my mother.

"Oh, Honey, he had too much to drink last night, so he's sleeping."

I suppress an eye roll. Here we are working our asses off, and my brother is sleeping. "Wake him up; he can help

Burt in here. While the three of us run into town, find a new caterer, and fix whatever else had happened." This is going to be a long day.

I was wrong. It wasn't a long day but also a long night. I didn't get back to the farm till ten at night. On the plus side, we have everything figured out for the wedding. Delivery for most things will be tomorrow; then, it's mostly just set up till the big day. I stare at the house, seeing the light still on and bodies moving around. Even if I had walked in there, I wouldn't have had any time with Conrad or myself. I feel a wheel of emotions bubble up inside me. It's all gone so wrong, and nothing is how I wanted it to be. With no desire to go inside, I head to the place where I feel the most comfortable. The barn. As soon as I open the barn door, the horse's heads poke out. Opus sees me and starts pawing at the ground.

I stop at the feed stall and pick up some sugar cubes before standing in front of Opus.

"Hey, boy. I missed you." I give his forelock a good scratch and feed him come cubes. His head nudges me wanting more attention.

I look out the barn door and see that it's snowing with the warm glow of the lights. It's such a beautiful scene, and for some reason, it saddens me. The emotions well up, and I can't seem to control them. I start to cry. They flow out. I'm not sure why. Maybe it's because of the holiday or how everything seemed to fall apart. I'm mad and frustrated about everything. But I'm also guilty. I lucky to even have any family members alive to celebrate. Conrad has no living family members. To say I have a mixed emotions is an understatement.

I hear footsteps coming down from the hall, and I look

up to see Conrad walking toward me. He looks concerned.

"What's wrong?" he sits next to me in front of Opus's stall.

I sob even harder at this point. "It's just all a disaster. I wanted to have a perfect first Christmas together, with the perfect gift, and nothing has gone the way I wanted it to go." I sob.

He hugs me tight, kissing the top of my forehead. "Darling, it's fine. This is all I need."

"What is?" I asked, confused.

He lifts my chin and wipes some of my tears away. "This. You and me. Having you in my life as my wife. No matter what happens in our busy lives, I have everything I need as long as we can do this."

He makes it seem so easy. Is it this simple? I suddenly feel Opus nudge my shoulder, looking for some attention. I watch Conrad slowly and warily reach up to try and pet him. The two never really get along. Opus always tries to take a bite out of him. But I guess this holiday would give us at least one Christmas miracle. Opus let Conrad pet him, and for a long minute as well.

"Well, I'll be. I thought for sure I might lose a finger."

"He's been in a better mood since his retirement. He's getting all fat and happy now."

"Well, he won the triple crown. He could have a gold plated stall if he wanted, and I'd be okay with it." He laughs.

I smiled at him, loving the light-hearted humour he brought to the conversation. It's exactly what I needed. We must have sat in the barn for hours, talking, almost catching up. We talked about the farm and the following year of training. That whole evening opened my eyes; this is all I need: nothing fancy or unique, but us. And for now, that's more than enough.

CHAPTER 6
CONRAD

I watch the chaos around me; we are finally here after the mad dash to get this wedding ready. Christmas Eve morning and Burt and Donna are getting married. The outside patio of our house is filled with wooden benches and red roses. It's a small wedding, just how they wanted it to be. I promised Burt I would ensure everything was ready, one less thing for the girls to worry over. From the noises I've heard upstairs, I don't want to add another worry to their list.

"So, how do things look?' Burt asks, walking up behind me.

I turn to him, "Looks all ready. We should go have a quick drink."

He looks appalled. "It's ten o'clock in the morning." He protests.

"Just a small one, tradition." I pressure him. "Come on. I have some in my office."

He rolls his eyes at me, but I'm doing this for his good. I can tell how nervous he is. A small drink will mellow him out.

"Fine. But just a small one." He caves easily.

I can't help but smile. I remember when the rolls were reversed. Burt was the one offering me a drink to calm down. I pour him a small glass before leaving to check on Donna.

When I entered the upstairs guest room, it was chaos, just like I thought it would be. I don't even see Penny anywhere.

"Oh Conrad, don't you look so handsome." Donna smiles at me.

She's wearing a white pantsuit, with a long white fur trench coat. She looks elegant and beautiful.

"Donna, you look stunning." I walk up and kiss her on the cheek.

"Thank you, dear. But tell me. How is Burt? Holding up well? Or is he getting anxious?" She asks worriedly.

I ease her mind. "He's looking forward to becoming your husband. Don't stress about a thing."

Penny suddenly opens the door. "Perfect timing." She gives me a quick kiss. "We are all ready for this wedding. Can you get Burt ready? The staff is already seated."

"Show time." I grin at Donna.

The wedding is short, simple and sweet. And exactly what Burt and Donna wanted. Based on the amount of work everyone put into this, you'd think it would be as big as a royal wedding. But as long as they are happy, I am too. I watched across the aisle and saw Penny tearing up with happiness. I'm also glad this wedding is over. Hopefully, the stress of the holiday will die down.

After the wedding, we move into the house for some food. I can already see Penny looking more alive and happier. Donna comes to stand next to me, passing me a glass of wine.

"Conrad, I want to apologize."

"For what?" I ask her.

"I know you and Penny wanted this to be a special holiday, and between your in-laws, my house disaster and the wedding, we all but highjacked this holiday." She lets out a sad sigh. "I can't imagine the pressure I added to your plates. I don't know how I can make it up to you."

I smile at her. "You can do something for me."

I've had something planned for the last few days, and I finally get to show her tomorrow. It took a lot of money to make this happen, but I'd do anything for Penny.

Chapter 7- Penny

As the night winds down, I can also feel the pressure of life on me. I honestly feel silly for worrying over such trivial stuff. I watch as Donna and Burt kiss, smile and laugh together. They are a perfect couple. The staff invited to the wedding left already, and my parents and brother went off somewhere.

"We're going to head upstairs now, dear." Donna comes up and kisses me on the cheek.

"Alright. You two get some rest. It's been a long day." I hug them both.

Looking around at all the mess, I decided to leave it for tomorrow. I pack away the leftover food and then speak to Conrad. He slipped out a little while ago; I assume his office. He's ever the workaholic. When I enter his office, I see him shuffling through some papers.

"What have you been doing? It's Christmas Eve; you shouldn't be working." I walk around the desk to sit on his lap. He wraps his arms around me and lets out a content sigh.

"I wasn't working, just finishing up some paperwork."

Before I can ask what kind of paperwork he stands for. I grip his neck, trying to hold on tighter.

"Where are we going?"

"We are going to take a bubble bath."

I love that Idea. We have a vast tub; I've used it several times but never in it together. What I didn't expect was the tub to be already filled with candles and some scented soap.

"When did you have the time to do all this," I ask when he puts me down.

"Right before you came to get me. I wanted to make sure everything was perfect for you."

He's so sweet. I turn around and give him a long passionate kiss. "Thank you."

When most people think of a romantic Christmas Eve with their partner, the good stuff comes after. But not in my case. I fell asleep as soon as I dried myself off and crawled into bed. The following day when I woke up, I felt utterly guilty about our sexless night. I know I need to apologize. When I turn over in bed, I see Conrad is already awake and smiling down at me.

"Good morning, beautiful."

"Sorry," I mutter with a yawn.

"For what?"

"For the lack of sex last night. That bath just totally knocked me out."

He chuckles and leans over to kiss my forehead. "I wanted you to sleep; the bath did exactly what it was supposed to do."

"I do feel much better than I did."

"Well, I want to make you feel even better."

"Not possible." I shake my head.

Conrad suddenly stands, grabbing my house coat and throwing it at me. "Put this on and come downstairs."

I feel a bubble of excitement start to form. I jump to my

feet and throw on the robe, ready to go in a second. Conrad takes my hand and leads me downstairs. It's still early in the morning, around six o'clock. We need to head out to feed the horses and start the stalls. When we get downstairs, I look around for something, anything. But all I see is our messy living room—the tree and decorations right where we left them.

"Notice anything?" Conrad asks.

"Not really," I say honestly.

"Alright, how about something missing." He hints.

It clicks, then. Donna and Burt should be up by now. Even on Christmas. My parents are also early risers; they've been up this time every morning they have been here. "Where are they? Sleeping in?"

"Probably, but not here."

I turn to look at him. "What do you mean?"

"I sent them on vacation." He grins.

I stare at him in shock. "You sent them on vacation. Donna and Burt and my family? All of them? When did they even leave?"

"I sent Donna and Burt on a honeymoon to Hawaii, and your parents and brother as well. They left late last night but will be back to celebrate New Years Eve with us."

I've been speechless for a long time. I don't even know what to say; what is there to say? I finally got my head around what was happening. "So, are you telling me we are alone here for the next five days?"

"Yes, but even better, all the farm chores are taken care of. I paid some staff wanting overtime triple pay."

I jump into his arms. This was precisely what I wanted, some alone time with my husband. "What should we do first?" I'm so excited my mind can't focus on anything.

Conrad pulls me into his arms, and suddenly the whole mood changes. His eyes are heated, causing me to flush with passion.

"How about we set a fire and make love in front of it like in those cheesy Christmas movies." He winks at me.

"I think that is the best idea you've ever had." And then I kiss him. Ready to show him just how much I love him.

We are lying in front of the fire, wrapped in blankets and each other's arms. This feels so right; it wasn't always like this with us; I remember those first few months of tension. I laugh about it now. But Conrad and I were meant to be, no doubt about it.

"I think I know the perfect gift to give you." I roll over to face him.

"Darling, you don't need to get me anything." He strokes my hair.

"I think you're going to love this."

"Well, now you've got my attention."

I sit up, pulling the blankets with me, and he does the same. Looking at his face, I don't want to miss his reaction. "Let's have a baby."

His eyes widen, and I can see a wave of emotions play through them. Excitement, fear, worry, happiness. I feel the same way.

"It doesn't have to be now or soon. I want you to know I am ready whenever you are ready."

He suddenly pulls me into a fierce hug and kisses me. "This is the best gift anyone could have ever given me." He mumbles into the side of my head. "I love you." He pulls back and kisses me again.

"Merry Christmas, Conrad."

"Merry Christmas, Penny."

And just like that, this highjacked holiday will become one of my favourites.

. . .

Chapter 8- Conrad

I look around the room to the crowded living room, thinking it was just like this only a week ago at Burt and Donna's wedding. During that time, Penny and I enjoyed alone time bliss. Christmas was just for us. We didn't leave the house; we just made love, overate food and napped. We napped. I don't remember the last time I did that, maybe when I was a child.

After Christmas, our days were quiet. We worked the farm together, got caught up with paperwork, and watched her train the yearlings. It may have been hard work, but we are used to that; the important thing is that we were together. Now that we've had our alone time, Penny was eager to get caught up with her family and the newlyweds.

Penny's mom stands beside me as I refill my drink. "Conrad, you're a good man." She gives me an affectionate hug.

"I appreciate that." I hug her back.

"I know this was a lot; we surprised you guys. And I know deep down Penny wanted something lowkey and special. I'm sorry if we caused so much trouble."

I'm not going to tell her just how much stress and worry this whole mess caused Penny. "Everyone got the holiday they wanted, and they are happy. That's all that matters." I reassure her.

Giving her one more hug, I step away and move to Penny. She's talking to her brother about the horse training year. "I'm going to steal her away," I tell Oscar.

"Surprised you even asked," Oscar smirks.

I grab her hand and pull her into my office. The floor-to-ceiling glass windows show the farm in all its winter glory. The decorations are still as stunning as ever.

"Why did you pull me in here?" she asks with a sexy smile. "Everyone is outside; we're not having sex right now."

I chuckle. "That wasn't what I was thinking." I pause, knowing that's not true. "I just wanted to have some alone time. We've been a part of this whole new year party." I complain.

She lets out a sigh. "I know but having our family away for the last week highlighted how selfish I've been. I have been so silly."

"I don't think you were selfish, but I do feel like some alone time all year round and not just over the holidays is what's needed." It's something I've been thinking a lot about. We were so burnt out and overworked and were banking on holiday to reconnect and recuperate. But in reality, we need to make time for that all year round. And I'm going to make it my mission to find that balance; it's even more critical now that we are thinking about having children.

"I can't believe I'm going to say this, but I will miss my family and having Burt and Donna as roommates."

"But just think about the big empty house we will have." I wiggle my browns at her making her laugh.

I pull her onto the office couch, and we cuddle while watching the snow fall outside the window. I look at the clock and see it's almost midnight. "Shall we return to the family?" I ask.

"I'm going to see Opus." She stands up.

I roll my eyes, but I shouldn't be surprised. Opus is her baby, and there is no changing that. "I'll come with you." I go towards the door to get our jackets from the closest, but before I even reach it, I hear the glass door of the office open. I watch Penny dash across the property to the barn, wearing her elegant pantsuit and heels.

"Hurry up!" she yells back at me.

Grabbing the blanket on the back of the couch, I run after her. My nice Italian loafers are getting ruined from the snow. The barn door is already open, and Penny is right where you can find her most days—sitting in front of Opus's stall—feeding his sugar cubes and giving him kisses.

Walking over to her, I wrap her in the blanket and sit next to her, making sure to give Opus extra space. I will never trust this horse, even if he has good days. I've had too many bites over the short time he's been here.

"I guess you two will never get along, huh?" she lets out a warry sigh.

"Sorry darling, wishful thinking." I look from her to the giant black beast. This horse has given me so much; I don't think I could ever repay him for it all. But if spoiling him is what makes Penny happy, then I help her with that.

I feel a slight nudge on my shoulder and look up to see Opus looking quite like a follicle. I'm still not fooled, but I try anyways. Reaching up, I try to pet him, and to my surprise, he allows it.

"New Year's Eve miracle." Penny muses.

And as if on cue, Opus tries to nip at me. "Asshole," I mutter, making Penny laugh. She leans against me and sighs in contentment.

"This is my happy place."

"Hey, I thought I was your happy place," I grumble, but she ignores me.

It always warms my heart when she says stuff like that. We've made a wonderful life together, and it's only just getting started. I look down at my watch and see it's only a few minutes till midnight.

"We should get back, ring in the new year with the family."

"Your right." She stands, giving Opus one last pet before reaching out her hand to mine. "Shall we?"

Grasping her hand, we head back to the house. "It's crazy to say, but I think this will be one of my favourite Christmases."

"That is crazy." I muse. "But next year will be better. I can promise you that."

Looking up at me, she smiles. "I'm holding you to that."

That's fine. It's a promise I'm not going to break.

EPILOGUE
PENNY

December, 2 years later

The wrapping paper is not my friend tonight. I've been trying to get all our Christmas gifts done so I can finally put them under the tree. I'm behind on my Christmas list. It's like this every year. But for better reasons than being busy with the farm. During the winter months, we hire extra hands, giving Conrad and myself a well-needed break. Even more so with Conrad Jr, that's arrived. He's only six months old and has kept us busy. As much as I loved being pregnant, I missed being able to ride and train the horses. Watching the trainer we hired to do it and coaching from the sidelines was a pain. It's not that the trainer was terrible; it just wasn't me.

"Hello?" I hear Donna call out; then she enters the dining room. "What's this? You still haven't finished wrapping?" it sounds like she scolded me.

"Please help," I beg. "My parent's brother is arriving in a few days, and this needs to be done."

Donna smiles and sits down next to me. "Where is Conrad Jr?"

"He's napping, I thought it would give me time to get this done, but wrapping paper hates me."

"You need a break, dear. I can easily handle this."

She doesn't need to ask me twice. I jump at the chance; I thank her with a kiss on the cheek before grabbing my coat and heading toward the barn. I go to Opus's stall to find it empty, then move to the outdoor padlock. I spot him playing in the snow like a little kid.

He's a beautiful horse and has produced us beautiful foals. His first round of babies is currently in training for the next race year. And they look nothing but potential. I cluck my tongue, calling him over. He comes trotting over, eager for his sugar cubes.

"Hey boy, how are you doing?" I scratch his face.

"Con still asleep?" Conrad asks, walking up beside me and putting his arm around me.

"Yes, Donna's in the house."

"Let me guess, you pawned the gift wrapping onto her."

"No!" I protest. "She offered, and I couldn't refuse."

He chuckles, leaning down to kiss me. "Your parents arrive in a few days; add Donna and Burt into the mix. Are you ready for another highjacked holiday?"

He's right. Even if Conrad and I have found a better balance to spend time with each other during the holidays, we've yet to find a way to prevent the takeover. But honestly, I don't mind. The first year was tough, but the last few have been better. Having a house full of the family always warms my heart.

"I'm ready. And my parents have been dying to see Con again."

"We just visited them at Thanksgiving."

"It's their first grandchild. Can you blame them?"

Conrad wraps his arm around me; we watch Opus eat his hay in the snow. Through the years, I still look back at that first Christmas together and shake my head at how I perceived what the perfect Christmas would be like. I was so naive and didn't realize just how lucky I was. As long as I have a family that loves me, they can hijack any holiday.

ABOUT MAY GORDON

May Gordon, bringing you sweet, sexy and safe reads! Happily ever after guaranteed!

Warning: This author writes what she likes to read. That means there will be instalove, OTT Heroes, and, brace yourselves, virgin characters at times. If none of those float your boat, you might want to find another book. If they do, you're in the right place.

A MERRY CREW CHRISTMAS

A NORTH SHORE CREW NOVELLA
FOR THE "OUR FIRST CHRISTMAS" ANTHOLOGY

BY VI SUMMERS

This novel is entirely a work of fiction.

Names, characters, businesses, places, events, locales, and incidents are the products of the author's imagination. Any resemblance to actual persons, living or dead, or actual events is purely coincidental.

Copyright © Vi Summers, 2022. All rights reserved.

All rights reserved. No part of this publication may be reproduced or transmitted in any form or by any means, electronic or mechanical, including photocopying, recording, or any other information storage retrieval system without the written permission of the author, except for brief quotations in a review.

This book is licensed for your personal enjoyment only. This book may not be re-sold or given away to other people.

Thank you for respecting the hard work of this author.

Cover design by: Y'all That Graphic

Edited by: Owl Eyes Proofs & Edits

Proofread by: Emma Kynaston

This book is intended for those 18 years and over.

It contains content of an adult nature.

This book is set in New Zealand where Christmas is during summer, UK English spelling is used, and flip-flops are called jandals.

It features the five couples from Vi Summers' *North Shore Crew* series.

CHAPTER 1
GAGE & LIL
~ THE WEEK BEFORE CHRISTMAS ~

GAGE'S POV

Elodie slammed her cereal spoon down onto the breakfast bar, making me jolt, then did it again to get the same reaction.

I raised a finger to my lips, trying my hardest not to crack a smile. "Shhhh, El, Mummy's asleep, remember? We need to be quiet."

"Quiet," she whispered—loudly—and widened her round hazel eyes. "More blueberries please," she sang at the top of her lungs.

I cursed under my breath and ran a hand down my face. "El, *whisper!*"

"Whisper," she repeated, barely at hushed levels.

Our little girl grew more like her mumma with each passing day, volume included.

"Now can I have more blueberries?"

I chuckled, unable to say no when she looked at me like that.

"Here you go. But leave some for Mummy," I cautioned, sliding the container to her.

"I leave some for Mummy," El told herself while taking a first, then a second fistful, barely leaving a third of the blueberries.

I snagged the container away and raised my brows at her. She popped a toothy grin that had me smothering another smile. Terrible-twos didn't have shit on the three-year-old sass my daughter possessed.

Shuffling footsteps in the hallway drew my eyes to Lil when she emerged, barely awake and squinting against the bright morning sunlight. She'd always been a terrible morning person, so I quietly gathered her into my arms and hugged her close.

"You're up early, Sunshine. Sorry if El woke you; I was trying to keep her quiet."

Lil snorted. "Good luck with that. And no, she didn't. I was too excited to sleep in. It's been forever since we've gone for a ride together."

I planted a kiss deep amongst the bundle of messy auburn hair on the top of her head.

The days of us jumping on my Victory and going for a carefree cruise together had all but disappeared since Elodie arrived. We'd planned today, but little did Lil know that I had extra plans for us—ones that I'd kept secret from her.

"I'll make you a cup of tea. Do you want muesli and blueberries too?" I offered.

Lil's eyes lit with gratitude. "Yes please."

"I saved you some berries, Mummy," Elodie said sweetly.

"Thank you, my little babe." Lil then turned to me. "Are we heading south to visit Lotte today?"

My heart both leapt and lurched. Lotte was my first love. My wife who'd been torn from this world decades too soon. Her traumatic passing sent me headlong into a three-year spiral, one where I'd given up trying to make it through the pain.

A family intervention saw me moving to Auckland, and it was during that hellish time that I'd met Lil.

She crashed into my life—literally—and dragged me kicking and screaming from the darkest of depths while healing me in ways I never thought possible. She and Elodie were now my entire world after my previous one shattered.

While guilt over moving on with my life gnawed at times, Lil had taught me that it was okay to openly talk about Lotte when I needed to, and it was her suggestion for Elodie's middle name to be Charlotte, in honour of my late wife.

I studied Lil intently, having a moment where reality didn't seem true. After vowing to never remarry, my heart had other ideas, and I'd proposed to Lil last year.

I carefully handed her a mug while answering her question. "Not today, Sunshine. I'll visit Lotte another day. Perhaps between Christmas and New Year."

"Lotte," Elodie sang before popping a blueberry into her mouth. She munched, then looked at me. "Can I see Lotte too?"

"No, sweetie. Just Daddy will visit her."

Her inquisitive eyes, identical in colour to Lil's, remained unblinking. "Why?"

"Because."

"Is she nice?"

I coughed away the stab in my chest. "She was very nice."

"Where does she live?" El asked.

I took a fortifying breath. This was the first time she had asked these kinds of questions and while I wanted to be honest, I was unsure of *how* honest.

"She's not alive anymore, El," I said gently, steeling my emotions.

A knot formed between her little eyebrows and she frowned into her cereal for a moment. "Is she dead?"

The kick under my ribs got harder. "She is."

"Yesterday?"

I let out a sharp puff of air. "No, sweetie. A long time ago. Before you were born."

"That's sad."

"It was the saddest," I murmured truthfully.

It was by far the hardest experience I'd ever had to endure. Nothing could have prepared me for losing the person I'd envisioned spending my entire life with.

Lil set down her mug on the counter and wrapped her arms around my torso, hugging me hard. She'd witnessed me grieve on more occasions than I cared to admit, and the one thing she never did was judge me for missing the hell out of Lotte. A deep down part of me was still heartbroken over losing her, but if I hadn't lost her, I wouldn't have met Lil or made Elodie. Either way, the double-edged sword stung.

I kissed the top of Lil's head again and paused, getting lost in the subtle sway of our bodies. She would forever be my home. My new path. And I couldn't wait for her ass to be nestled behind mine as we rode northbound later this morning.

* * *

"Hold the fuck on properly, Sunshine," I growled through my teeth while my fingers flexed on the handlebar grips.

The last thing I wanted was to lose my world all over again in another motorcycle accident. And today of all days.

"I am," she replied through the Bluetooth connecting our helmets. Her voice held the vibrations from the open road beneath us.

"Clamping your thighs tighter on mine isn't classed as holding on. Hands on my waist. C'mon."

Once on a straight, I reached behind me and fumbled until I had one of her hands planted on my hip. "Keep it there, Lil. Please."

"I just love how free it feels. God I've missed our biking trips."

"I've missed them too." My snicker was lost to the vibrations. "And you know what else?"

"What's that?"

"There's a packet of M&Ms in my pocket."

Lil's gasp came through the Bluetooth. "For me?"

I chuckled heartily. "Yeah, Sunshine, for you. But only if you hold on with both goddamn hands."

A wicked grin spread across my mouth when they immediately fastened on my waist.

She laughed. "You know I'll do anything for M&Ms."

While complex under the surface, Lil wore her heart on her sleeve and was easily pleased. One thing I learned early on when we were still locked in a love-hate friendship was that there was no use in apologising with flowers; the way to the feisty redhead's heart had been through large bags of colour-coated chocolate.

An hour into the ride, I slowed and pulled into a vineyard nestled amongst the rolling hills.

Lil's weight shifted behind me as she took in the tree-lined driveway. "Hey, this is the vineyard we looked at for our wedding."

"Is it?" I played the fool.

"Yeah. Remember; the one we loved but it was too damn expensive."

I hummed despite grinning to myself. "Do you think they'll let us eat M&Ms on their lawn?"

Lil laughed. "Who cares? It's probably going to be the only way we can afford to dine here."

"I booked us a table for lunch, babe."

She gasped. "You did?"

"Yup." I clicked down a gear and cruised through the sealed corners, then rolled to a stop in the parking area on the top of the rise.

I braced the bike while Lil climbed off, then swung my leg over. "Excited?"

She wrestled her helmet off, then bounced on the balls of her feet. "Oh em gee, so excited. I hope they do seafood." She then gasped. "And crème brûlée!"

"I'm sure they'll do both, babe." I chuckled while wriggling out of my helmet, then welcomed the hard kiss Lil planted on my mouth. It sent me stumbling back a pace until I regained balance, and I made sure to hold her tight while I kissed her properly.

Once we'd stripped from our motorcycle gear, I took her hand and hurried her out of the summer's heat. A friendly young man looked up from the reception desk and smiled.

"Welcome to *Rolling Vines Winery*. How can I help?"

"I have a lunch booking under *Westbrook*."

He quickly scanned the booking screen and his expression turned triumphant. "The Ellersly Nook is ready and waiting for you. Right this way."

"Ellersly Nook?" Lil whispered once the receptionist was a few steps ahead.

I shrugged. "I just requested an outdoor table in the shade."

Our escort led us into the summer sun and down a pebbled garden path. When we came to an open yet secluded nook in the garden, he gestured to the white table beneath the high leafy canopy.

"This is your nook. Your waiteress will be along in a few minutes with iced water. In the meantime, please relax and take your time perusing the menu."

"Thank you so much," Lil gushed, already reaching for her seat before I could be chivalrous.

I sat opposite her, picked up the menu and laughed. "Looks like you're in luck, Sunshine; they do a fresh seafood platter."

Lil slapped her menu down dramatically. "Done! Sign me up, Batman—I'm getting that."

Chuckling, I leaned to the side and extracted the packet of M&Ms from my shorts pocket. "Pre-lunch snack?"

Lil already had her hand out before I finished the sentence. "Hit me with a handful!"

I glanced around. "Like, cock and balls handful, or–"

"Gage!" Lil laughed. "For fuck's sake, no, not cock and balls!"

"Shhh, Lil! Your voice carries! I swear, if we get kicked out of here for fornication, you'll regret it so bad."

She flared her eyes and spoke without moving her mouth. "Then feed me the goods, dammit."

Snorting and ripping open the bag before she took my cock and balls and severed them from my body, I poured until her palm almost overflowed.

She tossed a couple into her mouth and exhaled in relief. "Mm!"

"You're an addict."

A couple more got chucked in. "I'm not even going to argue with you."

The instant we heard footsteps on crunching gravel, Lil threw back the entire handful. With cheeks bulging like a chipmunk, she was forced to remain mute while I ordered the seafood and an orange juice on her behalf, then a steak and beer for myself.

When our waitress left, Lil chewed furiously, then hissed, "Oh my god, I feel like I just broke all the rules."

I snorted. "Because you did. And you looked guilty as fuck while doing so. More?"

"Hit me," she stated, snapping out her palm. "No regrets."

The large bag of M&Ms was finished well before our lunch arrived, and by the time we'd eaten and finished our drinks, I was shifting nervously in my seat.

Lil's eyes narrowed. "Do you need the toilet?"

"No." I coughed into my fist. "Just waiting for my steak to digest." I paused for a second, then stood. "Actually, give me five."

She looked a little stunned at my abrupt change, but smiled and nodded nonetheless. "Okay, I'll order us dessert if the waitress comes back while you're gone."

"Sounds good, babe." I didn't have the heart to tell her it wouldn't be needed.

Instead of using the bathroom, I strode to the main reception and asked the guy who welcomed us to tell Claudia we were ready for her.

He clicked his fingers in understanding and assured me that she would be at our nook in a few minutes.

Nerves gathered and pooled in my stomach as I returned to Lil, and I knew the strain showed on my face.

She frowned from behind her sunglasses as I eased into my seat. "You seem tense. Are you sure you're okay?"

I gathered her hands in mine and toyed with her engagement ring. "I'm fine, I promise. Just thinking about how much I love you."

The sharp angle in her shoulders eased and her pretty

smile reappeared. "I love you too. And thank you for lunch. Did you see the waitress while you were up there?"

"I did; she'll be down in a moment."

Lil vigorously rubbed her hands together. "Bring on the crème brûlée."

I ran a hand over my smile. Butterflies like no other swept through me when a new woman appeared, picking her way carefully along the path with a covered platter balanced in her hands.

When she entered the grassy nook, she looked up and smiled. "Lil and Gage?"

"That's us," Lil replied politely.

"Hi, I'm Claudia, your cake maker."

"Oh, I'm sorry, I think you've got the wrong people. We didn't order—"

"Sunshine," I cut in softly, and her confused gaze snapped to me.

"But we didn't book a cake maker…"

My smile wavered anxiously as I shifted to her side of the table. I ran my hand up and down her thigh and swallowed thickly.

"Lil, there's something I haven't told you. I saw how disappointed you were when you realised this place was out of our budget for the wedding, but I made some inquiries, and well… they had an unexpected cancellation, so… I made a booking."

Lil's mouth worked open and closed and tears sprang to her eyes. "But you didn't want a big fancy wedding again."

"Big, no, but I want your special day to be as fancy as you want it to be."

"It's your day too," she countered.

"Of course. But while it's our wedding, it really is *your* big day. I want you to have everything you've ever dreamed of. Aside from horses; I'm allergic," I added with a half-cocked smirk to lighten the mood.

Truth was, I didn't take much notice while Lotte was planning our wedding. We were young, and I didn't care for the details. I now regretted not being as involved as I should have been during the process. I took it, and her, for granted, and that's something I wouldn't let happen again.

Lil gifted me with a watery smile and squeezed my hand. "If that's what you want…?"

I double-squeezed back. "It is." I then looked to Claudia.

She took it as her cue to proceed. "Let's get into tasting some wedding cake flavours, then, shall we? Vanilla or Lemon Curd to start with?"

"Lemon Curd," Lil and I replied in unison.

I looked at my girl and grinned. My heart tripped and my palms grew damp. Her smile reassured me I was doing the right thing by her, and the overwhelming love in my chest told me I was doing the right thing for me.

CHAPTER 2
TRAV & AINSLEY
~ CHRISTMAS EVE-EVE ~

AINSLEY'S POV

I opened the bathroom door and almost shat myself. "The fuck! Trav! *Travis!* There's a *goat* in the house!"

A white one, with glassy yellow eyes that were borderline horrifying. I briefly slammed the door closed, trapping me *inside* the bathroom and away from the goat, then whipped it open to yell at Trav again.

"Travis!"

His laughter found me from out of sight. "Is she inside again?"

"Again?"

"Yeah, again." He casually strolled down the hallway and stopped to scratch the animal's back. "You remember Betty, don't you?"

My chin tucked back. "Betty?"

"Yeah, Betty." He flared his dazzling blue eyes like I should remember. "My friend's baby goat I looked after when you first came to Auckland. This is her—she's all grown up," he added with an air of pride.

"She's fucking huge! Too big to be in the house."

The peak of his cap hid his face as he rubbed at the back of his neck. "Yeah, she seems so much bigger when she's inside, but she jumped the barrier I put up at the door so I'm not sure how to keep her out…"

I scoffed. "Can't you tie her up? Or shut the door?"

When Betty attempted to come at me again, I squeezed the door shut as far as I could while still glaring at Trav.

"Seriously, get her outside. I'm staying in here until she's *out* of the house. And if she craps on the floor, it's your problem, not mine."

He did nothing but laugh. "You thought she was cute when she was little."

"She was!" I exclaimed. "Now she's big with creepy eyes."

"Yeah…" He took a moment to admire them. "They're weird aye." When his focus lifted to me, some of the amusement slid from his face. "I'll take her outside."

"Thanks," I deadpanned.

I waited until they were gone before rushing to our bedroom, just wrapped in a towel, and shut the door tight. The last thing I wanted was for Betty to come at me while I was naked.

Barely a minute later, Trav barged into the room and leaned against the door with a lazy smirk.

I paused while moisturising my legs. "What are you up to now?"

One thing I learned about Travis O'Brian from the first day I met him was that his next move was hard to predict. Being married to him was like being on a constant sugar rush and being forced to ride the highs and lows associated with that.

"Lookin'," he drawled.

"Perv."

He chuckled and pushed off. "It's not perving when it's mine."

I looked up from my bent position and arched an eyebrow. "Yours, huh?"

"Yeah. Because we're married now."

Snickering, I flipped him off with my wedding band finger.

"Look, even Betty wants a peep show," he laughed, pointing at the window behind me.

I glanced over my shoulder and shrieked to find Betty with her front hooves on the outside window ledge, giving me a glassy side-eye.

"How long is she staying here for?" I cried, hiding behind the curtains while hastily whipping them closed.

"A week."

"A week! Trav!"

He lifted his palms. "Chloe was in a jam. No one else could look after her."

"Don't goats look after themselves? They're farm animals. And are we even allowed to keep a farm animal in the suburbs?"

Trav shrugged. "I dunno. But Chloe does, so I figure it's fine here too."

"So, Chloe lives on the North Shore?"

"Well, not *technically*... but it's practically the same thing."

I cursed under my breath and dug through my underwear drawer for my favourite pair. "It's really not."

"Tomayto, tomahto," he replied with a flippant hand gesture. "Anyway, I need to shoot out again."

My foot paused poised above the leg hole of my panties. "Now where?"

"Christmas shopping. I hope I haven't left it too late." He grimaced. "Town is going to be fucking intense."

"I'll come and help."

"Nope. Where I'm going is a secret, even from you."

Although partially relieved that I didn't have to brace for the Christmas Eve-eve shopping rush, I wasn't exactly thrilled about being left at home with a full-grown goat.

"What the hell am I meant to do with Betty while you're out shopping?"

Trav laughed long and hard, then shrugged. "Don't let her in the house?"

"Travis!" I exclaimed through my laughter. "That's the shittest advice *ever.*"

"Yeah, sorry babe, it's all I got. Call it practice for when we have kids."

"Oh my god." I tugged up a pair of little denim shorts. "If we're resorting to looking after a goat in preparation for having children, then we're one hundred percent screwed before we've even got kids."

Trav's eyes darkened and he closed the few steps between us. "All I heard was screwed, and I accept your offer."

More laughter escaped as I playfully batted him away. "I thought you were going shopping?"

"Shopping can wait. It's sex time."

I went to deny his ass, but let out a scream when his shove sent me tipping backward onto the bed.

He smirked. "That'll do perfectly. Now, off with your clothes."

Giving me zero time to take them off myself, Trav gripped the waistband and yanked them down in one swift movement, leaving me naked and catching my balance on the edge of the mattress.

Within a blink, he cast his clothing aside and stood before me in all his inked glory. He smirked and nudged my legs open with his knees, then leaned forward to blanket the length of my body with his.

When he eased into me, we released a mutual sigh of pleasure.

"See—" he grinned and wiggled his eyebrows— "makes you forget all about Betty, right?"

"Oh my god!" I giggled, making Trav emit a half-choked sound as the pressure from my laughter tried to force his dick from my body.

He playfully slapped a hand over my mouth. "No laughing, dammit. It makes my dick feel—" He gagged again as my laughter increased.

"Dammit, Lee, it's impossible to focus."

His continued mutterings kept my mirth alive until the air finally changed.

It thickened and sobered. Stole the remaining hilarity and gave way to uninhibited arousal. I ran my fingers up his bare torso while linking my ankles firmly on his lower back.

Uncovering my mouth, Trav set his hands either side of my shoulders and arched high above me, eyes now burning with need. He tugged until my ass was off the mattress, then shunted into me hard with a punishing rhythm.

"Fuck, I love you and your body," he hissed, taking my breasts in his hands and squeezing them.

I let out a little snicker and received a harder warning thrust.

"No laughing," he panted. "This is serious business."

I couldn't help it; another giggle slid free. Before I could lock more down, Trav pulled out, flipped me onto my stomach, and pushed my face into the bed cover.

"Laugh into the blankets so you don't distract me," he growled, adding a cheeky slap to my ass.

My attempt to counterargue ended in a long moan and

my knees automatically shifted wider as he hit a particular sweet spot deep inside.

"Oh my god. There. Keep going."

"Not so funny now, is it," came his taunt, laced with an audible smirk.

"Shhh."

A dirty snicker sounded behind me and his fingers bit harder into the creases of my hips. "That's it, baby. Let me fuck you."

My fingers found my clit and rubbed while I focused on the orgasm conjuring within. Slow at first, then quicker with each rhythmic thrust exactly where I needed it. The rush of pleasure tore through me without warning and my guttural cry filled the room.

Trav's groans increased until his rhythm faltered. I welcomed the last hard thrusts as he rode out his release and shook violently with a "jjjjjjjdddddddgggttt," sound.

It made me giggle and smirk over my shoulder. "Good?"

"So fucking good," he breathed out, then graced me with a half-cocked smile. "I'd do ya again."

He eased out and landed another slap to my ass, and I followed him into the bathroom while checking out *his* ass. It was void of tattoos, unlike the rest of him. We were both covered: arms, torsos, backs, legs. It was a shared addiction and one that would never wane.

Catching me looking, he smirked. "Now who's perving?"

I threw his words from minutes ago back at him. "It's not perving when it's mine."

The shit-eating grin I loved pulled wider and his dimples appeared. "Always has been from the moment I saw you the first time. It was the one and only time I've banged a skeleton."

Despite giggling, our eyes snagged and memories—both good and bad—resurfaced. So much had happened between that night and when we met again. The Ainsley from our one-night stand was leagues apart from the woman I was now. While time had passed and healed, there were still parts of me I'd never get back.

"I'm glad we found each other again," I murmured.

Trav's expression softened. "Me too, baby. Being married wouldn't be the same without you."

I flipped him off while sitting on the toilet, then met him in the bedroom when I was done. Once we were dressed, I whipped the curtains open only to be reminded of the current 'situation'.

"Ah, Trav... Betty is eating the grape vine."

A string of curses trailed in his wake as he rushed outside, and I happily stood at the bedroom window laughing my ass off as he tried to redirect her attention elsewhere.

I hung out of the window and called, "Think of this as practice for when we have kids."

"Kids don't eat the garden plants, Ainsley! Ouch, and kids don't have horns," he sassed after Betty nudged him with hers, sending me into another fit of giggles.

On a dreamy sigh, I shook my head and felt my heart fill with love. Trav was an absolute clown, but I wouldn't have him any other way. Goat and all.

CHAPTER 3
NICO & BROOKLYN
~ CHRISTMAS EVE-EVE ~

NICO'S POV

I felt eyes studying me as I assisted a client through her second set of bicep curls and lateral raises.

Through the mirror, my gaze locked with Brooklyn's. She lingered at the entrance to the gym, and I smiled despite unease gathering in my gut. Her expression pulled the knot of dread tighter.

After giving me the stink-eye, she strutted into the gym, wearing workout tights and a little cropped tank that held my attention, and lay on the leg curl machine.

My client's puff of exertion snapped my focus back to her. "Two more, Adele, then you get a rest."

I lightly touched the dumbbells in her grasp while glancing at Brooklyn over my shoulder. An unchecked growl left my mouth when I saw her getting instructions from a client.

Possessiveness had me torn between being professional and properly focusing on Adele, or storming over and telling the guy to get the fuck away from my wahine [woman]. Either way, I was distracted and jolted when Adele all but dropped the dumbbells after completing her set.

"Nice pushing through," I murmured and motioned to the awaiting kettlebell. "Rest for one, then twelve kettlebell squats."

My attention briefly cut back to Brooklyn and what I saw pushed my anger to the forefront. I pointed at Adele while keeping my eyes glued to Bee.

"Grab a drink. I'll be back in two minutes."

Setting Brooklyn in my sights and seeing red when the guy lightly slapped the back of her thigh, I came to a close stop beside him.

"Hey, bro. What's going on here?"

Brooklyn rolled her eyes while the guy got chatty as if he hadn't just had his fucking hands on my girl.

"Hey, man. Just helping Brooklyn out. She's a newbie so I'm showing her the ropes."

I puffed myself up and crossed my arms over my chest, staring him down and trying hard not to be a dickhead.

"She ain't a newbie, brother. She's my girlfriend and I'd appreciate you keeping your hands *off* her. This spot right here?" I pointed at the back of her thigh. "Is for my hands only."

He paled and snapped his palms up. "Fuck. I'm sorry, man. I didn't realise. Honestly."

"It's fine," I assured him with a clap to his shoulder. "And I'll take over from here."

When he nodded and returned to his workout, I whirled on Brooklyn and threw my arms wide. "What the fuck was that?"

She rolled her eyes again. "Since when do you hover when I workout?"

"He had his hands on you."

"Hand. And he was demonstrating what muscle group I was working."

"You already know that," I growled.

She got up from her stomach and came chest-to-chest with me. I scoffed under my breath, amused that she didn't match me physically, but outshone me by miles in the attitude department.

Her brows arched high. "And what are you gonna do about it?"

"What's with you, babe? I know you're tired, but c'mon. This is next level."

She'd been working her ass off lately to fit in as many clients as possible. Everyone wanted haircuts before Christmas and the late nights were taking their toll. On both of us.

"Just go back to your gym bunny." She shoved past and started squatting with her ass facing the floor to ceiling mirror.

Enough was enough. As she came out of a squat, I ducked and threw her over my shoulder. Ignoring the attention her screech drew from the light scattering of clients working out at nine-thirty at night—getting in their last workout before the gym closed for a few days over Christmas—I strode over to where Adele waited.

"Last set, Adele. Do ten instead of twelve with the dumbbells, then move back to the kettlebell. I'll be back in five."

She looked from Bee's ass to me and grinned. "Take your time. I'm finishing up anyway. I'll see you after Christmas."

I chuckled. "And working extra hard, no doubt."

"With the amount of food I'm planning to eat, you know it."

"Thatta girl. Laters, Adele."

Readjusting Brooklyn squirming on my shoulder, I laid a slap to her ass as soon as we hit the hallway.

"Fuck you," she spat and bucked, causing my grip to falter as I took the stairs.

"Quit squirming or we'll both be going down," I warned.

Once in our office on the walled-in mezzanine floor above the gym, I set her on an office chair and bobbed down in front of her.

My hands splayed around her thighs as I implored, "What's going on, sweetness?"

Her exhausted brown eyes locked with mine and made my heart drop. "Do you ever feel like we're just locked in a never-ending cycle? You know, like… work, barely eat, barely speak, sleep, then wake up and do it all over again? It feels like I never get to see you. We're both always working so hard."

I let out a tortured sigh that echoed the ache in my chest. "I know we are, babe; it's our busiest time of the year. But look around at what we've built. We're smashing it, and all the hard work is paying off."

Her stoic expression cracked and gave way to uncharacteristic emotion. Tears escaped before she could swipe them away. "I just miss you."

"Missing me isn't enough of a reason to flirt with clients when you know it'll rile me."

"I wasn't flirting." She shook her head and pressed her palms to her eyes. "I just hate that I'm all over the place at the moment. I'm exhausted plus PMSing so hard right now. My feet are killing me and I've hardly eaten since breakfast. I just… I'm just done and super bitchy."

With my heart panging, I picked her up and lowered

myself onto the office chair. There, I cradled her on my lap and hugged the fuck out of her.

"I got you, sweets. It's been a hustle, that's for sure. I'm looking forward to some time off too." I checked the wall clock: 9.40 p.m. "Only twenty minutes to go before we can head home. Until then, I'mma make you a protein shake and we're gonna sit here while you drink it."

The little nod against my chest made me smile. "Chocolate please."

"You got it, Queen Bee."

I placed her on the chair and headed to the small kitchen. Fuck, it hurt to hear how close she was to breaking point. She was right though: in our determination to make our combined businesses successful–hers the hair salon and mine the gym–we'd lost sight of us.

That fucking killed me; especially after fighting so hard to find myself again and accept Brooklyn's unconditional love when I didn't believe I deserved it.

While making her shake, I thought hard. I used to worship the ground she walked on. I'd give the world for her, and as I handed her the protein shake and resettled her on my lap, I vowed to make the most of our Christmas break together and be the man she deserved. Her Christmas present was part and parcel of that.

"I love you, baby," I murmured into her hair.

"And I love you too. I'm sorry. I'm just finding it tough at the moment."

I hummed in acknowledgement and slowly swayed us from side to side.

Looking out over *Quake Fitness* through the mezzanine window gave me a great sense of pride. I'd named it in honour of my best army mate who we'd lost in combat during an ambush in Afghanistan a couple of years ago. Me and Quake had always hit the gym together yet naming mine after him didn't seem enough. So, when his daughter was born—six months after he was killed—I'd also created a trust fund for her to take the pressure of his widow Willow. Thinking of them all still formed a heavy wedge deep in my throat.

"I'd do anything for you, Bee," I whispered thickly. *"Anything."*

Her caring eyes met mine and searched. She'd grown to recognise when my demons simmered close to the surface, and she eased away from my chest, ready to distance herself.

"I know you would. Do you need a second alone?"

"No, babe. I'm thinking, but I'm okay."

She nodded and the tension slid from her shoulders. Her arms looped around my neck brought a sense of peace. While my wahine was fierce, she had softness that brought solace to my soul.

I inhaled her perfume and released a deep sigh. "There's only one guy left and he's finishing up now. Let me close up downstairs, then I'll take you home."

Despite my intentions, I made no move to stand. I was shattered, too, and finding the energy for one last closing push before a few days off was increasingly hard.

Brooklyn sensed my reluctance. "Do you want me to close up for you?"

"No way. You stay here and I'll be back in ten."

I kissed her after I stood, then paused at the top of the stairs to look back at her. Sitting in the office chair with her legs tucked up and the shake resting on one knee was exactly where she needed to be.

The sight made me smile, because after all the shit we'd been through, she was my one and only. Always. No gym bunny would ever change that.

"I love you, my queen."

She looked around the side of the shaker and gave a weary smile. "I love you too, Packman."

As I made my way down the steep stairs, the knowledge of what I had planned for Christmas morning pumped me up. I couldn't wait to give Bee the most important present to date.

CHAPTER 4
MICKEY & KIMMIE
~ CHRISTMAS EVE-EVE ~

KIMMIE'S POV

I tapped my fingernails on the reception desk, waiting for my only client of the day to arrive. It was a straightforward head and shoulders portrait for a business portfolio, so all going well, I'd be finished and home before lunch.

I still didn't understand why it was urgently needed two days before Christmas, but the guy was insistent on the booking.

Right on time, my studio doorbell chimed and pulled my attention to the entrance.

"Mickey! What are you doing here?"

My heart skipped a beat when he grinned widely and shut the door behind him. "I was in the neighbourhood, Babykay."

I rolled my eyes. "You're never in this neighbourhood."

"Well, I am today." A primal look entered his gaze as he caged me against the desk with his arms.

Despite my pulse spiking, I pushed on his chest. "I'm

waiting on a client, Mickey. We're not doing this here or now."

A devilish smirk cocked his mouth. "Don't suppose the booking is under Wayne Chadwick?"

My eyes flared in surprise, then narrowed sharply. "Have you been hacking my booking system?"

A low chuckle vibrated against my mouth as he pressed his lips to mine. "No, baby."

"Then how do you know about the booking?"

"It's for me."

I pulled away just enough to bring him into focus. My eyes flicked between his. "For you? Since when?"

"Since I thought it would be fun. I got Scotty at the station to book for me so you wouldn't know."

"Mickey, this is meant to be a *paid* session, not you fooling around and wasting my time."

"Of course I'll pay."

My eyes narrowed again, then skimmed his clothes. "So, you're wanting headshots? In your fire department uniform?"

"Uh… yeah, kinda." He grinned and pushed off the desk, then pulled me to my feet. "And then I'll take you out for lunch before we collect Xave from your parents."

"You have the afternoon off?"

His smile widened. "Yup."

I shook my head yet allowed him to lead me into the studio. "But why?"

A wicked glint flashed in his eyes when he glanced over his shoulder. "So you can experiment with your first couples boudoir shoot."

Nerve-induced warmth unfurled in my stomach. "Are you serious?"

"I'm here, aren't I?"

My pulse fluttered. "You'd do that for me? Let me photograph you?"

"Us. You'll be photographing us. And yeah, of course."

Those belly-butterflies and skipped heartbeats made me breathless. "Mickey, I can't partake. I haven't done my hair and the underwear I'm wearing certainly isn't sexy."

The rushed explanation whispered to a close as he wove his hands through my long wavy locks.

"You don't need either of those things, Babykay; you're beautiful."

My smile couldn't be stopped. I looked into the stormy hazel eyes of my childhood friend and held his gaze. We'd been through so much growing up together. The past three decades harboured torment and heartache, but also a love that endured time and situations we shouldn't have had to face. I'd always loved Mickey. Through our highs and lows, and even when I'd given up hope of us having a future together, I'd loved him hard.

Gripping his forearms, I leaned up to kiss him. "Thanks —even though I don't feel beautiful."

Having a one-year-old son who ran us ragged left little time for me to look, let alone *feel,* my best.

"You're always beautiful to me," Mickey murmured, then kissed me hard and quick. "So, where do need me?"

I pointed to the white backdrop I'd prepared. "Over there, but I'm going to swap it out for black. Make it edgier."

He snorted before grabbing the back of his shirt and whipping it over his head. "We'll be getting edgy enough, princess."

Laughing, I snatched his shirt from mid-air when he lobbed it my way, then tossed it back at him. "Not what I mean. And put this back on; I want to capture the undressing."

Impatient mutters came from within the material as he re-dressed. I snickered at his mussed hair, loving that it was unruly and tousled when his head popped through the neck hole.

After getting the camera set up and the backdrop switched, I instructed Mickey to stand in the centre of it, fully clothed while I did lighting checks.

His scowl deepened with each bolt of bright light from the flash heads. "This isn't how I imagined this would go."

"Why's that?"

"I thought we'd be naked by now."

I scoffed while adjusting the focus, then met his gaze above the camera. "If we're doing this, we're doing it right."

More mutters came until I commanded, "Okay, stand up tall and angle sideways toward me."

He complied, then looked at me for further instruction.

"Now grip the back of your shirt like before, and slowly tug it over your head."

A wicked little smirk touched his lips. "Finally."

"And clench your other fist," I added, smiling when it immediately balled above his head.

Sounds of my camera clicking filled the space until Mickey stood with the shirt casually hanging from his fingertips.

"Now keep a hold of it like that and tilt your head back a little. Like you've just realised that we aren't having sex during this photo shoot," I teased.

As predicted, Mickey's expression darkened and the harsh, broody glare was heaven for my artistic eye.

"That's hot," I murmured.

"We'd better be fucking after this, Babykay. The anticipation has already got me half-ready to go."

"We have sex all the time," I reasoned.

"Not like this we don't!"

My subtle smile had him growling. I didn't have a plan for how far we'd go during this session, but he didn't know that. I liked to keep him hanging and force him to relinquish control.

"Next pose—you don't need the shirt. Tilt your head back again and grip your neck with the hand closest to me and fist the other around your waistband. Eyes closed and look like you're enjoying it."

"More than you realise, princess."

The photographic gods shone on me today, because holy shit my fiancé was a natural.

"Now look at me from the corner of your eye," I instructed after clearing my throat.

Mickey added a slow roll of his tongue across his lower lip, and that was the moment I cracked a little.

Pushing the first licks of arousal away, I turned his body face-on to the camera, then released the button and zipper of his pants.

He set his hands on my hips and drew me close. His hips greedily jutted forward as his voice lowered. "Are we doing kinky shit now?"

"Not yet." Those two words, more breathless than I was proud of, rekindled his broody impatience.

Extracting myself from his tempting embrace and pushing him to arm's length forced me to regain focus.

"Now fist both sides of your open pants and tense your arms. I want you to tease like you're shoving them down, but don't give too much away. I don't want to see peen."

Mickey snorted. "You always want to see my dick, Kimmie."

"But my camera doesn't, so keep it covered," I sassed, lifting the camera once more. "Look down…" *Click.* "And look up at me with a smoulder." *Click.* "And—hey! Stand still!"

Ignoring my exclamation, Mickey kept stalking in my direction. He barely stopped before roughly cupping my face and kissing me until I fought to breathe.

"Photo shoot is done," he hissed. "I want you *now.*"

"But what about the boudoir shots?"

Darkened irises searched mine before he snapped. "You've got five minutes. After that, the rules don't apply."

"Keep your pants on and go wait for me out there." Flustered, I gave him a little push to send him on his way.

My fingers shook as I connected the camera to the tripod. My breath shallowed as I set it to auto focus, and my pulse galloped as I plugged in the remote shutter release. I removed my tank and long skirt, then held my breath as I stepped out from behind the last remaining barrier between us.

He waved me over with a seductive sweep of his hand, then clasped my face between his heated palms again.

Click.

He took his time kissing me, tenderly and sweetly, all while the camera shutter clicked in the background.

"Where do we start?" he whispered huskily.

"We already have," I breathed out.

Mickey dashed a quick glance at the camera, then back to me. Passion and affection brought the copper flecks in his eyes to life and lured my lips back to his. When he boosted me into his arms, my legs wrapped around his waist, and the bite of his fingers on my hips spurred us on.

The remote between my fingers remained forgotten until he lowered me to the floor. I gasped from the chill and goosebumps spread across my body.

"Pose for me," Mickey gritted out, smoothing his hands up and down my thighs.

Elongating my arms above my head and arching my back, I tilted my chin high and closed my eyes while subtly pressing the camera remote again. I gave Mickey no instruction, and didn't need to. He kissed his way down my stomach, then licked a path from my panty line to my belly button.

Heat from his torso washed over me, and I opened my eyes to find him hovering above and on the verge of losing control.

Click, click, click.

His roughened palms planed up my arms until his entire body caged mine.

Click. Click.

I took one last image before his fingers pried the remote from mine.

"Five minutes is up, Babykay. What we're going to do next doesn't need to be documented."

He pushed up onto one arm while shoving his pants and underwear down. My fingers traced lines down his sculpted torso, then up the ridges of his flexed abs. As soon as he wrenched my underwear to the side, my knees fell wider to accommodate his hips nestling close.

Mickey let out a long, satisfied groan as he eased into my body. "You're so fucking wet and tight," he murmured.

I sent a quick thank you to the Kegel trainer I'd invested in before giving myself over to the fantasy of having sex on my studio floor. Mickey visibly held back until the beginnings of an orgasm danced with each strategic roll of his hips.

"You're getting close, yeah?"

"Yeah," I breathed out.

"Tell me when."

Countless time passed before my eyes squeezed shut of their own accord. "Soon. Really soon," I panted, holding onto the orgasm as it rapidly grew, willing it to hurry up and consume me.

Mickey picked up the pace. "Fucking hell," he growled.

As I tipped over the edge, he lost the last of his restraint and thrust into me with reckless abandon until I cried out from the pain-tainted pleasure.

I came hard and long, riding out the prolonged orgasm while Mickey chased his own. With a final hard thrust, he buried deep and arched.

"Holy fuck," he panted, resting both palms either side of my shoulders and hanging his head. "Charge me double for the shoot, baby. That was one hundred and ten percent worth every fucking dollar."

I managed to snicker through the sated bliss. "I can't accept money for sex; I'm not in that industry."

"Just as well because I'm the only one you're allowed to shoot and fuck at the same time."

I ran a fingernail over his nipple, making it pucker. "And I'm the only person who *you're* allowed to be photographed with while fucking."

A ghost of a laugh escaped as he pulled out and sat back on his haunches. "If you let me do you like that every time, then I'm going to need a weekly booking." His wicked smirk reappeared. "How are you placed for next week?"

Laughing, I got to my feet. "Next week we'll be at the beach with the crew, so I'm afraid I'm unavailable that day."

Mickey growled and snagged me by the ankle. "Better make the most of our session today then. Take off your bra."

Despite lifting my eyebrows and giving him an *excuse me?* look, I unfastened my bra and let it hang loose over my breasts.

"Just FYI: double the sex equals double the charges."

Mickey stood and kicked out of his pants and underwear completely. "Send the bill to Wayne Chadwick."

I threw my head back and laughed, and Mickey set his mouth on the tender spot beneath my ear. "And this round is *completely* off camera."

CHAPTER 5
MACE & JESS
~ CHRISTMAS DAY ~

MACE'S POV

I woke to snuffling and a tiny fist bumping against my cheek.

"Merry Christmas, Daddy," came Jess's sweet voice.

A wide smile wove across my mouth before I cracked an eye open. When I did, my heart filled infinitely more to see my little man Cree lying on Jess's pillow, facing me.

"Morning, my boy," I murmured, nuzzling his cheek, then leaned over him to kiss Jess. "Merry Christmas, Bright Eyes."

Her gorgeous smile set my world alight. "Our first Christmas as a family of three," she whispered.

"And it couldn't have started any better. How long's he been up for?"

Jess stifled a yawn. "Forty minutes. It's early but there's no point in going back to sleep since it's going to be a big day."

"What's the time?" I murmured, flicking Cree's fist back and forth as he gripped the tip of my forefinger.

Hints of sunshine were already lighting the room, so it was at least daybreak.

"Just before six," she murmured while watching my hand. "I can never get over how tiny Cree's fist is next to yours."

"Some day, his will be just as big." My eyes flicked from my son's to Jess's. "Some day this will be him, having his first Christmas with his beautiful wife and little boy."

"Or girl."

I smiled at the thought. "Or girl."

Jess tickled Cree's cheek with her sparkly red nail and gazed at our son with pure love.

Looking her over, I hummed around the kick in my chest. This girl had been worth the pain and the fight. Without either, I wouldn't have her today.

"I love you, babe."

Her deep-brown eyes met mine and smiled. "I love you too."

Careful not to bump our son, I reached for Jess and pulled her until she lay along the length of my body. A hum low in my throat slid out before I could stop it. We hadn't had sex in a few months and I was barely refraining from putting the pressure on her now that Cree was eight weeks old.

"Mace," she warned when my dick hardened with absolutely no coaxing aside from the feel of her silky skin on mine.

"I can't help it, babe. It's been so long."

"I know it has, but I'm just not ready yet…"

My arms tightened around her and I leaned up to kiss her. "I know; doesn't mean I don't miss it though."

Jess giggled and lovingly ran her hands down my face. "I've missed it too, but I'm scared. Especially after the stitches."

While my body bore scars of my own battles, Jess's was marked and marred after a long, hard labour. She'd needed stitches and almost required a blood transfusion after losing ungodly amounts. The thought alone had my fingers protectively tightening on her hips.

"I'll wait as long as you need; you know that." It just might be longer—selfishly—than ideal.

Jess giggled. "Don't *pout!*"

I cocked a lopsided smirk. "I'm not."

"You were. *Yes, he was,*" she added to Cree.

My little boy made a happy, gurgling noise just like he did whenever he heard his mumma's voice.

"How about I put little man back to bed then make us some breakfast? What do you say, sweetheart?"

Her eyes lit up. "Yes please. Then presents?"

I chuckled. "Yeah, babe, then presents. Bagel or breakfast muffin?"

She thought for a moment with her plump lips twisted to the side. While she pondered, I smoothed a long blonde strand of hair away from her face and tucked it behind her ear.

"Cream cheese and bacon bagel, please."

"You got it. Go have a shower while I get Cree and brekky sorted."

"Thank you," she breathed out and climbed from bed.

I lightly pinched her ass cheek peeking out of the bottom of her boy-leg underwear and laughed when she batted my hand away.

"Your ass is so fucking hot," I growled, then frowned when she groaned.

"It's so out of shape it's not even funny."

Jess popping her booty and looking back at it had me releasing a tortured exhale. "Babe, you're *killin'* me over here."

Her eyes flicked up and a devilish little grin appeared. "I'm allowed to check out my own ass."

"Not when I can't control this!" I blurted and flung back the sheet, revealing an erection within my underwear so hard the ache had me feeling sick.

Jess smothered her laughter behind her hand and rushed for the bathroom, calling out a string of apologies in her wake.

Cursing my predicament while scrubbing both hands down my face to shift the focus away from the arousal, I turned to Cree who stared at the ceiling, cross-eyed as if staring into a faraway land.

"What do you reckon, little dude? Mumma's too much of a tease, eh?"

"I heard that!" came Jess's indignant yell.

Laughter vibrated in my chest. Sex or no sex, I was still one of the happiest men alive. Right up until Cree's little face scrunched and turned red, then the sound of him pooping made me stare in horror.

"You couldn't have done that ten minutes ago when Mumma was sorting you out?" I asked while tickling his little belly.

He grunted and squirmed, then fussed immediately after filling his nappy.

"Yeah, I know, little dude."

Begrudgingly, I rolled from bed and pulled on a pair of boardies. I baby-talked to Cree while carrying him to the nursery to change his nappy, then took my time cuddling him before laying him in his little bed.

A little bit of shushing helped him settle enough for me to leave, and when I padded from his room into the hallway, I caught a fleeting flash of Jess's naked body in the reflection of our bedroom mirror.

I froze and held my breath, all but begging the Lord to

give me a goddamn break.

"Mace?"

My swallow was thick and painful, and my voice came hoarsely. "Uh... yeah, babe?"

"Can you help me with something?"

I cursed while putting one foot in front of the other, then almost dropped dead upon reaching the threshold of our room. Jess lay under the sheet with it pulled up to her chin, watching me with wide, nervous eyes.

I tried to play it cool while praying this would pan out the way I hoped. "What can I, uh... *help* with?"

She gnawed on her lower lip. "I need to get the first time over with."

"I thought you'd never ask," I joked, shoving down my boardies and underwear, then tearing away the bed sheet and all but diving between her legs.

Her shriek of laughter filled the room before petering off as my movements slowed. My heart raced as I leaned over her, propped up on my elbows while cupping her rose-tinted cheeks.

"All jokes aside, are you sure? This isn't because of what I said before, is it? While I'm impatient to have you again, I don't want you to feel pressured."

"You're not pressuring me. I just want to have sex on Christmas morning with my husband." A cheeky little grin cemented her words.

"You're sure?"

"Yeah," she breathed out.

I trailed a hand down her neck and over her breasts, groaning again when my dick hardened impossibly further.

"You've got to be gentle though," Jess added.

"I will. Can I touch you down there?"

When trepidation filled her eyes and accompanied her

subtle head shake, I diverted my hand away from her inner thighs.

"Roll over, babe. I'll give you a massage."

She snickered. "I know how your massages end, cowboy."

"That's exactly why I'm giving you one," I drawled, shifting so she could flip onto her stomach.

Bottle of massage oil in hand, I straddled her legs and poured a generous amount down her spine, smiling as she wiggled against the sensation. Smoothing my hands over her body had always felt good, but damn, sex-deprived me was panting and on the cusp of combustion ten seconds in.

I made short work of spreading the oil from her shoulders to her ass, then oh-so-thoroughly worked it in.

Jess snorted. "I have other places besides my ass, Mace."

"I know," I murmured, not tearing my eyes off where I massaged the plump mounds. "Just being meticulous."

"Meticulous!" She scoffed and twisted to arch a brow at me.

"Yeah." I grinned. "Meticulous."

A ghost of a laugh wove from her mouth before she fell silent. I felt the air shift with each centimetre I pushed the boundaries by gliding my thumbs deeper between her ass cheeks.

My groan of longing mixed with her breathy one. Her shoulders relaxed as she focused on what felt good. Soon, the sweet sounds of wet arousal met my ears with each pass of my thumbs.

"Fuck, I can't wait to have my tongue and fingers inside you again," I hissed.

A low hum of acknowledgement vibrated under my palms, then her legs shifted under me. "Let me roll over."

Becoming nestled between her open knees, I smoothed

my palms over the silky flesh on her inner thighs and continued up the curve of her waist.

"You're beautiful, babe."

The look in Jess's doe eyes had my heart kicking. "You're just saying that."

I shook my head while tenderly skimming across her breasts. "I mean every single word."

She arched into my touch when I drifted across her inner thighs again, then gripped both my wrists to still them.

"I'm ready," she whispered.

I gulped. "Actually?" Fuck, my voice shook with hopes and dreams about to come true. "Don't you want to come?"

"No. Today I just want to tackle the first time postpartum. Slowly though," she reiterated.

Nodding, I braced myself on one arm and gently smoothed the head of my dick through her arousal, scrutinising her expression the entire time.

"Is that okay?"

Jess nodded and gave me a wavering smile. "I'm a little scared."

"Of it hurting?"

She nodded again and bit down on her lower lip as I began to ease into her.

Each time she winced, I froze and held my breath, patiently waiting for her body to adjust and relax again.

"Still okay?" I breathed out once seated deep.

Jess's eyes flicked around the room as if looking for answers on the ceiling. "I think so. It feels weird." Her gaze found mine. "Does it feel different for you?"

I wriggled a tiny bit and smiled when she giggled. "A little spongier, I guess."

"It'll be all stretched and out of tone."

Kissing away the crinkle between her eyebrows, I gently rocked while blanketing her body with my own.

"It's perfect. So perfect, in fact, that I don't think I'm going to last long."

Her arms wrapped around my shoulders, pulling me into the crook of her neck. I inhaled her scent, getting lost in everything about my wife as if this was my first time with her.

I barely moved, barely thrust, barely so much as *breathed* before an orgasm threatened. "Oh fuck," I muttered, voice shaky and tense.

Surprise lit Jess's tone. "Already?"

"Yeah, already, babe. It's literally been months and there's no holding this back."

I kissed her and thrust a fraction harder while pulling at the reins of my control. I promised her tender and slow, but fuck, as good as it felt, holding back was agonising.

"That's feeling good," she breathed out, opening her legs a fraction wider for me.

"You're telling me," I growled, then couldn't stop the long, low groan that gathered in my chest. It tore from my throat as my release hit like a goddamn freight train.

"Holy fuck," I panted. "That one took me by surprise."

Sparks of worry appeared between Jess's brows. "Was it okay?"

"Babe, are you kidding? You witnessed how fast I came; don't tell the crew—they'll make fun of me," I joked around a breathless laugh. "Was it okay for you?"

I welcomed her red nails trailing down my arms. "A little uncomfortable to begin with, but not as bad as I was expecting."

"Gee, thanks," I drawled, smirking.

Amusement danced in her dark-brown irises. "You just wanna be told how great you are."

"Well…" I shrugged. "My ego could do with a little stroking."

She laughed and gently squeezed my face between her hands. "Oh, trust me; there's absolutely nothing wrong with your *ego,* cowboy."

I sat back on my haunches and cupped my junk. "How can there be when I've got a beautiful wife and a perfect son. That's an ego trip right there."

My laughter died when I glanced between Jess's legs. Immediate concern pulled my brows low. My eyes flicked to her face, then down again.

"Uh, babe… there's blood."

Jess pushed up on her elbows and peered down her body. "How much?"

"A little."

"Is it gushing?"

"No. Wait there and I'll grab some toilet paper."

After hastening to the bathroom and back, I handed Jess the tissue and waited while she wiped and inspected it. Having a doctor for a wife at times like these sure put my mind at ease—especially now that we had a baby to care for.

"Oh, that's fine," she concluded off-handedly, scrunching the paper. "Only a little blood mixed with your come."

I frowned harder. "So it's *my* blood?"

She snickered. "No, it'll be mine. Just from it being tender inside and semi-recent after birth."

I partially relaxed and eyed her carefully as she climbed off the bed. "So, it's okay?"

"It's absolutely okay, I promise."

"Thank fuck," I breathed out. "Come shower with me, then I'll make you breakfast as promised."

She smiled and held my hand on the way to the bathroom. Once standing on the cool tiles, I touched her waist, gaining her full attention.

"Thank you, babe."

She arched a brow. "For the sex?"

I smirked devilishly. "For putting me out of my misery."

* * *

I showered quickly to get a head start on breakfast before Jess emerged. I had Marjorie (my coffee machine) fired up and warming, and the pan heating for the bacon when I heard a scuff at the front door.

On high alert, my senses and body instantly primed. Ash and Hana—Jess's sister and niece—weren't due to come around for another couple of hours, and I would have heard Chippy's voice by now if they'd arrived early.

I rushed to the door and peered through the peephole. Shock pulled a sharp inhale into my lungs as a tall, lean male figure retreated down our garden path.

Without thinking or having a plan, I whipped the door open and called out, "Hey."

He froze but didn't turn around until I called his name.

"Mo."

Dressed in black leather from jacket to boots, with his greying hair tied in a small ponytail at the back of his head, Mo Rivers appeared exactly as I remembered him—sans the gang vest. While not making himself visible to me since mine and Jess's wedding a couple of years ago, I knew Mo kept close tabs on his daughters from afar.

My eyes fell to the bags of gifts he'd left on our doorstep, then cut back to him as he turned to face me.

"I didn't think you'd be awake yet," came his low tone as he eyed me up and down.

"Been awake for a while... babies have a habit of doing that."

Interest sparked beneath his scraggly greying beard, though he didn't pry further into my obvious opening.

He hesitated, as did I. Our history wasn't great; I was beaten to within an inch of my life by his gang thugs, yet he was the reason I still had my life. If it wasn't for him, I'd be long dead.

I stepped outside and quietly closed the door behind me. He remained rooted to the spot as I approached.

"Look, Jess doesn't know you're here."

He held up his hands. "I didn't mean to draw attention to myself. I'll get going."

"No, that's not what I mean."

Mo's dark-brown eyes bore into mine. "What did she have? A boy or girl?"

Pride welled deep within. "A boy."

"A boy," Mo breathed out and pressed his knuckles to his sternum as if it ached from the news. "I have a grandson."

I grinned as my chest puffed further. "You do. Do you..." I hesitated again before clearing my throat. "Do you want to come in and meet him?"

The unknowns were plenty. Even if he did accept, I wasn't sure that Jess would be okay with it. But after seeing my dad meet his grandson, I felt compelled to give Mo the same opportunity. Cree was, after all, the latest in Mo's bloodline.

Mo worked his fists open and closed as his expression turned wretched. He'd vowed to stay away from his girls to keep them safe, so to break that rule was visibly tearing him down the middle.

"Will she mind?" he murmured, referring to Jess.

I shrugged. "I honestly don't know. But she still cries for you from time to time. Regardless of what she says, she misses you badly."

Mo nodded and inspected his boots. "I left for them."

"I know."

His dark eyes cut to mine and held an edge of plea. "I'd like nothing more than to meet him."

"Cree. His name is Cree."

"Cree," Mo echoed, nodding and seemingly pleased.

I flicked my hand. "Come inside, I was just making coffee if you want one?"

He nodded and followed as I returned barefoot to my front door. A harsh curse immediately left my mouth when I opened it to find the forgotten pan smoking with heat. I rushed to turn it off, then returned my attention to Mo edging into the house as if it was the last place on Earth he wanted to be.

He set the gift bags inside against the wall and nodded at them. "Open those later. There's some for Ashley and Hana too."

"They're coming around later this morning," I supplied needlessly. "So... coffee?"

Fuck, having an actual conversation with him was tense. The last conversation we'd had consisted of me telling him to go fuck himself and him taunting me to stay alive.

"Thanks," came his single word as he pulled out a seat at the table.

Before I could give Jess a heads up about our visitor, her voice called down the hallway.

"Mace! Something's burning!" She rushed out with concern set deep between her eyebrows, then did a double-take at Mo sitting poised at the dining table ready to bolt.

The colour drained from her pink-tinted cheeks and her stricken gaze cut to me. "Wha...? What's he...?"

Panted words refused to form as her eyes snapped back and forth between me and the father she hadn't seen in nearly two decades.

Her lower lip quivered around a single word. "Dad?"

Mo cautiously rose to his feet and barely took a step toward her. I held my breath, unsure of how this would pan out. It could go either way—both me and Mo sensed that.

"J-bug," he whispered thickly.

It made Jess crack. The first sob left her chest and looked as painful as it sounded. I moved to her side and she immediately gripped my arm hard; Christmas-coloured nails gouging multiple half-moons into my skin.

"It's okay, sweetheart. I found him outside leaving gifts, so I invited him in to meet Cree, but *only* if it's okay with you."

The shock in her doe-eyes faded to give way to gratitude. With a subtle nod of acceptance, she released my forearm and took a tentative step toward her father.

The instant he opened his arms in invitation, Jess flew into them and sobbed her heart out. He clung to her, just as she clung to him, with the most afflicted expression on his ruddy face.

"Christ it feels good to hug you again, J-bug."

Jess hiccuped a sob. "You too. Merry Christmas, Dad."

"Merry Christmas." Mo's watery eyes lifted to meet mine. "Best goddamn Christmas I've had in years."

I nodded an acknowledgement, then silently excused myself, giving Jess and her father a minute alone while I went to get Cree from his cot.

By the time I returned to the living area, Mo was knuckling away his tears and Jess constantly palmed hers dry.

Mo pressed a hand to his chest and inhaled a shuddering breath when he saw me, then reached with trembling arms as I offered Cree his way.

"Mo, meet Cree Aiden Rivers Westbrook." I spoke each name deliberately, knowing two of them would hit him square on the heart.

His teary eyes found mine and searched. "After *my* Aiden?" He took his grandson into the crook of his arm and stared in awe.

I nodded and fought to lock down welling emotion. It meant the world to Jess for one of Cree's middle names to be after her missing brother—Aiden—and Rivers was their childhood surname.

"Yup," I stated hoarsely.

Jess's sniffle pulled my attention her way. I took her in my arms and kissed her forehead. "You okay, sweetheart?"

"Yeah," she whispered shakily. "I just never thought I'd see him again... Thank you for giving us this and giving him a moment with Cree."

"You're welcome, Bright Eyes. It was time," I admitted.

However, if I'd found Mo on our doorstep a year ago, I would have told him to fuck off and never come back. The wounds of my treatment while being held captive were still raw. But something changed in me since seeing my own dad hold Cree in his arms. Something that, since becoming a father, I now understood. It was suddenly important for me to give them both a chance to meet. Albeit, Cree wouldn't remember, but we could at least tell him the story of him meeting his grandfather on the morning of his first Christmas.

"Dad?" Jess murmured while remaining in my arms. "Just this once, would you like to stay for breakfast?"

The man standing in our living room tenderly cradling

our baby was a far cry from the hardened gang member he was every other day of the week. His sharp expression softened and the hard lines on his face eased. A warm smile even broke out.

"I'd really like that, J-bug. If that's okay?" he asked, flicking his focus to me.

I eyed him carefully before nodding. "It is. Bagel or breakfast muffin?"

"Either will be fine," he murmured, gazing down at Cree again.

Jess smiled at me with gratitude, and I kissed her forehead again. "Go catch up with him while I make breakfast."

"Thank you," she whispered and rose on tiptoes to plant a kiss on my mouth. "For everything."

When she shifted to Mo and asked him to join her on the couch, I watched until they were both settled, then left them to their cherished moment.

While setting Marjorie to brew again and cleaning out the burnt oil from the pan, I started second-guessing my actions. Fuck, I hoped I wouldn't regret inviting him into my house, much less feeding him.

Much to my horror, a car pulled into the driveway and I cursed; they were at least two hours early.

Jess's stricken eyes met mine and her panic grew with each of Hana's footsteps running to our front door. It flew open before I could meet her at the threshold and my eight-year-old niece barrelled in without greeting.

"Where's baby Cree?" she demanded. "I miss him!"

I chuckled. "You saw him two days ago, Chippy. And Merry Christmas; c'mere and give me a hug."

Her arms wrapped around my waist and we squeezed tight. I took a second to enjoy the calm before the storm hit. My eyes flicked from Mo in the living room to the front door as Ash rushed in, flustered and looking guilty.

"I'm so sorry for arriving this early. She's been up since five and pestered the hell out of me to see Cree. Even her Santa sack wouldn't distract her long enough." She grimaced apologetically.

"It's fine, Ash, honestly. We've been up for a while too. Merry Christmas."

When Hana left my arms, Ash stepped into them. I kissed her cheek before murmuring against her ear, "There's something I need to tell you, but I'm not sure how you're going to take it."

Her dark-brown eyes, exactly like Jess's, held a weight of worry. "Oh my god, *what?*" she hissed.

"Ah… well, we had a visitor this morning."

Ash's face drained of colour. "And?"

Wordlessly, I angled her toward the living area. Jess rose to her feet, though remained at her father's side. Mo remained on the couch cuddling Cree. Hana had tucked herself unusually close so she could pet and kiss her baby cousin, but Mo's eyes locked with Ash and never left.

"We let him in," I whispered.

Ash's gasp cut through the room and she backed up a pace. "Hana, honey, come over here, *now!*"

"Why, Mum? I want to hold Cree. Is it my turn yet?" she asked Mo with an expectant expression, not realising he was her grandfather.

His attention flickered from Ash to Hana, and softened impossibly further as Hana gave him her best puppy-dog eyes.

"It is." He adjusted his hold on Cree and waited until Hana set herself up cross-legged on the couch.

Mo handed him over with gentle care, then slowly rose to his feet, hovering close until Jess moved in to take his place.

Mo seemed to take a fortifying breath before rising to

full height and turning to his youngest child. His throat worked and his eyes held pain like I'd never seen before.

"My baby girl," he whispered hoarsely.

Ash tucked close to my body, slightly behind and using me as a human shield. "You're not here. This isn't real. You're *gone!*" she hissed.

He shook his head and cautiously approached. "I've been out of sight, but never gone. I've been watching over you and Jess for years."

"How *dare* you!" Ash surged forward and lashed out, palm connecting with his face with a loud, sharp *slap*.

Hana's little eyes bulged out of her head. "Mum just hit that man!"

Jess's quiet murmur soothed the worry while I hovered, poised to intervene.

"How dare you! You *abandoned us!*" Ash seethed. "Mum couldn't handle it and Aiden has never been found. You single-handedly destroyed our family!"

"I've never stopped searching for your brother, and never will."

"That doesn't bring him back!" she cried.

While Jess remained racked with guilt over what happened to Aiden, Ash had taken their father's abandonment the toughest. She'd had to fight the hardest to find herself. While in recent years she'd conquered her drug addiction and stepped up to be an admirable role model for her daughter, her internal scars were still jagged and raw.

Mo's jaw ticked as he visibly locked down his heartache. "I did what I thought was best at the time. I thought leaving would prevent you from being dragged into my world, and it fucking broke my heart when you ended up there anyway."

"It was *your* fault," Ash wailed, voice pitching with despair. "Our family fell apart because you left, and Jess was left to pick up the pieces. *He—*" she exclaimed, pointing at me, "—has been more of a father figure than you ever were. If it wasn't for Mace, I wouldn't be here today, and neither would Hana, or Jess, or Cree…"

Ash pounded her fists against his chest, crying and sobbing with each hit that Mo stood steadfast and took. Her cries grew louder as her strikes softened, until she fell against his chest and sobbed her heart out.

Mo encased her in a strong hold. His tears silently streamed into her hair, and he gripped harder when her legs gave out.

"I'm so sorry, my baby girl. I'm so fucking sorry," he chanted, over and over.

I backed away and let him console his daughter, then relaxed a fraction further at seeing Hana so besotted with Cree that her mum falling apart was nothing but background drama.

When Ash's sobs eased and Mo's murmurs quietened, I finally left their space and squatted down in front of Hana.

"What do you want for brekky, Chippy? Cream cheese bagel or bacon and egg breakfast muffin?"

Her dark-brown eyes met mine. "Can I have a bacon bagel?"

I chuckled and affectionately squeezed her little knee. "You can have whatever you want."

"And a Marjorie hot chocolate?"

A snort passed through my grin. "I thought you'd never ask. Cree's not allowed the foamy milk this time though, okay?"

"Okay." Her cheeky grin created my own.

Hana had already been through so much in her short life and was resilient as hell, but she'd shone infinitely brighter once life settled down.

I rose to my feet and kissed Jess's forehead, and had

barely set foot in the kitchen for my third attempt to make my family breakfast, when another of Hana's questions ground time to a halt.

"Is Grandpa going to stay for breakfast too?"

CHAPTER 6
NICO & BROOKLYN
~ CHRISTMAS DAY ~

NICO'S POV

"Babe, wake up, Santa's been!" I stood at Brooklyn's side of the bed and nudged her, chuckling when she buried further into the pillows.

"Awww, c'mon, Queen Bee."

Her voice came muffled. "It's early!"

I scoffed. "Hardly."

Albeit I'd been awake for a while, the suspense of her gift was killing me. I needed her to open it before the anticipation drove me insane. My pulse sky-rocketed just thinking about it.

Impatient and not wanting her to drift back to sleep, I whipped away the bed cover and bit her ass cheek through her tiny sleep shorts. She jolted and squealed into the bedding, then glared fiercely over her shoulder.

I grinned from above. "Oh good, you're awake. Mōrena, babe."

"I'm awake *now*. How rude!" She tossed a pillow at me

then savagely pulled the cover over her, giving me a *"what you gon' do about it"* look.

Smirking, I ripped it away again and had her over my shoulder before she could so much as think about reaching for it.

Her fighting my hold was pointless—I was so much bigger than her and she weighed nothing compared to what I lifted during workouts.

"Oh my god, put me down! Your shoulder is digging into my bladder and I need to pee!"

Diverting my direction to the bathroom, I set her down on the linoleum floor and hovered.

She shot me a dirty look. "You're not watching me pee."

I snorted. "I'm not watching; I'm waiting."

"Impatiently."

Lifting my hands, I retreated before I riled her too far. Christmas morning or not, Brooklyn would kick my ass with her stormy attitude if I kept pushing.

I strode into the lounge and set my hands on my hips. The massive box that didn't fit under the tree had me pursing my lips. Maybe I'd gone a little overboard. I mean, there were layers to this gift. *Many* layers. Perhaps too many.

While I waited, I set up my phone to record the unwrapping and my heart gave a hard kick of anticipation when I heard the toilet flush.

I met Bee at the bathroom door as it opened and hustled her back to the vanity.

"For fuck's sake, what now?" she exclaimed through laughter.

"Teeth, babe—we're brushing them."

She accepted her brush after I put toothpaste on it despite asking, "Why?"

"You'll see."

I chuckled at the roll of her eyes, which momentarily settled the churning nerves in my stomach. When Bee set her toothbrush down and declared she was done, I rushed to spit, then propelled her into the living room.

"You're so pushy this morning," she grumbled, leaning against my splayed hand between her shoulder blades and trying to slow the pace of her footsteps.

"I'm excited." This was our first Christmas living together, and it was going to be one we'd never forget. For good reasons, I hoped.

She muttered something about Neanderthal, then cut off with a gasp. "Is that for me?"

I grinned so hard it hurt. "Yeah, babe. I've been dying for you to open it."

Her eyes roved over the massive box. I'd used three rolls of gift wrap on that one alone.

"Can I open it?"

I laughed. "That's why I woke you up. But first, Merry Christmas, sweets." Wrapping her in my arms drew a contented sigh from deep in my chest.

Bee hugged me hard. "Merry Christmas to you too. I love you."

"And I love you back."

She looked up at me from under her thick, dark lashes. "Do you want to open yours while I open mine?"

I shook my head. "No, I want to watch this. Get into it already."

She let out a little squeal as she ripped at the layer of gift wrap. I handed her a pair of scissors to cut open the boxing tape, then smirked when she opened the box flaps.

A suspicious glare was cast my way. "Are you serious?"

"Yep." I grinned as she extracted a second large wrapped box.

With more wrapping discarded and a third wrapped box revealed, I snickered again when irritation cracked through Bee's amusement.

"Nico!" she exclaimed when the fourth box, the size of a shoe box, still hadn't revealed the precious gift.

I sat beside Bee when she dropped onto the couch. Unbeknownst to her, this was the perfect position for things to come.

The fourth box revealed a fifth, then a sixth, and by the time the seventh sat in the palm of her hand, her fingers shook.

"Neek?" My name held a tremble that wasn't there before.

"Open it, baby," I gently urged.

Slowly, agonisingly, with tears already shimmering in her eyes, Brooklyn unwrapped the last layer to reveal a ring box. She inhaled a shuddering breath and searched my face for meaning. "Is this…"

I plucked the box from her hand and dropped to one knee before her. Her hands flew to her mouth and failed to hold back an astonished sob.

Numbly, I flipped the little lid open and cleared the thickness from my throat. "This has been a long time coming, eh?" I smirked. "Brooklyn Aroha Andrews, my queen, will you marry me?"

Unexpectedly, her eyes narrowed. "Is this because of my meltdown at the gym?"

I scoffed. "Wanna tell me where I got the time to get this designed and custom-made especially for you, paid for, then wrapped in a shit-ton of boxes, one day out from Christmas?" I arched a brow, then softened my voice. "This wasn't a spur of the moment decision, sweetness, and not one I took lightly. I've had it planned for months."

"Really?"

"Really, babe. So, what do you say? Wanna get married?"

Bee nodded and blinked away her tears. "Yeah I do." She then pointed at herself. "Because this bitch has waited long enough for you to lock her down."

Laughing heartily and filled with monumental relief, I plucked the ring from its case and slid it onto her shaking finger.

"It's beautiful," she gushed.

"Just like you."

She rose with me as I stood, and I sealed my lips over hers, claiming not only her heart and body, but also her hand in marriage.

CHAPTER 7
TRAV & AINSLEY
~ CHRISTMAS DAY ~

TRAV'S POV

"Argh, this place gives me heartburn," I grumbled, rubbing at my chest while driving one-handed through the gates at my parents' house.

"Your mum is getting better," Ainsley reasoned. "Compared to when I first met her."

"Yeah, she's less of a judgemental bitch than she was, but there's still room for improvement." I pulled to a stop without skidding and kicking up their driveway stones like I normally did, and scoffed at my brother's Audi already sitting pride of place in the parking spaces.

"Fletcher is such a fucking show pony."

Lee snickered and arched a brow at me. "I'm sensing a little jealousy."

"Oh pa-lease, there is literally nothing about him I'm jealous of. This car is worth more than his twice over."

Fletcher was my older brother and had a rod stuck so far up his ass I bet he felt like he was sucking cock all day. Though, word on the street—i.e. gossip from our mother—

was that Fletch had found himself a new girlfriend that didn't fit his usual stuck up standards (my words, not hers).

The one and only thing I was looking forward to during this Christmas lunch was seeing if Mum's hypercritical tongue had been correct, or grossly blown out of proportion.

I met Lee at the forest-green-and-gold-striped hood of Rhiannon. Rhiannon was our 1969 Pontiac Firebird Trans AM. While I loved Maxine to death—the Chevy Impala that had popped my restoration cherry—the Firebird had always been my one true unicorn car. When one fell into my lap, I all but begged Ainsley to let me buy it as a restoration project we could work on together.

With only 697 ever being manufactured, this '69 model was as rare as fucking hen's teeth, and lucky for me, Lee fell in love with minimal convincing. *But* I did have to sell my other car-woman Maxine first.

"Is that everything?" Lee asked, eyeing the presents in my arms while she juggled platters of food.

"Yeah, I think so. Lead the way, Goat."

She snorted at the nostalgic nickname. "You're using me as a buffer again, Freak."

"I'm not. Ladies first, remember." Plus, it gave me a chance to stare at her ass as she climbed the steps to my parents' front door.

The little tank and shorts jumpsuit showed so much of her skin and ink that I was sure my mother would purse her lips. Good thing Ainsley didn't give a fuck—she stayed true to herself, always.

We didn't bother with ringing the bell before entering the house. Succulent scents of Christmas ham, roasting turkey, and freshly baked bread greeted us.

We kicked off our jandals and padded barefoot into the expansive kitchen, living, and dining area.

"Hi guys." Ainsley beamed. "Merry Christmas!"

Mum and Dad rose to their feet and hugged her after the food had been removed from her hands.

"You're looking well, Ainsley. Merry Christmas, dear. And you, Travis, Merry Christmas."

"You too, Mum." I set the gifts on the counter and hugged my parents, then wiggled my eyebrows in silent acceptance when Dad offered me a beer.

"You're not going to get drunk before lunch, are you Travis?" Mum admonished. "And take your hat off inside."

I paused with the bottle poised at my lips. "Dunno yet. If lunch is still hours away, then yes, I'll be drunk before lunch."

Her glower made me snicker, then add, "Lunch smells great by the way."

The compliment and removing my cap smoothed her over enough to switch the focus. "Ainsley, you've outdone yourself with these food platters. Shall we set them out now?"

Lee aimed a pointed look at me. "I think that's a good idea."

While her and Mum fussed over the pre-lunch snacks, I passed Dad and casually strolled over to Fletch and his new bird.

My brother rose to his feet and grinned. "Well, look what the cat dragged in," he drawled, giving me a hug.

I pulled back and looked him over; all boat shorts and swanky polo shirt. "Yeah, I agree; it's a fucking disaster."

Mum reprimanded me about my choice of language, while Fletch scoffed and rolled his eyes.

"Whatever." He reached for the wavy-haired beauty at his side. "Travis, this is Megan. Megan, this is my little brother, Travis. The reckless one."

"The fun one," I corrected while hugging her in greeting.

She laughed lightly. "It's nice to meet you. I've heard so much about you from Fletch."

I waved my beer around. "Forget everything he's told you; it'll all be a crock of shit."

"Travis!" Mum barked, coming over with the hors d'oeuvres. "Mind your *language!*"

"Sorry, Ma."

After her and Ainsley set the platters down, I introduced Lee to Megan. "Lee, this is Megan, Megan, this is Goat."

"Goat?" she exclaimed with a burst of laughter, then snickered again when Ainsley backhanded my stomach.

"Ignore him," Lee sassed. "I'm Ainsley, but you can call me Lee."

They hugged, then Megan's eyes pinged back and forth between us. "You guys are…" She waved a hand. "You're the same but different."

I grinned and threw my arm around Lee's shoulders, then pointed at Fletch. "Little bit different from this cleanskin, huh?"

"Yeah, heaps," Megan murmured, now openly comparing me to my brother.

"Travis is our free-spirited son," Mum explained as her and Dad sat on the couch in the blind-filtered sun.

"That's Mum's way of saying that Travis is the problem child," Fletch drawled.

I scoffed and threw myself onto the couch beside Lee. "No, that's her way of saying I refuse to fit into the mould. Unlike you."

My father finally weighed in. "Boys, enough."

"How about we do gifts?" Mum suggested optimistically.

My hearty laugh broke free. I couldn't wait for this part. "That'll be fun," Megan declared.

"I think we should do ours last," Lee warned. "Trav did the shopping and wrapped them before I got a look, so I literally have no idea what you guys are getting."

I smirked, barely able to sit still. "Oh, I dunno... I think we should do ours first."

"Go on then," Fletch chuckled.

I all but skipped to the bag of presents I'd left on the kitchen counter and eagerly handed them out, putting an extra flourish into Fletcher's.

"Do yours last."

His eyes narrowed suspiciously, yet him and Megan waited until Mum and Dad had opened their gifts. Megan went next, thanking me and Lee with a smile while holding up a spa voucher, then all attention shifted to Fletcher.

He grumbled and muttered about this being a set-up (because it was), then choked on an inhale and let out a booming laugh. "You got me a bag of *dicks?*"

"A bag of *chocolate* dicks," I corrected. "Now when people tell you to go eat a bag of dicks, you can proudly tell them that you've been there, done that, and got the breath to prove it."

"Well, I *never*," Mum breathed out while Dad failed to hide how funny he found it.

"Oh my goooooodd," Lee groaned from behind her palm. "Really, Trav?"

And the part that had me laughing so hard that I had to set down my beer to hold my stomach? Megan eyeing the bag and urging, "Open them, Fletch! We can all have a Christmas dick."

Lee lost her shit, wheezing with laughter so hard she curled into a ball, and Fletch, bless him, cracked up while shaking his head at his missus.

Yeah, I'd made up my mind about Megan; she wasn't his usual type… she was so much better.

* * *

We hit Mum and Dad's pool after lunch, and while we waited for the girls to change into their swimsuits, Fletch swam up to me with a stupid-as-fuck grin on his face.

"So, what do you think of Megan?" he opened with.

I glanced sideways at him. "You don't need my opinion, bro."

"I want it." An expression I hadn't seen on him before passed over his face. "She's… different. *More.*"

I set my beer bottle behind me on the pool tiles and reclined on the first step. "Fine. You're so much more relaxed than you ever were with Kate or Hazel. You're not as douchy either."

He shocked the hell out of me by laughing, then dropping his voice. "That's because I took your advice."

My focus cut his way and I squinted at him from under the peak of my cap. "What advice?"

His smile pulled wider. "About sampling *other* tastes…"

A wave of water radiated out from my body as I sat up quickly and leaned toward him.

"Where the fuck did you meet her?" I hissed as dread formed in the pit of my stomach. I sure as hell hadn't ever suggested he go down to hooker town.

"At the speedway," he whisper-exclaimed like it was some kind of outrageous confession.

A loud laugh fell from my open mouth. "Say it like it's a sin, why don't you?"

"But you were right, Travis," he implored. "She's uplifting and assertive without being a bitch. She's wild and fun and down for anything—and I mean *anything,*" he drawled and smirked. "And get this…" He leaned in and flicked his sunnies down so I could just see his eyes. "She has a *tattoo!*"

I feigned a horrified gasp and pressed a 'scandalised' hand to my inked chest. "Not a *tattoo!* How uncivilised!*"*

He brandished his middle finger while I leaned against the side of the pool to catch my breath.

"In other words, you're fucked?" I wheezed after I finally stopped laughing.

His nostrils flared in annoyance. "Yes, Travis. I'm *fucked.*"

I took a long swig of beer and eased into the water again, this time sitting with my back against the pool lip. Our silence was filled with Ainsley and Megan's voices in the background, then a hand appeared above the pool gate to unlock it from the inside.

Me and Fletch stared in silence, both barely breathing as our women entered the pool area wearing bikinis and sunglasses.

Ainsley never failed to make my heart lose its steady rhythm, and my mouth salivated while watching her test the water temperature with a dip of her pointed toes.

Without taking my eyes off her, I murmured out of the corner of my mouth, "I'm so fucked too, Fletch."

"Well, let's cheers to being fucked," he drawled.

When his fresh beer bottle thrust into my peripherals, I clinked mine against it, secretly over the fucking moon that he and I finally had something in common to bond over: our love of hot, inked women.

CHAPTER 8
THE ENTIRE CREW
~ CHRISTMAS DAY—CHAPTER 1 ~

LIL'S POV

"Yay, more presents!" Elodie cheered from the lounge window overlooking the front yard.

I joined her and laughed at Trav staggering his way up the driveway, arms laden with brightly wrapped gifts and Ainsley jogging to catch up.

Meeting them at the door, I whipped it open and stepped back to allow Trav to barrel through.

"Who wants presents?" he yelled, hyping El up.

"I do, I do!" she sang while following him like he was the Pied Piper.

Ainsley groaned as she hugged me. "Sorry, he's drunk."

I laughed and squeezed her back. "I expected nothing less. I assume lunch with his parents wasn't great?"

"It was surprisingly good. Him and his brother had this crazy bonding moment over Fletcher's new girlfriend, then they both got happy-drunk."

"Oh fuck," I snickered, leading her into the lounge where Trav and Elodie knelt under the Christmas tree, shaking the presents.

"Yeah," Lee deadpanned. "Their mum was trying so hard to be chill, but in the end, me and Megan decided it was best to hit the road before the boys got too rowdy." She studied Trav for a moment and smirked. "How long do you think it'll take the guys to notice their matching shirts?"

I giggled and met her hushed tone. "Gage is super reluctant to wear his. He's still needing some convincing…"

Her light-green eyes danced with amusement. "Is that why he's not here?"

I scoffed. "He's here but needed an afternoon nap. Let me go wake him."

"I'll stop these two from opening the presents early," she drawled, walking over to Trav and Elodie.

Their combined laughter and fun banter grew distant as I tracked down the hallway to our bedroom. I paused at the door to enjoy the fleeting moment of peace within the festively chaotic day.

Gage slept on his back with one arm above his head, hand furled into a loose fist. The other rested on his stomach, rising and falling gently with each steady breath.

He'd changed dramatically over the years. The night he'd turned up to a crew party, he was nothing but an angry, broody stranger. Now his smile lit the world more often than not and it warmed my heart knowing he'd found his happy. He sure as hell deserved it.

My past had broken me for a time, and then on a second occasion when Jono returned in a vengeful rage, but Gage's history was utterly devastating in comparison.

I silently crossed the room and softly laid a hand on his shoulder. He woke with a large inhale and a sleepy smile.

"Hey, Sunshine."

"Hey yourself. Good sleep?" I perched on the side of the bed when he shuffled across.

He hummed. "I needed it." A twinkle of desire entered his eyes as he smoothed a hand up my thigh. "Is El asleep too?"

I snagged his fingers before they dipped under my sundress. "You wish. I left Ainsley supervising her and Trav to make sure they don't open the presents prematurely."

Gage scrubbed his free hand over his face. "Fuck."

"Yeah."

"But, we have a few minutes alone…"

I narrowed my eyes when both of his palms smoothed around my waist.

"We cannot fuck while we have guests."

He scoffed. "When the hell has that ever stopped anyone before?"

"Not the point. We're hosting."

"So? Our house our rules, and right now, my rule is that I want to be inside you. It's been forever."

"Oh pah-lease, it's been like, two days."

"Two days too long," he murmured gruffly and pulled me on top of him.

My knees automatically fell wide and straddled his hips while firm fingers grabbed my ass.

Pushing onto extended arms, I rocked my pelvis a little and sighed dramatically. "Unfortunately, I don't think we have time."

"Fuck that. We have time." Gage tossed me to the side and pinned me on my stomach. He hissed in impatience while shoving up my sundress to expose my booty. His fingers flicked beneath my underwear and teased my slit. "Damn, Lil, you're more than ready for me."

I craned my neck and smirked over my shoulder. "But are *you* ready?"

He grabbed my hand and shoved it against the erection straining within his shorts. "What do you think?"

"I think you'd better take those off."

Gage wasted no time in complying with my suggestion. He whipped my underwear down, then kicked out of his clothing from the waist down. When he knelt behind me on the bed, I angled my hips high but kept my knees together.

"You'll wear the Christmas shirt?" I asked, during his time of weakness.

He groaned and slid the head of his dick between my cheeks. "I'll wear anything you ask me to, Sunshine, just let me in."

The millisecond my knees moved wide, he slid into me with a long, low groan of satisfaction. My back arched to take him deeper and I eagerly meet each thrust with a breathy gasp.

"I want you to come around me," Gage hissed, reaching for my clit.

"I want to, too, but I'm not sure I can with the time pressure."

He pulled out without warning and flipped me onto my back. His hungry kisses consumed me while I welcomed him back inside my body.

Since having Elodie, we'd learned to snag each intimate moment when it arose. Often those rounds of sex were much like this one: hurried and laced with urgency to finish before our little blessing threw ice on the sexy time.

Gage held my legs wide while watching himself slide in and out, then flicked his eyes up to mine. The visible thirst in his dark irises made me smirk and reach between my legs.

A deep hum of approval rumbled. "Tell me when you're getting close."

"Yeah," I breathed out, riding each wave of pleasure as it heightened.

The vein in Gage's neck bulged as he fought to hold back until I'd started tipping over the edge, and it took several merciful minutes before my fingers worked their magic.

"Oh god," I moaned right before my orgasm hit.

Gage anchored my legs wide as he thrust his way to his own release. He arched and shuddered, then stilled with his fingers still biting into the fleshy part of my thighs.

Our breathless panting filled the otherwise silent room, until something thudded against the outside of our bedroom door.

I giggled, whereas Gage ran a hand down his face and grumbled, "I swear to God if that was a bottle of mouthwash…"

"Oh, Trav's drunk, by the way."

He snorted. "Nothing new there. But seriously, how the fuck does he still have bottles of mouthwash?"

I shrugged. "Maybe he restocked."

"Christ help us all," Gage deadpanned, easing out and cupping his dick.

I followed him to the en suite bathroom where we cleaned up, then went in search of my discarded underwear.

Once we were both redressed and Gage had assured me there were no cum stains on my dress, I paused with my hand on the bedroom door handle.

"Shirt, Gage."

"What shirt?"

My smile widened into a shit-eating grin. "The Christmas shirt you agreed on wearing before we had sex."

He eyed me through a narrowed glare and snatched up the offending tee. "Damn you and your sorcerous ways." The grumbling continued while he shoved his arms through the holes and wriggled until his head popped out. "This is the fucking *worst!*"

I snickered and smoothed my hands over his chest. "It's cute. C'mon, let's go."

Gage gave my ass a hard squeeze as I opened the door, then cursed when he spotted the bottle of mouthwash Trav —presumably—had tossed there.

I snatched it from the floor so El wouldn't drink it, and tracked down the hallway with Gage's mutterings following me into the lounge.

"Yaaay, Mum and Dad are back," Trav cheered to Elodie, catching the mouthwash bottle I tossed his way.

A little crease appeared between El's light brows. "Where did they go?"

Trav snorted. "To funky town."

Our daughter, bless her, turned to Gage, and put on her best Daddy's Girl eyes. "Can I go to funky town?"

I failed to suppress a burst of laughter. Gage, however, paled ten shades before recolouring red.

"No," he snapped. "Not until you're over thirty and married."

She pouted as she thought, then turned her round hazel eyes on Trav. "Have you been to funky town?"

His laughter increased. "I have."

"Is it fun?" El asked.

"Best town known to man," he crowed, earning a subtle kick from Lee.

Desperate to reroute the conversation, Gage made a scene by rushing to the window. "Oh look, Neek and Brooklyn are here!"

Our daughter's focus immediately shifted, and she rushed for the front door.

"Thank *Christ* for that," Gage hissed. "I swear to god, Travis, if you mention funky town again, I'm going to maim you. And why the *fuck* are we wearing matching shirts?"

Ainsley and I burst into fits of laughter as the guys studied each other, then cracked up again when Neek appeared—also wearing the same t-shirt: red with gold tinsel stitched to each nipple area, with the caption 'Merry Christmas Tinsel Tits' written in script across the chest.

CHAPTER 9
THE ENTIRE CREW
~ CHRISTMAS DAY—CHAPTER 2 ~

LIL'S POV

"Heeeey, cool shirts, brothers!" Neek chuckled in his man-giggle way and pointed to Gage and Trav. "The girls stitched us up, eh?"

All going well, Mace and Mickey would turn up wearing matching shirts too.

"You sneaky little she-devils. I see what's going on here!" Trav exclaimed, rolling from the floor and smirking at me. "Your idea, I presume?"

I feigned innocence and finished hugging Brooklyn. "Absolutely not. It was a collective agreement amongst the girls, and don't you dare give Mickey or Mace a heads up. Any of you," I warned with a finger point around the three guys.

Gage shook his head and ran a hand down his smile. "I knew you were up to something, Sunshine."

"You're welcome." I grinned and twisted from side-to-side, making my red sundress brush against my thighs.

Nico's man-giggle had us all smiling wider. "Won't

breathe a word, sweetness," he promised while embracing me tight. "Merry Christmas, Lil."

"Merry Christmas too. Good day so far?"

His green eyes sparkled as he grinned down at me. "The best; ask Bee about it."

I turned my attention to Brooklyn to see her grinning and bouncing on the spot.

"Oh my god, guess what?" she blurted.

My energy immediately matched hers. "Oh my god, tell me!"

"Eeeeep," she shrieked and held up her left hand, wriggling her fingers to show off a gorgeous new engagement ring.

Ainsley and I gasped and rushed towards her. "Shut up! Oh my god, guys!"

A gorgeous solitaire diamond sat proudly between two tear-drop shaped pounamu (greenstone) gemstones, and the dark gold band shone in the afternoon summer sunlight.

"It's absolutely stunning," Ainsley gushed. "Congratulations!"

"Thank you. Neek designed it himself," Brooklyn beamed.

Neek, looking pretty damn pleased with himself, added, "The pounamu is from my ancestral lands. The kaumātua [a Māori tribal elder] at the marae [a Māori meeting ground] blessed it then gifted it to us."

"Aww guys!" I cooed, blinking the tears from my eyes. I gathered Brooklyn, then Neek, in for another tight hug. "Best Christmas ever!"

"Thanks, Lil. It's about damn time, right?" Brooklyn laughed with a sassy flick of her long, black-and-deep-green hair.

Brooklyn was definitely the prissy one of the crew, but hot damn she was fierce. While being a little younger than the rest of us, she'd shown incredible loyalty to Neek when he returned from Afghanistan broken and unhappy.

She giggled. "I feel like I've finally joined the grown-ups club."

"Ha," I burst out. "Trust me when I say that none of us 'grown ups'," I air-quoted, "have any idea about what we're doing. We're all totally winging this. Besides, you and Neek have businesses—that's totally grown up."

"Yeah but, you know... Marriage and babies is a whole other ball game."

"Marriage no, babies yes," I admitted, casting a look toward El where she sat playing with a freshly unwrapped gift.

"Elodie! Where did you get that?"

Her eyes snapped from the *Wonder Woman* figurine to Trav. "Uncle Trav said I could open one now."

"Trav!" Ainsley cut in, then turned to me. "And I just want to note that I shopped for the kids whereas Trav shopped for the adults and he's refusing to tell me what he got. I apologise in advance."

Trav's laughter filled the lounge. "And you'll all be *thanking* me after dark, if you know what I mean."

Brooklyn smirked. "So, not kid friendly?"

Travis's grin split wider and he popped the P on, *"Nope.* They are not."

* * *

The guys were on their second beer—aside from Trav—by the time Mace and Jess arrived.

"Party's here!" Mace called.

Jess appeared first, looking exhausted, followed by Mace's shit-eating grin. After he'd dropped a kiss on my cheek and I'd fought my way out of his bear hug, I gave

Jess a massive squeeze. I missed working with her in ED and we hadn't had a decent catch up in a long time.

"Merry Christmas, how are you doing, hun?"

She gave me a tired smile. "It's been a random, amazing, exhausting day. Dad had breakfast with us this morning."

My jaw hit the floor, and I darted a glance at Mace. "What! Like, your *actual* Dad?"

Jess nodded with tears shimmering in her eyes. "I came out of the bedroom to find him standing in the dining area."

"Wait—" I shook my head. "He just randomly let himself into the house after years of zero contact?"

She looked to Mace, who cradled Cree in his arms while saying hi to everyone. "No. Mace invited him in to meet Cree. I've never felt my heart shatter and heal at the same time, and I still can't believe it happened."

"Are you okay that Mace let him inside?" I asked cautiously.

"I'm incredibly grateful," she admitted.

I gave her another hug and didn't let go until Mace muscled his way between us. "Bring it in, Lil Bean."

"Merry Christmas, Tinsel Tits. Jess was just telling me about this morning."

Mace rubbed one tinselled nipple area, then the grin slid from place. "Crazy, right? Mo was the last person I expected on my doorstep at 6 a.m."

I lifted Cree from his arms and snuggled him close. "So crazy. Was it just a one-off or does this mean he's back in your lives?"

Jess looked to her husband. Mace's features were clouded. "At this stage it's a one off; he's still rolling with the Lucifer's Guild, and I'm reluctant to let him get too close. Especially since Ash and Hana arrived in the thick of it."

"Oh no!" I hissed.

"Yeah." Jess nodded solemnly but perked up, trying to shake the oppressive feelings before they drained our Christmas spirit. "And on that note, where are the mocktails, Lil?"

Rolling with her change of topic, I went to hand Cree back to his daddy, then diverted him to Ainsley's arms when she swooped in and all but snatched him from me.

Laughing, I led Jess to the kitchen. "I nearly lost a limb!" I joked. "And I need make another slushy batch; Brooklyn spiked the first one with vodka. Oh, go ask her about her news!"

Jess's eyes sparkled with curiosity. "What news?"

"I can't say. You need to find out for yourself."

"I'll be back," she declared, then hurried over to Brooklyn.

"Yo, Lil, when's Mickey and lil' Kim getting here?" Mace called as I loaded frozen berries into the blender.

"Do I look like their pocket diary?" I sassed.

He smirked. "If it's in a pretty red case, then yes."

"You know you can text him, right?"

"Yeah, but you're…" He waved his hand about. "You know, in his head."

"Uh huh," I deadpanned, despite channelling Mickey—my twin—through my mind.

<Where are you guys? Everyone else is here and Mace wants updates.>

We'd been connected this way for as long as I could remember, and I had to admit that it was pretty convenient at times.

His reply popped into my head. *<Be there soon. We had a fight.>*

<About?>

<Kimmie wants me to wear a fuck-awful Christmas shirt with Tinsel Tits written on the front!>

I laughed aloud. *<Just wear the fucking shirt, Mickey, and get your asses here ASAP. We're all waiting for you guys. Trav's pestering us about opening presents more than El is.>*

<On our way soon, just trying to smooth shit over with Kimmie before we leave. And just give him another beer.>

I let out a snort while pouring orange juice into the blender. *<He's at least eight beers deep already.>*

As if summoned by our internal conversation, Trav's tattooed arms slid around my waist and his chin landed on my shoulder. "You're my favourite, Lil Bean."

Laughing, I rested my head against the side of his. "I heard you say the same thing to Brooklyn not even two minutes ago."

"That's because you're all my favourite, besides Lee. She's my ultimate favourite because she lets me see her boobs and p—"

"Trav! I know what she lets you see, and I do *not* need explicit details."

He roared with laughter and released me from his hold, then leaned his ass against the counter. "But I like the details."

"Yeah, but I'm sure Ainsley doesn't want us knowing them."

With a shrug that signalled a change of subject, Trav dropped a bomb. "We're gonna start trying for a baby."

A pang cut through my chest and my gasp made his eyes flick over my shoulder, then back to me. "Keep that on the down-low, Lil. I wasn't meant to say *anything* but I had to tell someone."

"Awww, Travie!" I cooed, shoving my own struggles

with secondary infertility aside. "Look at you all grown up. You're going to be the best daddy."

His chest puffed with pride and his dimple-depth grin pulled wider. "Gage, Mace, and Mick do such a great job… I just hope I can live up to expectations."

"You're going to be a great one," I reassured him with an affectionate forearm squeeze.

Trav's gaze went all goo-goo and I dashed a glance behind me to where Ainsley cuddled Cree.

"She looks good holding a baby, doesn't she?" Trav murmured, a million miles away.

"She does. Go join her, Travie. And your secret's safe with me."

"Thanks, Lil. And that's why you're my favourite."

I laughed and playfully kicked his ass when he stepped away from the counter. "Get your ass out of my kitchen."

"You love me," he sang, dancing his way around the kitchen island.

"Yeah, Trav, I do."

I couldn't not love him even if I tried.

CHAPTER 10
THE ENTIRE CREW
~ CHRISTMAS DAY—CHAPTER 3 ~

LIL'S POV

"Thank feck we're finally here," Mickey breathed out, carrying a sleepy Xavier on his bent arm.

I peeked around his shoulder at my stormy little nephew. "Hi again, Xavie."

"He fell asleep on the way home from Mum and Dad's and I just woke him. He'll be wild for a little bit," Mickey explained.

"Aunty Lil doesn't like being woken up either," I whispered to Xave, who was fifteen months old.

"Still savage, huh?" my brother teased.

"Savage A F," I deadpanned. "About as savage as Kimmie looks right now."

Mickey's face turned indignant. "She forced me to wear this vomit-worthy shirt, and now I see why." He cast a narrow-eyed glare around the guys. "You know I hate matchy-matchy, Lil."

I laughed and got a little sassy. "It's Christmas, so suck it up."

His lips pursed hard, letting his irritation be known. The

longer he studied me, the more prominent his frown became.

"What's that look for?" I tucked my chin back and asked. Mickey felt something, I could see it in his expression.

"Uh, Lil, I think you're–"

"Yay, presents time!" Elodie cheered in the background.

"In a second, El," I called as Kimmie came to my side. I hugged her despite seeing her barely an hour ago at Mum and Dad's.

"What was it you were about to say, Mickey?"

He waved me off. "Nothing that can't wait. C'mon, it's presents time."

After giving Kimmie a tight smile and affectionately rubbing his hand up and down her back, he plucked up a beer and sat with Xavier.

"Ugh," Kimmie exclaimed, leaning on me as if unable to go on living. "I would have maimed him if he continued to refuse to wear that damn shirt. Honestly, Lil, it was almost the death of us."

"He's always been a bad sport; you know that."

"And I guess no guy really likes being called tinsel tits," she laughed.

I snorted. "Gage was growly as fuck about it too; I ended up bribing him."

"With what?"

"My vagina," I whispered.

Kimmie let out a full-bodied laugh as I led her into the kitchen and poured her a glass of wine. "That always works."

"You should have tried it with Mickey."

"Ugh," she burst again. "We'd passed that point. The thought of his penis coming anywhere near my vagina made me want to grow wolverine daggers inside it."

"Dayum, girl. And people say *I'm* savage."

I handed her the wine, and she paused before taking a sip. "I think he simply wore it to shut me up."

"The guys will look back and laugh about it. We always do." I waved my hand. "Come sit; I don't know who's more impatient for presents—El or Trav."

Kimmie giggled. "Trav has always loved gift unwrapping."

Smiling, I shook my head and made my way over to Gage. I snagged his beer bottle from his grasp and dinged it again my glass.

"Presents time!" I sang, then laughed when Trav and El let out matching whoops of celebration.

The entire crew—ten adults and three children—shuffled until we were in one large circle around the living area, with Trav and El self-appointed Santas by the Christmas tree.

Trav hastily took a swig of beer then raised his hands. "Okay, we're going to do mine and Lee's ones last. Got that, munchkin? Green sparkly presents last, okay?" he confirmed with Elodie.

She nodded seriously, then cheered when Trav handed her the first gift. "This one is for Neek and Bee, from Mace, Jess, and Cree."

El scurried off, all but threw the gift at Mace, then ran back to Trav for another. This continued until she couldn't hold off opening her pile of presents any longer, and Trav chose that moment to hand his gifts out.

"Don't let the tiny people see them," he warned, dashing his head toward El.

"Sounds ominous," Mickey mumbled.

Gage held our gift while eyeing Trav. "I swear to God, Trav, if this is a box of mouthwash, I'm going to lose my ever-loving sh—"

Trav fought to swallow his mouthful of beer before he spat it out, and cracked out a hearty laugh. "Those are saved for special occasions, bro. Like earlier." He winked, making Gage snort and cut his dark eyes to me.

I tilted my head to the side. "He has a point."

"You're both messing with me, Sunshine."

"You love it."

He smirked. "I love *you*."

I leaned closer as Gage unwrapped our gift, then let out a scandalised gasp. "Travis!"

His blue eyes shone with enthusiasm. "You like?"

"I uh…" Laughing, I couldn't form words, so plucked up the leather bondage set, ball-gag included, and widened my eyes. "Are you serious?"

He shrugged. "Gage always complains you're too loud and sassy, so, problem solved. You're welcome, bro," he added to Gage.

"Oh my god, Trav!" Lee exclaimed, as Brooklyn held up two pairs of matching nipple clamps and a fox-tailed butt plug. "I'm so sorry, guys. I had no idea."

Kimmie let out a massive laugh and had to set her wine down to hold her stomach.

"You're a dead man walking, Travis," growled Mickey, brandishing his brand new cock-pump like weapon.

"Thought it might help in the small peen department," Trav teased.

Mace's low rolling laughter shifted the attention to him. "Oh, we'll definitely be using these later, Bright Eyes."

Trav smirked. "It was hardest buying for you two since —I *assume*—Jess still has all her gear from working at the strip club."

"Wait, *what?*" Brooklyn exclaimed, flying forward in her seat and darting astonished looks between Jess, Mace, and Trav.

"What's a strip club?" came El's sweet, innocent voice.

I felt the blood drain from my face.

"It's like funky town," Trav explained without missing a beat. "Anyway, I know you have a thing for when Jess takes charge, so, if the shoe fits and all that shi–iiiitzu," he hastily amended after Mickey gruffly cleared his throat.

Brooklyn held up her hands to call order. "Wait wait wait. Girl, is he for real?"

Jess's cheeks coloured. "Yeah, he's for real. I worked my way through Med School, then more recently when my sister got caught up in a not-so-great situation."

"But, hun, we don't really talk about it in front of—" I dashed my head sideways at El, and whispered, "These walls have ears."

Understanding lit in Brooklyn's expression and she studied my daughter. "I bet if I whispered the word *l.o.l.l.i.e.s*, she'd hear straight away."

"Don't you dare," I warned. "With the amount of sugar that one has consumed today, we're all doomed later."

"But look how angelic she is."

My voice turned wry. "Don't let it fool you, Brooklyn. You haven't had the pleasure of dealing with the demonic chuckie doll yet."

She laughed and sipped her drink, then barely held it in when Elodie piped up, "Chuckie! Hey, Trav, can we go to the beach?"

"Sure thing, little miss."

"Trav! You know she asks you because you always say yes."

His blue eyes hit mine, filled with mischief and shenanigans. "Can we though? And make a fire and roast marshmallows? Please tell me you have marshmallows, Lil Bean!"

Mickey waved an arm from side to side. "Yo, it's

summer. There's a fire-ban in place across the entire region."

"Pffft," Trav scoffed. "You're a firefighter: you can put it out if needed. Besides, we'll literally be right by the water."

"Nope. Sorry, bro. Ain't happening."

Collectively, our eyes pinged back and forth between Mickey and Trav, who pouted, then pouted some more when Mickey's resolve refused to ease.

The corner of Trav's mouth twitched. "The old Mickey would have."

My brother rolled his eyes. "The old Mickey would have done a whole lot of shiz, but this one," he pointed to himself, "doesn't want to lose his job over breaking the most important fire rule of summer."

"Which is?" Trav challenged, crossing his arms over his chest.

"No fires during a fire-ban, Trav!"

He threw his arms wide. "Just pretend you had no idea."

"How about I fill up your diesel truck with petrol and pretend I had no idea?"

Trav's face turned ashen. "There's no pretending with that. It literally fucks the engine."

"Fucks!" El chirped in the background, sending Mickey's irritation a notch higher.

"You proved my point; about the fire *and* the reason why you need to stop swearing around the kids."

Trav waved his beer around while we laughed. "Okay, point taken. And El, you can't be cussing, little miss. Adults only."

She kept playing with her latest gift—a glitter wand. "But you do."

Everyone roared with laughter, then harder when indignation hit Trav's face. "I *am* an adult."

"No, because you're fun. Not like Mumma."

I lurched forward and slapped a hand over my mouth, quickly swallowing my sip of mocktail. "Hey! I'm fun!"

Her judgy little eyes briefly cut to me. "Nah, not really."

"The audacity!" I gaped in disbelief, then pointed at Gage. "That's on you, Batman."

His deep laughter gave way to a dry tone. "Says the one who practically cloned herself. I mean look at her. That sass comes directly from you, Sunshine."

"And we know where her audacity comes from," I countered with a sassy lip-pout.

As if our three-year-old hadn't unwittingly caused enough adult drama, her next question pushed my mortification to new levels.

"What's this for?" she asked, holding up Brooklyn's fox-tailed butt plug.

Thank god Bee snatched it away at lightning speed, allowing me to glare at Travis. *"You* can explain that."

He at least had the sense to look guilty. "It's for dress up, little miss. And one you're only allowed to use once you're over eighteen."

"Travis!" both Gage and I yelled, bewildered and mortified.

Gage stood with purpose. "I can't even handle the thought of that. Who's keen to light a fire on the beach?" he asked, mercifully taking us back to safer turbulent waters.

Ignoring Mickey's outburst of all the reasons why we couldn't, I was the first on my feet. "I'll get the marshmallows."

CHAPTER 11
THE ENTIRE CREW
~ CHRISTMAS DAY—CHAPTER 4 ~

LIL'S POV

We loaded up our truck with chiller boxes full of food and drinks, as well as beach chairs, buckets and shovels, towels, sun umbrellas, plus the children, and Gage and Jess drove to the beach while the rest of us walked the few blocks. Trav insisted on taking the Christmas tree with us, and garnered dozens upon dozens of honks and whooped cheers from passing cars during the journey.

We were set up with drinks in-hand, sitting around our illegal, soon-to-be beach fire with the damn Christmas tree precariously dug into the sand, when Trav made an announcement.

"Okay, I've got a plan," he said, stacking kindling within a rock circle.

"Uh huh, which is?" I asked.

"If we get arrested, we *all* get arrested. They simply have to take all of us, including the kids, or none of us."

Mace barked a laugh. "It doesn't work like that, bro.

Did you not learn anything from when you and Mickey got arrested?"

Trav threw his head back and roared with laughter. "Now there's a throwback!"

"Drunk and disorderly, wasn't it?" Neek chipped in with a man-giggle.

Gage snorted. "Yeah, and me and Lil had to bail them out in the middle of the night."

Mickey pointed his beer bottle at him and quickly glanced around to ensure no children were within earshot. "And while the three of us were laughing our asses off about it, Lil threw the biggest bitchfest ever."

"I thought someone was hurt, Mickey! You literally gave me emergency vibes."

He shrugged. "Because we wanted to be bailed out ASAP."

I flipped him off. "I can't wait for the time when *I'm* arrested and need you to bail me out at 3 a.m."

Gage's sharp gaze cut to me. "For fuck's sake, Lil, getting arrested should not be something you look forward to."

Trav snickered. "She can take one for the team if the cops show up tonight."

Grinning, I laid my head on Gage's shoulder. "You know how I roll: uterus to the wall."

Mace spat his beer and boomed with laughter. "What the fuck, Lil Bean? No one ever says 'uterus to the wall'!"

"*I* do, because I don't have balls."

"Jesus Christ," Gage muttered, running a hand down his face while Ainsley offered me a fist bump.

Trav dashed his head my way and addressed Gage. "You're marrying that, bro. It's not too late to back out. Run while you still can."

Despite the giggles, I brandished my middle finger, just

as Brooklyn, Kimmie, and Jess returned from their walk with the kids.

"Uh, what did we miss?" Kimmie asked, handing Xavier to Mickey.

Trav paused rearranging the firewood. "Lil talking about her uterus."

"What's a utis?" Elodie asked.

Gage nudged my side. "That's a question for you, Sunshine."

I gathered El onto my knee and hugged her, automatically slipping into nurse-mode.

"It's the part of our bodies that carries our babies inside us," I explained simply. When El looked at Gage's stomach, I snorted. "And only girls have them."

She looked around the crew and I could see all the little cogs clicking into place inside her head.

After confirming that, yes, Jess, Brooklyn, Kimmie, Ainsley, myself, *and* herself all had uteruses, because yes we were all girls—with vaginas (which I also had to confirm)—she seemed content and easily distracted by Trav asking for a lighter.

All eyes flicked expectantly to Mickey. While he'd quit smoking while Kimmie was pregnant, the habit of carrying a lighter hadn't passed. Ironic, for a firefighter.

He rolled his eyes and tossed it Trav's way, complete with a warning: "When I get fired, we're coming to live with you."

With a whoop, Trav flicked the flame to life and showed El how to light the smaller kindling before adding thicker pieces. My heart smiled as I watched them. Trav would be an awesome dad one day.

<*Lil?*>

My eyes flicked to Mickey as he entered my psyche.

<*Yeah?*> I internally asked back.

<*You're pregnant again.*>

Gage felt me startle and smoothed his hand around my inner thigh. He gave it a double squeeze of reassurance while continuing his conversation with Kimmie.

My focus homed in on Mickey. He'd always had the ability to feel sensations (mostly pain) that belonged to me.

<*How sure are you?*>

His eyes flared a little. <*Pretty fucking sure. It's the same feeling I got when you were first pregnant with El.*>

<*Oh shit!*> I fought the tears as they sprang to my eyes and blinked hard to clear them.

Mickey's face saddened. <*I take it this isn't good news?*>

I shook my head. <*It's the best. I haven't been able to conceive since El. Are you sure you're sure?*>

Visible relief swept through him. <*Abso-fucking-lutely sure. But do me one massive favour this time around, will you?*>

My eyebrows bunched at the centre. <*What?*>

A smirk tugged before he took a swig of beer. <*Have a fucking epidural. I thought I was going to die while you gave birth to El.*>

I grinned and snickered behind my hand. <*I'm thinking about having a natural home birth with no pain relief at all this time.*>

His eyes immediately narrowed. <*Sadistic bitch.*>

<*Love you. And thank you for telling me. I hope it sticks.*>

He straightened and nodded. <*It'll stick, and I love you back.*>

Gage's fingers idly rubbing on my inner thigh returned my focus to him. An overwhelming wash of love came over me as I studied his profile. My fingers delved into his beard and angled his chin my way.

When I set my lips on his, he drew me close and tenderly kissed me despite the audience.

"What's gotten you all soppy, Sunshine?" he murmured against my mouth.

"Just loving you," I whispered.

I felt him smile and welcomed his lips pressing to mine again. We ignored the crews' snickers and dirty mutterings, and allowed ourselves a moment.

If Mickey was right like last time, come nine months' time, we'd be a family of four.

The crew had come a long way over the years. We'd started as a close group of five and had overcome obstacles most people wouldn't dream of facing within their lifetime. We'd pulled each other through heartache and loss, built each other up, and fought for one another during the greatest times of need. We were more than just a group of friends. Blood or not, we were family.

Feeling my throat tighten with emotion, I thickly called for everyone's attention.

"Guys! We need to do a toast."

I waited until everyone had a drink raised above the small flickering fire, then thrust my glass into the fray.

"Here's to the greatest damn family the world has ever seen. Here's to the crew—I love you guys. Merry Christmas!"

"Merry Christmas!" everyone cheered above the sound of bottles and glassware clinking together.

Gage's worried eyes found mine. "Are you sure you're okay, babe?"

"I really am." Vibrations of adrenaline surged through me, making my voice tremble. "Let's just say that next year, we'll have at least one new crew member."

His eyes darted around the group, found Mickey watching us, then cut back to me. "Wait. Did he just...?"

I nodded. "Yup."

"*Again?*"

"Again."

"Did you know already?" Gage hissed.

"No. He literally just told me," I whispered back.

A heavy exhale left Gage's mouth before it split into a world-tilting grin. "Fucking hell. C'mere, Sunshine. Best damn Christmas present I could ask for."

He wrapped me in a hug and kissed me hard. When I came up for air, I glanced at the crew and wholeheartedly agreed.

Best damn Christmas ever.

THE END!

I'M NOT CRYING, YOU'RE CRYING!

The crew has owned my heart and ruled my head since I wrote them back in 2017! I'm so excited to have *finally* written their Christmas story. I hope you loved them just as much as I do!

If you want to read more of their individual stories, the entire *North Shore Series* is available on Amazon and free to read with Kindle Unlimited. There's a reading order, so start with Gage & Lil in *Ride For Me*.

OTHER TITLES BY VI SUMMERS

(All are available in Kindle Unlimited)

https://authorvisummers.com/

The North Shore Crew Series

Ride For Me

Break For Me

Lie For Me

Fight For Me

Burn For Me

The Seven Thousand Miles Duet

Living for Today

Dreaming of Tomorrow

Montana Cowboys

Montana Moonshine

Salvation Society

Oblivion

Driven World

Boost

Hades Horsemen MC

Slade

Phoenix Force

Hellfire

Standalone

Amor Prohibido

ACKNOWLEDGMENTS

Husband: Because I love you (except for when you tell me to calm down when I'm being spicy, *narrows eyes and shakes head*). LOL. Xxx

L.M. Reid: Thank you for including me in this amazing anthology. I have you to thank for the crew's Christmas story finally coming to fruition. I'd still be procrastinating over it otherwise, haha. Much love. Xx

Beta Readers: Nicole, Marnie, and Dana. Between the video calls, the McJokes, and random chats, you ladies are epic AF! Thank you for using your precious time to give me critique and feedback. I appreciate the hell out of you! Much love. Xx

Editor: Jenny at Owl Eyes Edits and Proofreading. Once again, you've been nothing but amazing through this entire process and I'm thrilled to be working with you once more. Thank you for putting my words through boot camp and whipping them into shape. Much love. Xx

Proofreader: Emma. Thank you for proofreading for me at short notice. I really should have organised it BEFORE you went on your month-long OE. Lol! Much love. Xx

Book Chat girls: You ladies never cease to be amazing!

Thank you for your support, your advice, and your friendship. So much love! Xx

YOU! (Reader Babes): Thank you for picking up this book and reading through to this point. Without you there is no me, and I'm grateful for us both being here! Much love. Xx

Until next time, Vi. Xx

ABOUT VI SUMMERS

Vi Summers hails from New Zealand.
She is a confetti queen, cheese fiend, tea addict, beard lover, and hot-mess Mumma, all rolled into one International Bestselling Romance Author.

When you read Vi's books, you can expect heat, heart and suspense.
In these gritty romances, Vi loves breaking her characters before putting them back together.

Connect with her on Amazon, BookBub, Facebook, Goodreads, Instagram, and TikTok.
https://linktr.ee/authorvisummers

Made in the USA
Columbia, SC
13 November 2022